"Micah, this is crazy—"

"Maybe," he interrupted. "Maybe not."

His big hand slid inside her panties, pushing them down. "Holly, you know you can stop me anytime. But I don't think you want to, so why don't you just let go for once?"

Holly knew she should push him away. It had been a crazy few weeks, and she was vulnerable. Given where her head was right now, it would be the worst possible time to jump into bed with Micah.

But her body was singing from an entirely different songbook than her brain. "Let go," Holly said in a whisper, more to herself than to Micah. She twined her arms around his back and lifted her face for him to kiss. "For just one night."

"V. K. Sykes has created a unique island removed from the chaos of the mainland, accessible only by ferry or private boat, and populated it with a community of strong-minded people who work hard, take pride in their heritage, and band together to celebrate the good times and get through the bad times as they protect and support each other...It's a place I want to visit with people I want to know. They've touched my heart and I'm now invested in their happiness. I can't wait to catch the ferry over for my next visit to Seashell Bay!"   TheRomanceDish.com

"Genuine emotions plus intriguing characters make *Meet Me at the Beach* constantly enjoyable, and V. K. Sykes always keeps the reader engaged during every entertaining scene. This author is a talented husband-and-wife writing team, and they perfectly balance duty with dreams for a very imaginative story."   —SingleTitles.com

ALSO BY V. K. SYKES

Meet Me at the Beach
Summer at the Shore

See You at Sunset

V. K. SYKES

FOREVER

NEW YORK   BOSTON

Copyright © 2016 by Vanessa Kelly and Randall Sykes
Excerpt from *Meet Me at the Beach* copyright © 2015 by Vanessa Kelly and Randall Sykes

Forever
Hachette Book Group
1290 Avenue of the Americas
New York, NY 10104

www.HachetteBookGroup.com

Printed in the United States of America

First Edition: February 2016
10 9 8 7 6 5 4 3 2 1

OPM

Forever is an imprint of Grand Central Publishing.
The Forever name and logo are trademarks of Hachette Book Group, Inc.

The Hachette Speakers Bureau provides a wide range of authors for speaking events. To find out more, go to www.hachettespeakersbureau.com or call (866) 376-6591.

The publisher is not responsible for websites (or their content) that are not owned by the publisher.

Acknowledgments

Our grateful thanks to our editor, Alex Logan, and to our publicist, Fareeda Bullert, and to all the hardworking folks at Forever Romance who helped us release *See You at Sunset* into the wild.

We'd also like to extend our gratitude to our critique partner, Debbie Mason, for her kindness, her sense of humor, and her uncanny ability to wrangle difficult plot points.

Finally, we'd like to thank our agent, Evan Marshall, for his unflagging support. Evan, you are a truly classy guy and we're so happy to be working with you.

See You at Sunset

Chapter 1

$\mathscr{H}$olly Tyler always looked forward to the ferry ride from Portland to the small island in Maine where she'd grown up. She loved stepping onto one of the gaily painted red-and-yellow boats, the stresses of her demanding job fading under the magical influences of sunshine, wind, and water. The boat ride was only forty-five minutes to Seashell Bay Island, the one place on Earth that served as a haven from her pressure-cooker existence in Boston. Even the simple ride over was way more relaxing than any high-end spa treatment or fancy massage that money could buy.

But on this unplanned and very unexpected trip, she suspected her hometown might turn out to be more of a minefield than a sanctuary.

Aunt Florence had suffered another panic attack last night—a bad one. It had landed her in the hospital in Portland, where Holly's other aunt, Beatrice, had spent the night with her. After racing up from Boston this morning and spending several hours with her two aunts, Holly had finally managed to catch a late-afternoon ferry to the island.

Now, as she stood on the upper deck, she inhaled deep breaths of the crisp sea breeze that swept across Portland Harbor. The crowded boat, full of shoppers and commuters, scythed through the deep blue water of Casco Bay, heading straight for the narrow channel between Peaks and Little Diamond Islands. Everything she saw was so familiar—every cove and inlet, every dock and marina, every cliff and beach. Since college, she'd returned to Seashell Bay for a vacation every August, and it was always a welcome retreat. Sixteen years after a semitrailer slammed into the rear of her parents' car in a sudden winter storm on I-95, instantly killing them both, the island still remained the only place where Holly felt completely safe and loved.

This year though, she'd told her aunts and her friends that she wouldn't be able to make it up to the island. She was in the middle of the biggest move of her professional life, leaving a successful firm of marketing consultants in Boston and moving to New York to partner with two hotshots in a new company with huge potential.

But life had thrown her a curveball, and here she was heading to Seashell Bay anyway. She absolutely had to be there for Florence. And Beatrice—the younger of her two aunts—was going to need Holly's help in running the Jenkins General Store until her sister was able to return to work.

Leaning against the ferry's starboard rail, Holly scanned the hundreds of lobster buoys that bobbed in the swells near an underwater shelf just offshore. Sure enough, she spotted her best friend Lily's orange-and-green colors a couple of hundred feet away. Nothing said home to her more than spotting those buoys. The Doyle family had been lobster fishing the waters around Seashell Bay for a couple of centuries, and Lily was one of a long line determined to keep that tradition unbroken for years to come.

As the boat approached the island, she could see thirty or forty people waiting on the big concrete dock, including a few construction workers from the new ecoresort, identifiable by their work boots and hardhats. Lily was there, along with Morgan Merrifield. And as soon as her friends spotted Holly, they started to wave like she was visiting royalty. Seeing their welcoming smiles made her heavy heart lighten.

Holly had grown up with Lily and Morgan, her two closest friends in the world. They'd bonded as little girls even before they attended the island's elementary school and were inseparable right through their years at Portland's Peninsula High. But after graduation, Holly and Morgan had headed off to different colleges on the mainland, while Lily began her lobster-fishing career on her father's boat.

Holly blew kisses to her pals and then let her gaze wander down the length of the pier. When she spotted the distinctive black-and-gold SUV of the sheriff's office parked at the end, her heart took a funny little skip.

Micah Lancaster.

The unsettling sensations she got whenever she saw Micah tugged at her stomach, this time intensified by a magnitude of about ten. Micah was one of her oldest friends, but something between them had changed last summer, and she'd been thinking for months about what it would be like the next time she came home.

Thinking about him so much over the past year seemed wrong, given that she was already in a relationship— sort of.

Micah emerged from his cruiser, his eyes hidden as usual by aviator sunglasses. He started strolling down the dock, shaking hands with some of the men and ruffling kids' hair as he passed. He towered over almost everyone, an awesomely brawny man with the demeanor of a friendly giant to his friends and neighbors, and that of an intimidating, take-no-prisoners cop to anybody who dared threaten the peace and security of the island.

And Holly couldn't take her damn eyes off him. Yes, she'd always known on some level that he was a truly hot guy, but it had never affected her before. Not since last summer, and surely not like it did now.

She was one of the first passengers to disembark once the deckhands had secured the gangway to the pier. Lily and Morgan politely hung back to stay out of the way of the throng. As soon as Holly reached them, they pulled her into a tight, three-way hug that went on for what must have been a full minute.

"Hey, sweetie, we sure missed you," Lily murmured in her ear. "But you're home now, and we're going to take care of you."

"I missed you guys too," Holly choked out through a tight throat. She knew how true it was that they would rally around her, and Florence and Beatrice too. Island people looked after their own.

Though Holly hadn't seen Lily in months, her friend looked exactly the same—lean but incredibly fit and sporting a gorgeous tan from working long days on her boat. She wore soft, faded jeans, a white T-shirt, and flip-flops. As usual, Morgan looked way girlier, her blond beauty showcased by her pretty white-and-green polka-dot sundress. Holly had last seen her beautiful, blue-eyed friend in January when Morgan and her hunky fiancé, Ryan Butler, spent a weekend in Boston doing a little sightseeing and taking in a hockey game. Morgan, a substitute teacher in Portland, also ran the island's B&B with her younger sister, Sabrina.

"How's Florence doing?" Morgan asked. "We're so worried."

"She's resting comfortably, thanks to the medication," Holly said. "It looks like they'll keep her in the hospital awhile because of her age and medical history. It was a pretty bad panic attack. It did a bit of a number on her heart."

Micah suddenly loomed up behind Lily, his tall, muscular body casting her friend's slender form in shadow. He was a bit like the granite cliffs that lined the island's southern coast—formidable, rugged, and potentially dangerous, at least to Holly.

"The law has arrived," Morgan commented drily. "Why am I not surprised?"

"Stow it, you two," Micah drawled in his deep voice, "or you'll be spending the night in a cell." He took off his hat and pushed his shades on top of his head. His short black hair was suffering from what Holly thought was a cute case of hat head.

"Hi, Holly. Welcome home." His warm smile softened the edges of his oh-so-masculine mouth. His dark gaze as he scanned her was even warmer. "Morgan told me you'd be on this boat."

"Hi, Micah," Holly said.

Okay, she sounded totally lame, but these days he made her feel like a tongue-tied teenager. Not surprising, given how hot he was. Micah had looked like a grown man since he was about fourteen or fifteen, way ahead of every other boy his age at school. Now he was almost thirty-three, two years older than she was, and maturity certainly sat well on him. An avid boater and outdoorsman, good at sports, good with tools, and always ready to lend a hand, Micah Lancaster was truly the walking definition of a man's man.

She fixed her eyes on his gold badge, a seven-point star that he wore just above his heart. Holly remembered all too well what was underneath his brown uniform shirt. She'd seen a lot of him last summer as she recuperated on the island from foot surgery. Micah had volunteered on more than one occasion to push her wheelchair around the quiet island roads to give her some much-needed fresh air. One sunny and very hot day, Micah had stripped off his shirt and draped it over Gracie Poole's mailbox, saying he'd pick it up on the way back. Naked from the waist up and with his khaki pants riding low, he'd looked nothing like the image he was careful to maintain when he was in uniform. And while he looked fantastic in his deputy duds, he was utterly, mind-numbingly sexy without a shirt. Holly had come way too close to saying to hell with the danger and giving in to the insane desire to lick every salty drop of sweat from his sculpted chest and washboard abs, and then going on from there.

Micah remained rooted in place, staring down at her and apparently forgoing the usual hug he gave her whenever she came home. That seemed to make her feel even more awkward. Besides—and she would die before admitting this—she'd been secretly waiting for his bear-hug greeting.

"What, no hug for your old pal?" she finally prompted in a teasing voice.

A flush seemed to glaze his tanned cheekbones, but his lips curved into a smile. "You bet there is."

His relieved look told her he hadn't been sure of his welcome. He probably thought she'd stay in touch after he'd been so considerate and helpful last summer. While Holly felt about two inches tall for practically ignoring the man all these months, the obvious crush he'd developed on her over the past couple of years made her worry about giving any sign that she'd be up for something more than friendship.

Because she wasn't, and if she told herself so enough times, she'd surely believe it, right?

Lily stepped out of the way, and Micah drew Holly into his brawny embrace. On her tiptoes, Holly air-kissed his cheek, her lips barely grazing his deeply tanned skin. Though he was always clean-shaven, his stubble was getting a little heavy by this late in the day. She breathed in the familiar, faint scent of aftershave and leather and told herself to dial it back. It would be so easy to get lost in the comfort of his protective embrace.

She forced herself to give his broad back a couple of awkward pats, hopefully sending a signal that she was ready to break the clench. Micah relaxed his grip and took a slow step back.

"Holly, I'm really sorry about Florence." He flipped his sunglasses back down, hiding the emotion she thought she glimpsed in his dark gaze.

"Hey, guys, it's broiling out here. Let's walk as we talk," Morgan intervened. She made a grab for the wheeled suitcase.

Micah had other ideas, taking the suitcase before Morgan's hand reached it. "I've got this. And I'll take your computer case too, Holly."

"The sheriff's office lives to serve," Morgan said wryly.

"I was pretty worried about Florence," Micah said as he matched his normally long stride to Holly's. "I got there right after the EMTs. Poor old gal was looking grim."

Holly fought back a surge of guilt. "I just wish I could have been here—for Beatrice's sake as much as Florence's. It was really hard on her too."

Micah nodded. "I thought about going in the rescue boat but figured I could be of more use by sticking close to Beatrice until we knew what was going on."

She gave him a grateful smile. "She told me you took her over to Portland in your boat and saw her safely to Maine Med. That was so kind of you, Micah. She was really touched that you'd do that, and so was I."

He gave an embarrassed little shrug. "That's my job."

Holly knew better. She doubted there were many cops who would go to the lengths Micah did for the people of Seashell Bay.

The four of them halted beside Morgan's red pickup truck, a Toyota of indeterminate but advanced age. "Beatrice told me she was sure it was the news of Night Owl applying for a building permit that sent Florence over the edge. Do you really think it's going to finally happen?" she asked Lily.

Lily would have more news, if anybody did, since her maternal grandmother, Miss Annie Letellier, scooped up information like a gigantic NSA satellite dish.

"If the town grants the permit, then yes," Lily said with a sigh. "The good news is that the company said they're only interested in the vacant lot beside the post office. I can see why, since there's no other property big enough and close enough to the landing for their standard-sized store. If the town selectmen say no to that location, I think that'll be the end of it."

That gave Holly a glimmer of hope.

Micah stowed Holly's suitcase in the truck bed and then leaned against the frame. "I guess you didn't expect to be back at all this summer, did you?"

Guilt twisted her gut into a tangle. "Well, I'd hoped for a couple of days in September, maybe. My New York partners and I have a business to set up, with some tight deadlines. I want to be there for my aunts, but it's going to be really hard for me to stay for any length of time."

Micah's eyebrows rose for a long moment, as if something had surprised him. But then his expression went carefully blank. "Well, let me know if there's anything I can do to help out with your aunts," he said. "See you at dinner tonight."

Holly cast a quick glance at Lily as Micah turned and strode off. Lily had invited her and Morgan to dinner—it was something of a tradition whenever Holly made it back to Seashell Bay. And this time, of course, Lily's husband and Morgan's fiancé would be there too. But Micah?

"You don't mind that I invited the deputy tonight, do you?" Lily asked sweetly. "Aiden and Ryan practically insisted."

Crap.

"Of course not," she said, forcing a smile. "Why would I?"

She'd avoided Micah for almost a whole year, but her reprieve was coming to an end.

Chapter 2

All Micah could think about was Holly. When she stepped off the boat, tall and elegant and more beautiful than ever, he'd wanted nothing more than to sweep her into his arms and carry her off, as if they were in some goofy romantic movie. Of course, what he'd wanted to do to her next was considerably more X-rated, so playing it cool had taken some doing.

He had to admit though that she'd looked a little worn out, which was hardly surprising given the circumstances. Her deep brown eyes had lacked their usual sparkle, and that made him even more determined to find something he could do to help both her and her aunts. He knew how much Holly had appreciated the things he'd done for her last summer, and the pleasure of her company had made it more than worth it to him. Helping her out was no chore.

Not that he hadn't been frustrated on more than one occasion, having to throttle back his lust to manageable levels. But the last thing he wanted to do was screw up their friendship, so he'd done what he had to do.

Before he could call it a day, Micah still had work to do,

retrieving an Easter Island statue that Daisy Whipple had lifted from Peggy Fogg's front yard. Daisy, the island's seventy-year-old kleptomaniac, remained the object of bemused tolerance and even grudging affection, at least from the old-timers. Micah had long ago lost count of the number of times he'd had to recover some item she'd stolen. Not that she was a break-in artist. No, she simply plucked whatever she fancied from people's yards when they weren't around, or sometimes even when they were. That was always good for a laugh, although some of the newer residents weren't really down with the joke.

Micah spotted the statue as soon as he stepped out of his Chevy Tahoe. The two-and-a-half-foot-high gray resin sculpture now occupied pride of place in one of Daisy's raised garden plots, butted up next to her tomato vines. She probably put it in that strategic spot in the vain hope that it might frighten marauding deer away from her vegetables. It was sure ugly enough, but in his experience, nothing deterred the deer short of an electrified fence.

Micah picked up the little statue, brushed some dirt and a curled-up worm off the bottom, and deposited it in the trunk of the cruiser.

"Do you think it's right to just up and take whatever you want, Micah Lancaster?" Daisy shouted from her half-open screen door. Short and round with steel-gray hair tied back in a ponytail, Daisy wore a cardigan over her dress in spite of the warm day. "How many times have I told you that you can't just waltz right in and steal my property?"

"Actually, ma'am, it's Peggy Fogg's property," Micah said politely. "She paid good money for it."

"Her property? Well, so *she* says," Daisy grumbled.

"I'll ask Peggy to show me a bill of sale before I let her have it," Micah said. *Sure I will.*

Daisy made a loud sniffing noise. "Well, you'd best see that you do."

Micah and Daisy had gone through this routine so many times that they didn't need a script. He tipped his hat to her and went to get back in the cruiser.

"Are you in such an all-fired hurry that you can't take time for a glass of lemonade, Deputy?" she called after him.

Micah smiled as he turned to face her. "Well, you do make the best lemonade in Maine, Daisy."

She nodded and then trundled into the house, returning moments later with a tall, iced glass of lemonade. They sat together on her creaky porch swing and talked about the weather and the deer problem for ten minutes before Micah decided he'd better get moving.

After thanking Daisy for her hospitality, he got into his car and headed back down the semi-overgrown path to Island Road, braking when he heard a rattling roar approach from his right. About a second later, a familiar golf cart buzzed by on the main road.

Rocket Roy Mayo—at it again.

Micah heaved a sigh and bumped up onto the road, turning on the cruiser's light bar. He flipped the siren on too, since Roy never bothered to look in his rearview mirror. Then again, he knew the siren might have no effect, since the old guy tended to shun his hearing aids, and the straining cart motor made as much noise as the average jetliner. Fortunately, about a hundred yards down the road, Roy figured it out and stomped on the brakes. The cart screeched to a stop and ended up with two wheels on the sloped grass verge.

Micah put on his hat and pulled his sunglasses down.

He strolled up to the cart and bent down a little to look at Roy. "Hell, Roy, is Miss Annie dying? Because that's the only good excuse I can think of for driving this thing like some idiot teenager."

Miss Annie was Roy's live-in girlfriend and the widowed matriarch of the Doyle clan. She and Roy seemed to have found a crotchety sort of happiness in each other's company.

Roy peered up with startling blue eyes that made Micah think of the North Atlantic in winter. Tall and wiry, he looked at least ten years younger than his chronological age. "Well, there's no excuse for harassing a ninety-year-old man either, Lancaster. Not when the only thing I could hit on this goat track is a deer, and the island would be a damn sight better off without both me and the varmint if I did."

"Roy, I have it on good authority that you're ninety-two. But never mind, because you could definitely pass for ninety."

The old dude bared his teeth or, more accurately, his dentures. "Ha, ha. I've always said you'd make a better comedian than a cop, and you're not even funny."

Micah laughed. "Be that as it may, here's the deal, Rocket Man. No more free rides. One more speeding offense and I'll have to finally confiscate your keys."

Roy gave him a pretty credible sneer. "Just try it, sonny, because I'll sue your ass off. And you know what else? I'll file an age discrimination complaint with the government too. Just watch me."

Both of them knew the exchange was mostly in fun. Despite some locals griping about Roy's driving habits, the old guy wasn't much of a threat to life and limb. While Roy often drove the cart too fast, he remained an efficient driver who slowed to a crawl whenever he neared the school or the busy areas around the ferry dock.

"Nothing like a litigious old codger to ruin my day," Micah said with an exaggerated sigh.

"There you go again. Ageism, plain and simple," Roy retorted.

"Yeah, yeah. So, how's Miss Annie?"

Roy shook his head, sending his wispy white hair flying around. "Right now she's got her knickers in a twist over that Night Owl store they want to build. Says it'll ruin the Jenkins sisters for sure."

Micah's mood went south just thinking about it.

"I figure most of our people should stay loyal," Roy went on, "but the frigging tourists and day-trippers won't give a damn what happens to Florence and Beatrice."

By *our people*, Roy meant the island families who'd founded Seashell Bay and lived there for generations—the Doyles, Flynns, Mayos, Letelliers, Coolidges, and dozens more. Micah wasn't sure he'd be included in Roy's cut. While he'd lived on the island all his life, his parents had moved here shortly before he was born, barely a blip in time by local standards, and his mom was now gone, living in Arizona with her second husband. The only Lancaster in an island cemetery was his lobsterman father, dead more than twenty years. Micah planned on being the second someday—way in the future, he hoped.

Micah propped a foot up on the cart's wheel well. "The Night Owl news had to be what sent Florence over the edge. When they applied for a building permit, it must have felt like a knockout punch."

"Yeah, but Florence is tough. And, hey, I hear Holly's on her way home now to help out." Roy gave Micah a sly grin. "I don't blame you for being sweet on that filly, Lancaster. Hell, if I was twenty years younger..."

Sweet on her.

That was one way to put it, though that old-fashioned expression hardly captured the way Micah felt about Holly. He wasn't sure exactly when he started looking at her as more than simply a good friend he'd known all his life. Growing up, he'd always figured he'd never have a chance with the willowy, auburn-haired girl who had drawn boys like flies to honey. He wasn't the smartest kid, and he wasn't one of the athletes who got a lot of notice. With his size and strength, he always made the team but never in one of the star positions.

Basically, he'd never thought he was good enough for Holly Tyler, so he hadn't even tried.

Later, she'd gone on to marry a hero—an army helicopter pilot—while Micah had become mired in an ultimately hopeless four-year relationship with another cop, which in retrospect should have been over in four weeks.

Micah snapped out of his brief reverie. "Holly got in half an hour ago," he said.

Now why the hell did I say that?

"Ha!" Roy cackled. "You were waiting for her boat, huh? Hell, I can't say as I blame you. That girl reminds me a little of Rita Hayworth. Not that a young buck like you would know who Rita was."

"Famous movie actress and dancer in the forties and fifties. I'm not a complete moron," Micah said. "Anyway, just go a little easy on the pedal, okay, Roy? And give my love to Miss Annie."

Holly quickly unpacked a week's worth of casual clothes. Her room was still a step back in time to her teen years, since her aunts refused to change anything. They wanted the old two-story clapboard house to always feel like home, even though she'd told them dozens of times to change whatever suited them. But if keeping the faded rosebud wallpaper and braided carpet made them happy, Holly was fine with that too.

The only significant changes since high school were the curtains and the counterpane, the eye-searing pink shades of her teen years giving way to the earth tones she'd later picked out herself. But the old furniture remained the same. The four-poster bed with its well-scuffed corners and its matching side table still faced the large window with its amazing view of the bay. The chest of drawers—a gorgeous oak antique—had come from her parents' bedroom. That old dresser had been handed down in her mother's family since the late nineteenth century. Mom had told Holly many times that she wanted her to have it after she was gone and, hopefully, pass it on to her own children. She'd thought about moving the historic piece to Boston but figured it somehow belonged in Seashell Bay, in the place her mother had loved so much.

The top of the dresser was bare except for a pink jewelry box where she kept a few pieces for her island visits, and a photo of Drew in a pewter frame. Her husband was posed in front of their Boston town house with his classic 1956 Harley, his proud grin as bright as the bike's polished chrome. She'd captured the image on his thirtieth birthday, less than a year before the Taliban shot down his Black Hawk in Afghanistan, killing him and every single soldier he was transporting on a rescue mission.

She had the same picture in a larger frame in Boston, and also a few casual shots of the two of them on the island. There were no pictures of her husband in uniform, even though a few of her friends thought that was kind of strange. But Holly hated looking at him in his army gear. While she would always be proud of his service to his country, she didn't want the daily reminder. She didn't need pictures, because the memories of his ultimate sacrifice were lodged deep inside, in blood and bone. Some days the pain was as real as it was four years ago.

And that wasn't the way she wanted to remember him.

She picked up the photo and kissed it for what had to be the millionth time.

Turning away from the heartbreaking image, she forced herself to focus on the present. Job one right now was getting the store in shape, which meant getting her aunts to agree to her ideas. Holly desperately wanted them to let her inject some actual cash into renovations too. She could afford it, while her aunts didn't have a dime to spare.

The old gals had always refused her previous offers of help, but things were different now. The doomsday clock was ticking, thanks to Night Owl. Now it was a matter of how quickly they could transform the general store into a business that would survive and prosper, instead of fading away to nothing more than a few photos preserved in the archives of Seashell Bay's historical society.

Holly knew she could do it if they'd let her. After all, saving businesses was basically what she did for a living.

The first thing she had to do was make a brutally honest assessment of the current state of affairs. She knew the store was in pretty rough shape, but until she got her eyes on the place—and especially on its financials—she wouldn't know the true depth or urgency of the problem.

She quickly ditched her city clothes in favor of a yellow

tank top, black yoga pants, and yellow Keds—her bee outfit, according to her aunts—and then headed across the narrow gravel path leading to the back of the store. As anxious as she was to get to work, she stopped to gaze for the first time in a year across the sparkling little bay and the strait that separated Seashell Bay from Long Island. The glittering waters looked as placid as a lake in the afternoon sun, and in the distance, she could just make out the gentle curve of Long Island's popular South Beach. The view never failed to fill Holly with a mix of tranquility and wistfulness. There was no vista more familiar to her than this one, and yet nothing she'd seen anywhere else could move her like this little corner of the world she still called home.

As usual, she had to pull hard on the brass knob of the store's weathered door to get the lock hardware to line up. She stepped into the storage area, making a mental note to upgrade the locks and the security system. Drew had once told her that cheap dead bolts like the ones at the store could be opened with a pick or a bump key in seconds, often leaving no trace of entry. That had given Holly nightmare visions of some scumbag slipping inside late at night when Florence was working alone in her little office behind the checkout counter.

With the increase in tourism and traffic to the island, it just didn't pay to take chances.

The storage area looked as well organized as ever, with metal shelf units lining three out of four walls. Beer sales were the store's bread and butter, so there were always plenty of cases of both local and imported beers on hand. But other goods were kept to a minimum supply of each product. Florence had always been efficient at keeping inventory, and thus costs, down. She knew what her customers wanted and when.

Holly pushed through the swinging door into the retail area. It looked exactly the same as it had last summer—and every year before that. Wooden shelf units of canned goods, chips, bread, cereal, and household necessities like soap and toilet paper occupied the center of the square store. Wine racks, a beer fridge, and a soda cooler took up most of the rear wall, along with souvenir T-shirt racks. There was a sad-looking old chiller with packaged meats and cheeses butting up against the seven-foot-high DVD shelf unit, its old discs crammed haphazardly within the limited space. The checkout counter had metal racks with stuff like candy, gum, lip balm, and batteries. A shorter counter behind the cash register held a two-burner coffeemaker with a storage cabinet and a small refrigerator underneath.

The modern cash register was only two years old and stood out like a sore thumb in the throwback shop. Holly had bought and presented the robust machine to her mystified aunts as an overdue replacement for the manual clunker they'd used for decades. She suspected that few of the new machine's powerful capabilities were being utilized.

Most items for sale featured small green price stickers laboriously applied each day by Beatrice. Her aunts had plenty of time to create and apply the stickers, and would die before they used a modern scanner at the register. Besides, Florence always maintained that their customers liked their old-fashioned ways.

Repressing a sigh, Holly pushed up the hinged section of the counter and passed through into the cramped office. She'd always reluctantly taken her aunts' word for the state of the store's finances. But those days were over now. She was no longer willing to back off in the face of Florence's unconvincing reassurances that the store was doing *quite all right*. Holly knew she would feel like a jerk for snooping, but it was the only way she could learn the truth and develop a plan.

Unfortunately, Florence was still in the Stone Age when it came to keeping records. Holly had bought her a laptop three years ago and some books on systems and software, but her aunt had eventually confessed that she wouldn't trust the store's records to some *darn machine*. Most of the accounts were still kept in bound ledgers, accompanied by folders full of printed receipts. Holly had no intention of wading through that mass of detail today. Everything she needed to know would be in their Portland accountant's profit and loss statements and balance sheets. Those documents would tell her if she was dealing with a sick patient or a critical one.

Or worse yet, the store could already be effectively DOA. The mere thought of the last possibility made her stomach do a sickening flip.

She dragged the old office chair over to the ancient four-drawer filing cabinet by Florence's desk. Opening the second drawer, she scanned a jammed row of buff file folders. Holly pulled out the one containing last year's reports from the CPA and started reading.

Fifteen minutes and two files later, she had a nauseating understanding of the Godzilla-sized disaster that currently loomed over her aunts.

Home for an hour or so until he had to head to Lily's for dinner, Micah had just popped open a beer and started to check the mail he'd picked up at the post office, when his cell phone rang.

His secretary always set calls to be forwarded to his cell at the end of the day. "Deputy Lancaster," he answered.

"Jesus, Micah, somebody broke into my house!"

"Fitz?" Micah recognized the young woman's voice, though it sounded half an octave higher than usual.

"Yeah, it's me. Sorry, I'm pretty freaked out right now."

"Okay, but slow down and tell me what happened."

He heard her suck in a deep breath.

"I got home from work, like, five minutes ago. My foot's been driving me crazy all afternoon, so I went to take one of my prescription painkillers and damned if the bottle was gone. That freaked the crap out of me, because I knew I'd left it on the bathroom vanity this morning."

Fitz was a bright and responsible woman. As far as Micah was concerned, her word was gold. "I'll be there in three minutes. Leave everything exactly as it is."

"Okay. Thanks, Micah."

His mind racing, Micah grabbed his hat, locked his door, and hurried out to the cruiser that was parked in his driveway. Unless Enid Fitzsimmons had suddenly gone loopy, it looked like a real crime had just been committed in Seashell Bay.

Micah made a tight turn onto a semi-overgrown path leading to a ramshackle cottage set back a couple of hundred feet from Yellow Grass Road. Fitz's place was in one of the island's least desirable locations. The homes on this winding, north-end lane offered no views of anything other than rather scrubby landscape. While most of them were at least well maintained, a few were serious candidates for demolition. Fitz, a young marine mechanic at O'Hanlon's Boatyard, had told him she bought the old Cavanagh place for pocket change in an estate sale. Since then, she'd been working hard to fix it up herself. She hadn't done much with the exterior yet, instead focusing on making the interior habitable after years of neglect by the previous owners.

Still wearing her grease-stained work coveralls, the young woman pushed open her screen door as Micah got out of the cruiser. "Can you believe this, Micah? Who the hell would rob *this* dump?" She swept her left hand around in a dramatic gesture.

Micah had to admit that Fitz had a point. It would take a pretty desperate—or stupid—thief to hit on a place that could only be described as modest.

"I know this sucks, Fitz, but I need you to focus," he said as she waved him to come in. "You can start by telling me if the doors were locked."

He put the odds of that at about 10 percent.

Fitz rolled her big green eyes. Red-haired and heavily freckled, she was cute rather than pretty, but with her sunny personality and dynamite little body, she never lacked admirers. Micah didn't date much but had asked Fitz out not long after she arrived from somewhere out west. They'd had one date—dinner at a Vietnamese restaurant in Portland—but nothing had sparked, at least not for him. Then again, no one had been able to ignite any true heat in him for years—no one other than Holly Tyler.

"Like I'd bother," she scoffed. "How many people on this island lock their damn doors? Hell, one of the reasons I came here was because it was supposed to be ultrasafe. Micah, this is crazy."

"No point in checking for signs of forced entry then," he said pointedly.

"Smart-ass," she grumped.

Micah scanned the small, neatly furnished living room. Nothing seemed out of place, as far as he could tell. "Take me through what you've found. What's missing?"

Fitz slipped past him, taking quick strides down the center hall. Micah followed.

She swung left into a bathroom that was tiny but had been completely redone. There was a new tub and shower combo, a small new vanity with a stone countertop, and updated light fixtures. The walls had been painted sunflower yellow, and fluffy blue towels hung on a rack by the tub.

Micah knew she'd done the impressive reno herself, including the plumbing.

Fitz pointed at the vanity. "The Vicodin was right there beside the liquid soap. I haven't moved it since I got it from the pharmacy two days ago. I won't take them at the boatyard, so I just down one in the morning and another as soon as I get home."

"Anything else gone from the bathroom? Any other meds?"

Fitz shook her head. "Nothing. I was hoping to stop the Vicodin tomorrow, even though the doctor gave me enough for a couple of weeks. It's making me a little dopey, and I've been worried I might do something really dumb at work."

"Okay, what else is missing? Any cash or jewelry?"

"I don't keep cash in the house, and I'm not exactly the Bling Queen of Seashell Bay, Micah. There isn't a damn thing worth stealing. I've got better things to spend my money on than that," she said in a dry tone.

Micah couldn't recall seeing her wearing any jewelry. And her watch was a Timex with a leather strap. "Like fixing up the place, right? You're doing a great job."

She gave him a tiny smile, then slid across the hall to the bedroom. It too had been updated. Blue paint, white roman shades, a sturdy-looking ceiling fan, and some coastal artwork. And a big sleigh bed with matching dresser, no doubt bought secondhand, from the looks of the worn and chipped surfaces.

But unlike the living room and bath, the bedroom was a mess. Clothes were strewn all over the floor, and the drawers from a small nightstand were upended on the bed. Micah glanced at the scattered piles of panties, bras, camisoles, and a single red thong, and then shifted his gaze back to Fitz, who had reddened slightly but shrugged.

"Obviously, he rifled through all those drawers." She pointed to the dresser. "Tossed my things around pretty good. I don't know whether he took anything or not. I don't count my damn underwear."

"Did he muck around in your kitchen cupboards too? People usually keep some spare cash there or in the bedroom."

"Yeah, a bunch of the doors were open, but he didn't make much of a mess there." Fitz started to look a bit queasy. "God, maybe he's one of those perverts who like to mess with women's underwear. I've read about creeps like that." Then she blew out a sigh. "But I guess I'm just being paranoid, right?"

He gave her sympathetic smile. "A bit. Try not to read too much into it, Fitz. I'm sure this guy was looking for cash and drugs. There's a pretty good market out there for opioids like hydrocodone and fentanyl."

While he cautioned himself to resist coming to conclusions before he even started his investigation, Micah's immediate feeling was that it might very well be a kid looking for a free high, not somebody trying to sell the stolen drugs. If money were the thief's primary objective, he would have passed on a house like this. There certainly were more inviting targets on the island than Fitz's run-down-looking cottage.

His gut told him somebody might have found out she had a Vicodin prescription and decided to make an easy score while she was at work. Probably knew she was one of a multitude of islanders who never locked their doors.

"When I think about some dirtbag putting his grubby hands all over my clothes, especially my underwear…" Fitz's eyes started to tear up. "I think I'm going to have to throw it all out. Every single thing."

Micah got it. Burglary victims always felt violated, and when they knew the thief had handled personal things like intimate clothing, many reacted just like Fitz.

"I hear you, and I'm sorry." He gave her shoulder a brief, comforting squeeze. "Now, who else knew you were taking Vicodin?"

"Well, I told Mike, just in case… you know, uh, he had a problem letting me keep working while I was on it."

That was her boss, Mike O'Hanlon. "Smart. Good for you."

She managed a smile. "And I told Jessie."

And that would be Jessie Jameson, another O'Hanlon's employee who was also one of the island's EMTs. Jessie would be about the last person Micah would suspect of committing a crime.

"Just those two," Fitz added with a frown.

Micah started back toward the living room. "I'm going to have to ask you to leave everything as it is for the moment. I'm going to see if I can get a crime scene team out here. I'm not real optimistic about that, but I'm going to try. In the meantime, I'll get my camera out of the car and take some pictures."

"Okay," she said. "Maybe I'll ask Jessie if I can bunk in with her tonight. I'm not feeling too good about being here right now." Her lip trembled slightly.

"I'm really sorry you have to go through this," Micah said, grimacing.

"Not your fault," she said. "I just hope you catch the bastard."

"I will," he said firmly, more to give her a sense of reassurance than anything else. Petty thefts like this one were notoriously hard to solve.

He strode out to his cruiser, struggling to tamp down his anger. Fitz was a capable young woman doing her best to hold it together, but the look in her eyes and the tremor in her voice signaled how much the break-in had rattled her. He couldn't help feeling a sense of responsibility for that—not so much in his head as in his gut.

There wasn't supposed to be any crime in Seashell Bay, especially nasty break-ins in broad daylight. There wasn't supposed to be a frightened young woman who now might wonder if her home would ever be truly safe again. Because once that sense of personal security was shattered, Micah knew it was hard to get it back.

And of course, news of the burglary would spread across the island like a bolt of lightning. Everybody would be asking him questions, offering advice, and freely promoting their theories about the perpetrator, expecting him to apprehend the asshole in short order. And everybody would be hoping that it would be a single isolated incident that would never be repeated.

Micah hoped so too. As much as he welcomed the chance to do some real police work, he hated the idea that any other woman —or man—on the island would have to suffer such a personal violation, or come under any kind of threat. And when he thought about that disturbing prospect, one woman was front and center in his mind.

Holly Tyler, who'd seen enough trouble and heartache to last a lifetime.

Chapter 3

$\mathcal{L}$ily, this place is amazing," Holly said, as she took in the high-end kitchen. She'd never been inside Aiden and Lily's new home, although the renovated Victorian was hardly "new." In fact, it had been in Aiden's family for generations.

Aiden's dad had moved into a tidy, brand-new cottage Aiden had built for him, and then Aiden and Lily renovated the much larger Flynn family home. Holly had been impressed from the moment she walked in the door. They'd stripped the old kitchen down to the studs and redesigned it with high-end white cabinetry and a huge, granite-topped center island. But it still retained an old-fashioned, homey appeal with lacy white curtains and the beautiful antique china that had belonged to Aiden's mom lovingly displayed in the new cabinets.

Holly, Lily, and Morgan worked at the center island on salad and fixings for barbecued burgers. In recognition of Holly's stressful day, Lily had assigned her the least challenging task of slicing the tomatoes.

The way she was feeling, even that was almost too much.

Holly was not just tired but heartsick over the depressing

financial situation at the store. She'd even thought of bailing on dinner, but she'd only seen Morgan and Ryan once in the last year, and Lily and Aiden not at all. Lily had planned the dinner as a joyful celebration of her long-overdue visit. She just had to suck it up and try not to kill the mood.

"Now we can finally talk," Morgan said as she expertly sliced a zucchini into a large wooden salad bowl.

After Micah arrived with his startling news, all they'd talked about was the break-in at Enid Fitzsimmons's house. Everybody had been a little shocked, though Aiden was right when he said that the island was changing and people had to get smart about locking their doors. Holly had been on her aunts about that for years, but they had never taken the threat seriously. Yes, Seashell Bay had always been a gentle, safe place, but with more tourists and day-trippers every year, and with a big new resort soon to open, the future was less predictable. Maybe this break-in would finally jolt Florence and Beatrice out of their complacent attitude toward security.

After they'd exhausted that unpleasant topic and the guys had started to drone on about baseball, Lily had rolled her eyes and declared it time for the three manly men to head outside and get the grill going. A glance out the window told Holly that they were now happily drinking beer and shooting the breeze as Aiden cleaned the barbecue.

"Talk about what?" Holly asked. She was fairly certain that burgers weren't the only things about to get a grilling tonight.

Lily finally looked up from ripping romaine lettuce into bite-sized pieces. "About whether you really want to be doing this, of course."

"Going to New York," Morgan added unnecessarily.

Holly stifled a sigh. "You both probably think it's insane to leave such a good firm and start a brand-new one. Well, hey, I do too." Truth be told, she'd been close to a nervous wreck since the day she'd said yes. "It's not like I went looking for this opportunity. But I've always wanted to start my own firm, and my gut tells me that if I don't grab this chance, I'll probably second-guess myself for the rest of my life."

It wasn't like she enjoyed taking risks. In fact, she pretty much loathed it. Making the decision to leave the security blanket of her Boston firm had been hell, and she'd spent weeks analyzing the pros and cons before finally signaling to her prospective partners that she was willing to accept their invitation to start up in New York. It was almost a miracle that they'd chosen to offer her an equal share of a company that had a chance to become a significant player in the industry. She simply couldn't pass up such an opportunity, even if it was a huge leap into the unknown.

"Not to be too grossly selfish," Lily said, "but it's pretty tough to think about you moving farther away from us. You didn't even make it home all that much when you were a ninety-minute drive away, so what's it going to be like when you move to Manhattan?"

Holly waved her paring knife. "Hey, it's not the West Coast, guys. I'll only be five or six hours away by car, or about an hour by plane. And I'll have more control over my life when I'm running my own company, so I might be able to get home more. Besides, it'll be awesome when you guys come visit me there. We'll go to Broadway plays and the fabulous museums and the best restaurants in the whole country."

Morgan said, "That all sounds fabulous, but we're worried that you're trying too hard to convince yourself."

When Holly opened her mouth to protest, Morgan held up a hand. "Sweetie, just don't let your new partners pressure you into doing something you're not completely sure is right for you. That's all we're saying."

"I won't, but I *am* committed to it." She was certain of that, though there were a ton of issues still to be worked out. That was why she had to be in New York as soon as possible.

Morgan waggled her eyebrows as she slid the last of the zucchini into the bowl. "Apparently not so committed that you've given your notice in Boston."

That was part of the strategy, not indecision on Holly's part. Her new partners, Cory and David, would work on getting commitments from existing clients before leaving their current firms. That rather sneaky part hadn't sat terribly well with Holly, but to the guys it was a deal-breaker. Fortunately, none of them had noncompete clauses in their contracts. "Yeah, I know," she said. "But that'll come at the appropriate time."

Lily wiped her hands on her apron, looking thoughtful. "Holly, is there something else pushing you to make this jump? Something you haven't wanted to talk about?"

"Is it about being close to Jackson?" Morgan asked. "Nobody could blame you for wanting that." She paused just a second too long. "I guess."

Both of her pals knew full well that Holly and Jackson Leigh had a relationship that wasn't much deeper than a topcoat of nail polish. But she was looking forward to living in the same city as the man she'd been intermittently seeing for almost two years. Jackson was handsome and rich and fun—well, usually fun—and he never pressured her. He just wanted to have a good time whenever they were together, and Holly was down with that. Jackson and her husband were opposites in almost every way, and that was one of the reasons she'd been attracted to him. That Jackson was nothing at all like Drew made it impossible to draw comparisons between them.

Because deep in her heart, she was afraid that no one could ever measure up to Drew.

It was time to fess up. Holly put down the knife and leaned against the countertop. "Honestly, guys, it's as much about leaving Boston as it is going to New York. The truth is that I don't want to spend the rest of my life with my stomach clenching and my eyes getting watery every time I see or do something that reminds me of Drew. And in Boston, about a million things do that."

Morgan grimaced. "Like Fenway Park."

Drew, a devoted baseball fan, had dragged Holly to many a Red Sox game, and Morgan had gone with them once too. Despite Holly's general aversion to professional sports, she'd always ended up having fun at Fenway because of Drew's knowledge, passion, and gentle humor. Now she was sure she could never go back there. Just passing by it was bad enough.

"Yes, and like cycling along the Charles," Holly said, her throat tight. "And strolling through the Common after dinner, and having a quiet Sunday morning coffee at the Wired Puppy. I can't do any of those things anymore. Whenever I try, it makes me feel like my life is over."

When her friends exchanged concerned glances, Holly rushed to fill the awkward silence. "Look, I know it's stupid to think that way. Drew spent way more time at Fort Campbell and on deployment than he ever did in Boston. It's just that...well, it was our home. The only home we ever had together. I still see him everywhere, and I don't think that'll ever change. I kept telling myself it would get better. That eventually all the good memories would push the pain deep enough to…" She didn't quite know how to finish, since her thoughts kept getting tangled up in her emotions.

Her friends waited patiently.

"I just can't be there anymore," she finally said.

Lily nodded, her eyes brimming with sympathy and sadness. "I'm sure I'd feel the same way if I were in your shoes."

"Me too," Morgan said. "Sometimes it still hurts to be at the inn, because I see Dad everywhere there. I can't even imagine what it would be like if I ever lost Ryan."

"Getting away does make sense," Lily said. "We just hoped you'd be heading north, not south."

Holly sighed. "In a perfect world—where I could transport my career anywhere I wanted—I'd rather be here with you guys than anywhere else on Earth. You know how much I envy you both." She stole a quick glance through the kitchen windows at Aiden and Ryan chatting around the monster barbecue, now belching smoke. "Especially now that you've hooked up with two of the hottest guys on the planet. Way to overachieve, guys."

Morgan reached across and gave Holly's hand a little squeeze. "Dare I say that Aiden and Ryan aren't the only superhot dudes in this little corner of the world? If you ever get tired of Jackson, you might want to cast your eyes closer to home. You never know what could happen if you did." She arched her brows, nodding toward the window.

"You know all the reasons it can't happen with Micah," Holly said firmly. "My career. His career." And there were other reasons too.

"Yes, yes, and the one-in-a-million chance that he could

get himself shot on the job," Morgan said, obviously reading her mind. "Even though that's about as likely as him getting hit by a bus crossing Island Road."

Holly couldn't help laughing. There had never been a bus in Seashell Bay.

Lily wasn't laughing though. "I get that you don't want to risk falling in love with a man who puts himself in harm's way, but you know Micah's almost more of a social worker than a cop."

Holly gave her head a decisive shake. "That might be true now, but will he spend the rest of his life here? Anyway, it's fruitless to talk about it. I do love Micah, but not in that way. You guys know that."

When Lily shot Morgan an amused glance, Holly had to clamp down on a little spurt of irritation.

"Do we know that?" Lily asked Morgan.

Morgan cut Holly a sly grin. "All I know is you practically melted when he strolled up to us at the dock today, and I sure can't blame you. Our Deputy Dawg gets hotter with every passing day."

Well, of course he was hot, and of course she lusted after Micah. A woman would have to be comatose not to. And while her heart might still feel locked in ice, Holly's body surely did not. But she intended to continue to keep an iron grip on those dangerous urges, just like she'd done last summer. While it was absolutely clear that Micah wanted her, she wouldn't risk destroying their friendship with some doomed summer fling—however wickedly tempting sex with Deputy Lancaster might be.

"Holly looks fantastic, huh?" Ryan said. "Pretty amazing, considering all that's going on."

"Hot as ever," Aiden chimed in as he scrubbed the grill with a wire brush.

Unbelievably gorgeous, as always, Micah thought but didn't say. "Yeah, but you can see how worried she is about Florence. She always keeps up a brave front, but we know her too well."

"And according to Morgan, she's been on edge for months about that career move," Ryan said. "I can't say as I blame her. Leaving a well-established firm like hers to start a new one from scratch? That takes some balls, man. And on top of that, she's moving to frigging New York."

"Yeah, well, the first I heard of any of that was less than an hour ago," Micah said, trying not to sound frustrated. Holly's girl buddies had clearly known about her plans but had kept their mouths shut—other than telling Aiden and Ryan, obviously. "At least she'll be in the same city as her boyfriend now."

Aiden glanced up and gave him a wry smile. "I'm not sure that factor had anything to do with her decision."

"Yeah?" He hoped he didn't sound overly curious. Micah told himself he shouldn't care one way or the other about Holly's relationship status. Too bad he did. A lot.

"Aiden's right," Ryan said. "That's the vibe Morgan gets, anyway. Holly never talks about the dude being part of the reason why she's moving. But, hey, one way or the other, it shouldn't stop you from making a move. If that's what you want."

Micah mentally sighed as he looked away to gaze at the ocean view. Apparently, everyone on the damn island knew he had it bad for pretty Miss Holly Tyler.

"Hell, when it comes to Holly, I'm not sure what I want," he finally said.

While that sounded lame, it was the truth. In his gut, Micah knew he wanted to be with Holly like he wanted to keep breathing. But he didn't want to wreck a friendship, and he sure as hell didn't want the sting of her rejection either. Actually, *sting* was way too weak a word. Micah knew that if she pushed him away for good, it would be a body blow—which was why he couldn't let her get into his head like he had last summer. No, this time he'd play it cool. Try to act like nothing much had changed from the time when they were just friends.

Because they *were* just friends.

"Dude," Ryan said, "don't be an idiot. She's sweet, and she's smoking hot. Who cares about her lame-ass boyfriend? What are you waiting for?"

Micah shrugged. "I wish that was all there was to it, man. You know Holly's always wanted a different kind of life. For her, the island is a great place to kick back once a year and get all nostalgic for a while, but it's not home. It hasn't been home for a long time."

Ryan shrugged. "You never know. After I enlisted, I never thought I'd come back to this place. In fact, I'd be in Texas now if it hadn't been for Morgan. And believe me, I thought about that a fair bit as we slogged through that last crappy winter."

That was total bullshit. Ryan was so head over heels in love with Morgan that it would take an invasion force to drag him off the island now. "I know. And that city boy came back too," Micah said, pointing at Aiden, "even though I thought we'd gotten rid of him forever."

Aiden snorted. "You wish, dude."

He and Aiden had been fierce rivals growing up, and Micah had been more than glad to see the back end of the big-shot athlete when he left Seashell Bay to play pro ball. Now though, since Aiden's return, they'd managed to become solid friends. Aiden was a truly good guy who'd already done a lot for Seashell Bay.

"That's my point," Ryan said. "It can happen to anybody, Holly included. This place is like some kind of freaking black hole, sucking you back in." His smile indicated he didn't mind that particular pull of gravity.

Micah inhaled deeply as a gust of wind swept in from the Atlantic and rustled the tangled bushes that grew all the way down the rocky slope to the beach below. "I might go the other way. Maybe break out of the vortex."

"Huh?" Aiden said.

Ryan stared at Micah like he'd lost his mind. "Say that again, because I couldn't have heard right."

Micah gave a wry laugh. "I'm just saying that I'm not sure I want to spend my whole life as a go-between for our resident kleptomaniac and her victims. Sometimes I'd like to be a real cop again. Like I was for a few years on the mainland after I got out of the academy. Maybe I'll even try for a detective shield at some point."

"Hey, you just got a real crime to solve right here," Aiden said.

"Unfortunately," Micah said. "But I doubt it's the beginning of a crime wave. At least I sure as hell hope not."

"So get a transfer into town," Ryan said. "You can live here and work in Portland, just like Morgan's doing."

Micah gave a slow nod. "Yeah, I guess I just have to pull the trigger one of these days and do it. But it's not going to be easy to leave. Taking care of folks here has been my life for a long, long time."

Aiden rubbed his chin, obviously pretending to look

thoughtful. "Well, I suppose if you want to do some real policing, you could always try New York. There are so many cops in a place like Times Square that you can't wave your arm without hitting one."

"Ha, ha. I guess I might do that if I was thinking with my dick instead of my brain," Micah said. *Not that I'd have a ghost of a chance with Holly anyway.*

"You realize you're totally in denial mode, right?" Aiden said.

"Nah. I'm just being realistic. Holly and I are worlds apart. When she's back here, it doesn't seem like that, but a vacation is a break from your real life. Nothing's changed when it's over."

Ryan gave him a friendly jab on the arm. "We get it. Look, if transferring to the mainland is what you want, go for it. But I'm guessing you want us to keep our mouths shut about that, right?"

Micah wasn't even sure why he'd told the guys, especially since he wasn't fully sure that he'd go through with it. But he guessed that, for once, he just needed to confide in someone. "Yeah, it's better that you don't say anything."

"Sure, but you know it won't be easy to get away from this rock, man," Ryan said. "I swear at least half the people here will sink any boat that tries to take you away from them. They really depend on you."

As their deputy sheriff and friend, Micah knew he had the islanders' trust. More than that, he had their respect and affection, and he'd spent years building that up. To quit wouldn't be an easy transition for them or him. But with every passing day, he was feeling the need for a change in his life.

Chapter 4

$\mathcal{M}$icah never called Detective Griffin Turner before nine in the morning unless it was an epic emergency. He and Griff had been in the same police academy class and had signed on simultaneously as patrol deputies with the Cumberland County Sheriff's Office over ten years ago. After a few years, their career paths had diverged—Micah heading to Seashell Bay and Griff going on to earn his detective shield. Even though he was a great cop and probably the smartest guy on the Cumberland County force, Griff had a seriously laid-back attitude and preferred to ease into the day.

So on the dot of nine, Micah settled behind his desk and punched in Griff's cell number.

"Well, good morning, Deputy Lancaster. Is this a social call, or do you need help getting some old lady's cat out of a tree?" Griff chuckled at his lame attempt at humor.

"If this was about a cat in a tree, you'd be the last cop I'd call," Micah said. "You'd probably get it down with a shotgun."

"Possibly true. You know I'd never have the patience for the trials and tribulations of island policing."

"Look, I've got a situation out here," Micah said, cutting to the chase.

"What's up?" Griff asked, immediately turning serious.

Micah quickly briefed him on the break-in and Vicodin theft. "I got hold of Crime Scene," he added, "but they said they didn't have the manpower to send somebody. No surprise there."

Micah was still a bit pissed off about that. To him, no crime in Seashell Bay was minor except Daisy's thievery, which he basically classified as short-term borrowing.

"Well, if you're calling me to get involved, you'll get the same answer," Griff said flatly. "You know we don't have the resources to investigate some chickenshit B and E over there. You'll have to handle it. Besides, I bet this wasn't even a forced entry. Nobody on that damn island locks their doors."

"I keep telling folks to lock up, but it's like beating my head against a brick wall," Micah reluctantly acknowledged. "Everybody knows it's a supersafe place, but with all the tourists and day-trippers, anything can happen."

"Look, buddy, if the only thing stolen was Vicodin, chances are pretty damn good that it was some local teen looking to score an easy high. Kids are raiding their parents' medicine cabinets every day of the week. And when the parents don't have drugs, they sometimes range farther afield."

"I know, and that's where I'm going to start. I just thought I'd see if you've had any similar thefts recently. On the islands, I mean, not in Portland. Obviously you've got that kind of thing all the time in the city, but it doesn't seem likely that somebody from there would come all the way out to Seashell Bay to look for drugs."

"No, we haven't had anything like that on the other islands," Turner said. "It's got to be one of your locals."

That stuck in Micah's craw big-time. "Like I said, it was worth a check."

"Good luck with it, man. And make sure you let me know if your crime wave out there continues, huh?" Griff said, twisting the knife.

"Not that you guys would show up in the bay for anything short of a full-scale terrorist attack," Micah responded. Too bad he was only half joking.

"Always a pleasure to talk to you, Deputy."

Micah stood, shoved his phone into his pocket, and grabbed his hat off the desk. Mary-Ann Crispo, his part-time secretary, was on the phone, so he just gave her a wave and ducked out of the office. It was time for his morning call at the Jenkins General Store to pick up a coffee. The old gals brewed a pretty good cup, but he mostly went to hear what people were saying. The news and gossip occasionally contained a useful nugget of information.

He also had to admit that he was more anxious to get to the store than usual. And that was because, this morning, a certain auburn-haired beauty would be serving him.

Holly had opened the store at eight o'clock, right on time. Though Beatrice had told her yesterday not to push herself for an early opening, Holly hadn't slept much, and there was no point in lying around in bed. All night, her restless mind had oscillated between worries for her aunts and the store, and for herself. The stress of seeing Florence and Beatrice in trouble, both physically and financially, had sharpened her nagging doubts about making the big move to New York.

Then again, she needed to stop thinking like a gutless wimp.

By ten o'clock, only two customers had shown up, mostly because word hadn't yet made the rounds that the store would remain open even without Florence and Beatrice. Peggy Fogg had confirmed that when she stopped by on her way to the post office. Peggy had picked up three tins of Tetley tea and two bags of her favorite gingersnaps, which Florence brought in especially for her. The other customer was one of the construction workers from the resort site. He'd stopped to pick up coffee and cigarettes on his way to the job.

It was a pathetically sad haul for the store.

After doing a little rearranging and restocking, Holly grabbed some sheets of paper from the office and started to sketch out some ideas for renovations. She was sitting at the sales counter, thinking about the best place to locate a bigger deli case, when the little bell over the screen door jingled and Aiden strode in.

"Morning, Holly," he said, craning his head sideways to stare at her drawing. "Already planning renovations?"

She mentally winced at the slightly skeptical tone to his voice. At dinner last night, they'd wound up talking a little about her aunts' reluctance to change, even though she'd been determined to focus on the good things about coming home, not the problems.

Aside from seeing her friends, she was running short on the good stuff.

She put down her pencil and smiled. "A girl can dream, can't she?"

Aiden was wearing a University of Southern Maine T-shirt that showcased his athlete's physique. He was gorgeous, ambitious, and, most importantly, a hell of a nice guy. Holly couldn't be happier for Lily, even if she was just a teeny bit jealous of the wonderful life her friends had created for themselves.

Aiden shot her a grin. "I hope that coffee's good and fresh, because I sure need a hit. After you guys left, Lily and I had a... well, late night."

Holly rolled her eyes. "Yes, it's fresh, but please spare me the details of your night, Romeo. And don't you feel a little guilty that you get to sleep in while my poor friend has to haul herself up before dawn to catch lobsters?" she teased.

"Of course, really guilty," he said with a sigh. "But somehow I manage to get over it."

Holly knew Aiden truly loved and appreciated his hard-working wife. She reached for a paper cup and quickly filled it.

Aiden glanced out of one of the long side windows that offered a view of the ferry dock. "I'm catching the ten twenty boat. It's just pulling in now."

"One cream, no sugar, right?" Holly said. The general store didn't go in for fancy self-serve stations for cream, sugar, napkins, or God forbid, soy or rice milk. The aunties kept a modest supply of fixings next to the pot and doled it out in careful increments.

"Perfect," Aiden said. "It's sure good to have you home, Holly. It's been way too long."

Holly felt herself blushing, not so much because of his compliment but because he'd just tapped into her guilt over her infrequent visits.

"None too subtle, dude," she said. "Yes, I'm a terrible niece and friend. Although you're one to talk—you didn't come home for years."

"Ouch, you got me," he said, dramatically clutching his chest. "Then again, I was an idiot, which you're definitely not."

"That's certainly true." She covered the cup with a lid and handed it to him. "And that'll be a buck and a half, buddy."

Aiden reached into his pocket and plunked down a ten-dollar bill. "Keep the change. Consider it a small contribution toward keeping this place going. The island needs the Jenkins General Store. I just hope people get their shit together and start supporting it more."

"Aw, that's not necessary, but thanks. You're such a sweetie." Holly rang the purchase into the register and put the money in the till. "But the next few cups are on the house."

"Forget it. And by the way, you're the furthest thing from a terrible niece and friend. A terrible niece wouldn't even be here, much less running the store to help her aunts. And you know that Lily and Morgan would love you to death even if you only came home once a decade."

Embarrassed and still feeling guilty, Holly shoved her hands in the pockets of her jeans and stared down at the floor. "Thanks, Aiden."

"Chin up, girl. Everything will sort itself out. See you later."

By the time she looked up, Aiden was heading out the door. But standing in front of him, pretty much blocking his way, was Seashell Bay's gorgeous deputy sheriff.

The guys exchanged a few words and a fist bump before Aiden strode off. Holly had to shake herself into action, partly because they were two of the hottest guys on planet Earth and any red-blooded girl would be struck dumb at the vision of all that hotness in close proximity, and partly because she tended to freeze whenever she saw Micah these days.

That development was incredibly annoying. The man had been one of her best friends all her life, and yet damned if she didn't feel like a nervous teenage girl when she thought about being alone with him, even in the store.

"Coffee, Deputy?" she asked brightly. As he strode up, she took a step back to lean against the back counter. The extra four feet of distance did little to diminish the impact of his overwhelming masculinity or the way his tall, muscled form seemed to make the store shrink around him.

"Hell, yeah. You know how I need caffeine in this high-pressure job," he said as he laid his deputy's hat on the counter. He flashed her a quick, charming grin. "It's getting hot out there already."

It was getting pretty hot inside the store too. She felt herself flushing, even though the store's aging but still-efficient air-conditioning kept things at a steady seventy-three degrees.

Hormones, dammit. And she wasn't anywhere near old enough to blame it on early menopause.

Since Micah took his coffee black, all Holly had to do was pour a cup, put a lid on it, and set it on the counter. And, yes, she was avoiding handing it to him in case their hands brushed. "There you go. I just made a new pot a few minutes ago."

Micah reached into his pocket and pulled out a small wad of bills.

Holly rolled her eyes. "Put your money away, my friend. It's on the house, as always. Cops and firefighters don't pay for coffee in this establishment."

Micah shook his head. "Maybe not before, but now

they do. At least this one does. Holly, I'm sure as hell not taking free coffee when Florence and Beatrice are obviously struggling."

As hard as her aunts had tried to keep the store's financial woes under the radar, Micah clearly knew they had more problems than the prospect of competition from a convenience store chain. Though the Jenkins General Store was looking tired, she suspected most people on the island had failed to realize how bad things were. Then again, Micah knew pretty much everything that was going on in Seashell Bay, often via Miss Annie, in whom Florence and Beatrice usually confided.

"It's just a cup of coffee, Micah," Holly said.

His expression was polite but implacable. "Doesn't matter. It's the principle. And I'm going to buy everything I can here from now on. No more picking stuff up in town just because it's a little cheaper. Islanders have been doing that more than we should."

He pushed a five-dollar bill across the counter. "And don't give me any change," he said with a little growl roughening his deep voice. Holly found it adorable—also totally sexy, which she would *not* think more about.

"You're a doll," she said as she picked up the bill. "But I'm not going to breathe a word of this to Florence and Beatrice. They'd shun me for accepting money from the law."

His grimace signaled his discomfort with the conversation. "They'll just have to get used to it."

He seemed almost as nervous as she felt. "Just how bad are things anyway?" he asked after a few moments of awkward silence. "There are rumors that the store might have a hard time surviving, Night Owl or no Night Owl."

Crap. The last thing they needed was that sort of damaging gossip.

"You know what, I think I could use some coffee too."

That was a lie, but she needed a moment to get herself settled, so she turned her back on him and reached for a paper cup. When she'd filled it and turned around again, Micah hadn't moved a muscle. He was just a brawny force of nature planted in front of her, his big hands resting on the counter as he patiently waited for her to answer.

When she didn't immediately reply, he blew out an exasperated breath. "That bad, huh?" he said. "It's written all over your face, babe."

She didn't know which was worse—the way his casually uttered *babe* sent chills rocketing down her spine or the fact that he could so easily read her. Then again, Micah had always been skilled at reading people, which she supposed was one of the reasons he was such a good cop.

No point in pretending with Deputy Hottie. "Quite bad. I did a little snooping through the files yesterday." She gave a nervous little laugh. "I know that's not very nice, but I needed the truth. My aunts just won't level with me when it comes to the store. It's like they'd rather quietly die than let people know they're in trouble."

His dark gaze warmed with understanding. "They're proud people. Most islanders are like that."

Yeah, but they were a little too proud sometimes. And that applied to her too. Maybe it was time she started asking for help, or at least a sympathetic ear. For some reason, she wanted that to be Micah.

"No kidding, and unless I can talk them into finally making some changes, I'm not sure the place will make it. They've been losing money for over a year, Micah. Florence and Beatrice still have some savings they built up in decent years, but when that kitty runs dry, all they'll have left is social security to live on for the rest of their lives."

If her new firm succeeded, Holly would gladly support them. But she knew they would hate that idea. They'd been so independent and so hardworking their entire lives. The situation was just massively unfair.

Micah grimaced again. "That would totally suck, but at least they'll have their house. You can still live pretty cheaply on the island if you don't have to carry a mortgage."

"If I know Florence, she'll try to mortgage the house rather than give up the store." She sighed. "I'm not sure her bank would go for it though, which might be a good thing."

He reached across and gave her shoulder a quick, gentle squeeze. "You'll think of something. And don't be afraid to ask for help, okay? Almost everyone in Seashell Bay would go to the mat for you and your aunts, me included."

Her throat went oddly tight, so she just nodded.

"Well, as much as I'd rather spend the whole morning talking to you," Micah said, popping the lid on his coffee, "I'd better go earn my salary. That break-in's not going to solve itself."

Disappointment flared surprisingly strong. It was silly to want him to stay, but his words had triggered a flood of awful memories that made her pulse start to race. She'd always felt completely safe in Seashell Bay, never having to even think about personal safety or loss.

"I feel terrible for the woman, Micah. She must feel so..."

Violated. Holly practically gagged on the word.

Micah loomed closer, his gaze narrowing with concern. "Holly, are you okay? What's going on?"

"Nothing," she said, flapping a hand. "It's just that it's such an awful thing to happen, especially to a newcomer."

"You got that right," Micah said. "Fitz was a little freaked out at first but seems fine now. She strikes me as a pretty tough customer."

Unlike me, Holly thought grimly. "The fact that someone *seems* fine doesn't mean they are. I'll bet she's hurting and at least a little scared."

He grimaced. "I know. I'm not always the best at picking up female signals."

Well, he was pretty adept at picking up *her* signals.

"That's a common male affliction, for which there is no cure," she joked, trying to lighten things up. "I hope Fitz has a friend she can talk to."

"She and Jessie are buds." He dropped his gaze for a moment, apparently thinking. "You know, Fitz always comes down to the Lobster Pot on Darts Night. Maybe you could check in on her. I'm sure she'd appreciate making a new friend." When he looked up, her stomach dipped with a funny little swoop at the sudden heat in his eyes. "You'll be coming, right?"

Holly nodded. "Morgan made it clear that she'll be dragging me to the Pot tonight come hell or high water."

"Good. Then I'll see you there."

"I'll look forward to it." Which was certainly the truth, Lord help her.

A moment later, his expression morphed back into that of a serious law enforcement guy. "Holly, I'm going to say this to you and everybody else on this island. You have to lock your doors whenever you leave home, okay? And keep them locked even when you're in the house. Let's try to make it at least a bit of a challenge for whoever this asshole is."

"I promise." Holly never left her doors unlocked, not anymore. Not after what had happened in Boston.

The drive to Barrington Point took Micah eleven minutes, at least three longer than usual since he had the bad luck to be blocked by a truck carrying Rex Fudge's old lobster boat. But instead of putting two wheels in the shallow ditch and roaring around the blockage, Micah forced himself to relax and use the extra time to think about Crystal Murphy's kid, Justin Gore.

Justin had graduated from high school last year after a tough slog. For most of his nineteen years, his mom had raised him by herself. His father, a drunk who had worked off and on at the wharf, had taken off to the mainland around the time Justin turned ten. Things hadn't gotten any better for the kid since. He was widely perceived on the island as lazy and careless and, so far, incapable of growing up.

Crystal's beaten-up trailer nestled in a pretty stand of beech and maple trees on a lane just off Island Road. Most islanders who lived in modest homes, even those that could rightfully be called shacks, tried hard to keep them clean and tidy. Not Crystal and Justin. Maybe Crystal was just too worn out by life to make the effort, and Justin apparently didn't give a damn.

The rickety wooden step at the door had sunk well down into the soft earth at an angle. When Micah stepped gingerly onto it, it rocked enough to almost make him lose his balance. He knocked twice on the screen door.

Justin appeared, rubbing a hand across his eyes. He was dressed in a faded black T-shirt and patterned black-and-white boxers. The young man was about average height but weighed no more than a hundred thirty pounds soaking wet.

"What?" he grumbled.

"Hi, Justin. Is your mom home by any chance?"

The young man shook his head, his black, curly hair drooping down onto his forehead. "Nah, she's got the day shift this week."

"Well, it's you I wanted to talk to anyway."

"Talk to me about what?" Justin asked warily.

"Mind if I come in first?"

"Mom doesn't like people coming inside."

Because it's a dump or because you've got a stash and she's protecting you?

Her son was the only family Crystal had, so Micah wouldn't blame her for trying to protect him. "Okay, we'll sit down at the picnic table then."

Justin stared daggers at Micah for about ten seconds. Then he shuffled sideways and slipped his feet into a pair of flip-flops before opening the door and stepping out. "I don't have any weed, if that's what this is about."

In the past couple of years, Micah had caught Justin smoking pot three times and each time had let him go with a warning. The last one had included the proviso that, if he caught him a fourth time, a charge would result.

Micah made a point of not going nuts if the local kids toked up from time to time as long as they didn't do it openly, and as long as nothing harder was involved. He figured a little marijuana was part of growing up. But he wouldn't put up with flagrant use. When he caught Justin and one of his pals brazenly lighting up down at the dock as they waited for Crystal's ferry to arrive—and there were about forty people on hand to smell the pungent odor—it had ended his patience.

He took off his sunglasses and sat down with his back to the sun.

"Okay, what?" Justin slipped onto the bench opposite Micah.

"Start by telling me everything you did yesterday from eight in the morning until five thirty. I've got plenty of time, so don't leave anything out."

Justin squinted hard, angling a hand against his forehead to shade his eyes. "I was right here all day, just like I am every day. Listening to music. Surfing the Net. Same old boring shit."

"I'm guessing your mom was at work since you said she's on the day shift at the restaurant."

Justin nodded.

"That means nobody can vouch for your claim that you were here all day, right?"

"Doesn't mean I wasn't," the kid said petulantly. "Where do you think I was?"

"Your mom still on those antidepressants?" Micah said, changing tack. "And she was on tranquilizers for a while too, as I recall." Crystal had never hidden her problems, especially not when she'd had a few beers down at the Lobster Pot. Seashell Bay folks sympathized with her because she worked hard and tried to be a good mom.

Justin shrugged. "You'll have to ask her about that."

"Any drugs in the trailer? Prescription or otherwise?"

"Not as far as I know."

Micah stared into the kid's light brown eyes, trying to make contact even though Justin was continually shifting his gaze. "Okay, then I don't suppose you'd mind me having a quick look around in there?"

"Mom wouldn't like that. She never lets people inside." Justin's eyes dropped, probably in embarrassment. "It's kind of a mess."

"I get it, Justin," he said gently. "But you're not a minor anymore. It's okay for *you* to give me permission. If you really don't have anything to hide, this whole thing could end right here. And believe me, I'm not going to judge you or your mom because of a messy house."

Justin thought for couple of moments and then made a gesture of resignation. "Okay, but please leave Mom's stuff alone or she'll kill me."

Micah breathed a mental sigh of relief. Justin wouldn't have agreed to a search if there was anything problematic in the trailer. Still, he had to go through the motions. "Best that you stay out here. It won't take long."

He headed inside the old double-wide, straight into the living room. The dining area and the kitchen were on his left. Heading past the kitchen and down a short hall, Micah found a decent-sized bedroom where clothes were strewn everywhere, like he'd expect in a teenager's room. But from the underwear he saw on the floor, he had no problem deducing it was Crystal's. The bathroom was across the hall, and another smaller bedroom was beside it at the end. That one was obviously Justin's, because it featured a common theme in late-teen male décor—posters of near-naked swimsuit models on the walls. A wooden table with folding metal legs supported a desktop computer, two monitors, a Wii console, and a rat's nest of black cables. The room was messy, though not as bad as his mother's.

Micah made only a cursory search of each room. In the tiny bathroom, he found a bottle of lorazepam and another of Celexa, which he knew was an antidepressant. Both prescriptions were ordered by a Portland doctor and filled a few weeks ago at Watson's Pharmacy, not surprisingly, he supposed, since it was right across the street from the restaurant where Crystal worked.

Justin, who'd been peering in the door, quickly moved out of the way to let Micah through. Micah took his sunglasses out of his shirt pocket and put them back on. "One more question, okay, Justin?"

The kid nodded.

"I know you're pretty plugged in on what's going down here on the island, so let me ask you this. Do you know any kids who like to fool around with stuff like Vicodin or Oxy?" Micah put his hand on Justin's shoulder. "Look, I know you don't want to be a rat, but you need to be honest with me now. I want to be able to trust you, and I'll never be able to do that if you lie to me about something like this."

Justin didn't hesitate, shaking his head hard. "Nobody on the island does that stuff. Not that I know of anyway. And that's the truth."

Micah had watched Justin's eyes and body language carefully. The kid gave no indication he was lying, but that didn't mean he wasn't.

"Okay, son, that's all for now."

Micah returned to his cruiser with some relief. He would have hated to dump more trouble on Crystal by having to arrest her son. But he was concerned too, because if Justin was indeed telling the truth about himself and the other island kids, it would mean his theory—and Griff Turner's—had just gone down the drain.

Chapter 5

$\mathcal{H}$olly's first dart sailed off to the right and missed the board. That pathetic toss earned her a raspberry from Bram Flynn and a mixture of groans and shouts of encouragement from the tables nearby. Sighing because she totally sucked at Seashell Bay's cherished pastime, she aimed her second missile. It hit the wire just below the number twenty but then bounced off and clattered to the floor. For the final attempt, she shut her left eye in the vain hope of sharpening her aim and sent the dart in a shallow arc toward the board.

Success! Somehow the dart not only landed inside the triple ring, it actually stuck, scoring twenty-four points. She pumped her fist in triumph as the dart wobbled, unsure whether to stay lodged or fall off to join its red-tipped mates on the floor.

Bram Flynn grinned as he retrieved the darts. "Even a monkey can hit a triple, time to time."

Bram had hounded her for the better part of an hour to play a match with him, though Holly suspected it might have more to do with getting a better view of her legs and other parts of her anatomy than it did with darts. She'd finally given in, if for no other reason than to shut him up.

"Are you calling me a monkey, you jerk?" She smacked Aiden's little brother on the shoulder as he toed the line. Describing him as a little brother was a hoot. At six five, *little* was not the appropriate adjective for Bram Flynn.

Bram's face got red, his mouth pulling down with dismay. "Jesus, Holly, I was just yanking your chain."

Holly knew that, of course, and she loved Bram, despite his history of ribald comments during her visits home. And she was thrilled that he was in control of the alcohol and gambling addictions that had almost destroyed his life.

"I know, you big goof." She threw a glance at Micah, seated with Lily, Aiden, Morgan, and Ryan. At the next table sat Morgan's sister, Sabrina, along with Miss Annie, Roy Mayo, and Father Michael Malone. "Micah, why don't you take over for me? I think I've humiliated myself enough."

Grinning, Micah tossed back the rest of his beer and stood. He'd already agreed to relieve her if she decided to bail. "Be glad to, if Bram can handle getting his ass whipped."

Bram rolled his eyes. "Lancaster, I could beat you if I threw backward over my shoulder."

"Okay, let's see you back up all that talk."

When Holly slid by him on her way back to her seat, Micah gave her butt a soft pat that practically froze her in her tracks. Though it was just a playful gesture and she figured no one would make anything of it, it struck Holly as almost possessive. And damned if she didn't kind of like it.

And it wasn't hard to imagine that big hand on the rest of her body either.

You wish, girl.

Then again, maybe that was two and a half bottles of Shipyard Ale doing the talking. She was already past her usual limit. If she was going to get a little blitzed though, tonight felt like a good time for it. A little de-stressing was definitely in order.

Trying for a casual smile, she eased back into the chair beside Morgan and across from Miss Annie and Roy.

No matter how hard she tried, Holly couldn't help eating Micah up with her gaze as he waited for his turn to throw. Maybe an inch shorter than Bram, the guy looked like an NFL defensive end standing next to a high school basketball player. Micah's superwide shoulders stretched the blue, long-sleeved Henley he was wearing, as did his sturdy biceps and muscular forearms. With his impressive size and totally ripped body, he was a dominating presence even among the man-mountains that generally populated the Lobster Pot.

"Holly, as I was saying before you abandoned me for that rascal Bram Flynn, I'll be darned if I can get a bead on those selectmen yet," Miss Annie grumbled, referring to the town councilors. "I've talked to all three, and not a one of them is showing his cards."

The matriarch of the Doyle clan turned her sharp gaze toward Father Michael, whose face was ruddier than usual, no doubt from the heat and the beer. Father Mike was the classic stereotype of the jovial, Irish American priest if there ever was one. "Father, you'd think it would be a no-brainer for those three old coots to get behind Florence and Beatrice, wouldn't you? But no, they say they want to get lots of *feedback* from people before they make up their minds."

She made the notion of feedback sound as appealing as a bucket of rattlesnakes.

"That's what you get for not running for selectman yourself, Miss Annie," Ryan drawled in a teasing voice from the other side of Morgan. "Actually, I think we'd all be better off if you ran the island as a benevolent dictatorship."

"Hell, I thought she already did," Roy said without a second's hesitation.

Miss Annie gave him a poke on his wiry arm.

"Granny, they're hardly old coots," Lily said from down the table. "Chester and Amos and Thor are all at least twenty years younger than you are. Besides, you always say you're not even old. Unlike Roy," she added with an evil grin.

"Lily Doyle Flynn, you know very well that age is relative," her granny shot back. "Chester's still got most of his marbles, but Amos Hogan can barely figure out where the town hall is, and Thor Sigurdsson isn't much better. They can still catch lobsters like nobody's business, but why in heaven they ever wanted to be selectmen is beyond me." Miss Annie's fluffy white perm practically quivered with frustration.

Father Michael made a gentle scoffing noise. "Oh, climb down from your soapbox, Annie. Some of us had to practically get down on bended knee to beg Amos and Thor to run since nobody else wanted to, other than Chester."

"Oh, I know, but who ever thought that prehistoric trio would wind up having to decide the fate of poor Florence and Beatrice?" Miss Annie raised her gaze to ceiling. "May the good Lord above help us all."

Despite the importance of the subject at hand, Holly was having a hard time concentrating. She kept getting distracted by Micah's back—or, to be more geographically precise, his very fine ass. How insane was that? Though she'd always looked at her friend with deep appreciation for his manly attributes, her reaction to him now felt quite different. She tried to tell herself that she was simply too tipsy to keep her guard up, and yet she knew that would be too easy an answer.

Damn hormones.

"Earth to Holly Tyler," Miss Annie said, waving her bony right hand halfway across the table at Holly. "Are you with me, dear?"

Feeling the heat of embarrassment rising up her neck, Holly managed a contrite nod. "I'm sorry, Miss Annie. I'm just a little tired and distracted."

"Well, no wonder. You must be worried sick about your aunts. I was saying that we need to start a petition drive to convince the selectmen to deny Night Owl their building permit. I'll draw it up, and you can get everyone who comes into the store to sign. And Roy can take it around the island to those folks who don't visit the store much."

"Hey, don't I get a say in all this?" Roy protested, winking at Holly.

"No, Ancient One, you don't," Miss Annie said firmly. She looked back at Holly and smiled. "Most folks will be glad to sign. Those three dinosaurs won't be able to ignore the will of the people after that."

Holly perked up as everyone nodded in agreement. "That's a great idea," she said. "I know how much Florence and Beatrice appreciate all your help. And so do I."

Miss Annie smiled and uttered a soft *psshh.*

Ryan stood up, pushing his chair back. "Okay, now that we've got our battle plan, let's get back to some serious partying. Morgan and I want to lay down a challenge to any pair that has the mistaken impression that they might beat us at shuffleboard."

"That would be Lily and me," Aiden said.

Ryan shook his head. "Forget it, dude. No, I was figuring the deputy could take us on. Joined by our sweet pal Holly, who we're so happy to have back on the island."

Holly saw Morgan turn in her seat and stare up at her fiancé, her icy blue eyes conveying what she thought of Ryan's mischief making. Her friend knew Holly would be uncomfortable being put on the spot like that.

Unlike darts, Holly enjoyed shuffleboard and was generally decent enough at it to hold her own, so that part didn't bother her. But she could barely believe Ryan's meddling. She opened her mouth to refuse but didn't get the chance.

"Sounds like a plan to me," Micah said. He gazed down at Holly, his dark eyes glittering with an unspoken challenge... and a whole lot of heat.

Holly, you are in so much trouble.

"We can't duck a challenge, can we?" he added.

When Morgan gave her an apologetic look, Holly waved a hand and got up from the table. She would not look like a wimp to her friends. Even more important, she would not disappoint and maybe even embarrass Micah by making some lame excuse for not playing. Not after everything he'd done for her. She simply had to keep her unruly hormones under control.

Good luck with that.

"Game on," she said, pinning on a smile.

*　　*　　*

Micah gave Holly lots of space as she made her way across the room to the shuffleboard table. It wasn't like him to jump in like that, accepting Ryan's challenge—not when it was clear that Holly was about to decline. But he just hadn't been able to resist the temptation to get close to her. He never could when it came to Holly Tyler.

Not that he wasn't tempted to whack Ryan upside the head for being so obvious. His buddy knew exactly how conflicted he was about Holly, and yet he still hadn't been able to resist playing matchmaker. Like plenty of islanders, Ryan wanted Micah and Holly to hook up. Not just for his sake but because it might pull her back to Seashell Bay.

Too bad Holly wasn't down with the program. Nor was she the type to want a casual summer fling. And when it came to Holly, neither was Micah. He wanted more than that, and was pretty well convinced he would never get it.

And she has a boyfriend. Micah forced that unpleasant thought away.

He kept his eyes pretty much glued to Holly's perfect ass as she slipped through the crowded tables. Her short, red skirt was hot enough to peel the paint off the Pot's walls. Her form-fitting white blouse showcased her trim waist and dynamite rack. Not for the first time, Micah couldn't help thinking that, looking the way she did—not just tonight but all the time—Holly could have virtually any man in the world. Add in a sweet personality, and it'd been no surprise that she'd ended up with a dude like Drew Tyler, a guy about as handsome as they came, not to mention a brave airman and a hell of a nice guy.

By the time he caught up with her, Holly was already lining up the shuffleboard pucks at one end of the fourteen-foot wooden table. "Ryan, since you issued the challenge," she said with a sly smile, "I assume you have no problem with Micah and me having the hammer to begin?"

Micah swallowed a grin. Players usually flipped a coin to see who would have the advantage of throwing the last puck—called the "hammer"—in the opening round. Holly had smoothly backed Ryan into a corner.

"No problem," Ryan said with a mock sneer. "You and my big doofus pal will need all the help you can get."

Morgan poked him in the side. "Play nice, you jerk."

"Babe, I love it when you talk dirty," Ryan said, pulling her tight against his side.

Holly laughed. "Hey, are we here to play shuffleboard or make out?"

Making out sounded pretty great to Micah. He couldn't help pointedly raising his eyebrows as he stared down at her. Holly's eyes opened wide as she realized her mistake, then a sweet flush turned her cheeks rosy. He almost laughed when she scowled back at him.

"Both sound good to me," Ryan joked.

Morgan rolled her eyes in exasperation. "Keep it up, buddy, and you'll be sleeping on the sofa tonight."

This time Micah did laugh, easing the tension.

Smiling, Holly shook her head at Morgan and Ryan's banter and gave one of the pucks a little spin. Micah lined up close behind her, breathing in the sweet vanilla scent of her silky hair. He was close enough to hear her exhalations of breath and to practically feel the rise and fall of her chest. Surprisingly, she didn't slide away from him, instead standing there with a hip cocked, spinning the disc slowly as she stared down at the table. Micah felt the blood in his head begin to flood down to territory below his belt.

Not good.

He forced himself to get a grip. "Holly, go ahead and throw whenever you're ready," he said, his throat a little tight. "We're gonna murder these guys."

That overblown declaration seemed to defuse the rest of the tension in her sweet bod.

"Murder?" she tossed out, only half turning around. "Goodness, that's hardly an appropriate thing for an officer of the law to say, Deputy Lancaster."

Micah didn't miss the slight catch in her voice, despite her flip words. Was he doing that to her? He sure as hell hoped so.

Man, how he wanted this woman. He could tell himself a million times over that it was batshit crazy, and even self-destructive, to think of Holly as more than a friend. He *had* told himself that, so many times that the words were carved into his gray matter. But his resolve always took a powder whenever he saw her. In fact, the more he vowed to put his feelings for her out of his mind, the stronger they seemed to get.

Holly inhaled a deep breath, and with a gentle spinning motion, she slid the puck down the table. The beads of silicone that had been scattered over the polished wood surface gave the puck a smooth glide until it finally stopped in the three-point section at the opposite end. Holly clapped her hands in delight.

"Great shot." Micah patted the slender curve of her hip. "You've always had a real sweet touch, Holly."

So much for his resolve to play it cool.

Holly swung around and eyed him cautiously. Micah

gave her what he hoped was a totally innocent-looking smile, just a *well done, teammate* look. The slight narrowing of her eyes told him he'd probably failed.

Morgan elbowed him. "Okay, it's time for the pros to take over."

Micah inadvertently bumped into Holly as he took a step to the side. She'd been moving too, and their bodies collided, his arm sliding over her breasts. Soft and oh so sweet, they felt amazing, even though the touch was momentary.

More blood drained straight south to his dick.

Holly practically jumped back, keeping her gaze firmly on Morgan and not on him.

"Sorry," he said.

"No worries," Holly replied. She refused to look at him, but he heard a slight catch in her throat.

Morgan slid a blue puck in a straight line down the board and knocked Holly's shot into the gutter. Micah made himself concentrate on the game instead of on his partner. He stepped up and wasted no time mirroring Morgan's shot, knocking her puck off the table.

They all played well through the rest of the first frame, falling into an easy rhythm. Even Holly seemed to forget her worries—and the sexual tension between them—long enough to get into the spirit of the competition, enthusiastically urging Micah on whenever it was his turn.

The score was tied, and Holly held the hammer in her hand. She was facing a board with Ryan's puck in scoring position and the next one belonging to her and Micah. If Holly could somehow manage to curl her last shot just enough to both knock Ryan's out and stay on the board, she and Micah would win the frame.

Micah didn't offer any advice because he knew she had it under control. She'd shown a deft touch throughout the game. He put her chances of making this moderately difficult shot at something like 70 percent if her speed was perfect. If not, the odds went way down.

Holly turned to him. "I could do this for sure if I wasn't half-lit," she said with a rueful laugh.

Micah leaned in. "It's good to be loose. You can't make tough shots when you're uptight." He gave her shoulder a quick squeeze. "You can totally do this."

Holly gazed at him for a long moment. She seemed... he searched for the right word... almost grateful for his support. As if she wasn't used to it.

That couldn't possibly be true. Everyone loved Holly, including, he had to assume, her boyfriend. If he didn't, the guy was a total tool.

Then she broke the moment by nodding and turned back to the board.

She spun the puck once and then launched her shot. It slid down the table on a perfect trajectory, slipping past the guard and hitting two-thirds of Ryan's puck, knocking it out. Holly's spun to the right and came breathtakingly close to the gutter but didn't fall off. That clutch shot gave her and Micah a total of five points, and they won the frame.

"Yes!" Holly cried. She swung around, eyes lit with excitement as she pumped her fist. "I can't believe—"

Those were the only words she got out before Micah grabbed her and hoisted her into the air until her eyes were a few inches above his. Without conscious thought, he'd lifted her and now held her about a foot and a half off the floor. She was so light in his arms that it had taken no effort at all. It was purely an instinctive response to the moment and to her joy.

Her eyes flew open wide as she sucked in a shocked breath, then she slapped her hands on his chest. She gazed down at him, her cheeks flushed and her silky hair falling forward to brush his cheeks. He felt a shudder race through her body as their gazes locked.

Embarrassed, Micah set her down, mentally cursing himself for acting like...well, like she belonged to him. As if he had the right to touch her like that, especially in public.

"I'm sorry, Holly," he managed. "I don't know what got into me."

Morgan's expression was as gobsmacked as Holly's, while Ryan just grinned and said, "Nice toss, man. Way to celebrate the win."

Holly tilted her head and studied Micah, looking puzzled rather than annoyed. To his amazement and relief, a small smile crept onto her flushed face.

"I'm glad we won the frame," she said, "though it makes me worry about what could happen if we end up winning the whole match. You might celebrate by bouncing me off the ceiling. You don't know your own strength, buddy."

Her joke unwound some of his tension. Still, Micah couldn't believe he'd made such an impulsive gesture. He was never impulsive. Unfortunately he'd drawn a hell of a lot of unwanted attention to the both of them now. Holly was a private person and hated that sort of thing.

"I'll behave myself," he said. "At least I'll try."

"Good, because I'd hate to have to handcuff the deputy sheriff in front of half the town," Holly said with mock severity.

When she turned away to speak to Ryan, Micah scanned the bar, expecting to be on the receiving end of weird looks and puzzled stares, especially since islanders thought of him as such a total straight arrow. Instead, he saw only smiles and even a few approving nods.

It seemed that his fellow citizens had no problem at all with the fact that their deputy sheriff had just taken matters into his own hands.

It gradually dawned on Holly that Boyd Spinney, Miss Annie's old foe in the last town fight, was making a public display of himself again.

She'd been so absorbed in the shuffleboard game—and in Micah, especially after he'd wrapped his big hands around her waist and lifted her straight up in the air—that she hadn't been paying attention to what was obviously a raucous argument going on back at their table. Spinney and his pal Cooper Frenette were hammering away at Miss Annie and Morgan, and Miss Annie looked about ready to murder the two men.

Micah took Holly's hand and wrapped his fingers around it in a comforting grip as he led her back to her seat.

"Dammit, Spinney's three sheets to the wind," he said, clearly annoyed.

Holly didn't know Spinney well, and she'd only met his fellow lobsterman Frenette a couple of times. But she did know that Spinney and Miss Annie had historically been like gasoline and open flame, and they were obviously taking turns yelling at each other. Spinney was in his mid-sixties and had a reputation for being even more opinionated and dogged in his views than Miss Annie, which really saying something.

As Holly and Micah approached, Spinney threw his arms up in the air in clear frustration. "Annie, you've got to stop being so pigheaded," he thundered. "Night Owl could sue both the town and the selectmen if they try to deny that permit. They've got no damn grounds for saying no. You're just causing trouble for nothing."

"What bull. Night Owl won't sue," Morgan said indignantly, putting her arm around Miss Annie's narrow shoulders. "They don't need Seashell Bay. Hell, I doubt they'd even *want* to come here if the majority of people were against it. So Miss Annie's idea makes good sense to me. Let's find out what people really think. Or are you guys scared to find out?"

Spinney's head jerked back. "Are you kidding? You people are crazy if you think there aren't a lot of people on the island who feel the same way as Cooper and me. Your problem is that you can't stand even the idea of change. I keep telling you it's like you're stuck in time. Like you're damn fossils."

"Stuck in time, my ass, Spinney," Morgan said, her eyes blazing. Ryan slid into position behind his fiancé, looking like a big muscled wall of intimidation. Still, he remained silent, letting Morgan fight her own battle.

Besides, it wasn't as if Morgan and Spinney were actually going to start duking it out.

"Anybody with half a brain wants to keep the good things we've always cherished," Morgan retorted. "Things like the Jenkins General Store. There's no reason why we need Night Owl. The stores we've got now can meet all our needs just fine."

Before Spinney could launch another rebuttal, Morgan cut him off. "And, hey, how about showing some loyalty, huh? Taking the side of a big corporation over Florence and Beatrice? You two should be ashamed of yourselves!"

Miss Annie joined in, wagging her finger at her foe. "Boyd Spinney, you can call me all the names you want, but this old fossil will have no part of anything that hurts the Jenkins sisters. And like Morgan said, you shouldn't either. Why should we line the pockets of some big mainland corporation that sticks stores every ten feet across the state of Maine? We've done just fine without places like that for a couple of hundred years, so we sure don't need them now."

Blowing out a loud sigh, Father Michael finally rose from the table. "Now folks, I don't think—"

Frenette moved to hover over the much shorter priest, his black eyebrows furiously pulling into a unibrow. "You people are just full of hot air. Times change, and the general store ain't up-to-date. Everybody knows that." He swayed a bit, clearly drunk. "If we're going to be honest here, the place is a stinkin' dump."

The shock of those words hit Holly squarely in the chest.

"Watch it, Frenette," Micah said in a cold voice, giving her hand a squeeze that she suspected was a signal for her to stay out of it.

But she couldn't. For Frenette to launch such a vicious insult against the store was too much. She pulled her hand free, ignoring Micah's growl.

"Stinking dump?" she said, going up on her toes and getting right in Frenette's grill. His beery, cigarette-stinky breath almost made her gag. "That's the way you talk about your neighbors? About two gracious ladies who've devoted themselves to this town? You ungrateful jerk!"

Frenette gave a loud snort. "Relax, okay? I'm not crapping on Florence and Beatrice, so don't go getting your little panties in a twist, dollface. Besides, I figure somebody who only comes around once a year shouldn't get much of say in island business anyway."

And there you have it, folks. The ultimate insult in Seashell Bay—to tell a native-born islander that they no longer belong.

Something in Holly's head seemed to pop, and every bit of fear, frustration, and rage she'd been suppressing came pouring out like a red tide.

"How dare you!" She flattened her palms on Frenette's chest and shoved, sending him reeling backward. The man's mouth gaped open as he windmilled to keep his balance. She launched herself at him again, making an instinctive fist.

"Holly, chill out!" Micah said sharply, wrapping his arm around her waist. He pulled her back with irresistible force, lifting her feet right off the ground.

"Leave me alone, Micah. I'm not taking that kind of crap from him. This is my home as much as his." Holly tried to wriggle out of his grasp, but his arm was an iron bar around her body. She probably looked as helpless as a worm on a hook.

"You need some air," Micah said, half carrying her past Frenette and Spinney. "And Cooper, you need to shut your mouth. Don't talk to Holly like that again—ever. Now, either sit down and shut up or get the hell out of here."

Chapter 6

*E*xhausted and light-headed from her attempt to unwind at the Lobster Pot, Holly closed her eyes as Micah's truck bounced along the rutted island road. A pounding headache might well be on tomorrow morning's agenda. On top of that, any attempts to forget her troubles had been undone by that nasty little fight with Frenette and Spinney.

Not to mention that she'd made a complete ass of herself in front of half the town.

She'd fully intended to hoof it home but Micah wouldn't hear of it. He joked that he'd tail her in his cruiser if she insisted on walking. Holly had laughed and capitulated. But an awkward silence had shrouded them on the short drive.

Holly picked her handbag off the floor and set it in her lap, getting ready to bolt. When he came to a stop in her aunts' driveway, she unbuckled her seat belt and shucked off his sheriff's office jacket. Micah had noticed her shivering in the stiffening breeze off the channel as they crossed the Pot's parking lot, and had whipped the jacket out of his backseat and wrapped it around her shoulders.

It smelled faintly of the aftershave he'd used for years—an outdoorsy, masculine scent—along with a subtle note of motor oil. That actually had her blinking back a sudden sting of tears. Micah loved cars and tinkered with all kinds of engines, as had her husband. It was a familiar, comforting scent, one she missed a lot.

Holly racked her brain for something to say after he turned off the ignition, preferably something breezy that might defuse the tension between them. Unfortunately, she seemed to be all out of breezy for the night.

She reached for the door handle. "Thanks for the lift. And I apologize again for acting like an idiot."

Micah had told her to forget it after her two previous apologies. But even his understanding attitude hadn't lessened her embarrassment.

"Hey, hold on a minute," Micah said. "I don't just dump ladies off in the driveway. You know me better than that." He smiled and started to open his door.

"I certainly didn't act like a lady tonight," she muttered.

"You're always a lady. And those jackasses deserved what they got and more."

God, he was such a good guy. She got out and tracked around the front of the Tahoe. Micah met her there, his elbow crooked in a gallant invitation. She smiled as she tucked her hand around his muscular arm, and they strolled slowly to the house and up the short set of steps to the front porch.

And with every step they took, her heart pounded harder from a mix of nerves and anticipation.

She didn't want to let go of him. Micah was a big, utterly masculine presence by her side, making her feel protected and cherished in a way she hadn't in a very long time. Yes, because of worry and maybe one too many beers, her defenses were definitely down. But at the moment, it didn't seem to matter.

"I think I'm still too wired to go to sleep," she found herself saying when they reached the front door. "Why don't I make us a cup of coffee? If you want to stick around for a bit, that is."

Ugh. Lame.

Under the yellow glow of the porch light, she could see Micah's eyebrows tick up. "Uh, sure, I can stick around. I'd like that." He paused for a couple of moments as a grin crept over his handsome features. "You make great coffee."

She didn't, at least not in the old drip pot in her aunts' kitchen. "You are such a liar."

She dug out her key, fumbling for a moment before finally getting the door open. Micah followed her in. "Glad to see you locked the doors," he said.

"I'd never flout your orders, Deputy," she teased, batting her eyelashes at him.

His eyebrows went up again. "Really? I'll hold you to that."

Oh, man. Now she was flirting with him. She obviously did need coffee to counteract the alcohol that had loosened her tongue.

"You think maybe I came on a little strong about locking doors tonight?" he asked as he followed her through the softly lit living room to the kitchen. "Folks at the Pot just want to relax and have a drink, and there I was going at them hammer and tongs about security."

"You only spent *half* the evening buttonholing people at the bar and haranguing them about it, so you were only a PITA for part of the time."

"Thanks for the support," he said wryly.

"Anytime, big guy," she said as she pulled out the giant tin of Folgers from the freezer. She was starting to miss her local Starbucks already.

Micah leaned back against the counter, looking at home in the old-fashioned kitchen. He often checked in on her aunts and spent time with them—another reason why she loved him so much.

Love. Her mind stumbled over the word. She had to force herself to focus on what he was saying.

"Too many people still don't take it seriously," he said. "They think Fitz's break-in must be just some jackass teenager looking for pain meds." He shook his head. "But I'm not sure it was a kid or a one-off."

Holly filled the coffee machine with water and flipped the switch. "It's understandable though. Seashell Bay's always been a safe place."

"Sure, but a guy like him knows that minor thefts can't get much attention from law enforcement. He might even think it's open season around here." His mouth flattened into an irritated line. "He'd be wrong."

"But the thief didn't actually break in there," she said, feeling queasy at the idea of a real problem in Seashell Bay. "She left her door open."

"True, but he might have broken in regardless. Depends on what he knew. Did he know Fitz had Vicodin? That she didn't lock up? She said nobody knew she had the pain meds other than a couple of people at the boatyard, and they're in the clear. Maybe the thief wasn't looking for drugs at all. Maybe he was really after money and just happened upon the pills."

"Didn't she tell you she had nothing much worth taking?"

Micah frowned. "That's why I keep thinking it had to be the drugs. It's hard to believe he picked Fitz's place at random, or just because she doesn't lock her doors. Not when half the people on the island don't lock theirs either."

"She didn't show up at the Pot tonight or I would have talked to her. Is she okay? It's hard to get over something like that."

Sometimes Holly wondered if *she'd* ever get over what had happened in Boston.

"She still seems a little freaked out. At least it looked that way to me when I dropped in yesterday to check on her."

A tight sensation lodged in Holly's chest. Why should she feel weird at the idea of Micah checking on Fitz? It was his job, after all. And in any case, shouldn't she feel relieved if he was becoming romantically interested in Fitz or any other woman instead of her?

The answer should be yes. Yet it didn't feel that way right now.

She waved him into the living room and brought in two mugs of coffee, setting them on coasters on the old mahogany coffee table. Micah settled into one of two Queen Anne wingback chairs that graced the room. Most of the furniture and decorative pieces in the house were antiques, collected during years of dedicated foraging by her aunts through little shops up and down the Maine coast.

Holly took the matching wingback at the opposite end of the coffee table. Best to keep some distance between them.

After taking a sip of coffee, Micah cocked an enquiring eyebrow. "Holly, can I ask you something?"

Uh-oh. That sounded like trouble. "Sure."

He ran a hand across the dark stubble on his chin. He obviously hadn't shaved since morning, and he looked just a little rough around the edges. And a whole lot sexy.

"Every time I talk about Fitz's break-in, you look kind of...oh, antsy, I guess. Are you really worried about someone breaking in here?" He gave her a reassuring smile. "I know I've been riding you about being careful, but you shouldn't give it too much thought. Even if the guy does strike again, it's unlikely he'll try here. This house is on the busiest road, for one thing."

Talking about her break-in was hardly her favorite topic, but if anyone deserved to hear the truth, it was Micah.

"I hate to admit it, but yes, I am worried."

Micah searched her eyes. "Tell me why."

She couldn't help a grimace. "I don't much like talking about it."

Though Micah's gaze remained intense, he didn't press her. Drew had been like that too. He never pushed; instead he just calmly waited her out when something was bothering her.

"But I will," she said. "To you."

He nodded.

"It happened on the Martin Luther King holiday weekend, during one of my New York..." Holly stopped before she said *weekends with Jackson*. Micah never said anything about him, but it was clear he didn't think much of Jackson. "Anyway, when I got back to Boston, my condo had been broken into and trashed."

He blinked in surprise. "Was the lock picked?"

"Yes, according to the cops. The thieves found the cash

I kept in a tea tin in the kitchen—about three hundred dollars. My iPad, camera, and some other electronics were gone too. Fortunately, I had my laptop with me."

"I'm sorry," Micah said in a sympathetic voice. "You said they trashed the place?"

"Well, they—or he—the police weren't entirely sure, did a real number on it. Every drawer and cupboard was emptied—in the kitchen, the office, the bedrooms, my bathroom. The closets too. Bottles were smashed, containers emptied. It was just a horrible, unholy mess."

She'd gone to a hotel that night and couldn't bring herself to return home for two days. Even then, she'd asked a friend from work to go with her. It wasn't so much that she didn't feel safe there anymore—though she'd never felt entirely comfortable since. It was the fact that thugs had invaded her space, pawing through her belongings. She'd found it so devastating that she'd filled a half-dozen trash bags with clothes and other things they'd handled, including most of the stuff in her bathroom. Some of the bags had gone to charity, others straight into the Dumpster.

Her friend had thought it a major overreaction and tried to talk her out of it. Holly had to admit that lack of understanding had hurt. She'd felt more alone at that moment than she had in a long time.

"The bastards do it because it's the fastest way," Micah said. "And the most thorough. Thieves just yank and dump so they can be in and out in minutes and not miss anything. Guys like that will be wearing gloves so they don't leave any prints."

"That's exactly what the police said."

He put his cup down and leaned forward. "Holly, I'm really sorry, but why didn't you tell me before?"

"I hate thinking about it, Micah. I don't know if I'll ever be able to forget it." She gave him an awkward smile. "I guess that makes me a wimp."

His gaze narrowed. "Not even close, so none of that bull. And I'm glad you told me now. No wonder you tense up whenever I talk about what happened to Fitz."

As a cop, Micah would intellectually understand how a victim would react. But no one could truly get the sense of personal violation without having gone through it. Certainly not a big, tough guy like Micah.

"After I settled down, I read up on the emotional impact of burglary," she said. "It seems it's generally much worse for women. The sense of violation and helplessness and the fear that it could happen again." She grimaced. "Or something even uglier."

"Most people see their home as an extension of themselves," Micah said. "If it's breached, they feel like they've been personally attacked even though they weren't there. And like you said, that's especially true for women." His jaw was set in a hard, tight line. "That's why I have to nail this asshole. I don't want anybody else in Seashell Bay to go through what you and Fitz have had to endure."

Holly couldn't hold back a smile. Knowing Micah, he wouldn't be able to rest until he made the island as safe as it could be again. He'd make it his personal mission, and that gave her a good deal of comfort when it came to her aunts. The old darlings were vulnerable. They'd always been careless about security, leaving barely adequate locks on both the house and the store. Florence had always heaved dramatic sighs whenever Holly brought up the subject, as if burglary only happened on the mainland, and Seashell Bay was protected by a magical force field.

"Florence and Beatrice need to start taking security more seriously," Micah said, mirroring her thoughts. "I'll bet they have some meds kicking around, don't they? With all their ailments?"

"I'm sure." Holly knew Beatrice had been taking a couple of medications for several years to help her cope with her rheumatoid arthritis, one of which was for the pain. "I'll check with them. And I'll talk to them again about replacing the locks. I'd just go ahead and get it done before they got back, but Florence would probably bar me from the island forever for being so bossy."

He rolled his eyes. "Yeah, like that would ever happen. Tell her I'll install the new locks myself, so it'll just cost her the price of the hardware." Micah drained the last of his coffee and stood up. "I'm sure you're tired, and I don't want to wear you out. Thanks for the coffee." He cut her a sly smile as she got up. "It was great, honestly."

She was a bit surprised that he'd taken the initiative to leave. "Yeah, almost as good as Starbucks. But thank *you* for the ride home, Micah. It was really nice of you."

When they reached the door, she touched his arm. "I think it was probably good for me to talk about the break-in. Especially to someone who gets it."

She opened her arms, waiting for Micah to give her one of his usual friendly hugs.

But she got something quite a bit different. He swept her into his embrace and held her tight against his brawny chest, one of his hands spread dangerously low, fingers brushing her butt, while the other hand stroked slowly down her spine. "We were damn good together tonight, weren't we?" His voice was a low rumble that made her shiver. "At shuffleboard, I mean."

Oh. My. God.

He wasn't just talking about shuffleboard. And Lord above, did he feel good wrapped around her. Better than good—it felt like what she'd been wanting for a long time. If he tried to kiss her now, Holly wasn't sure she could resist.

And that would lead to some very bad things, especially given his clear state of arousal.

She stretched up and gave his bristly cheek the briefest of pecks.

"We were the best," she whispered. Then she wriggled a little to let Micah know she needed to break away.

She felt a sigh move through his body before he let her go. "I'll be thinking about that," he said. Then he turned and strode down the steps to his cruiser.

Holly shut and locked the door. She sagged against it as she sucked in an unsteady breath. She would be thinking about it too, probably all night.

Chapter 7

$\mathcal{A}$n evening ride in Lily's lobster boat had always been a highlight of Holly's summer vacations. The girlfriends made it an annual event to mark the day Lily had cobbled together enough money to buy the green-and-white craft that was her pride and joy.

Morgan had met Holly at the ferry when she got back from the hospital, and the two had carried the treats Morgan had prepared to the floating pier where Lily waited with her skiff. As they motored out to *Miss Annie*'s mooring, Holly had filled them in on her aunt's condition. Both the psychologist and the attending physician had cleared Florence to return home tomorrow, subject to one last round of blood tests. That had been a welcome piece of news.

Lily headed out of the channel, maneuvering *Miss Annie* around the colorful buoys running parallel to the shore, and skillfully avoiding the lines that connected the buoys to the lobster traps far below. When they reached the middle of the sound, she pointed the bow toward the darkening east and killed the boat's diesel engine. Westward from the stern was tiny Pumpkin Knob, and beyond that were Peaks and Great Diamond Islands, the lights of their houses starting to twinkle into life. It was a familiar scene to all of them, but no less beautiful because of it.

Holly sank into one of the aluminum chairs that Lily had brought aboard for the evening. A beer in her hand, she propped her bare feet up on the stern rail, while Morgan and Lily settled on either side of her. They were all wearing shorts, and of the three pairs of legs resting on the gunwale, two were deeply tanned while the other— Holly's—were still way too pale for her liking. It was hard to get a tan when all you did was work.

They held a peaceful silence for a few minutes as they watched the sun sink slowly over Portland, throwing gorgeous streamers of orange, pink, and purple to color the sky. A gentle northwest breeze heralded the arrival of crisp, clear days ahead. Holly inhaled deeply, loving the salty tang of the coastal air.

Living in downtown Boston, she missed that clean scent. She did not, however, miss the pungent smell of lobsters, fish, and bait that was so much a part of Seashell Bay life. As thoroughly as Lily hosed down *Miss Annie*'s deck at the end of every fishing day, that funky scent still lingered. Holly had no affinity whatsoever for the lobstering way of life, something that influenced everyone on the island, even those who didn't work directly in the trade. It always made her feel like a bit of a Seashell Bay fraud, which was probably why she'd overreacted to Frenette's snarky comment at the Lobster Pot.

Despite her mainland sensibilities, she adored the island, and her family and friends meant everything to her. Still, she felt like she was on the verge of drifting farther away from her roots. The move to New York would be a game changer in her life and would bring consequences she could barely guess at—for herself, for her aunts, and even for the store.

And then, of course, there was Micah. She'd lain awake for hours after he left last night, tossing restlessly. As much as she didn't want to admit it, she'd wanted to have sex with the deputy. Badly. She'd wanted nothing more than to drag the wonderful hunk upstairs to her bedroom and have her way with him all freaking night.

It wouldn't have taken much dragging either. Not with what she'd felt going on below his belt. She'd killed herself not to let it show, but that impressive contact had pretty much stolen her breath. And it had tempted her like nothing in a long time.

Yeah, you totally forgot about your boyfriend then, didn't you? Remember him, Jackson Leigh?

She really had no reason to feel guilty about Jackson. Though they weren't exclusive, Holly hadn't slept with anyone else since they'd started dating. But she'd bet the bank that Jackson had. After all, they only saw each other every few weeks, and the guy was a total player. It was one of the reasons she'd decided to move to New York, so she could figure out once and for all if she wanted some kind of future with the guy.

Morgan gave her a gentle poke on the shoulder. "Don't you guys wish we could do this all season? Once a year isn't nearly enough."

"Amen to that, sister." Lily raised her can of iced tea in a toast. "For me, Casco Bay, a beautiful sunset, and hanging with the two best women on the planet—it just doesn't get any better than that."

"Not that we want you to feel any guilt for leaving us, Holly," Morgan said sardonically. "Not one tiny bit."

"There's no point since I'm already drowning in it," Holly said, unable to hold back a sigh.

Lily frowned. "Come on, you know we're just teasing you. You'll come back in your own time. It may take a while, but you will someday. Just like Aiden and Ryan."

"Because escape can only be temporary, right?" Holly said. "The lure of Seashell Bay always sucks you back in."

"But not just yet, huh?" Morgan pulled the corners of her mouth down to make a sad face. "How does it go? If I can make it there, I'll make it anywhere, it's up to you, New York, New York," she sang.

Holly shook her head. "You make it sound almost like a funeral dirge. But I really do have to give it a try, guys." She'd staked everything on this once-in-a lifetime chance to make it to the top echelon of her profession.

Lily gave her bare leg a pat. "We understand, darling. We wish like crazy that you were here, but we really do understand."

Their understanding and acceptance just made her feel worse. Weepy, even. What the hell was wrong with her?

Time for a subject change.

"Let's talk about the store for a minute," she said. "I spent most of the day thinking about some improvements we could make. God knows I had plenty of time in between serving the rare customers."

"Something that will bring it into the twenty-first century, hopefully?" Morgan said.

"For sure," Holly said. "Tinkering isn't going to be enough to make the store profitable again. The orientation needs to change, especially if Night Owl sets up shop."

Lily looked thoughtful. "Are you thinking in terms of something other than a general store?"

"You know *general store* is just a quaint name for it, Lily. It hasn't been that for decades, if it ever was. It's a convenience store and not much different from Night Owl, at least in essence. Just smaller, dowdier, and with less product."

"I suppose you're right," Lily said. "Dad told me it used to carry hardware and fishing supplies and some fabrics too. But that was way back when. Before your aunts took it over, I think."

"Now it's basically a convenience store with a little tourist stuff thrown in," Morgan added. "Like those incredibly ugly lobster T-shirts."

"I love those shirts!" Lily said indignantly.

Holly knew her pal wore them regularly, as did many islanders.

"I'm sure Night Owl will carry the T-shirts and other cheapo tourist stuff too," she said. "The bottom line is that our store needs to look different and be different. It can keep selling some of the same things that Night Owl and the seasonal store carry, like basic groceries, beer, and wine, but it needs to give people access to some products they can't get unless they go all the way to Portland. Especially the tourists who are going to show up once the resort gets going. I guarantee they won't want tacky stuff."

Holly pulled her feet down off the rail and sat up straight, feeling more enthusiastic. This was what she was good at—figuring out how to make business thrive. "Night Owl isn't about catering to the tourist trade, other than supplying them with chips and soda and cigarettes. To be different, we need to give people stuff they can't find anywhere else on the island. And if they come to our store to buy those things, they might even end up getting their beer, wine, and groceries there too."

"Huh," Lily said. "So you're thinking about focusing on tourists? That would be a sea change."

"I know," Holly said. "I can't deny there would be some risk."

"I can see your point though. There definitely are going to be a lot more tourists, and most of them should be pretty well-off."

"Exactly. Take souvenirs and gifts. There's not much worth buying on the island right now, so tourists do that kind of shopping on the mainland. What if we were to start sourcing and selling some quality goods by Maine artisans? God knows there are enough of them."

The idea had formed when Holly thought about the local Blueberry Festival. Every year at that event, a couple of dozen artists and craftspeople—almost all from off the island—set up tents and booths for the weekend. They produced and sold quality goods ranging from paintings and photography to jewelry, glass, leather, and woodworking. Those artisans always did a brisk trade at the festival, and most came back year after year. What if her aunts made their goods available in the store all year long? It could become a real showcase for artists and artisans from around the state.

"It sounds good, as long as Florence and Beatrice could source and manage that kind of inventory," Morgan said. Her expression, however, registered doubt.

Holly had been thinking about that. "I'll help them as much as I can when I'm here, and I could do some work remotely too. And don't forget how shrewd Florence has always been in dealing with suppliers."

"What are you thinking of getting rid of so you'll have room?" Lily asked.

Holly had a tentative list in her head. "The gas pump has to go, for starters, though that's not a question of space. It should go because it's a relic and an eyesore, and there's not that much profit in it. Night Owl is going to take most of that business anyway."

"All true," Morgan said. "I can't tell you how many times I've felt like kicking the hell out of that cranky old pump. I swear it's older than I am."

"Ha! It's probably as old as Gramps," Lily scoffed.

Holly didn't think she was exaggerating by much. "That horrific DVD collection has to go too. And the T-shirts."

"Not the T-shirts!" Lily protested.

"Stay with me, sweetie," Holly said, patting her hand. "As for groceries, I'm going to suggest cutting back to not much more than half the floor space. We should continue to carry most of the basics but stock only a couple of best-selling brands of each product."

"I bet some of the regulars will be pissed off that they can't buy their favorite brand of detergent," Morgan said.

"They'll get over it. In truth, they probably buy most of that stuff in Portland at Hannaford's or Costco anyway. Our store should mainly be for people who run out or who don't want to shop in the city on any given day. People like that can't expect to have a full range of brands. We're not a supermarket."

"Logic, I like it," Morgan said. "But people on Seashell Bay get pretty emotional about this sort of thing. As much as I hate to admit it, we are pretty resistant to change."

"Time to get with the program, buttercup. It's that or the store goes belly-up," Holly said. "I'd like to put in a deli bar too, with a focus on high-quality meats and cheeses and fresh sandwiches. And I'm even thinking about a commercial espresso machine."

"Seriously?" Morgan said.

"Sure. You can't get a good cup of coffee on this island. A lot of tourists and day-trippers go into withdrawal when they can't get their daily latte or macchiato. It could be a real win for us."

"That's going to change, because they'll be able to get good coffee at the resort," Lily said, sounding apologetic. "The restaurant will have an espresso machine. Aiden and I figured people would go crazy without it."

Damn. Holly hadn't thought about that. "Okay, but still, when those folks are out and about, they might drop in the store for coffee, don't you think? Plus there are the day-trippers who may not even go near the resort."

"I think your ideas are really creative and make a lot of sense," Morgan said. "Sure, there's risk, but we all know something significant needs to be done."

"I agree," Lily said with a decisive nod. "It may be risky, but look at Aiden and me. We're throwing everything we have into the ecoresort. Sometimes you have to listen to your heart and just go for it."

"Ryan and I will help promote the store to the tourists and kayakers at the B&B," Morgan said. "We'll make sure everybody knows where they can buy the good stuff while they're on the island."

"We'll do the same thing at the resort too," Lily said. "In fact, we can put the store's info in our brochures about things to do on the island."

God, no wonder she loved this place so much. No matter what, your friends and neighbors had your back.

She relaxed into her chair and put her feet back up on the rail. "Thanks, guys, you're the absolute best. I can't tell you how much your support means to me." She paused for a moment. "Now, I don't suppose you'd like to help me get my aunts on board with the plan, would you?"

Because that would be the most difficult hurdle of all.

Chapter 8

Micah had spent yesterday interviewing the island's teenagers and college-age kids. Unfortunately, it had all added up to a big fat zero. Nobody owned up to seeing Justin Gore or anyone else with prescription pills. Time after time, the kids sang from the same songbook—that Justin was troubled and angry but probably wouldn't have the guts to break into somebody's house. Nor would any of the other kids.

And that was probably all true. Most parents on the island kept a pretty close eye on their kids and tended not to put up with a lot of crap when trouble did crop up.

So yesterday evening Micah had retreated to the rocking chair on his front porch to put back a couple of beers and think hard about where to take the case. One obvious group of suspects was the construction crew at the resort. There were at least thirty guys on-site at this stage of construction, and almost all of them came from the mainland. At the very least, he should check their whereabouts on the day of the burglary.

He was just now finishing up interviews with the first

batch of workers in the makeshift lunchroom at the construction site and had a dozen more to go. He was focusing on the ones under forty, leaving out the handful of older guys on-site, at least for now. Aiden had made it clear that Micah was to receive full cooperation from the staff.

Opening the door to the lunchroom, assistant site superintendent Mike McGee ushered in a rough-looking dude with a scraggly beard and hair that hung down almost to his shoulders. The guy gave Micah a resentful stare as he took off his hardhat and raked a grimy hand over his flattened black hair. Both his arms were covered in ink, with the tattoos running up under the sleeves of his black T-shirt. Dragons seemed to be his preferred artistic theme.

"This is Jace Horton," McGee said.

"Thanks, Mike. Have a seat, Mr. Horton."

Horton thumped down onto the gray metal chair.

The guy's personnel file contained only three sheets of paper. Jace Horton was twenty-nine years old, lived in South Portland, and had worked at unskilled construction jobs since high school. He'd started to work at the resort site in February.

"I need to ask you a few questions," Micah said. "Should only take a few minutes."

Horton shrugged.

"Where were you on Tuesday between eight in the morning and five thirty?"

"Right here," Horton said in a bored voice. "I started work at seven thirty and I didn't leave until five thirty. Got a couple hours' overtime. That's been happening a lot lately."

The answer was so quick and thorough that it sounded

rehearsed. "Okay, we'll check your time cards just to confirm that," Micah said. "Did you leave the site at any point
before quitting time?"

Again, Horton didn't hesitate. "Yeah, I went to my buddy's house to eat lunch and have a beer. He's got a car. "

"How long were you off-site?"

"Half an hour. That's what we get for lunch, and the
fucking foreman watches us like a hawk."

"You go there a lot?"

"Often enough. Can't drink beer on the job, right?
We're out here busting our asses all day, and a guy gets
thirsty for a cold one. Who doesn't want to get away from
the job for a few minutes if he gets the chance?"

"Sure. So what's your buddy's name?"

"Logan Cain. We're on the same crew."

Micah lifted Horton's file. Cain's was next in line. He
slid it open and scanned the top sheet. "So Cain lives on
the island."

"Yeah, maybe three minutes from here."

The address was Fortune Lane, a dead-end road in the
middle of the island. The house was a well-maintained
and nicely furnished rental cottage owned by Sally Christopher. Micah remembered Ryan telling him that a laborer
and his girlfriend had recently rented a cottage.

"Anyone else there when you guys had lunch Tuesday?"

Horton shook his head. "Nope."

Micah made a note to ask Griff Turner to run a criminal record check on Horton, as he had for another guy he'd
interviewed. The simple fact that Horton had left the site
on the day of the burglary made him a suspect.

"So, Mr. Horton, you ever run into trouble with the
law? Any arrests?"

"Long time ago," Horton finally said after a long pause. "Just some juvie stuff, and that doesn't count." He paused again, as if deciding whether to say more. "And there was a bogus conviction for possession of stolen goods."

"Bogus?"

"Totally. I was just keeping some stuff for a friend. Doing him a favor. It was all bullshit."

Micah would check that out. "Okay, that's it for now," he said, getting up.

Horton shrugged again, then lazily pushed up from the table and strolled out. It was weird that the guy hadn't even asked why he was being questioned. In Micah's experience, it was usually the first question people raised when confronted by a cop. Most of the other workers had asked immediately.

Horton's buddy, Logan Cain, strode in a few seconds later, a smile on his deeply tanned face. According to his file, Cain was only twenty-five, but Micah figured he looked more like thirty. Unlike Horton, he was big, well groomed, and what most women would no doubt call good-looking, with dark, spiky hair and a small silver ring in his left ear. The guy had an easy smile and the confident swagger that suggested he didn't spend any lonely nights unless he wanted to.

Unlike Horton, Cain had no visible tattoos, but he had plenty of muscles and his hands were covered in nicks and scars.

When Cain extended his hand, Micah gave it a solid crunch. The grip elicited a blink and a quick, indrawn breath, as if Cain were surprised. When a guy looked that laid-back going into a police interview, it always raised Micah's antennas.

He started off with questions about Cain's background. The guy had grown up in Bangor, went to community college there, and then worked construction in two other Maine cities before landing in Portland a year and a half ago. During last year's bad winter, he'd been laid off. When Micah asked him how he'd found the Seashell Bay job, he said Horton—whom he'd met on a previous job—had told him about the opportunity. He'd worked at the resort since February, and in May had decided to rent a cottage on the island. He liked the slow pace of Seashell Bay and had convinced his reluctant girlfriend to give it a try, even though she had to commute by ferry to her job in Portland.

"You're a lucky man to live here, Deputy," Cain said with a friendly smile.

"Tell me what you did on Tuesday," Micah said, putting a little steel into his voice.

Cain closed his eyes for a couple of seconds. "It was another long day with a couple of hours' OT. After work I went straight home, had a beer, helped the girlfriend with dinner, and watched a little TV. Same old, same old."

"When did you sign out?"

"I guess it must have been about five thirty. Like I said, we got about two hours' extra work."

"Did you leave the site at any point during the day?"

Cain raised his eyebrows. "Didn't Jace tell you?"

"Please answer the question."

"Jace and I went to my place for lunch. We were back here at noon, if that's your next question."

Cain obviously had a brain and wasn't the least bit nervous.

Micah would verify the accuracy of Cain's claim as to

when he came and went from the site, as he would every other employee's. The crews were required to record their arrival and departure times, signing in and out with the guards on duty at the gates.

"Did anyone other than Horton see you during the half hour you were gone from the site?"

Cain shrugged. "Guess not. Hell, we just went to my place, ate a sandwich, drank a beer, and got back to work on time." He sat up straighter and locked his gaze on Micah's eyes. "What's this about anyway, Deputy?"

Micah had been careful to keep that information from all the guys he'd interviewed so far. There was no need for them to know unless they didn't have solid alibis, and the first wave of guys had them, with the exception of Horton and one other. Most had been working long days as the construction bosses pushed to make up for time lost due to bad weather.

"Since you live on the island," Micah said, deciding to gauge Cain's reaction, "maybe you heard about a burglary at a house on Yellow Grass Road."

Cain barely reacted. Just a slight curl of one corner of his lips. "Actually, I didn't. I try to mind my own business, though people around here do like to gossip, don't they?"

Micah decided to try a different tack. "If you're like most construction guys I know, you must get hurt a fair bit on the job. You're used to dealing with pain."

Cain was clearly surprised by the abrupt shift in direction but recovered quickly. "Actually, most of my pain comes from my girlfriend." He winked at Micah. "You know what I mean?"

Asshole. Micah's instinctive dislike of him grew. "Ever been arrested?"

"Never," Cain said.

"Maybe you and Horton spent your lunch hour breaking into that house," Micah said abruptly. "You don't have much of an alibi, and your buddy has a criminal record. Possession of stolen goods, no less."

Cain's gaze flickered, then he look irritated. "So you just assume that everybody with a criminal record is a liar?"

Micah gave him a bland smile. "Okay, that's it. For now."

Cain stood quickly and left the room.

Micah stayed seated, thinking. His spidey senses were definitely tingling when it came to Cain and Horton, but he had to caution himself against letting his gut feelings send him down the wrong path. Since he had to conduct this investigation with little support from the rest of the department, he'd better be sure to get it right.

Chapter 9

$\mathcal{A}$s Holly stowed the vacuum cleaner in the hall closet, a sharp rap sounded on the door. She took a quick glance out the front window through the venetian blinds and saw the sheriff's office cruiser parked in the driveway.

Crap. She looked a mess.

Pulling the scrunchie off her ponytail, she shook her hair loose and then glanced down at her pink scoop-neck tank top and white shorts. Thank God they didn't look too horrible after a couple of hours spent tidying up her aunts' house.

"Hi there, Deputy," she said brightly as she swung open the door. Her heart skipped a few beats at the sight of Micah in his sexy cop's uniform, complete with handcuffs on his belt. Man, was he a fantasy come to life.

"Am I interrupting?" he asked. "Seven thirty probably isn't the best time to drop in. Have you had dinner?"

Was he about to ask her out if she said no? Holly wavered between wanting an invite and being afraid of one. She instinctively came down on the side of caution.

"I had a salad earlier," she said, lying. "And I was just

doing a little cleaning. Under the circumstances, I'm happy for the interruption."

"Good." Micah stepped inside. As usual, his stubble was heavy at this time of day, and he was wearing a slight frown. In fact, he looked pretty tired.

"Long day?" she asked.

Micah's smile was wry. "More cats to rescue than usual."

"Yeah, those darn cats."

"Actually, I spent most of the day at the resort site interviewing guys about the break-in at Fitz's place," he said. "Then I got HQ to run criminal record checks on some of them. "

She should offer him a beer. Island hospitality demanded it, which was as good an excuse as any. "Why don't I get you a cold beer and you can sit down and tell me about it?"

His face broke into one of those easy, warm smiles she found so appealing. "I didn't come to talk about the case. But, sure, a beer would hit the spot." He glanced down the hall toward the kitchen. "Could we go out on the deck? It's a real nice evening."

"Of course, though I'm afraid it's a bit of a danger zone out there. It's getting pretty decrepit."

Holly led him to the kitchen and retrieved two bottles of Shipyard from the fridge. Micah slid open the patio door and stepped out onto the battered deck that ran almost the full width of the house.

The harsh coastal weather—the rain and the salt and the brutal winters—had combined with the passage of time to render most of the deck unusable. Looking down at the rotting, crumbling boards made Holly sad. She'd spent a lot of happy hours out here in her teens and twenties, her bare feet resting on the low rail, a glass of lemonade or beer on the table beside her, and a thriller or romance novel in her lap. The view of the glittering water and the islands in the bay was both breathtaking and soothing. Sadly, the deck had become yet another casualty of her aunts' need to economize.

As with so many other things, Holly had practically begged them to let her pay for the necessary repairs. And as usual, the answer was no. Florence had admitted she was afraid to go out on the deck anymore and missed being able to sit out there. But she remained adamant that she'd pay for the repairs herself when they could afford it. Which would probably be never.

"As for the case, there's not much to go on so far." He took a long drink, one hand resting on the rail.

"Better be careful, Micah. If that rail gave way and you fell, the county would probably sue my aunts for negligence."

Micah rolled his eyes and then gave the rail a yank, causing it to wobble. "The state of this deck is exactly what I came over to talk about."

She frowned. "It is?"

"I've been thinking about things I could do to help Florence and Beatrice. And what I'd really like to do is build them a new deck." Micah shrugged, as if already hearing her aunts' objections. "I must owe them for about five thousand cups of free coffee by now, after all."

She smiled. "Well—"

He cut her off. "I'll pay for the materials and do the work myself. Your aunts have always enjoyed sitting out here. A view like this shouldn't go to waste, and those two more than deserve it for all the good they do for the island."

Because the conversation was starting to make her feel way too emotional, Holly decided to go for light-hearted. "Okay, you seriously win the vote for nicest guy on the planet. Although way to make me feel guilty, dude."

Consternation pulled his brows down. "Holly, I never—"

She poked him in the arm. "I'm kidding. I think it's a wonderful idea, and I'd be happy to help with the costs. I just hope you have more luck convincing them than I've had."

Micah glanced out toward a passing ferry heading for the dock, its decks loaded with passengers waving at friends and relatives onshore. Then he settled his gaze back on her, and the intensity made her stomach go fluttery.

"I'm not going to take no for an answer," he said. "Your aunts are proud, and pride is important. We all know how deep it runs here on the island. But letting your neighbors help out and take care of you in tough times is important too."

Like he took care of her last summer when she was injured. Like all her friends had taken care of her.

He crossed his arms over his broad chest, silently challenging her.

"Okay, I'm with you," she said. "I'll hog-tie Florence if she gives you any trouble."

Micah's warm laugh rolled over her, turning her flutters into pinwheels. God, she loved his laugh.

"I'd pay a lot of money to see that," he said.

She held up her arm and flexed the muscles in her bicep in a silly imitation of a bodybuilder. "I'm tougher than I look. And by the way, I intend to help you with the deck. I have zero experience with power tools, but I can fetch and carry like nobody's business."

"Great. Now, how's Florence doing anyway?"

The question wiped away her smile. "Beatrice called this afternoon. Florence's blood work is off, so they're going to keep her a while longer and redo the tests."

"She'll hate that, but at least she's getting some much-needed rest." Micah turned and started to carefully test the boards of the deck with his foot. "I was just thinking—what if we converted the deck into a screened porch?"

"Micah, that's an awful lot of— "

"Expense," he finished. "Not as much as you might think. Anyway, if we enclose the deck, your aunts can enjoy the fresh air and the view even when it's raining. And we could replace the screens with windows when summer's over so they could use it all through the fall."

Holly studied Micah's face. It was radiating determination. *Oh, what the hell.* "Honestly, that sounds like a slice of heaven, but it would take a huge amount of your time. It'd be a lot to ask of you."

"If we're going to do it, let's do it right." He came back to stand beside her and carefully rested his hand on her shoulder, almost as if he expected her to jerk away. His palm was callused and a little rough. It felt wonderful against her bare skin.

"I'm counting on you to help me talk them into this," he said.

"Of course I will," she said, forcing a smile. "I don't know how to thank you, Micah. It's a truly amazing and thoughtful plan."

Only her desperate fear of where kissing might lead them—*up to my bedroom*—stopped her from launching herself at him. But they *were* friends, and that friendship was important. The last thing she wanted to do was screw that up.

He shrugged. "It's no big deal. How about I take some measurements now? That way I can get started right away on ordering some of the lumber. And since I've got the day off tomorrow, I might as well get going with the demolition."

His sexy voice somehow made demolition sound like a ton of fun.

"Go right ahead," Holly said. "But aren't you hungry? You obviously haven't had dinner."

"It won't take long," he said. "I'll just get my toolbox out of the truck."

"I could throw together something quick, like pasta and sauce," she said. "And a salad? How does that sound?"

Dumb, that's how it sounds.

She was acting like Micah was still just her old pal, and she was just inviting him to stay for a casual meal. Though she'd done that many times over the years, what she was feeling now was anything but casual.

His eyebrows ticked up. "Sounds great, but only if you join me."

She gave him a mock scowl, trying to keep things light. "I told you I'd already eaten. Are you trying to make me fat, Micah Lancaster?"

He laughed. "A salad doesn't count."

His smile faded, and the look in his eyes changed from amused to smoldering as his gaze trailed over her body, lingering briefly on her chest before dropping to her hips and legs. "Besides, I don't think a little pasta could even begin to mess with perfection."

The dark tone of his voice sent her heart rate up to

jackhammer level and made her realize just how much trouble she was in.

Because she didn't have much food in the house—and because she'd needed to get away from Micah for a few minutes—Holly had popped next door to the store and picked up some basics, including a box of rigatoni, a jar of tomato sauce, and a quart of chocolate ice cream. Fortunately, she still had some salad fixings from her trip to Whole Foods yesterday after her visit to the hospital. She knew Micah wouldn't complain about the hastily prepared, plain dinner. Fancy for him was anything that didn't come out of a freezer or a can.

And he absolutely loved chocolate ice cream.

As she prepared the meal, she snuck frequent peeks at him through the patio doors. He seemed as focused and precise about measuring the deck as he was about everything he did. Micah's strong, comforting presence made her feel utterly secure whenever he was around.

With one eye on the pasta that boiled on the range beside her, Holly worked on the salad and warily probed her own feelings. It had been a long time since she'd felt like this around a man—since she lost Drew, to be exact. In some ways, Micah was a lot like her husband, although Drew had been more intense. He'd been the kind of man who charged through life full bore.

With Drew, every trip home from overseas or from his stateside base had been a celebration. Making dinner while he puttered around the house or worked on his motorcycle had been a blissful refuge from her demanding and frenetically paced job. She'd loved nothing better than a quiet evening at home with the man she loved, cocooned from the demands of their busy lives. But soon Drew would leave again. The quiet times had been only a temporary respite for both of them.

Still, she missed those moments with an intensity that could still make her body ache with longing. And no matter how much fun she had with Jackson or how involved she was in her job or new partnership, the ache never fully disappeared. Some days, in fact, her life felt pretty shallow, especially in comparison to the one she'd led with her husband.

And what would her husband have thought of a man like Jackson? That question nagged at her, and she didn't think the answer was one she'd want to hear. *But Drew had really liked Micah, as Micah did him.*

She jerked her head up at the sound of the patio door sliding open.

"Wow, you look pretty intent there. Does it take that much concentration to make a salad?" Micah said in a teasing voice as he strode through the kitchen with his toolbox.

Holly eyed his very fine butt as he passed her. His back and shoulders were pretty darn impressive, too. "Micah, you know very well that I'm more than a little challenged when it comes to kitchen duties. As are you, as I recall."

"Bullshit," he called over his shoulder. "I'm totally challenged, but you sure aren't. And what you're making now smells great."

That was a big stretch, but it made her smile. It was nice to be appreciated. "I really should have offered to buy you dinner at the Pot. This isn't much of anything."

He turned and looked at her. "I'm glad I have you all to myself for once. Most times when we've had a meal together, it's been with a crowd." Then he winked at her before disappearing through the front door.

Holly was still thinking about that wink as Micah came back in and went upstairs to clean up. When he returned to the kitchen, he opened the bottle of red wine she'd set out and poured each of them a glass.

"Think it'll be a problem if I start right in on the deck?" he asked. "I was thinking that Florence will probably want peace and quiet, at least until she gets back to work."

Holly shook her head. "I doubt that a little hammering will bother her. Besides, she's going to be on enough anti-anxiety medication to tranquilize an elephant."

"You told me she hated that stuff."

"She does, but she looked pretty blissed out yesterday," Holly said drily.

She grabbed a pair of cloth napkins and a handful of cutlery and headed through the arched doorway into the dining room to set the table. "By the way, you still haven't told me whether those criminal record checks turned up anything. I have to say that the thought of some creep skulking around the island looking for places to rob makes my skin crawl."

Micah was leaning against the kitchen counter, wineglass in hand. She sidled around his big body to get to the stove, resisting the silly impulse to brush up against him.

"After what happened to you, anybody would feel that way," he said. "The main thing is to keep your doors and windows locked all the time. Everybody here has to get used to doing that. But try not to worry."

She decided not to mention minor details like how easy it would be for an intruder to smash the glass in the door and twist the dead bolt open. Besides, the slight frown on his face as he stared at the patio door suggested he was thinking the same. Still, she appreciated his attempt to reassure her.

"So has Aiden got any ex-felons working for him over there or not? Micah, I won't melt into a terrified puddle if you tell me the truth." At least she hoped not. She took a gulp of wine for fortification, just in case.

He gave a reluctant nod. "Only one guy had a rap sheet. A dude all tattoos and attitude. He was convicted of Class D petty theft when the Portland cops found stolen computer equipment in his apartment. Horton probably planned the theft with the buddy that did the actual break-in, though they couldn't make that theory stick. He served four months in county jail for that one. Plus he'd done time in a juvie facility before that."

"Gee, that sounds swell—not. I don't get why a contractor would hire somebody like that."

"Experienced laborers can be hard to find during construction season, and it's worse here in the islands because of the long commute," Micah said. "Then there's the fact that some contractors like to give guys like a Horton a break if they've had some history as a good, reliable worker. It's not a terrible thing to do."

She sighed. "I guess that makes some sense." She drained the finished pasta. "But he still hardly sounds like a good hire."

"A buddy at the site is giving him an alibi. I'm not necessarily buying it, but it'll hold up unless there's evidence that they're lying."

"That's why you said there's still nothing to go on."

"And there may never be." He hesitated. "Unless there's another break-in."

Chapter 10

"Aunt Florence, you are *not* going back to work," Holly said, gripping her teacup with white fingers. "You fell in the hospital, remember? When you tried to get out of bed without any help. Or are we just supposed to pretend that didn't happen?"

That awful little episode had kept her aunt in the hospital for a few days longer than expected. Fortunately, the fall wasn't the result of a ministroke, as the doctors had originally feared, but simply as a result of too much antianxiety medication. Once the docs had sorted out the right dosage, Holly and Beatrice had been able to bring Florence home—with strict orders to rest.

Naturally, the old gal had only walked through the door a few hours ago and she was already issuing orders and being a hardhead.

Florence adjusted her old wire-rimmed glasses and gave Holly a glare. "What else am I supposed to do? Lie around on the couch like a lazy dog? Or watch soap operas? You know me better than that, Holly Tyler."

That was a pretty mild retort by Florence standards.

Holly suspected that the only reason she hadn't ramped up the volume to combat level was the meds the psychiatrist had prescribed, combined with the strain of her illness. In fact, Holly could hardly believe how frail her darling aunt still looked. Her face was pasty, and she'd lost five pounds off her already thin frame. But it was a good sign that Florence had a fair amount of spirit left in her.

"The doctor told you not to go back to work for at least ten days," Beatrice said in a firm voice, patting her elder sister's slender, blue-veined hand. "He was very clear about that."

"That quack?" Florence scoffed. "I bet he tells every patient the same thing. Probably pushes a little button inside his coat and a tape recorder says the words so he doesn't have to trouble himself." She gave a dismissive snort. "He doesn't know *me*."

Holly sighed. "Aunt Florence, you know how much I love you, but I swear I'll lock you in the house if you so much as try to set foot in the store. I've lost too many people I love already, and I'm darn well not going to lose you. Especially not because of your pigheadedness."

"Holly's right," Beatrice said. She hardly ever took on her sister, but the recent scare had clearly rattled her. "You have to do what the doctor ordered. If not for your own sake, then for ours." She was obviously repressing tears.

Florence opened her mouth as if to argue but then closed it again. A couple of moments later, she gave a small nod. "You two should be ashamed of yourselves. Guilt-tripping me like that." She managed to crack a small smile.

"So you'll take your medication and rest while Beatrice and I run the store?" Holly asked.

Florence took a delicate sip from her teacup. "We'll just see how it goes. I'm not making any promises."

Holly relaxed back into her chair. That phrase represented as close to capitulation as she was ever likely to get from Aunt Florence.

Florence redirected her gaze to her sister. Beatrice, her small, neatly dressed figure ramrod straight as always, stared back at her, obviously determined for once not to cave in to her big sister. Aunt Beatrice was as sweet and mild as Florence was feisty and strong-willed.

"But Holly's leaving in a few days, Beatrice," Florence said. "So I'll need to get back in the saddle at least by then. You've never been comfortable running the store by yourself."

Beatrice suddenly looked sick. She'd clearly forgotten that minor detail.

"I'm not leaving for a while," Holly said, patting Beatrice's hand.

While Beatrice could handle most day-to-day tasks at the store, like unpacking and stocking shelves and manning the cash register, she'd never wanted to have anything to do with the financial side of the business and didn't like having to deal with suppliers. Because Florence was always there, she'd never had to.

Beatrice looked dumbfounded. "But you have to be in New York soon, don't you?"

Holly had been wrestling with that problem from the moment she first set eyes on her aunt at the hospital. She'd hoped Florence would bounce back quickly so she could keep her stay on the island almost as short as she'd originally planned and then get down to New York. But now that she was back home, she realized that her schedule was a lot less important than her responsibility to her aunts.

David and Cory wouldn't be happy, to say the least, and she mentally cringed at how that phone call was likely to go. But Holly wasn't about to leave until Florence was healthy and back in the saddle.

"I can make some adjustments," she said. "The most important thing is for you to get well, Aunt Florence."

Beatrice reached over and gave Holly's hand a squeeze. "God bless you, dear."

"Thank you, Holly," Florence said in a tight voice. Florence didn't do emotion very well, but Holly could see that she was struggling to hold back tears.

"You'll take advantage of the fact that I'm here for a while and just rest up, right?" Holly asked. "Because you need to totally relax if you're going to keep your blood pressure down."

"That's what the damn pills are for," Florence scoffed.

"Aunt Florence—"

"Yes, yes. I'll rest, and I'll try not to bother you at the store," Florence said, waving a hand. "But I'll tell you one thing I'm going to do. I'm going to get on the phone and talk to every single soul I know about that Night Owl permit. Those blockheaded selectmen need to get an earful from people who don't want to see our store pushed out by a damn chain."

"Oh no, please don't. That would jack up your blood pressure for sure," Holly said. Just the idea was no doubt sending *her* blood pressure up through the roof.

Florence gave a smile that suggested Holly was still a silly eight-year-old girl with skinned knees who didn't know much at all. "On the contrary. I just know all the support will cheer me up. And in any case, would you rather I showed up at the store every day? Because that's what's going to happen if I don't keep busy fighting Night Owl."

Her aunt had always been a tough negotiator, and Holly knew when she was beaten. "Fine, as long as you don't overdo it," she said in a resigned voice.

"Now what about all those plans you have for the store?" Florence said. "Beatrice told me she just happened to see some drawings you've been working on."

"Florence!" Beatrice exclaimed. "You weren't supposed to say anything!"

Crap.

"Why don't we just park that discussion for a few days," Holly said with a placating smile. "We'll see how you're feeling then."

"Oh, bosh!" Florence snapped. "You really think I'm going to be able to rest knowing that you're plotting some kind of . . . revolution? I know very well where you're coming from, Holly. You made yourself quite clear last summer. You think we're just a couple of old fogies who want to keep living fifty years in the past."

"I never said any such thing," Holly said. Okay, she'd thought it, but she'd jump off the high bluffs on the other side of the island before admitting it.

Florence waved away her protest. "Holly, dear, just tell me. If my damn heart doesn't kill me, all this suspense will."

"You'd better go ahead, Holly," Beatrice said morosely. "You know how she gets."

Florence's faded blue eyes narrowed to slits behind her glasses as she silently radiated disapproval of her sister and niece. *Wimps* was what Holly could clearly hear her thinking.

Resigned, Holly stood up. "All right, let me get my sketches."

She retrieved the set of drawings from her room. When she returned, Florence was at the kitchen counter, screwing the top back onto a fifth of Johnnie Walker. As Holly watched in horror, her aunt picked up a glass containing two fingers of whisky and started back to the table.

"You're certifiable," Holly said. "You know you shouldn't drink while you're on antianxiety and pain medications. You're going to end up flat on the floor."

"Yes, Dr. Tyler," Florence said sarcastically, "but as Rhett Butler famously said, 'Frankly, my dear, I don't give a damn.'" She raised the glass as if toasting. "Scotch is the best treatment for anxiety. Always has been, always will be."

Holly was appalled but figured it might at least soften Florence up a bit while she presented her ideas.

As it turned out though, Florence's face looked pinched and her thin cheeks were flushed through the entire presentation. Holly wished she'd put her foot down and refused to talk about it at all.

"These are just preliminary ideas," she said. "The details can wait until you're feeling better."

"Oh, phooey. I feel fine. This is doing the trick." Florence held up her glass approvingly. Then she pointed down at the sketches. "Aside from the fact that those changes look like they might turn our store into some kind of tourist trap, there's the minor matter of cost. I appreciate all the work you've done, Holly, but you know we could never afford anything like that. We don't make enough profit these days to even buy that fancy coffee machine you're talking about."

Holly had planned for that response. "Aunt Florence, Aunt Beatrice, you've never wanted to let me give you anything, but this time you really must. I'll beg if I have to. Since Mom and Dad died, all the giving has been from you to me, so it's high time for me to finally give something back. Believe me, I can afford what this would cost, and nothing would give me more pleasure than to do this for you."

She meant every word—no one was more important to her than her aunts. Holly had made an excellent salary for years, had saved a good deal of it, and still hadn't touched a cent of the military insurance payout she'd received after Drew's death. There was no better way to spend her money.

"Please let me do this for you," she pleaded, her throat going tight with all the love she felt for them. "For *us*. I'll be devastated if you say no."

Beatrice turned and looked at her sister with a steadfast gaze. Florence held that look for several moments, but then let out a sad little sigh. Holly knew how hard it was for her to ignore the generational legacy of self-reliance and pride that all the islanders valued so highly.

"You're far too generous, dear," Florence said, "and you should be worrying about *your* future, not ours. After all, you're starting your own business. But we love you, and we'll certainly think about everything you've said. Yes, we'll think hard, won't we, sister?"

Beatrice gave a mournful nod, obviously not terribly hopeful.

Holly didn't blame her. There was too much wiggle

room in Florence's reply, so it was time to double down on the guilt.

"I hate to have to say it," Holly said, "but my plan might be the only way for the store to survive. If I can't do something to help you save our family treasure, I'll feel like a complete failure."

And as tired as the old store was, she did feel like the historic Jenkins General Store was a Seashell Bay treasure. It was hard to imagine the island without it.

Florence pushed herself up from her chair with grim determination. "You certainly shouldn't feel that way, dear. But we'll talk later. Right now, I could use a little nap."

When Holly moved to help, Florence waved her off. "I'm not dead yet." She took a few slow steps to the patio door and peered out at Micah, who'd used the extra few days her aunt was in the hospital to forge ahead with the new porch.

On arriving home, Florence had grudgingly accepted that the project was too far along to turn back. Holly had formed the distinct impression that her aunt was in fact secretly pleased that Micah had taken charge.

Florence pursed her lips, looking thoughtful. "My, my, that Micah Lancaster looks even better without his shirt on, doesn't he? Quite a treat." Then she cut Holly a sly grin.

"Nice, Aunt Florence. Real nice," Holly said sarcastically.

The hell of it was, Florence was totally right.

After her nap, Florence had pulled Beatrice into the living room for a discussion of Holly's plans. Not wanting to intrude, Holly had headed upstairs to her room, although she'd been tempted to sit at the top of the stairs and eavesdrop. She'd barely managed to restrain herself.

But her self-discipline utterly failed when it came to staring down at the construction project going on behind the house.

Or, more precisely, staring down at Micah in all his half-naked, sweaty glory as he labored on the new porch. Even though it was almost dusk, he was still working away, doing all the heavy slugging involved in mixing and pouring concrete to set the new support posts. The rays of the setting sun lit up his bronzed body like it was gold. Holly was mesmerized by the flex and bulge of his biceps as he easily lifted big sacks of sand, his cargo shorts riding low on his narrow hips. He turned his back to her, his massive shoulders gleaming with perspiration, every gorgeous muscle lovingly outlined as if by a master craftsman. She had to resist the insane urge to drag him out of sight behind the house and lick every square inch of his awesome body.

Get a grip, you pervert.

Ever since their dinner a few nights ago, Micah had kept a bit of a distance between them, which she hadn't expected. Oh, he was as friendly as always, but his focus was firmly on the job and not on her. Holly would frequently slide open the door and ask if she could get him something to drink or help him in any way. The answer was usually yes to a drink but no to her assistance. He seemed determined to do most of the work himself, although he'd finally promised she could join him in hammering down the porch floor once they got the support posts and beams underneath squared away.

Naturally, she'd offered to help with that too, but he'd

given her a firm no, telling her that Ryan was coming over
tomorrow to lend a hand. Maybe he thought she was too
much of a wimp or a city girl to get her hands dirty. That
had her mentally wincing. She'd known for a long time
that Micah had a thing for her, and she realized that in
some weird way she'd come to emotionally depend on
his feelings for her. The notion that he might think less of
her, for any reason, was more disturbing than she cared to
admit.

She sat down on her bed with a sigh. Life was getting
way too complicated, and her growing feelings for Micah
weren't making things any easier. It was time to end her
trip to Seashell Bay as soon as she could. Now that Florence was settling in at home, Holly figured she might be
able to make her getaway in time to avoid really creat-
ing friction with her new partners. It would take maybe
a week or ten days to get most of her ideas for the store
moving forward—if her aunts agreed—and then Florence
and Beatrice would have to take over. Florence would
be champing at the bit to get back to work by then anyway. And even if Florence wasn't up to full speed, Morgan
had said she'd be happy to help out at the store, since she
wasn't teaching until later in the month. There was no one
as organized or better able to whip the place into shape
than Morgan.

For now, Holly simply had to keep her head down,
work on the store, and ignore Deputy Lancaster as much
as possible—especially when he wasn't wearing a shirt.

She was getting her laundry ready to do a load, when
Beatrice called up the stairs. "Holly, we're ready to talk
again now."

When she joined her aunts in the living room, Florence

and Beatrice were sitting primly on opposite ends of the sofa. Holly took one of the wingback chairs and tried not to look as nervous as she felt.

"We've come to a decision," Florence said, pushing her glasses higher on her nose. "As much as I hate to admit it, we're scared to death that the Night Owl permit might get approved. And we aren't so old-fashioned or naïve as to think it won't mean we're in a lot of trouble."

Encouraged, Holly nodded.

"So yes, we'll accept your generosity—just this once," her aunt went on, giving Holly a tight smile. "Though we're terribly ashamed to have to take your hard-earned money."

"Well, you shouldn't feel that way, Aunt Florence. You shouldn't ever—"

"But we're not in favor of everything you want to do," Florence interrupted.

Frig. It wasn't like she'd presented her aunts with an all-or-nothing, take-it-or-leave-it deal. But her ideas did hang together. "Okay, such as?"

"Putting in a deli counter and even one of those ridiculously expensive coffee machines might make some sense," Florence said. "I suppose that's the sort of stuff people want these days, even here on the island. And we were going to get rid of the DVDs anyway at some point."

"Good, that's good," Holly said.

"But we're just not comfortable with the idea of making the general store cater more to tourists than to our own people. We won't have room for our regular stock, and our loyal customers won't be able to find what they want. Then they'll start going somewhere else—like to Night Owl." Her aunt's mouth quivered a bit. "If, God forbid, they do get their permit."

Holly took a deep breath. "Okay, I get your concern. I think we can keep most of the same products, though we'll need to reduce the number of brands."

She explained her ideas in more detail, and the aunts rebutted with what they could live with and what they couldn't. After a half hour of pushing and pulling, they reached a cautious consensus. Holly's biggest concern at this point was the potential for backsliding when she left the island, but they'd just have to cross that bridge when they came to it.

Finally, Florence gave a satisfied nod. "Good. Now there's just one more thing we need to talk about."

Holly bit back a groan. "Yes?"

"The thing is, dear," Beatrice said apologetically, "we can't see how the two of us could possibly put all those changes into place. Especially if Florence isn't completely up to scratch for a while. So—"

"So the only way we can see all this working is if you're able to stay here long enough to see the changes through," Florence finished.

Holly swallowed hard against the sensation that her stomach had decided to take a stroll up her throat. Stay long enough to see the changes through? That would probably take several weeks—maybe even a couple of months if they expected her to line up all the new suppliers. And there was no way that could work for her. Not with her New York partners breathing down her neck and her Boston firm expecting her back too.

"Aunt Florence, Aunt Beatrice, I'm so glad you're going to do this. And I'm sure I can get almost all the basics in motion while I'm still here, like contracting for the necessary renovations and the new equipment."

"I hear a *but* coming, don't I?" Florence said.

"Well, I do have to get back to Boston soon, and I have to meet my obligations to my new partners in New York too." Holly forced a smile, even though she felt panic rising inside her. "I'm balancing quite a few balls here. I'll do as much as I can by the time I have to leave, and Morgan is willing to help you as much as she can after that. I've already discussed it with her."

Florence's eyes pinched shut for a moment, as if a wave of pain had passed through her. "Holly, Morgan's a wonderful girl, and she certainly knows how to run a bed-and-breakfast. But she's not you. You've been helping with the store since you were a little girl. You know the business inside out." She glanced at Beatrice, who looked ready to cry, then heaved a huge sigh. "Oh, well, I suppose if you have to go, you have to go. Beatrice and I will manage. We always do."

God, talk about the mother of all guilt trips. Did she think her life was complicated before? Now she had to completely steer her aunts through this crisis without blowing the deal with her new partners. All she could do now was pray that somehow she could make it work in the time she had left on the island.

Good luck with that.

Chapter 11

$\mathcal{W}$hat an evening," Micah said, breathing out a contented sigh as he gazed into the deepening dusk over Casco Bay. The only sounds were crickets chirping, the occasional frog croaking, and waves gently sloshing on the rocky shoreline.

Holly glanced up at him, a warm smile lighting up her gorgeous features. His pulse hammered in his veins, like it always did when she looked at him like that. Sometimes he imagined her sweet smile was like a secret, intended only for him.

"Perfect weather and another sunset to die for," she said. "And it's so, so peaceful here. You can almost forget there's a big, bustling world going on over there on the mainland."

He and Holly had strolled down to the landing after he finished his work on the porch for the day. "It's great to be able to cut out all the background noise of the city and focus on the things that really matter."

When she paused for a second, he wondered if he'd offended her. After all, she was a city girl through and through.

Then she smiled at him again. "Like friends?"

"Sure. Like everybody and everything you love. Everything you really care about."

"Yes," she said, sounding wistful.

"Holly, you could have that again too, if you stayed."

As soon as the words were out of his mouth, he regretted them. "Sorry, I shouldn't lecture you. I know you love the city and what you're doing."

"Well…on most days I do."

That was a bit cryptic, but then she turned away, as if signaling the end of that particular topic.

"Hey, let's go hang out at the dock for a while," she said. "It'll be deserted until the next ferry comes in. We could even make believe we're waiting for a boat to take us anywhere in the world we want to go. Remember how we all used to do that when we were kids?"

Some kids had named exotic places like Tahiti or Hawaii or Africa, while others—mostly the girls—wanted to go to romantic cities like Paris and Rome. For as long as he could remember, Micah had always said he'd go to the Arctic, maybe taking the Northwest Passage and ending up in Alaska. Most kids had thought he was nuts, but severe and remote lands had always fascinated him. They were difficult and challenging and incredibly beautiful.

Just like the woman standing beside him.

"Good idea. How about some ice cream first?" Micah nodded toward the seasonal store at the foot of the shallow hill.

"Awesome. You know I can't resist Sam's almond mocha."

Unlike the Jenkins General Store, which sold only packaged ice cream, Sam Appleby's Island Market carried big tubs in various flavors. Micah ushered Holly into the tiny store that shared a one-story concrete building with Josh Bryson's repair shop. Open from May until October, the store's niche was tourists and day-trippers, plus any island resident that wanted to snag some bread, milk, or beer after getting off the ferry.

"Hi, Sam," Holly said with a wave. "We're in serious need of some of your ice cream. Almond mocha for me and chocolate for the deputy, please." She looked up at Micah. "In a cone, right?"

"Always," Micah said. Yeah, he was pretty predictable.

Appleby, a pleasant-faced man of about fifty with wiry gray hair, stopped loading beer into one of his coolers and headed behind the ice cream counter. "You got it, Holly. How's Florence doing?"

"Much better, thanks. I practically had to chain her up to keep her out of the store."

"Glad to hear she's okay." Sam grabbed a sugar cone from a tall container. "People are guessing it was the Night Owl thing that took her down. If that's true, I can understand it. I'm worried as hell too."

"It didn't help, that's for sure," Holly said.

"Lots of people have signed Miss Annie's petition," Sam said, nodding toward a clipboard on the counter, "including some day-trippers who really appreciate the local merchants. Maybe the selectmen will deny Night Own the permit if we keep up the pressure." He handed Holly her cone, wrapped in a napkin.

"The response has been good at our store too. And Aunt Florence is working the phones like crazy." Holly rolled her eyes. "Man, she would have made an awesome Borg Queen."

Both Sam and Micah laughed.

"I think Miss Annie's already buttonholed everybody

on the island," Sam said. But then his face turned somber. "I hope so, anyway. There's no way my place can survive with a Night Owl store in Seashell Bay. Hell, they'll probably drive both our stores out."

"Not if we can help it, Sam," Micah said.

As a rule, Micah stayed away from controversial issues as best he could. He needed the respect of all islanders, regardless of their political beliefs or their stands on local issues. But the threat posed by Night Owl was making it damn hard to keep from speaking out. The idea of Sam and the Jenkins sisters losing their stores and livelihoods to some corporate chain made him sick.

"I appreciate that, Micah." Sam patted down a double scoop of chocolate ice cream and handed the cone over. "And there's no charge for the cones."

Micah shook his head as he pulled out a five and two ones from the pocket of his shorts and pushed them across the counter. "Have a good evening, Sam."

With an apologetic smile, Sam picked up the cash as Micah and Holly headed out.

"I'm glad you insisted on paying," she said as they made their way to the dock.

"He didn't put up much of a fight—not like you did over the coffee," Micah said wryly. "Seriously though, losing the store would be a huge blow to him and Sarah. But the corporate honchos at Night Owl headquarters won't lose any sleep over them or your aunts."

Holly linked her arm in his, and a zing of energy shot through his body.

"It's just business to them," she said. "That's why I'm trying as hard as I can to make sure Florence and Beatrice are able to survive even if Night Owl comes here. I'm glad they're willing to try some new things, but it's still going to be a battle to bring in enough real change."

Micah pulled her in closer, relishing the feel of her slim, warm body next to his. She'd often linked arms with him in the past, but now it felt different. Like they might be lovers out for an evening stroll. That deeply appealing idea, combined with the nicely curved hip nestled against him, had certain parts of his anatomy taking notice.

Down, boy.

"Your aunts have been doing the same thing for a long time," he said, trying to focus on the conversation. They turned onto the deserted dock. "It's not surprising that they're a bit scared of change."

"True, but when so much is at stake, you have to take some risks. Look at me. I'm giving up a really good, secure job to strike out in a new venture in a different city. That's not exactly easy either."

"That's brave for sure, but don't forget that they're twice your age. They don't have much room to make mistakes."

"I know. Believe me, I'm feeling the pressure. From everywhere."

When they reached the end of the dock, both leaned against the black iron railing and stared silently out at the deepening dusk and the lights winking to life on the neighboring islands. Micah demolished his cone, but Holly was taking her time. He loved watching her tongue curl around the smooth mound of ice cream. As could be expected, how could he *not* imagine that sweet mouth and pink tongue all over him?

He had the feeling she knew it too. And from the little glances she kept darting his way, she didn't seem to mind.

Now that was interesting.

"I hope I don't sound like I'm whining," she said after a while. "I hate pressuring my aunts, and I know how hard it is for them, but I'm just trying to do my best before I have to leave."

"I'm sure they know that. And I'm really happy you're staying longer." They'd dropped arms to lean against the railing, but she was still close, her shoulder and hip still resting against him. Micah decided to test the waters a bit.

"A guy could get used to having you around, you know." His voice came out low and raspy.

Holly seemed to hold her breath, then let out a quiet sigh. "I wish I could be here a lot more. Every single time I come back, I feel the same way. But then I go back to Boston and get all caught up again in my job and my life..."

She moved to put a little space between them.

Dammit.

Ryan had mentioned that Holly didn't seem all that keen on her boyfriend, but maybe it was time to finally find out the status of things while he had the chance.

So he said, "I guess your boyfriend must be happy you're moving to New York."

Holly's brain scrambled to find the right words. Micah had obviously assumed her remarks about her complicated life had included Jackson's role in it. In fact, she hadn't been thinking about her boyfriend at all.

She'd been thinking about Micah and how he fit—or didn't fit—into her life.

"Actually, I suspect Jackson may be almost as nervous about it as I am," she said.

"Seriously? He should be doing a nonstop happy dance. I would be."

That surprised her. Clearly, her old pal had decided to put himself out there a bit.

It was also clear that Micah didn't understand her relationship with Jackson. That certainly wasn't his fault, since they'd never really talked about how she felt after Drew was killed or the way she'd decided to try to rebuild her life. She'd been shut down for years, guarding herself against a repeat of the pain of that devastating loss. Sure, she'd talked to Lily and Morgan about it—wailed and cried, more like it—but Holly wasn't comfortable with public expressions of emotion or grief. She'd been that way after the deaths of her parents too. In both cases, the sudden losses were too horrible to express in words or tears. For her, talking about the pain had never eased it. Only the passage of time had partly accomplished that reluctant miracle.

She dropped the remains of her cone in a trash container, her appetite for it gone. "Micah, it doesn't work that way between Jackson and me," she said, wiping her fingers on the napkin.

He leaned against the railing, crossing his arms over his chest. His T-shirt was stretched tight over his biceps and his amazing shoulders. "I know things are complicated for you. If you want to talk about it, I'm here for you."

She had to smile. He wasn't just there for her—he was always there for everyone on the island who needed a helping hand or a sympathetic ear.

Or a kick in the ass if that was what the person needed.

"It works because Jackson and I are hardly ever in the same place," she said. "When we started dating, neither of us had any expectations, and that was exactly what I needed. Because, well…" She trailed off, not sure how to say it.

"Because it could never compare to what you had with Drew," he said quietly.

She peered up at him, but it was now dark enough that she had trouble reading his expression. "Right," she said.

"So I guess that means you don't love him."

Wow. Micah was really putting it out there tonight. When he spent all that time with her last summer, he'd pretended Jackson didn't exist. They both had.

She blew out a sigh and averted her gaze. The lights of a ferry cut through the twilight a couple of miles down the bay, heading toward the city. "Micah, I'm still not...I'm not ready for a real relationship yet. Not like I had with Drew."

At least that's what she told herself whenever she was with Jackson. But maybe that was because it was Jackson.

She wandered over to the opposite side of the dock, looking down at the motorboats and skiffs that were tied up at the floats. Micah followed her, silent and strong, a comforting presence at her back. She could feel his warmth behind her, and suddenly she wanted to feel his arms around her.

"All I know for sure is that you deserve to be happy," he said in a soft rumble. "Drew was a great guy—the best, really. But I'm sure that at some point he'd want you to move on and find happiness again. The real thing." He paused. "You know he would, right?"

Holly glanced up at Micah. He towered over her, radiating concern and...well, love.

And that scared the hell out of her.

Chapter 12

$\mathcal{H}$olly had opened the store at eight o'clock and had managed less than thirty dollars in sales in two hours. More than half of that came from Roy Mayo buying gas for his golf cart and also picking up a six-pack of beer. And he'd dropped off another stack of petitions that Miss Annie had printed out.

At least the lack of traffic had given her lots of time to make phone calls and plan out the renovations to the store.

Her next call was to Brendan Porter, the local carpenter and cabinetmaker. Brendan was always busy, and Holly worried that she'd have to resort to using some contractor from Portland—not a good situation if she wanted to get the bulk of work completed before she left. She simply had to talk Brendan into taking on the project.

"Holly," he said over the whine of a power saw in the background, "how are you? How's Florence?"

"She's coming along. Thanks for asking, Bren. I'm calling on the chance that you might be able to free up a few days to do some renovations on the store. We need to make some changes, especially with the Night Owl situation."

"That's great, but how soon are you talking about? My schedule's jammed."

Holly quickly explained the situation, emphasizing the need for some urgency.

"You said about four days' work?" Brendan asked in a slightly skeptical voice.

"That's my best estimate. I want to move a couple of walls to expand the retail space, plus install new counters and a big deli case, which is already on order. Then just a few small cosmetic things."

"Holly, can you give me a second?"

"Sure." She held her breath while he put the phone down, no doubt to check his schedule. If he said yes, she was going to owe him big-time.

Brendan came back on. "How about if I get a good start this weekend? I was planning to get in a little fishing, but this is more important. And I figure I can put off next week's job for a few days. Those folks will understand when I tell them it's for Florence and Beatrice."

Holly sagged against the register counter in relief. "That would be perfect. And God bless you, Brendan. You're the best. I owe you one."

"None of that, now," he said in a gruff voice, clearly embarrassed. "When can we discuss the plans in detail?"

"Any time you've got available."

"Meet you at the store around six today?"

"Perfect."

"See you then."

She let out a ghost of a laugh, hardly believing her luck. For once, something was going right. But that was the way things worked on the island. Friendships and loyalties ran deep, and people made sacrifices for neighbors in need.

People like Brendan were stark reminders of how different Seashell Bay was from Boston or New York. Holly didn't even know the names of most of the people who lived in her small condo building.

She poured herself another cup of coffee and punched in Jackson's office number. She rarely called him at work because he never picked up. Today, she would be more than happy to just leave a message.

To her shock, he answered on the second ring. "Hols," he said, using the nickname she'd never much liked. "What's up? You back from the boonies?"

As usual, he sounded like he was listening with only half an ear. She could picture him checking the stock market on his phone or tablet as he paced around his thirtieth-floor office in the Madison Avenue skyscraper that housed his family's wealth management firm.

Holly grimaced. He was always ragging her about her attachment to *that backwater island*, though he usually managed to say it in a rather jesting voice. Jackson just couldn't comprehend how anybody could even vacation in a place like Seashell Bay, much less live there. She doubted he would stay anywhere that didn't have a luxury hotel or rental property—bedsheets with at least an eight hundred thread count—and certainly nowhere that didn't have reliable high-speed broadband.

"I'm still at home in Maine." She emphasized *home*. "That's what I'm calling about, Jackson. To tell you I'm not going to be able to make that party next weekend. I'm sorry, but it can't be helped."

One of Jackson's billionaire clients had invited them to a blowout birthday party for his wife at their summer estate in Newport. Jackson's company helicopter was going to ferry them up there in the morning and return them to New York late in the evening. Holly hadn't been that keen to go, but he'd insisted. Since it was only for the day, she'd agreed.

"Ah, shit. Why not?" he said, irritation lacing his voice.

"Hey, thanks for asking about my aunt," she said sarcastically. "She's doing better."

His sigh filtered over the phone. "Sorry, babe. I'm a jerk. But I did listen to your messages about it."

He paused for a second. "So, if she's feeling better, why can't you come with me to Newport?" His tone had switched back to annoyed.

"I'm working on some critical renovations to my aunts' store, and I'm under terrible time pressure," Holly said, trying to keep her voice level. "You know I have to be in New York to meet my new partners as soon as I can. I'm hoping to be far enough along here in a week or so to be able to leave, at least for a few days."

"You can't even spare one day?" Jackson said. "Hell, I could bring the chopper up there and pick you up. We could stay the night in Newport, and I could fly you back up first thing Monday morning. Easy."

She frowned. Why was he being so persistent? Did he really want to see her, or was he just giving her a hard time for standing him up? "I'm afraid I can't even spare a day."

"Come on, Hols, we hardly ever see each other. You're not going to make me go to the party alone, are you?" he said in a cajoling voice.

"It's just a party after all, Jackson."

She had no doubt that he could—and would—pull up his contact list and find half a dozen willing beauties who'd be thrilled to party with him in Newport. The

fact that such a prospect bothered her not at all emphasized once again their lack of emotional investment in the
relationship.

Which was pathetic on both their parts.

"Honestly, Hols, I miss you." He heaved a dramatic
sigh. "You're the only woman who doesn't want more
from me than I can give."

That wasn't exactly a ringing endorsement. Then again,
he'd never told her before that he missed her. She didn't
know what to say.

"Besides," he added, "I'm sure you could use a little
fun right now. You're stuck up there on that rock with all
sorts of stress weighing you down. It comes through loud
and clear in your voice. If you come with me to Newport,
I'm sure I'll be able to get you relaxed and, uh, thoroughly
satisfied. When have I ever let you down on that score?"

She couldn't deny that some hot and heavy sex might
indeed be what the doctor ordered, and she and Jackson
had always been physically compatible. But now the idea
of getting naked and sweaty with him was definitely more
of a turn-off than a turn-on.

Holly knew exactly whom to blame for that and had no
intention of going there. She forced away the all-too-arousing
picture of her naked body plastered on top of Micah's.

"Oh, you're just fishing for compliments," she said in a
breezy tone. "But as much as I hate to miss Newport and
spending time with you, I'm afraid I just can't leave my
aunts right now. Not even for a day."

He snorted. "And that's your final answer?"

How many times do I have to say it?

"I'm sorry, Jackson. I'll probably see you in ten days
or so."

"We'll see," he said after a moment's pause. "Anyway, I gotta take this other call now. Bye."

Holly stared at her phone for a moment before putting it down beside the cash register. *We'll see?* What the hell did that mean?

There was no point in speculating. She had too many problems to deal with to start tying herself in knots about Jackson. And her next phone call was going to be even more trying.

She dialed David Kramer's cell number.

"You're still in Maine?" he said in lieu of a greeting.

"Yes, David, and we need to talk."

"Shit, I don't like the sound of that."

"Yeah, I'm really sorry, but I'm going to have to be here a bit longer than I thought."

When he groaned, Holly could envision David rolling his eyes toward the ceiling. "Jesus, Holly, we've got a schedule, and we're starting to run out of time. We can't keep this thing under wraps much longer—not when we're approaching our key clients every day. Once we make the announcement, all three of us are going to have to be on the phones and meeting with those clients nonstop."

Holly had been staring grimly at the floor through his minitirade, but she looked up when she heard the door open. Micah strode into the store, his eyes narrowing as he took off his sunglasses. He stopped halfway and pointed back toward the door, silently asking if she wanted privacy.

She waved him to come in.

"It just can't be helped, David. My first responsibility is to my aunts. It always will be, for as long as they need me."

"Define *a bit longer*, please."

"A week or ten days. But I can't give you an ironclad guarantee. Look, I'm still totally committed to our partnership," she said, hating that she sounded almost desperate. "I just need a little time, okay?"

"Yeah, family is family. I get it. But don't forget that one of the reasons we made you the offer was because you weren't tied down and said you didn't intend to be—just like Cory and me. We all agreed that we'd give the business a hundred percent, remember? And that makes this a bad start, Holly."

"I know. I'm sorry." She hadn't felt bad at all at not seeing Jackson. But this...she just hoped David and Cory didn't get so frustrated that they gave up on her. "I'll make it up to you guys, I promise."

Kramer didn't speak for what felt like a full minute. "I'll talk to Cory. I'm not sure he'll be as understanding as I am."

"I'll get there as soon as I possibly can," Holly said.

"Make that *very* soon," he said before hanging up.

Holly set her phone down on the counter, closing her eyes for a moment as she took a couple of cleansing breaths.

"That sounded pretty grim," Micah said quietly. "They're putting the screws to you?"

Holly opened her eyes to take in the sympathetic expression in his dark gaze. She forced a smile. "Let's just say they're making me feel more than a little guilty."

"For taking care of family? That sucks, if you ask me."

Micah would be the last person to put business before people. *Welcome to my world, dude.*

So many of the people Holly worked with paid lip service to the importance of family but invariably opted for work and career whenever pushed. She adored her creative job but hated that aspect of corporate culture, although she understood it. But having lost her parents at an early age and then having been saved by her aunts, she could never take the attitude that work should come before family. She was as invested in her work as anyone, but family mattered more than anything.

"I can't really blame my partners for thinking that I'm not pulling my weight. There's an awful lot at stake for all of us, both financially and in terms of our reputations."

Micah looked skeptical but didn't argue. "Just let me know if I can help with anything, okay?"

She smiled at him, and this time the smile was genuine. "I will. Now, what can I get you, Deputy?"

"Actually, I just dropped by to ask you about Lily's party tomorrow night. Why don't I pick you up and we go together? It'd be great to show up with the sweetest girl in Maine on my arm." His mouth curled up in a playful and confident grin. "Besides, that way you can drink as much as you want and not have to worry about some dumb cop pulling you over on the way home."

Holly had planned on driving herself to the party to celebrate Aiden's promotion to head coach of the University of Southern Maine baseball team. But it seemed silly to refuse Micah, even if he did make it sound a bit like a date. Then again, Micah was about the only person in her life right now who made her feel like everything would be okay.

"Your logic is impeccable as always, Deputy Lancaster," she said. "But just don't get any ideas if I *do* get a little tipsy and out of control."

The warmth in his gaze morphed into a smoldering heat. "I can make no promises—not when it comes to you."

Whew. She was suddenly feeling quite hot under the collar of her starched sleeveless blouse. There was no way she should be flirting with him, but she just couldn't seem to help herself. Besides, given everything going on in her life, she did deserve a little fun.

Right now, a Seashell Bay summer party with her friends—and the sexiest cop on the planet—seemed just the ticket to take her mind off her troubles for a while.

Chapter 13

$\mathcal{H}$unkered down over Florence's desk, Holly checked over her list of artisan contacts. She'd gotten through all of them because there'd been so little traffic in the store all day. For all the promises of support from locals, it didn't seem to be translating into increased sales.

She knew she had to project confidence, but deep down she was scared. Her only comfort was the knowledge that doing nothing would likely mean the end of the store.

One positive note was that almost every artisan she'd talked to so far had been enthusiastic about her plan to sell their work. Holly was particular thrilled about a young woman from Stonington who created the most beautiful stained glass suncatchers, most of them with coastal Maine themes. Holly was convinced that tourists would eat them up. She just had to stay focused on the positive, for everyone's sake.

When she heard the screen door open, she dropped her pen and pushed back from the desk.

"Holly? You here?"

What the hell? "Jackson?"

She stumbled out of the office and slammed to a halt behind the counter. It really was her erstwhile boyfriend standing in front of her. If the pope had dropped in to pick up a quart of milk, she probably wouldn't have been much more surprised. And she suspected she would have been way happier to see His Holiness.

Jackson raked a hand back through his longish black hair, carefully trimmed by a stylist who didn't take out his scissors for less than four hundred bucks. He wore a bespoke dress shirt with the sleeves rolled up to the elbows, along with a dark blue silk tie. His suit jacket was slung over his shoulder, and the knot in his tie had been casually loosened.

He might be sweating a little, and his suit looked like it could use a pressing, but Jackson Leigh was still one of the handsomest men Holly had ever known. His dark, mischievous eyes and infectious grin had always been able to pull her back into his orbit, even when his sometimes-arrogant personality had turned her off. Physically, he was absolutely magnetic. It was the only way she could explain his appeal.

"Surprised?" he purred, like the cat that ate the canary. He flipped up the counter gate and swept her into his arms before she could move a muscle.

He kissed her hard as his hands slid down to grab her ass. "I told you I missed you, Hols. I bet you can feel how much, right?"

Yikes. She could feel his erection all right, which was so not good. Anyone could walk in on them right now, including one of her aunts.

Holly wedged her hands against his chest and gently pushed him back. She was overwhelmed, but not in the way he'd obviously hoped. She simply didn't need any more complications or high-maintenance people to manage.

And Jackson was *very* high maintenance.

"What are you doing here?" she asked, mentally wincing at the shrillness in her voice. "And how did you get here anyway? I wish you had called me first before just showing up."

His dark brows narrowed. "That's not exactly the warm welcome I was hoping for, Hols, I came a hell of a long way to see you, babe." He made a ridiculous pouting face. "Had to, since you wouldn't come see me."

Holly brushed her damp palms down the legs of her capris. Now she was sweating even more than he was. "Did you walk over from the ferry?"

"The ferry?" he echoed with disbelieving smirk. "Are you kidding me? My helicopter landed over by the dock."

Of course.

She cleared her throat. "Is this just a whirlwind hello and good-bye?" she said, trying for a smile. "In and right back out again, as usual?"

He moved in for another kiss, this time trailing his lips down her neck. "No, Sierra booked a room at some little B&B. Said it was the only place on the island. I wasn't sure you'd want to spend the night in Portland, though it would be a hell of a lot better if we could. I doubt there's much privacy in some chickenshit little B&B."

Sierra was Jackson's personal assistant and also occasional bedmate, if Holly didn't miss her guess. "I'll bet she booked you into the Merrifield Inn under a false name, didn't she?"

"She said it would be best to not give my real name if

I really wanted to surprise you. There are no secrets in small towns, right?"

That was for sure. Morgan would have given her an immediate heads-up if he'd used his real name.

"How long are you planning on staying?"

Jackson gave her a curious look, obviously catching her less-than-enthusiastic tone. Then he shrugged. "Overnight. I figured I could use a little break, and I wasn't lying about wanting to see you. And meet your friends. It's time, don't you think?"

The party.

Holly had wondered a few times about how Jackson and her friends would react to each other when they finally met, but it had always been questionable that it would ever happen. And she'd always thought that was probably a good thing.

On top of that, Micah wouldn't be happy. She was supposed to be going to Lily and Aiden's party with him tonight.

"I'm touched that you'd come all this way, but like I told you on the phone, I'm really behind the eight ball. I can't leave the store all day, so I won't be able to spend much time with you, Jackson."

He'd started to browse the store, glancing at the food shelves. "That's okay, as long as I've got you all night."

I can't deal with that problem right now. "My friend Lily is throwing an important party tonight. I have to go."

"Great," Jackson said. "I can meet everyone in one shot. That makes it easy, right?"

Micah had to read every paragraph two or three times before the words sank in. His mind just would not focus.

As he often did toward the end of the day at the office, he was studying *Criminal Investigation: The Art and the Science*. The criminal justice textbook was a bible for detectives, used by numerous police departments as prep for the detective exam. Micah had been reading it for so long he'd gone through two editions.

Mary Ann had gone home hours ago, so the tiny station was quiet. Then again, the phones were quiet this time of day too, as always.

He sighed and shut the book, too preoccupied over the lack of progress on the Fitz break-in to effectively study. Plus, he couldn't stop thinking about his date with Holly, though he guessed it was stupid to call it a date. What would happen tonight was anybody's guess, but he hoped he could ease her a little farther down the path of what seemed to be a cautious, mutual flirtation.

For now, he needed to stow those thoughts and keep his mind on work.

He'd spent some time tailing Jace Horton and Logan Cain, following them twice from the resort site to Cain's place on their lunch break. Horton had waved to him a couple of times, a taunting sneer on his face. Neither man had done anything unusual, although Horton always managed to look nervous and furtive as hell. But he always came in on the ferry and went straight to the site. Cain drove to work each day and gave Horton a lift to the dock at the end of their shift. It frustrated Micah that he had no probable cause to search the house, because nothing about those guys sat right with him.

Just as he got up for a coffee refill, the station door swung open and Holly breezed in, gorgeous as always in snug-fitting capris. His pulse rate immediately jacked up a few notches.

"I saw the cruiser parked out front," she said with an apologetic smile, "so I thought I'd talk to you here instead of on the phone."

Something seemed wrong. "Sure. Want some coffee?"

"Thanks, but no."

Now Micah was officially getting a bad feeling about tonight. "Grab a chair in my office. I'll be right there."

"Micah, I have to get back to the store."

"Okay. Then just spill it."

When she flinched, he regretted his edgy tone. "Jackson showed up at the store half an hour ago," she said. "Completely unexpected, obviously."

That sucked big-time. "And?"

"He said he wanted to surprise me. Well, it worked," she said drily. "I almost keeled over."

Apparently not from joy, if he was reading her expression right. "He probably thought you'd be thrilled."

Her smile was pained. "He's just staying one night—at the Merrifield Inn."

"The B&B's not exactly his style, is it?" Micah said, trying hard to keep the disappointment out of his voice. "Are you still going to the party? I mean with him, of course."

"I really don't want to miss it. Lily and Aiden..." She let her voice trail off.

"Of course," he said. "No problem." What else could he say?

She raised a hand, as if to pat his arm, and then let it drop to her side. "Thank you for being so understanding, Micah."

He shrugged. "Well, he's your boyfriend, and he's come a long way."

"Yes," she said, dropping her gaze.

"The poor guy's going to feel like a fish out of water around here," he said, trying to be generous about it. "Like I'd probably feel at one of your New York parties."

That brought her gaze back up. Her gorgeous blue eyes looked a little flinty. "Jackson's a big boy. We don't need to worry about his delicate feelings. Anyway, when have Seashell Bay folks ever been anything but friendly?"

"Never."

Holly cast an anxious glance toward the door and then back at him.

"I'll see you there tonight," he said, giving her an easy way out.

"Sure." She started to turn but then stopped and faced him again, still looking unhappy. "I really am sorry, Micah."

He shook his head. "You have nothing to be sorry about. I'll look forward to meeting him."

Holly let out a sarcastic little snort before opening the door. Micah rarely lied, but she clearly knew he'd just told a whopper.

Chapter 14

"Your friend Morgan is seriously hot," Jackson said as Holly pulled into the driveway of Aiden and Lily's gorgeous old Victorian. "And sweet too. I had no idea that one of your best friends owned the B&B. I'd figured she'd be pissed off to learn about my little ruse and the fake name, but she couldn't have been nicer."

"Yes, she's a sweetie," Holly said, repressing a flare of irritation. Jackson *was* trying to be nice, after all. "But if you'd be more comfortable at a Portland hotel, feel free to move. Morgan wouldn't mind at all if you decided to cancel."

Jackson picked some apparently invisible lint off his crisply pressed black slacks. "Hols, if I didn't know better, I'd say you were trying to get rid of me." He raised his eyebrows in an exaggerated lift.

Busted.

"Don't be silly," she said.

They got out of Florence's car and climbed the stairs to the wraparound front porch with its pretty white rocking chairs. Normally, the serenity of the rather isolated place calmed Holly down, but tonight she was as nervous as a Collie in a thunderstorm.

"I hope I'm not underdressed," Jackson said.

Underdressed? She knew his pale pink shirt—perfectly rolled up to just below the elbows—was made to measure by a London tailor, and his loafers were Prada. The white gold Rolex on his left wrist screamed wealth.

"These are plain working people, Jackson. That classic watch on your wrist might be worth as much as Lily's lobster boat."

"I doubt it," he scoffed. "Anyway, you're certainly going casual tonight."

There was a hint of judgment in his tone. She'd decided to wear a red, scoop-neck tank top with a belted black skirt and flat sandals. "Is that a bad thing? This is home, after all, and these are my closest friends." Holly rang the bell before opening the door. "I told you it was a casual barbecue. No big deal."

"I guess I'm still having a hard time getting my head around this being home for you," he said. "You seem so different here than in New York."

"It's a different world."

Jackson snorted. "Tell me about it."

"Come in, you two," Lily said as she hurried down the hallway toward them. She hugged Holly and then, smiling, extended her hand to Jackson. "And you're Jackson, of course. Welcome to Seashell Bay."

Holly had introduced Jackson to Morgan at the B&B, guilty that she had to drop such an unexpected bombshell on her friend. She'd managed to get Morgan aside for a few moments and asked her to call Lily to give her the heads-up on Jackson. Morgan had given her a sympathetic pat on the back and then dealt with Jackson with her easy innkeeper's charm.

Thank God she could always depend on Lily and Morgan to have her back.

"Great to meet you, Lily." Jackson's gaze flashed over Lily with undisguised interest. With her deep tan and trim figure, Lily looked amazing in a dandelion yellow sundress, so Holly couldn't entirely blame him. Still, did he have to act like such a player with her friends?

"Well, it's about time you showed up on our island," Lily said jokingly, though Holly knew she meant every word.

Jackson just smiled.

"I'm ready for a drink," Holly said. *Or maybe six.*

"Most of the people are out back." Lily took Jackson by the arm. "Aiden's grilling burgers. I'll let him take over the introductions, and then you boys can talk about sports and such while Holly helps Morgan and me in the kitchen."

Lily winked at Holly and then dragged Jackson away.

Relieved to have a break, Holly followed them and then took a right turn into the kitchen, where Morgan and Micah were talking and drinking beer. Morgan was scooping avocado dip into the center of a glass veggie tray. As soon as she saw Holly, she grabbed another Shipyard from the fridge, opened it, and shoved it into Holly's hand. "I'll bet you totally need this," she said.

"You have no idea," Holly said. "Hi, Micah."

Her favorite deputy, dressed in jeans and a black Polo shirt, definitely looked out of sorts—like he could chew up nails and spit out staples.

"I guess that was the famous Jackson Leigh who just sailed by," he said in a flat voice.

The last thing Holly needed was another cranky male. "Be nice, Micah. He is our guest on the island, after all."

"Uninvited guest," Micah said. "But, yeah, I'll be *nice*."

Morgan punched him on the shoulder. "This is hard enough for Holly, you big jerk. Don't even think about getting into some stupid male contest with the Come-From-Away."

Micah clearly had to wrestle his irritation under control. "No worries," he finally said. Then he turned and strode out the back door into the yard.

"Sorry, sweetie," Morgan said. "But he's upset. He told me he almost didn't come."

"I know and I hate it," Holly said. "I'm furious with Jackson for thinking he could just breeze in like this." She shook her head. "I suppose I should be thrilled that he dropped everything to come visit me. And I guess it's a real problem that I'm not."

"Well, if Ryan and I were separated for weeks on end and he helicoptered up here to spend a day or two with me, I'd be dragging him up to bed in a second, regardless of what else was going on."

"I can't totally blame Jackson for doing this," Holly said, starting to pick nervously at the beer bottle label. "I just wish I could talk him into taking a hotel room in the city tonight."

"There's not a lot of privacy at the Merrifield, that's for sure," Morgan said.

Holly's stomach had been tight for hours thinking about what would happen later tonight. Refusing Jackson after he'd made such an extravagant gesture would make him crazy and might spell the end of their relationship. Was she ready for that?

"Right now I'm just trying to get through the evening," she said. "I'll figure that part out later."

Morgan shot her a startled look. "Whatever you say." Then she glanced behind her out the window. "You saw Micah just now. This is tough for him."

"I know." Micah was the last person she'd ever want to hurt, especially after all he'd done for her and her aunts.

But it was more than that, and she knew it.

Don't think about that now.

"I'd better get outside and see what Jackson is up to," she said. "He's probably trying to sell Aiden on one of his investment schemes by now."

"Good idea. And try not to worry about Micah. He's got plenty of friends here, and you know he'd never do anything to embarrass you."

"No, but Jackson might."

Micah had kept his eye on Jackson Leigh for the better part of an hour. Aiden had introduced him to the stockbroker, and the tense conversation had lasted only about fifteen seconds before Aiden figured out he'd better keep the Come-From-Away moving. Holly had appeared a few minutes later and had pretty much stuck close to her boyfriend. He made a point of having his hands all over her, including several pats to the ass. She hadn't looked happy about it but didn't abandon him either.

Aiden broke away from his brother and joined Micah, Ryan, and Josh at the edge of the crowd of forty or so people that had gathered in the yard. "So, what did you think of the great Jackson Leigh?" Aiden's sarcastic tone made his own assessment clear.

Micah shrugged. "Since he seems to view me as some kind of redneck idiot, I'd say I'm not about to sign up for his fan club."

He didn't like the way the guy treated Holly either—as if she were some sort of pampered possession to parade around on his arm.

"Actually, that's pretty much how he's treating everybody, though some of the women seem to think he's a charmer," Aiden said. "As far as I'm concerned, the guy's a raging asshole."

"He seemed interested enough in talking to you though," Ryan said.

Aiden snorted. "Only enough to tell me how much the hotel and resort business sucks. He said the profit margin on a resort like ours would be minimal and that he could have made Lily and me ten times as much if we'd had him invest our money instead. He said he had lots of professional athletes as clients and had made them all rich."

"What did you say?" Micah asked.

"That our resort was more about community than about making money."

"That must have been when I saw him laughing," Micah said sarcastically.

Aiden grinned. "Actually, it was. Jesus, I thought Holly was going to haul off and slug the moron. She was squeezing his arm like a fucking tourniquet."

The tension in Micah's shoulders eased a bit. He'd seen that and hoped that his eyes weren't deceiving him.

A minute later, when he noticed that Miss Annie had dragged Jackson to a corner of the patio beside Aiden's huge barbecue, Micah excused himself. He eased his way through the crowd and drew Holly off to the side of the garden so they wouldn't be heard.

"You sure don't look like you're having fun," he said. But despite the frown marking her brow, she looked so

damn beautiful—simply dressed and with her hair drifting in a silky wave to her bare shoulders—that breathing
didn't come easy.

Holly's gaze shifted toward Jackson. Miss Annie was
wagging a finger at the CFA, obviously delivering one of
her famous lectures.

"Jackson's already pretty drunk," she said in a tight
voice. "I'm going to have to get him out of here soon
before he does any more damage."

"What did he say that got Miss Annie going?"

Her shoulders went up around her ears. "I'm not sure I
should tell you."

"Well, if you don't, Miss Annie will."

Holly blew out a sigh. "Jackson probably thought he
was making a joke. For a genuinely smart man, he can be
so stupid at times."

Micah waited her out in silence.

"Oh, whatever," she said in a grumpy voice. "He made
a couple of dumbass remarks about Seashell Bay. That it
looked like the place didn't realize it was the twentieth
century, much less the twenty-first. The idiot," she finished under her breath.

Well, the guy wasn't exactly the first mainlander to say
something like that. But Micah could tell that the thought-
less remarks had embarrassed Holly in front of people she
cared deeply about. From the look in her eyes, he figured
she was pulling her punches, afraid to tell him the full story.

"I don't get it, Holly." He probably didn't have the right
to say this, but they'd been friends forever. "You and Jackson just don't add up. But I guess everything looks different when you're back in the city." He paused. "I only hope
the guy doesn't end up hurting you."

She looked down at her feet. "Don't worry about me, Micah. I'm fine."

She sure didn't sound fine. He let his instincts take over and reached out to gently grasp her shoulders. Holly looked up into his face, her eyes both troubled and questioning.

"You'd rather be somewhere else right now, wouldn't you?" he asked.

When her lower lip trembled, he thought it told him everything.

"We could just go," he said. "Leave the party right now and let Morgan and Ryan take Jackson back to the inn. You're not responsible for the guy, and I don't think you really want to be with him anymore. Not after what I'm seeing here tonight." He let one hand drift down her bare upper arm, stroking it. It felt like satin under his fingertips.

"Am I wrong?" he prompted as she stared at him, wide-eyed.

"Oh, Micah," she whispered. She shook her head, as if she couldn't talk.

Suddenly her eyes darkened as she looked over his shoulder. "Shit. Here he comes."

Biting back a curse, Micah turned. Jackson was elbowing his way toward them in a hurry, knocking a drink out of old Roy Mayo's hand and prompting Roy to let out a choice curse word. Ryan was right on Jackson's heels, and Morgan was hurrying to catch up to her fiancé.

"Am I interrupting?" Jackson said to Holly in a nasty tone as he burst into her personal space. "I damn well hope so, given what seems to be going on over here."

"Jackson, please don't start," she said from between clenched teeth. She took a quick step back.

The guy's face went red. "Don't tell me what to do. I'm getting you out of here right now."

Okay, enough from you, asshole.

Micah moved closer, just enough to cause Jackson to reluctantly retreat a step. "So, here's the thing. You're our guest on the island, and you're Holly's friend. That means we'll overlook your rude behavior this one time. But listen when I tell you that you'd better not speak to her like that again."

Jackson let out a derisive laugh. "Or what, Mr. Deputy Sheriff of Butthole Island? You going to arrest me or something?"

Holly and Morgan sucked in horrified gasps, their eyes popping wide simultaneously. Ryan took an angry step forward, but Micah shot out an arm and held his friend back.

"Jesus, Hols," Jackson said, apparently oblivious to his girlfriend's stunned reaction. "I knew this town was going to be some kind of lame-ass throwback, but I didn't think I was going to get lectured by a crazy old lady and some bruiser hick deputy. Christ, I've only been here a few hours, but I totally get why you wanted to get the hell out of the place. Shit, I'd have run away when I was in kindergarten."

He snorted out a laugh, apparently thinking he'd said something hilarious. Sure, the guy had been drinking, but that didn't excuse his behavior.

Holly was on top of it. Her hand shot out and grabbed the front of Jackson's shirt. "We need to talk in private, Jackson. Right now."

Her voice made it clear that Jackson Leigh was about to get a major shitkicking.

Jackson didn't resist as Holly pulled him into the house, down the hallway, and out the front door to the porch. The idiotic grin on his face signaled his pleasure that she'd rescued him from the Seashell Bay rubes, as he would no doubt label them. Maybe he even thought the two of them would head straight to the B&B and get naked between the sheets.

In his freaking dreams.

She rounded on him as soon as she closed the front door behind them. "What the hell were you thinking, Jackson? How dare you insult your hosts? My friends? Me?"

His head jerked back. "I didn't insult you, babe. Hell, I'm sorry I called that old lady crazy, but she came at me like I was some grubby kid. I didn't come all this way to be lectured by some old bag about *proper manners*." He put air quotes around the words.

Holly felt like her head was going to explode. "Old bag? Miss Annie is worth at least ten of you. And what about insulting Micah? He's my lifelong friend, Jackson. He has the right to try to comfort me when I'm upset. Are you saying he isn't even allowed to touch me?"

"Yeah, well, I think the deputy might be more than just your friend," Jackson snarled. "Tell me he's not, Holly. Or do you think I'm as stupid as these morons you grew up with?"

Unconsciously, her hand had curled into a fist. Startled, she shook it out. "Dammit, Jackson, just shut up. Look, I don't want to embarrass you by making you leave, but I will if you don't promise to act like a decent human being for the rest of the evening. Or *I'll* leave, if you'd prefer."

Jackson studied her for a few moments before turning away to lean on the porch railing. Holly watched as he stared up at the star-filled sky for a solid minute.

"It's a beautiful night, isn't it?" he finally said, turning back to her. His voice had gentled and his smile was the entrancing one she'd come to know so well. "It's so quiet out here too. I suppose this place is actually pretty romantic—in its own bucolic kind of way."

Oh God, another major mood swing. Sometimes Holly felt like she couldn't keep up with the back and forth. And although she was glad he'd calmed down, romance was the last thing on her mind right now.

She crossed her arms over her chest and kept quiet, assuming Jackson had more to say.

"I was going to wait until later tonight to say this," he said. "When we were alone at the B&B. But I guess I'd better get it out now—since you're so bent."

Holly stiffened. She supposed she was *bent*. She was sickened and furious.

He gave her a placating smile. "Just listen, Hols, okay? Look, we both know we're not into commitments. We agreed on that a long time ago. But that doesn't mean I don't want to be with you more than just a weekend here and there. We haven't seen much of each other lately, and it's making me realize how much I miss you."

Holly frowned. "What are you saying, Jackson?"

He gave her the wry, charming smile that used to move her but now seemed so practiced. "Just this. I've been thinking about how it doesn't make much sense for you to pay a fortune for an apartment in New York when I've got a ton of room at mine. And you've got to admit I live in a hell of a nice building."

Holly couldn't have been more surprised if he'd pulled a big diamond ring out of his pocket.

"Move in with me, Hols," he said. "I think I'm ready to give it a try. Let's see how it works."

When he took a step forward, his arms reaching for her, she took a quick step back. Her mind could barely process his...offer? Jackson had always made it clear that he didn't want to live with anyone, even her. Nor she with him, truth be told. That had never been part of their deal.

"What exactly is it that you're willing to give a try, Jackson?" she asked cautiously. "What kind of a relationship are you talking about? Like roommates?"

He snorted. "Give me a break, for Christ's sake."

"What, then?"

"What do you want, an engraved invitation on a gold plate? Asking you to move in is a hell of a big step for me, Hols. You know that." He threw up his hands, "Hell, I thought this would make you really happy. You're the first woman I've ever asked to do this."

"Well, thanks for the honor," she said with a tinge of sarcasm. "But are you talking about sharing our lives? I mean truly sharing?"

In her life with Drew, they'd shared everything, including their deepest emotions.

"Because that's what...living together...implies to me," she went on. "Otherwise we really would just be roommates. Or friends with benefits." The thought of that filled her with distaste.

Jackson shrugged. "I'm not sure what *truly sharing* means. That's pretty vague stuff, Hols."

She blew out a frustrated breath. "Well, how about the fact that a big part of my life is right here in Seashell Bay? These are my people, Jackson. You can see that, can't you? Yet you obviously think they're just a bunch of hicks and old hags."

Jackson peered at her like she was speaking a foreign language. "Hey, we don't have to be joined at the hip, do we? Why do I have to tag along when you come north, or have anything to do with this place? I've never dragged you out to California and inflicted my family on you, have I?"

"No, you haven't. And doesn't that tell you something?"

He waved a hand. "You're just pissed off that I'm not crazy about this damn island. So what? I don't care if you want to spend time here. Just because we live together doesn't mean anything has to change."

Now that it was staring her in the face—or pouring over her like a bucket of ice water—Holly could only think of how boring and meaningless that sort of arrangement sounded. Her relationship with Jackson had been right at the time, and she was grateful to him for that. But she didn't want a future with a man who wanted no part of what amounted to half her life, and who had no intention of sharing the whole of his life with her.

Thanks to him, she'd reached the fork in the road tonight. It was time to make a choice.

"But that's just it, Jackson," she said in a quiet voice. "Everything does have to change. And my answer to your offer is thank you, but no."

Micah shook his head as Ryan offered to get him another beer. "I've got to get out of here, man. If I see that jerk again, I might have to drill him. And then I'd have to arrest myself."

Micah shook hands with his buddy, quickly thanked Lily and Aiden, and then said good-bye to Morgan, who didn't look surprised when he said he was leaving. "Holly and Jackson went into the house, right?" he asked her.

Morgan squeezed his arm. "Yes, but don't worry, Micah. She can handle him."

"Of course she can. I was just asking so I wouldn't run into them as I leave. I'll go around the side of the house."

She winced. "Yuck, I hate this."

"Tell Holly I'm sorry, okay?"

"I will, but you've got nothing to apologize for. You were the gentleman here, not Jackson Leigh."

"Thanks, Morgan." Micah hugged her and slipped through the crowd, making his way to the stone path that ran along the side of the house. It was pretty dark now, with only the glow of the porch lights at the front and rear to guide his way.

He had no intention of going home just yet, since he knew he'd just sit there feeling like crap and worrying about Holly. Instead, he'd probably make a few circuits of Island Road and some other streets, making sure all was well in Seashell Bay, and then drop in at the Pot. Sit at the bar and nurse a couple of beers. Maybe talk some to owner Laura Vickers or the bartender, Kellen Dooley, if they weren't too busy serving customers.

As he neared the front of the house, he heard Holly's voice drifting back. She and Leigh were talking on the porch, and she was telling her boyfriend that *everything had to change*. The words were clear as crystal, and they stopped Micah in his tracks.

"This is bullshit," Leigh said, his voice rising. "If you're not ready to move in with me, let's just keep things the way they are. I'm fine with that."

Would Holly really move in with that asshole? That would royally suck.

"But I'm not fine with it," she said. "Not anymore. This isn't what I want, and it sure isn't what I need. I've been stewing about this for a while, Jackson, and I have to tell you that it's just not working for me anymore. In fact, I don't think it's good for either of us. " Her voice dropped to a murmur, and Micah had to strain now to hear.

You shouldn't be eavesdropping, dude. But he quickly told his conscience to shut the hell up. He'd feel bad about it later, but right now he wanted—needed—to know how Holly felt.

"I'm sorry, Jackson," she said quietly. "Truly."

"That's bullshit, and please don't tell me what I need," the guy retorted. "You're in some kind of goddamn emotional fog, and it's because of this stupid island. You'll snap out of it once you get away from here. Jesus, if I had my way, I'd load you in my helicopter right now. We could be in New York in a couple of hours, and it's time you went back. Your aunt's out of the hospital, and you need to be back in the city to meet with your partners. If you don't wise up, you're going to blow the hell out of some really good things. Your job. Me."

"You really don't get it, do you? You don't get family, you don't get obligation, and you sure as hell don't get commitment."

"Commitment?" Leigh said with a loud snort. "Hols, I thought that was the last thing you wanted."

"I'm talking about commitment to family and friends. The only roots I have are in Seashell Bay, Jackson," she patiently explained. "They're very dear to me, and you obviously don't get that."

"I'd say your career is pretty damn dear to you. And I thought I was *dear* to you too. Obviously I was dead wrong."

Holly's exasperated sigh was clearly audible where Micah stood.

"Look, I truly am sorry," she said, "but this isn't getting us anywhere. I can take you back to the Merrifield Inn now, or I can ask Morgan to take you later if you want to stay at the party. But one way or the other, I'm going now."

"Yeah, you are. You're going with me. We're going

someplace where we can sit down and talk this out. Come on, let's go."

"Jackson, no. Talking will just make things worse. Please, I want you to leave." Her voice rose. "And let go of my arm right now!"

Okay, enough was enough. Micah charged around the end of the porch and bounded up the steps. Her face red with anger, Holly was still trying to yank her arm from Leigh's grasp.

"Let her go." Micah growled. "Right now."

"Fuck off, Mayberry," Leigh snapped, not letting go. "This is none of your business."

Holly glanced at Micah, her eyes blazing with anger. "I've got this, Micah. Don't get in the middle."

"He's hurting you." He took another step closer. If the asshole didn't release Holly's wrist in the next five seconds, he was going to spend the night behind bars. "What you're doing to her is assault, Leigh, and nothing would give me greater pleasure than to lock you up."

"Jail me for arguing with my girlfriend?" Leigh said. "Oh, that's hilarious." But despite his brave words, he relaxed his grip, and Holly yanked her arm free.

Micah gently rested a hand on her shoulder as she came to him. "Let me see your wrist."

"I'm fine, Micah. I just want to leave." From Micah's side, she gave Leigh an ice-cold stare. "You can find your own way back to the B&B. Or better yet, call your pilot and get him to fly you back to New York tonight. I don't ever want to see you in Seashell Bay again."

Micah narrowed his gaze on the other man. "You heard the lady—it's time to go. I'll find someone to drive you back to the inn."

"Like I said, fuck off. Nobody orders me around. I'll leave when I'm damn well ready." Leigh took a step forward, shot out a hand, and shoved Micah. Shoved him hard enough to knock him slightly off balance.

What an idiot.

Micah grabbed Leigh's shoulder and spun him around, twisting his right arm behind his back and shoving him up against one of the porch columns. "Holly gets the last word on this, asshole."

When he looked over, Holly's mouth was gaping open. "Shall I arrest him for assaulting both you and a police officer?" he asked.

She shook herself, as if coming out of a daze. "No, let him go, Micah. He's not worth your trouble." Then she pointed a finger at Leigh. "But if you're not off this island tomorrow morning, I *will* press charges."

Micah reluctantly let him go.

"Screw you both," Leigh growled as he turned to face them. "You blew a great thing, babe. And you'd better not think you can walk this back when you change your mind."

Holly stared at him. "Well, I'll try not to lose too much sleep over that." She turned to Micah. "Micah, would you take me home? I'm too angry and upset to drive. I'd probably end up in a ditch."

"You bet I will."

In an instant, Micah's entire world had just changed for the better.

Chapter 15

*L*ike Caesar, Holly knew she'd just crossed the Rubicon—a critical line she couldn't recross. Jackson Leigh was going to be just part of her history from now on, a history she'd mostly like to forget. "Micah, could we just drive around for a little while?" She stared off into the darkness of the forest that lined both sides of the road.

"Whatever you like," he said. "I'm here for you."

She managed a smile but didn't look at him. "I really don't want to have to explain to my aunts why I look like a strung-out crazy woman. Besides, I'm not up to explaining what happened at the party, at least not yet."

Holly had promised her aunts she'd bring Jackson over in the morning to meet them. That, obviously, was no longer on.

They drove in silence for a few minutes until Micah turned onto a narrow wooded lane that curved away from the wash of his headlights. "I know you want to drive around more, but I thought we could stop here awhile and take a little walk. It's still a beautiful night, despite that bullshit at the party."

"Too beautiful to let Jackson completely ruin it," she

said. She peered ahead, finally recognizing where they were. "This is the old Carney place. That New York TV producer owns it now, right?"

"Yeah, Jerry Foreman. He tore down Carney's old house and built a summer home. Well, I guess *mansion* would be a better description. It's a shame that his family only uses it a few weeks a year."

"I've seen it from the water a couple of times," Holly said. "It's gorgeous. And the view has always been spectacular from the point."

The property was on a narrow peninsula at the south end of the island that offered stunning views to the south, east, and north. When she was a teenager, she'd been friends with Jocelyn Carney, as had Micah and nearly everyone else their age. The Carneys had moved away some years ago when Jocelyn's father had been forced to look for work on the mainland.

"Jerry and I have become good friends," Micah said, stopping the car in front of a massive garage.

"Really? You never mentioned that before."

"He was grateful for a solid I did him last year. He started inviting me over to use his home gym after I mentioned once that I like to work out. Now we spend some time together whenever he's on the island." He got out and came around to help her out of the Tahoe.

"Cool. Maybe he'll give you a bit part in one of his shows: You'd make a great TV cop because you look so…"

"Big?" he said drily.

"Intimidating," she said. "But only to the people who don't know you."

"Yeah, just ask Daisy Whipple. She roasts my ass every time I see her." He laughed. "As do half the people on this rock, especially the older ones."

Holly smiled, loving that he didn't mind the ribbing he took from some of the locals. Micah was secure enough in himself not to mind the teasing. He knew it came from affection.

He led her through a breezeway between the house and garage. It opened into a huge, sparsely treed rear yard that sloped gently down to a long dock. The vault of the sky arched overhead, thick with the stars of the Milky Way, and a half-moon softly lit their way down to the dock. The ocean shimmered in front of them, almost as still as a lake on a windless night.

"Well, Jackson doesn't frighten easily, but I could tell he was afraid of you."

"He had some reason to be," Micah said. "Nobody's going to grab you like that when I'm around—not even your boyfriend."

Holly hated violence of any kind, even in contact sports. It was ironic that she'd married not just a soldier, but one trained for the most dangerous missions. She'd forced herself to suck it up because she simply couldn't help falling in love with Drew. But she'd never dealt well with his deployments, terrified every time he went overseas. Her worst nightmare had come true when he died on a mission.

She sighed. "I never thought Jackson was the type of man who would rough me up, but the way he flipped out tonight, I really have to wonder." She stopped and shook her head, mortified. "What was I doing with a guy like that? How could I not see it?"

Micah took her hand. "You were still grieving when you met him. I'm sure that explains a lot. Let's just try to forget that guy for tonight. You've been through enough."

Holly clung to his hand, loving the way it engulfed hers.

Even more, loving his warmth and generosity. He was a friend she could rely on no matter what. "That sounds like an awesome plan."

"Jerry rebuilt the Carneys' old dock a couple of years ago," Micah said as they stepped up onto it. "But it looks pretty much the same, doesn't it?"

She nodded, peering ahead. The dock extended out into the Atlantic, with light fixtures on poles at both ends. As they walked side by side along the boards, Holly could hear the waves very gently sloshing against the pilings and smell the salty tang of the sea air. She loved that sound and scent, having always taken comfort in them. They whispered *home*.

"We did some crazy things here when we were kids," Micah said, his grip firm on her hand. "Remember?"

"Micah, I'd hardly call jumping off a dock crazy," Holly said, though she knew what he was getting at.

"We sure had some fun when Mr. and Mrs. Carney went on trips."

Jocelyn Carney had liked to party. When her parents went off to visit family on the mainland—as they regularly did in the summer—Jocelyn had no hesitation in turning her home into party central. Diving off the dock had been one form of entertainment—underage drinking and pot smoking had been others. Even Micah, the straightest arrow in the quiver, had indulged, though not as much as most guys.

Skinny-dipping in the ocean was a favorite of the more adventurous kids but certainly not Holly. Her eternally straitlaced aunts would have grounded her until doomsday, had even a whisper of something so outrageous gotten out.

"It made me pretty nervous sometimes, because some of the guys would get so drunk or stoned that it made me afraid they'd hit their head on the dock and drown." She wrinkled her nose at him. "I was such a wuss."

Micah laughed. "I would have pulled them out."

Holly knew he would have. Micah always looked out for everyone, even way back then.

He let go of her hand and wrapped a muscled arm around her shoulders, pulling her into his side. She snuggled in, telling herself she was simply keeping warm.

"We had some good times though, Holly," he said, his voice low and gravelly. "We were young, and everything was still ahead of us."

Her throat went tight. She remembered moments of happiness in her late teens, and many of them were spent with friends here at the Carneys' place and other island hangouts. But the shroud of her parents' deaths had never slipped off her shoulders for very long. And back then she remembered thinking a lot more about the past than she did about the future. The world outside the cocoon of Seashell Bay had seemed like a very scary place. It was a view that didn't really change until she went away to college in Boston.

Micah let out a quiet sigh, obviously reading her. "I'm sorry, Holly. Sometimes I forget how hard it was for you back then. I shouldn't be trying to walk you down memory lane."

"No, no, it's fine." She slid her arm around his waist and leaned into his shoulder. "You always seem to know what I'm thinking, don't you? I might put that down to cop instinct if I didn't know you'd always been that way."

"I guess I was born to be a cop."

"Maybe, but you were always different, Micah. Most guys were so focused on the girls' boobs that they didn't have a clue what we were thinking or feeling. You were way more tuned in. Lily and Morgan and I always noticed that. We've talked about it before."

"Now I know why my ears get hot whenever you're back on the island," he joked.

Hot was a very good way to describe him, and not just his ears.

She slipped out of his grasp and pulled him down to the end of the dock. She leaned out over the railing, staring down at the calm waters below. It was deep here at high tide—deep enough to make diving safe and fun. Under the soft glow of the light fixture over her head, she could see that the water level was almost up to the high tidemark on the pilings.

"Hmm, I wonder what the water temperature is tonight?" she said.

Micah gently bumped her shoulder with his. "Probably in the low to mid-sixties. Great minds think alike, because I was just contemplating a dip."

"What? No, I wasn't thinking of taking a dip. Really."

He tilted his head to look at her, his eyebrows lifting in silent question.

Okay, I was, but...

"We're not eighteen anymore, Micah."

He grinned. "No, but there's no law that says we can't act like we are for a while." He yanked his shirt over his head, draping it over the railing.

Startled both by his action and the proximity of his incredibly ripped and naked chest, Holly just stared at him. When he started to undo his belt, she managed to find her voice. "Deputy Micah Lancaster, what are you doing?" She winced at the slightly screechy tone to her voice.

"What does it look like? Look, nobody could see us

out here on the point even in daylight. And I'd like to note that I'm off duty." He kicked off his shoes, then shoved his jeans down and stepped out of them.

All he had on was a pair of black boxers that fit him like a second skin. Though she couldn't help a brief glance at his *very* impressive package, Holly tore her eyes away. But, oh man, did she want to keep looking.

"I can't believe you did that," she said.

"Sure you can. Come on, Holly, be crazy for a few minutes—you've earned it tonight." He slipped past her to the swimmer's ladder.

Her heart pounded out a crazy rhythm as she greedily took in Micah's broad shoulders, muscular back, and fine butt. He glanced back, gave her a quick grin, and arced down into the water with perfect form. On top of everything else, he was a great swimmer and a powerful one. She wouldn't have anything to worry about if she followed him in.

No, no, no. What a cosmically bad idea that would be—both of them wet and basically naked. But still she moved to the ladder, as if pulled by a magnet. Micah broke the dark surface of the water and raked a hand back to clear his eyes as he bobbed in the gentle waves.

"It's nice and warm," he said. "What's wrong, Tyler? You chicken or something?"

No, dammit. She wasn't—not anymore.

"Those are fighting words, Lancaster," she called down to him as she pulled her tank top over her head and dropped it at her feet. She kicked off her sandals and wriggled out of her skirt, deliberately not looking at him. Irrationally, she was really happy that her lacy red demi bra and hip-hugger panties were both new, stylish designs from Victoria's Secret.

She stood poised at the top of the ladder, where she'd stood countless times before. Holly had no fear of the ocean, having jumped and dived off Seashell Bay docks and piers all through her childhood. She'd never suffered anything worse than a black eye Brett Clayton inadvertently gave with his elbow as he surfaced beside her.

After a quick glance down at Micah, who was staring up at her with his mouth hanging open, she aimed a little to his right and launched herself into a dive.

She came up spitting salt water and shrieking. The water was *not* warm—it was freaking cold. "You lied about the water, you rat," she yelped.

He swam closer. "Since when did you become such a wimp?" he teased.

Holly splashed water at him. "Officers of the law are supposed to always tell the truth."

Micah gave her a sly grin. "Are you still cold?"

She didn't miss the heated intent in his gaze. *You are so playing with fire, Holly.* But she didn't care—not tonight anyway.

"Am I still shivering?" she scoffed.

"I can fix that." He pulled her in, plastering her against that wet, gorgeous chest of his. Holly couldn't resist. Didn't want to resist, because it felt too damn good— better than anything she'd felt in a very long time.

She snaked her arms around Micah's shoulders and treaded water along with him.

"Does that help?" he whispered in her ear. His bristly chin brushed against her cheek, making her shiver even harder.

"You have no idea," she choked out.

"Mmm, wrap your legs around my waist, babe. Then you can just float with me."

She was vaguely aware that he was pulling her with him, but didn't fully realize what was happening until he turned and gently pressed her against one of the dock's pilings. Micah's arms protected her back from rubbing against the rough, moss-covered wooden post. He pulled her close, and the filmy fabric of her bra was like nothing against the rock-hard heat of his chest. Her nipples, already stiff from the cold water, ached with a delicious heat from the contact.

When she sucked in a startled breath, one of his hands slid down to her ass and he kissed her hard. She didn't even try to close her lips, taking him right in.

And, dear sweet Jesus, did he ever taste wonderful. She'd dreamed about kissing him for so long. And not the friendly, quick kiss on the cheek or the occasional peck on the lips they'd shared as friends. She'd wanted *this*. Hot, glorious, messy, and so damn passionate that it blasted every rational thought from her brain. She'd wanted Micah's tongue sweeping into her mouth, his lips devouring hers like he'd never wanted anything more in his life than what they were doing right now.

Holly wound herself around his big, muscled body, getting as close as she could. With his strong arms and the buoyancy of the water supporting her, she could crawl right on top of him. And everywhere they touched, every point of contact—and there was a *lot* of contact—her skin burned with heat. Even in the water, she could tell she was getting hotter and wetter between her thighs, getting ready for him. She clamped her hands on the sides of his head, holding him still as she indulged in leisurely kisses that slid from one to another, never seeming to end.

When he breathed out a sexy groan against her lips and slid a hand down the back of her panties, cupping her,

Holly broke away on a gasp. She stared into his eyes. Even in the deep shadows underneath the dock, she could see that his gaze had gone heavy-lidded and oh so possessive, taking every bit of strength from her trembling muscles.

It would be so crazy to give in to him, but she wanted it, wanted *him*, more than anything she'd wanted in years. Her heart pounded out a surging, driving rhythm that silently urged her to take more. *To take everything.*

"Let's go back up," Micah finally whispered.

Holly simply nodded, all out of words. She grabbed the edges of the ladder and found an underwater rung with her feet. She rested there for a moment, trying to gather her wits after that mind-blowing string of kisses.

"Don't worry, I've got you," Micah said. His big hands grasped her hips. "But if it's easier, we could just swim back to the shore."

Holly didn't worry about falling, not with Micah right behind her. There was no way he'd let her get hurt even if her grip faltered. "I'll be fine." She started climbing.

"You have the most beautiful ass in the history of the world," Micah said in a husky voice.

"Well, you're certainly getting a good view of it," she joked.

"And feel of it," he said, applying a gentle squeeze.

Her breath seized again. She loved the feel of his hands on her, but what was going to happen when they made it back up onto the dock? It was clear that he'd only broken it off in the water because he wanted to get even busier on dry land. And so did she.

She scrambled up and turned around to extend a hand down to Micah, her breath coming in shallow pants, partly due to exertion but more a result of her nerves. After all, it seemed she was about to take one of the biggest risks of her life.

And Holly hated taking risks—especially emotional ones. In her experience, they only led to heartache. Then again, she'd played it safe with Jackson and that had turned into an epic disaster, hadn't it?

Micah grasped her hand and hauled himself up. Before she could even say a word, he pulled her against his dripping body. His erection felt long and thick and so very hard against her belly.

"Micah, this is crazy—"

"Maybe," he interrupted. "Maybe not."

His big hands pushed her panties down. "Holly, you know you can stop me anytime. But I don't think you want to, so why don't you just let go for once. Stop worrying and let go."

Holly knew she should push him away. It had been a crazy few weeks, and she was vulnerable. The breakup with Jackson had been the icing on the cake. Given where her head was right now, it would be the worst possible time to jump into bed with Micah.

But her body was singing from an entirely different songbook than her brain. Boy, was it ever singing.

"Let go," Holly said in a whisper, more to herself than to Micah. She twined her arms around his back and lifted her face for him to kiss. "For just one night."

Something dark flashed through Micah's eyes, then he smiled at her. "For just one night," he echoed before nuzzling her mouth.

A few seconds later, she came up for air. "Your place, I presume? We can hardly barge in on my aunts."

Micah's laugh came out deep and wicked. "I was thinking, why wait?"

She pretended to think about that—not an easy thing when his big, warm hands were sliding all over her wet skin. "Uh...okay," she stuttered when his fingers slipped between her thighs.

The truth was that she wanted him inside her and she wanted it now. It was totally crazy, but doing it out here on the dock—the same dock where they'd hung out as teenagers all those years ago—somehow felt not just insanely sexy but absolutely right.

Holly stepped out of her panties and reached for the waistband of his boxers. When she carefully eased them down over his straining erection, Micah sucked in a deep breath and grabbed at the front clasp of her bra. Unhooking it easily, he slid the straps off her shoulders and dropped the scrap of lace and nylon to the wooden planks.

"You're so beautiful," he breathed as he gazed down at her. "You can't believe how many times I've imagined what you looked like underneath all those tight shirts and bikini tops. As a perverted teenager, of course," he added with a grin.

"You mean the adult Micah has never had even one lewd thought about me?"

His hand drifted up to caress her breast. "Only about a million," he whispered.

She rested her hands on his hips, gazing up at him. "Me too," she whispered. "About you."

She'd had an epic crush on him when they were teenagers, but she'd always been too afraid of screwing up their friendship. Then she'd moved away to school, and those feelings had faded under the impact of time, distance, and her new and busy life—a life that had soon enough led her to Drew.

Still, there'd always been a spark deep down with Micah,

a cherished memory of that first schoolgirl crush on the best boy in Seashell Bay.

But there was nothing girlish about what she felt for him now. And there was damn sure nothing boyish about Micah Lancaster. He was all man, and so nakedly gorgeous that she could hardly catch her breath.

When she reached up to slide her hands around his neck, he gently pushed her arms away.

"Let me play for a minute, babe," he murmured in a low, raspy voice. His sexy tone was almost enough to send her over the edge.

"O . . . kay," she stuttered when his hands moved up to cup her breasts.

Her still-damp nipples were already tight, aching points from the night air and from the urgency of her lust. When his long fingers finally closed over them and gently tugged, sensation zinged straight to her core. It forced a cry from her throat.

Micah let out a husky, satisfied laugh when she clapped a mortified hand over her mouth.

"Oh, damn," she muttered. "Do you think anyone could have heard?"

He pulled her hand away and turned it over, pressing a kiss to the middle of her palm. "The closest house is half a mile away. You can make as much noise as you want."

"Good." She had no intention of curtailing the evening's activities, but nor did she want half the island knowing she was doing the nasty out here with Micah Lancaster.

"Then again," he said in a thoughtful tone as he flicked his thumb over her nipple, "sound does carry a long way over water."

She smacked his arm. "You big jerk—"

She lost her breath—and her words—when Micah dipped down and fastened his mouth over her nipple, sucking hard. Pleasure bolted through her, weakening her knees, and she had to grab his shoulders to keep from tumbling down to the smooth boards under her feet.

He clamped one hand on her ass, lifting her up. For the next few minutes he drove her crazy, teasing her breasts. She squirmed against him, pressing her hips against his erection, trying to find just the right angle to assuage the growing ache between her thighs.

Finally, when she couldn't take it anymore, she clamped her hands over his ears and forced his head up. "Micah, you're driving me insane."

He slowly straightened, holding her away from him as his fiery gaze swept over her body. Her breasts felt hot and swollen, and part of her wanted his mouth on them again. But she needed more—much more. She needed him to make love to her now.

"You're really something, babe. I think I could spend the rest of the night playing with those sweet breasts of yours." He swooped down and sucked one of her nipples back into his mouth for a brief taste.

"As good as that sounds," she managed in a squeaky voice, "I need more."

She reached down and wrapped her fingers around his thick length. He let out a harsh, trembling breath.

"I need you inside me," she whispered.

He bent down, resting his forehead on hers. "I need that too, babe. More than you can know."

When he let her go, she immediately missed the heat pouring off his body. It was a mild night, but she still shivered in the slight breeze that wafted over her skin.

Holly cautiously eyed the planks under her feet. She wanted Micah so badly that every muscle in her body was pulled tight with lust, but suddenly the idea of doing it on the dock—without even a towel underneath her—was somewhat less than enticing. With her luck, she'd probably end up with a splinter in her butt.

Holly mentally sighed. *When did you turn into such a wet blanket?*

"So, how do you propose we do this?" she asked as he rummaged in his pants pocket.

He glanced up, no doubt hearing the hesitation in her voice. "Afraid of getting a splinter in that sweet ass of yours?" he teased. "Don't worry, I won't let that happen."

She propped her hands on her hips and scowled at him. "Do you always read my mind like that? It's really annoying."

He eyed her with appreciation as he flipped open his wallet. "Hate to break it to you, honey, but that nasty glare is pretty much offset by your smoking-hot and very naked body."

"I'll take that as a compliment." She nodded at the condom he pulled out of his wallet. "Well, someone came prepared."

Thank goodness. Holly had been so caught up in what was happening—so caught up in him—that she hadn't even thought of protection. She needed to dial back the emotional intensity a few notches. Micah was as dangerous to her as a riptide, threatening to wash away what little control she still had left.

But as she watched him sheath his big and hard and gorgeous erection, she had to admit it would be a pretty terrific way to go.

He gave her a wicked grin. "I'm an officer of the law. I always come prepared."

"I'm glad someone did," she muttered. Now that they were finally going to do it, she couldn't help feeling just a bit nervous. Because it was Micah, and he knew everything about her. There wouldn't be a hope in hell of hiding behind their old, easygoing friendship after tonight.

Yeah, tonight she was crossing the Rubicon in a big, big way.

"Hey, you," he said, "come here." He slowly drew her in. "You're going to let it go just for one night, remember?" he whispered.

She nodded and pressed a kiss to the center of his brawny chest. Now that he had his hands back on her body, desire spiraled up in her again, twisting her insides into a delicious ache. "Sounds like a plan, big guy."

"Thank God," he said with a rough-sounding laugh.

A moment later, he had her down on the dock with him. Before going flat onto his back, he lifted her so she straddled his hips.

"There, no chance of splinters in your ass," he murmured. "Plus, I still get to play with you this way."

She lost her breath when his hands came back to her breasts, plucking and teasing the rigid tips. She was splayed over him, her thighs spread wide. His erection slipped between her folds, sending a bolt of sensation cascading through her body. Holly moaned and rocked against him. It was so hot and delicious that she knew it wouldn't take her long to come. In fact, it felt so good she was almost tempted to bring herself to climax right away, saving the main event for later.

And, boy, was there a lot to save for later.

They indulged themselves, him playing with her breasts and stroking his hands over her body, and Holly rocking against him. Too soon she felt herself starting to come, and she suddenly realized she didn't want that—not without Micah inside her. She'd waited a long time for this, denying herself for what seemed like forever, and she didn't want to get there without him.

He suddenly tilted her forward, taking her mouth in a hot kiss. "Ready, babe?" he rasped out against her lips.

She huffed out a quiet laugh. "You have no idea."

His hands came to her hips and lifted her. Holly positioned herself over the broad head of his erection, then started the slow slide down. She clutched at his arms, her lips parting as she sucked in a startled breath.

He was huge. And amazing. So damn good that she suddenly found herself blinking back surprised tears.

Micah groaned as her hips came flush against him, his eyelids fluttering shut. He held her still, as if drinking in the moment. "You're gonna kill me, babe. You feel so damn good."

She nodded, even though he couldn't see her. When she started moving, his eyes popped open. Slowly, then with increasing urgency, they moved against each other. Soon Micah was all but pounding up into her, and Holly was right there with him. Need built between them with ferocious energy. Everywhere he touched her, bolts of electricity raced beneath her skin.

Then, when she was close, so close that it almost hurt, Micah slicked his fingers between her thighs and she broke. Holly threw back her head, her back arching and her eyes wide open, and stared upward as she came hard.

At the exact same moment, a falling star streaked across

the night sky, a trail of fire burning bright against the stars.
She blinked, stunned for a second. It was unbelievably
crazy timing, and it felt so corny she had to laugh.

Make a wish and make it count.

But then Micah was pulling her down, kissing her with
an almost desperate passion and shaking as he too came.

As Holly curled herself around him, a wish did drift
through her mind—a wish that he would never let her go.
A wish that Micah would keep her right here in Seashell
Bay, safe, warm, and cherished, where nothing could ever
hurt her again.

Despite the incredible time they'd spent at Carney's dock,
Micah felt empty the moment Holly gunned her car out
of Lily's driveway. Their scorching kiss as they'd parted
made him regret even more that she'd told him she couldn't
spend the night at his place. To say that she'd burrowed her
way into his heart was a massive understatement. Micah
was well and truly gone when it came to Holly, and there
was no use pretending otherwise.

Besides, the sex had been damn near epic, just as he'd
always known it would be.

Micah's cell rang. Maybe she was missing him already
and calling now from her car? He laughed at that optimistic thought as he glanced down at his call display.

Delbert Rideout.

Not only was it late, but Del wasn't like some folks
who called in the hope that the deputy sheriff would drop
everything and look for their lost cat. Hell, he didn't even
own a cat or any other kind of pet. All the widowed lobsterman did was work sunrise to sundown and then spend
his evenings at the Lobster Pot, shooting the breeze at

a big corner table with half a dozen other grizzled bug catchers.

"Hey, Del, what's up?"

"Shit's up, Micah. Some bastard got into my damn house tonight and stole my money."

Micah jammed on the brakes and made a U-turn on Island Road. "Somebody *broke in*?

"Uh, well . . ."

"You're telling me you left your door open?"

"You've given me that lecture more than once, son."

Yeah, but it didn't sink in. "Look, I'll be right there, Del. Don't touch anything, okay?"

Micah pulled into Del's graveled driveway about two minutes later. Like many island homes, his was set back well off the road in a dense thicket of trees. The two-story clapboard house, its white paint more peeled every time Micah saw it, had been in the Rideout family since the early twentieth century. Del already stood at the open porch door, swatting away mosquitoes as he waited.

"You're okay, right?" Micah asked after he stepped inside. Del was in his midsixties but looked older, the rugged life of lobstering having taken its toll. Add to that the tragic loss of his wife to a heart attack five years ago, and it wasn't surprising the guy seemed grizzled and worn. But he was still a burly, barrel-chested man who held his own every year in the arm-wrestling contests at the Blueberry Festival.

Del started toward the back of the house. "I'm fine, but I'm pissed off, I'll tell you that. The son of a bitch found my cash stash and took it," he growled over his shoulder. "Every last dollar."

Micah wanted to drive his fist through the nearest

wall. Fitz's break-in was bad enough. To have another one this soon in Seashell Bay was damn near inconceivable. "Where did you keep the cash?"

When they reached the kitchen, an old-fashioned farmhouse type, Del waved a hand at the refrigerator. "In the freezer. Inside an empty ice cream carton."

As hiding places went, Micah had seen a lot worse. "How much was in there?"

Del's eyes went to slits, as if a bolt of pain had shot through him. "Over four hundred bucks. I was saving up to take...to go on vacation in Florida this winter."

"Sorry, Del," Micah said, feeling for the guy. "Anything else missing?"

Del shook his head. "I checked around pretty good. Nothing else I can see gone."

"What about those pills you've been taking for your foot?" Micah asked. It was a small fishing town, and everybody heard about accidents at sea. So he knew about the medication Del had been taking for the pain from the injury he'd suffered when his sternman had dropped a heavy trap on his foot.

Del reached into the pocket of his khaki pants and pulled out a pill bottle. "I had them with me."

"Percocet, right?"

Del nodded.

"You weren't drinking, were you, Del? You know you can't drink when you take pain meds."

"Hell, no. I spent the whole evening at Molly's place. Brought her over a couple of lobsters and damned if she didn't invite me to stay for supper, so I did. All I had to drink was some of that fancy, bubbly water she likes."

Micah smiled. He'd heard rumors about Del and Molly

McMillan, a sweet widow of a long-dead lobsterman. If they were getting together, it was great news. "I think the guy might have been after your pills. After all, you do go out to the Pot almost every night. He probably knew that but didn't think you'd take the pills with you."

Del screwed up his mouth. "So you're saying this is like the one over at Fitz's place?"

"You're both on pain meds."

"I take them with me whenever I go out. I can't go without a pill for more than four hours, tops. The foot's still real bad, Micah." He pointed down at his right shoe, a loose-fitting loafer.

Micah figured there wasn't much more he could do tonight at this late hour. Tomorrow morning, he'd canvass the neighbors to ask whether they'd seen anyone hanging out near Del's place or a strange car parked nearby. But the odds of getting any useful information were slim. This house was secluded and separated from its neighbors by hundreds of feet, and the woods were thick.

"Okay, Del, you should try to get some sleep. I'll come back tomorrow and take a statement. And start locking your doors, okay?"

Del shook Micah's offered hand. "Yeah, yeah. But what in hell is this island coming to anyway, Micah? Nobody used to have to lock a door. Never." He gave a disgusted snort. "If I wanted to live in the damn city, I'd move there."

"I'll find this guy and put him away, Del. I promise you that. But the world's changing, my friend, and so is Seashell Bay. The days of unlocked doors might be coming to an end."

And nobody hated that any more than Micah.

Chapter 16

$\mathcal{I}$n between serving an encouragingly steady stream of morning customers, Holly tried to focus on getting the store ready for the temporary shutdown needed for Brendan's renovations. Fortunately, Morgan and Sabrina would be over soon to help her with the heavy work.

Despite downing a shot of Florence's scotch as soon as she got home last night, she'd hardly slept. She'd lain there with her eyes clamped shut, her stomach tight, and her mind whipsawing between the ugly scene with Jackson and the awesome sex with Micah. For a few minutes, the world had seemed suddenly right when she was locked in Micah's arms, swept away as he made love to her. And it *had* felt like he was making love, not just taking her oh-so-willing body in some frenzy of pent-up passion.

Yet as right as it had felt with him, and as liberating as it had been to *just let go*, her doubts had reared soon after. And she'd known that's what would happen, even though she'd tried to deny it. She'd just added another complication to her already seriously complicated life.

Mostly though, she worried about how it all would affect Micah.

When she told him she couldn't spend the night with him, he'd accepted it with wry good humor. She'd taken a quick shower at his place, then he drove her back to Lily's house to pick up her car. They'd parted with a short but very steamy kiss. Micah had clearly wanted to linger, but Holly had managed to pull out of his arms and jump into her car for a quick getaway. She had no desire to run into Jackson in the unlikely event that he was still at the party, but mostly she was spooked by her sexcapade with Micah.

She'd taken the coward's way out, and that didn't make her feel good.

So she'd been obsessing for hours over what she'd say to Micah the next time they saw each other. Chances were that he'd be back at work on her aunts' porch this evening, so she'd have to deal with the situation then if not before. No matter how she imagined that conversation, nothing she could say sounded right to her.

She was rearranging some boxes of canned goods in the storage room when she heard the front door bell jingle. Brushing her hands against her jeans, she hurried back into the store but then skidded to a halt.

Jackson.

"Morning, Hols," he said with his usual confident smile, as if their relationship hadn't imploded last night.

"What are you doing here, Jackson?" She walked backward toward the counter, keeping as much distance between them as she could.

He moved closer, still smiling. "The chopper's waiting, so I need to get out of here in a minute. But I didn't want to leave before talking to you again."

Wearing one of his summer-weight gray suits along with a white shirt and dark blue tie, he looked immaculate, ready for some high-powered meeting back in New York.

Holly just nodded, waiting for him to say his piece and fervently praying that Micah wouldn't happen to drop by to pick up coffee in the next few minutes.

He leaned against the counter, looking rather contrite, if she read his expression right. "Last night totally sucked, Hols. And I'm sorry."

Actually no, only some of last night sucked.

She nodded again.

"I'm sure we both said things we regret," Jackson said.

When Holly crossed her arms over her chest and narrowed her gaze, Jackson looked flummoxed for a second. Then he let out a dramatic sigh. "Ah, hell, baby. We've been good together for a long time. Wouldn't it be stupid to let one off night screw it up?"

Holly hadn't known what to expect from him, but this half-assed apparent attempt at an apology felt ridiculous. "It was a *really* bad night, Jackson. I can't be with you after the horrible way you behaved."

His mouth went flat. "I suppose it's because of whatever the hell you have going on with that thick-necked idiot of a deputy. Christ, Hols, is that the best you can do? I mean, yeah, this place is a total backwater, but surely you could do better than him."

Jackson wasn't fit to shine Micah's boots.

Holly clenched her fists shut against the almost irresistible impulse to throw something at him. And there were a lot of potential missiles within easy reach. "Jackson, please don't start."

He shrugged. "Oh well, I guess you're allowed to do stupid shit sometimes. God knows I'm no saint. Look, I just wanted to tell you that when you get back to the city, you should give me a call. Because I know that woman at the party last night wasn't the Hols I've known all this time. It's just this place—it always messes with your head."

"Unbelievable," Holly said.

He gave her a tight smile. "Just don't take too long to make up your mind. I won't be waiting around forever."

What did I ever see in this jerk?

The problem was, she obviously hadn't *seen* him enough. During the limited times they'd spent together, he'd been almost always lighthearted and charming and fun, with the occasional flash of arrogance. Holly had a strong and sickening feeling that the Jackson Leigh that had revealed himself at Lily's party was the real article, and that certainly didn't reflect well on her.

"Have a good flight back to the city," she said. "And don't let the door hit your ass on the way out."

Jackson stared at her for a couple of moments, then turned on his heel and stalked out.

When Micah finished with the last of the porch windows, he put down the caulking gun and eyed the general store next door. Holly was working only a few steps from him, and yet the distance between them yawned as wide as the Grand Canyon.

According to Beatrice, she and Holly had spent most of the afternoon getting the store ready for the renovations, with help from Morgan and Sabrina. Beatrice had gone home by late afternoon, and Morgan and Sabrina had taken off to tend to their B&B guests. Holly apparently intended to keep working through most of the evening.

Micah had deliberately avoided the store, wanting to give Holly some space. Like he knew the sun would rise in the east, he knew she'd be questioning—and probably regretting—what they'd done out on Jerry's deserted dock. He suspected it had been as mind-blowing an experience for her as it was for him.

It had changed everything between them.

When he wasn't thinking about Holly, of course he was thinking about the break-in last night at Del Rideout's. After taking Del's statement first thing in the morning, he'd briefed Griff Turner and then interviewed all the neighbors in the vicinity of the burglary. As he'd feared, no one had seen or heard anything unusual last night.

As gut-wrenching as a second break-in was, at least it told him that the thief had to be plugged in when it came to who was taking meds in Seashell Bay. Because he didn't believe for a second that cash was what the guy was looking for at the Rideout place. Del lived more modestly than most, and his place, like Fitz's, sure wouldn't be one any thief would target for a grab of cash, jewelry, or other valuables. No, it was clear to Micah that the guy was after Del's pain pills. Like a lot of people in town, he obviously knew Del was taking them for his injury. Unfortunately for the thief, he didn't know Del never left home without them.

After washing his hands in the kitchen, Micah said good-bye to Florence and Beatrice and headed out to his cruiser. He glanced over at the little general store as he got in. It was lit up on the inside, though the fluorescent lamp over the ancient gas pump was off. That would normally be an indication that the store was closed, except that particular bulb had been burned out for weeks.

He sat for a few minutes with the big engine idling as conflicting arguments jostled around inside his head. His pride, usually the loudest voice, told him in no uncertain terms to leave Holly alone. If she'd wanted to see him, she'd have come over to the house while he was working, if only to say a quick hello. She would have seen his cruiser every time she glanced out one of the store's side windows.

Pride didn't seem to be winning the battle though. His teeth clenched at the idea of not talking to her tonight—of not holding her in his arms. Last night had been everything he'd ever dreamed it would be. He'd had his share of women over the years, and there'd been some pretty great, if a bit infrequent, sex. But making love to Holly had been on a whole other level, because his heart and mind had been just as into it as his body. Maybe that sounded dumb, but the emotions he'd felt were too big to put into words.

And now the thought that it might have been just a one-off was turning him inside out.

Micah drove next door and stopped in front, shutting off the engine and yanking out the keys.

Enough with giving her space.

He'd been giving her a freaking ocean of space for years. Last night, for the first time since he'd known Holly Tyler, he'd figured he might actually have a chance with her, so he might as well find out here and now if that was more than wishful thinking.

Because if being with Holly—truly being with her— were just wishful thinking, he needed to try to rip her out of his heart once and for all.

*   *   *

Holly had been nervously watching Micah's parked cruiser all evening. A dozen times she'd thought about going over to talk to him and had even headed toward the door more than once. But her anxiety and simply not knowing what to say had pulled her back.

She hated feeling so awkward. She loved Micah—was possibly falling *in love* with Micah—but there were so many complications that freaked her out.

When she heard the Tahoe's engine start up, she felt a brief moment of relief, a coward's respite. After what seemed like a very long time, she heard him pull out of the driveway and went to look. But instead of driving away, the SUV stopped directly in front of the store and Micah got out, looking like a man on a mission.

Holly bolted away from the window and hurried into the tiny restroom, where she whipped the scrunchie off her ponytail. She shook out her hair and tried to style it with shaking fingers. Her face and neck were flushed and sweaty from packing and lugging boxes to the storage room. In her now-dirty yoga pants, tank top, and sneakers, she figured she must look like she'd spent the day jogging around the island in the hot sun before rolling around in the dirt.

When Micah rapped sharply on the door, she inhaled a few deep breaths and walked back across the store to open it.

"I'm afraid we're closed, Deputy," she said, forcing a smile as she stepped back to let him inside. "No coffee for you."

So lame.

Micah came in and closed the door behind him. His

smile looked forced too, though his gaze zeroed in on her skintight pants with a spark of interest. "Hey, Holly. I just wondered if there was anything I could do to help you. It looks like you've put in a really long day."

God, he is so wonderful. Holly, what is wrong with you?

As he towered over her, she couldn't help thinking how amazing that brawny body had felt wrapped around her.

She kept her gaze firmly fastened on his face. "You've had a long day too. Are the porch windows all set?"

He nodded.

"That's so great. It shouldn't be long now until the aunties can enjoy it, right?"

"Just a few details left." He glanced around the nearly empty store and frowned. "I really should have been here helping you tonight."

"Oh, no. I'd rather you finished up over there as soon as possible."

The conversation felt so strained that Holly wanted to throw up. Micah let out a tired sigh, perhaps thinking the same thing

"Babe, we really should talk about last night."

This is not going to turn out well. "I know," she said, dropping her gaze to the floor.

"How about a walk?"

"Sounds like a good idea." At least going for a walk meant they wouldn't have to stare at each other as they talked. "I guess I can leave the rest of the work until morning."

Actually, the store was in a perfect state of readiness. All she needed to do tomorrow was unlock the door for Brendan and his assistant.

Micah waited outside while Holly shut off the lights

and locked up. They headed up Island Road, the soft dusk of evening falling around them.

"I saw Leigh fly out," he said. "Hell, that damn helicopter practically blew Roy's golf cart into a ditch. I thought the old guy was going to have a stroke, he was so pissed." His disgusted tone said everything Holly was thinking about her ex-boyfriend too.

"I'm sorry about Roy. Jackson had to get back to work this morning."

"Good. I hope he never sets foot in Seashell Bay again."

"I think you can bet the house on that."

He gently stroked her shoulder, unconsciously, she thought. The touch of his callused hand on her bare skin was electric, and it brought everything they'd done on the dock rushing back with blazing intensity. Nerve endings fired from her scalp down to the soles of her feet.

She sighed. "Micah, about us...we let things get out of control last night. And it was totally my fault. I got too emotional at the party, and I shouldn't have let myself... uh, get carried away like that."

Even in the fading light, she couldn't miss the stark pain that flashed across his features. It felt like she'd been kicked in the gut.

"Hold on," he said. "Are you saying what happened between us was just a reaction to what Leigh did?" His voice was thick with disbelief.

Part of her wanted to say exactly that and hopefully be done with it. But she knew it would be a lie. And she hoped she was done with lying, especially to herself.

"No, of course not."

"Then what was it?"

Holly didn't know the whole truth. Her feelings for

Micah had grown so strong. And sure, she'd fantasized for years about having sex with him, so that was a bonus. But she'd been a total mess last night, and so very vulnerable. That was no way to start a relationship—especially with an old friend, one who lived in a very different world. She simply didn't have room for that kind of emotional intensity in her life, not right now anyway. And Micah, just by being Micah, would demand emotional intensity.

"I'm not entirely sure," she said. "All I know is that it shouldn't happen again."

Micah lifted a brow at her choice of words. "Shouldn't, or won't?"

"What I'm trying to say is that it didn't really change anything, Micah. Our circumstances, I mean. How could it?"

Then how come it feels like everything's changed?

"Now you're going to lecture me about our different worlds again," he said, shaking his head. "I understand, Holly. I really do, but circumstances can change, you know."

"Yes, but we have to be realistic. My heart will always be here in Seashell Bay, but it hasn't been my world since I was nineteen."

He was quiet for a few moments before answering. "I've been thinking a lot about transferring to the mainland at some point—maybe going for my detective shield. Hell, I could even end up in New York."

"Oh God, no," she blurted.

Micah stopped and stared at her. "I'm sorry?"

She flapped a hand. "I didn't mean it like that."

"Then what did you mean?"

Holly had never worried much about Micah's safety. Yes, he was a cop, but policing in Seashell Bay—and rural Cumberland County before that—had always meant that he faced little danger on the job as far as she could tell. Becoming a New York City cop, however, or a Portland detective, struck her as a whole lot riskier. She simply could not love another man who carried a gun and put himself in harm's way.

"I can't believe you'd ever live anywhere other than Seashell Bay," she said.

"Because I'm too stuck in my ways?" Sarcasm laced his voice. "Too resistant to change?"

"No, because you love it too much," she countered. "Not to mention the fact that the people here love you and need you."

That was all true, of course. But she also had to admit that the idea of Micah making such a move, partly for her sake, made her extremely nervous. It was too much, too fast.

Silence fell between them as they passed the empty fire hall and then the Lobster Pot. The bar's parking lot was full, and rock music bled out through the Pot's leaky front door. But once they got out of range of the music, all Holly could hear was the shushing of the waves against the rocky shore and the incessant chirp of crickets. An owl hooted from a tall stand of pines on their left. It was a warm evening, and under other circumstances, it would have been a lovely night for a stroll with the hottest guy in Seashell Bay.

"Okay, I'm just going to say it," Micah finally said. "Holly, I've never felt about anyone like I feel about you—not even close. I didn't think something like last night would ever happen, but I'm damn glad it did. And I'd like to believe that you feel something more than just friendship too. Something strong enough to build a future together."

Holly blinked in surprise. Coming from Micah, the most taciturn guy she knew, that kind of heartfelt statement was pretty much a Shakespearean soliloquy. He was not someone who put himself out there like that—certainly not when it came to women.

But how could she talk about how she truly felt when her life was so messy? All she knew was that she had to find some emotional distance before she damaged their relationship beyond repair.

"I've never heard you talk about your feelings for a woman before," she said, deflecting. "Not even about your relationship with that Portland cop. Gina, wasn't it?"

"She was a county deputy like me, not a Portland cop."

"Oh, right. Sorry." Holly had only met Gina two or three times, back when she and Drew spent some vacation time in Seashell Bay. She remembered forming the distinct impression that Gina wasn't a fan of the island. None of the locals was ever sure why the relationship had ended though, because Micah had always refused to say a word about it.

"That's old news, Holly," he said. "Look, maybe what we did last night hasn't changed anything for you, but it sure as hell feels like it's changed a whole lot for me."

She nodded, feeling more miserable by the minute. Still, after last night, Micah deserved the truth. "I understand."

He squared his shoulders, as if already preparing for the hit. "Look, I'd just like you to admit that someone like

Jackson Leigh is not what you really want. I've watched how you look at Morgan and Ryan, and Lily and Aiden too. I think *that's* what you really want. You want what your best friends have found."

When he paused, giving her the chance to respond, Holly just shook her head. What did he expect her to say?

Micah blew out an exasperated breath. "What they found right here on the island," he said, driving his point home.

Holly felt something inside start to give way, and it didn't feel good. She'd built up a lot of emotional firewalls over the last four years, but those defenses had already started to falter last summer when she'd come home to recuperate and bask in the love and support of her friends. While she'd done that and then some, she'd been happy to leave and return to her life too, return to the job and the work that she loved.

But Lily's wedding to Aiden, followed by Morgan's engagement to Ryan, had affected her more deeply than she'd let herself admit. She refused to be the girl who envied the happiness of her friends, or the one who needed a guy to be happy. But she could feel a sea change taking place within her. The emotional status quo was beginning to feel...unacceptable.

For years, *she'd* been the married one, the lucky girl who'd snagged a wonderful, brave man who loved her as much as anyone could hope to be loved. But time and death had turned that upside down. Now her friends had wonderful futures stretching out before them, while Holly had had one true love in her life and didn't know if she had the courage to risk another.

"Micah, I would be so, so grateful if you would just let

it go. Please. I feel like I'm being interrogated right now, and I can't deal with anything more than what's on my plate already." She hated the desperate note to her voice, but she really needed out of this conversation.

Coward.

Like he'd done so many times in the past, Micah rescued her. His brawny arms wrapped around her in one of his wonderful bear hugs. Then he let her go.

"You're right," he said. Even in the twilight, she could see the pain in his gaze. "I was a dick to push you. I promise I'll back off and give you all the space you need."

He really was the best guy she knew, while she was a total jerk. She had to force down tears to answer him. "Micah, I don't know what's going to happen between us, I truly don't. But just promise me that you'll always be one of my dearest friends, no matter what happens. I don't want to lose that. I can't."

He flinched, obviously not happy to be relegated to the friend circle in her life. But then he pulled up the warmest smile she'd ever seen on his oh-so-masculine mouth. "You'll never lose me, Holly. I'll always be there for you."

Chapter 17

$\mathcal{T}$he Seashell Bay Town Hall was a modest affair, and although the meeting room was scrubbed and tidy, the cracked vinyl flooring and the graying, chipped tiles in the suspended ceiling spoke to its advancing years. Holly could still remember when the building had gone up when she was a kid. Back then, she'd thought it huge and impressively modern. Now, like the Jenkins General Store, it seemed so much smaller and a little shabby.

"So many people," Beatrice said, scanning the room. She'd taken a seat in a row near the back. Florence had squeezed in next to her, and Holly had claimed the aisle seat.

"Let's just hope our folks are in the majority," Holly said.

She was impressed that islanders had shown up in such large numbers to let the town selectmen know how they felt about the Night Owl application. Well over three hundred people had signed Miss Annie's petition, and scores had come to tonight's special meeting to have their say on the building permit application. Later this week, the selectmen would hold their regular meeting and make a final decision.

At a narrow table up front were Selectmen Chester Buckle, Thor Sigurdsson, and Amos Hogan. Chester sat in a tense, rigid posture, while Thor and Amos had pushed back their tilting chairs and looked relaxed as they chatted. From the front row, Miss Annie was giving the selectmen a combination of sweet smiles and meaningful glares. Beside her were Roy, Lily, and Aiden on one side, and Morgan and Ryan on the other. The six formed a formidable team that would be vocally supportive of Holly's aunts.

Three rows ahead of Holly, Micah was sitting beside Enid Fitzsimmons. Fitz was a pretty, lively girl with a compact, athletic body. She looked to be in her midtwenties and appeared *very* comfortable talking to Seashell Bay's deputy sheriff.

The second Holly had seen Fitz and Micah chatting away, their heads intimately close together, Holly's already nervous stomach had started to cramp. She knew she had no business being jealous, not after the message she'd delivered to Micah, but that didn't make it any easier to see what a cute couple those two made. In fact, she had to clamp down hard on the impulse to march up to Micah and physically pull him away.

In the four days since their walk along Island Road, she'd seen Micah only once. That had been for about five minutes when he'd shown up at her aunts' house to adjust the door on the new porch. Other than that awkward encounter, he'd become a ghost. Not that she blamed him. While they'd pledged their continuing friendship, she had no doubt they'd both come away from that conversation feeling like crap.

"Look at Thor and Amos chatting away up there as if they were just having a beer at the Pot," Florence said grumpily. "You'd think those old bug catchers would be taking this more seriously, wouldn't you? They're probably griping about the price of diesel fuel or some such fool thing."

Holly patted her aunt's hand. "Now don't go getting your blood pressure up, Aunt Florence. The meeting hasn't even started yet."

"Well, it's about time it did." Florence inched forward on her metal chair and stretched her neck high. "What are we waiting for, Chester?" she called out.

When a smattering of people started to applaud, Chester got to his feet. "I didn't want to start without the representative from Night Owl, but here he is now."

A tall, thin man in a blue suit strode confidently down the aisle to take a chair off to the side of the head table.

"I'd like to introduce Mr. Kevin Archer," Chester said. "He's the local district manager with Night Owl."

Smiling broadly, Archer waved. "Hi, folks. Thank you, Selectman Buckle. I'm pleased to be here."

Chester quickly outlined the events that had led up to the meeting, and ended by opening the floor for questions and statements. When a dozen hands went up, Chester pointed at the island's most irrepressible octogenarian.

"I won't say everything that's on my mind tonight," Miss Annie said, hitching up her jeans. "You all know my position on this application, since I was the one who put together the petition." She pointed to the stack of papers piled in front of Chester.

Chester flashed an apologetic smile at Miss Annie as he squared up the stack.

"A huge number of us have already signed the petition, making it crystal clear that we don't need or want a Night Owl store," Miss Annie continued. "So I don't see why we need to have much of a debate. I say the people have spoken, and it's time to put an end to this nonsense."

Even before she resumed her seat, the crowd began to buzz. Holly was surprised that Miss Annie hadn't delivered one of her typically blistering tirades but had instead opted for a short, strong plea based on the strength of the petition. The only problem with that was unfortunately a lot of islanders had declined to sign too.

Though Morgan's hand had shot up right away, Chester instead recognized Boyd Spinney, a vociferous Night Owl supporter. Though Spinney wasn't exactly a beloved figure in Seashell Bay because of his noisy backing of the doomed car ferry proposal, he commanded the respect of the pro-development crowd.

Spinney tugged on his jacket and sucked in a deep breath, as if preparing for a pitched battle. "Chester, Thor, Amos—let's face it. We just can't keep blocking every proposal that would bring some new business to Seashell Bay."

He then launched into a lengthy recitation of all the development projects that had failed to get off the ground over the past quarter century. He ended with a mournful reference to the sad fate of his pet project, the Bay Island Properties resort and housing development that had been deep-sixed by the defeat of the car ferry referendum. "I know a lot of you folks were against the Bay Island project, and I respect that. But you know what thumbing our noses at them earned us?"

"A reprieve?" Aiden said sarcastically.

"A Nobel Prize?" Jessie Jameson shouted out.

"A new ecoresort?" Lily chimed in.

Spinney glared. "Yeah, sure, you folks think it's funny. No, what it earned us was a reputation for being a real bad place to do business."

A number of people jeered or groaned.

"You know it's true," Spinney said loudly. "I figure it's almost a miracle that a corporation like Night Owl would want to set up shop on our shores. I'm just thankful that they do, and you should be too. This place deserves a modern, well-supplied store that addresses *all* our needs. It would be a pure blessing not to have to run to the mainland every time you need to shop."

That was a huge stretch since a convenience store—however big—would hardly eliminate the need to go into Portland to shop. Still, Spinney got a fair bit of applause when he sat down.

Florence grasped Holly's hand. "I'm afraid he's got quite a lot of supporters here."

"So do we," Holly said stoutly.

From the crowd's reaction, she thought that certainly well more than half were against the permit. The selectmen, on the other hand, were another matter. By tracing the long history of islanders' reluctance to embrace mainland businesses, Spinney seemed to have made his point effectively.

Morgan spoke next, focusing on the value of loyalty as well as the ability of the existing stores to adapt to islanders' needs instead of corporate directives. Her staunch, heartfelt support left Holly blinking back tears. Beatrice started sniffling into her hankie.

Unfortunately, Morgan was followed by four speakers

in a row that supported Night Owl with varying degrees of enthusiasm. The last speaker, Heywood Calhoun, a main-lander who owned two vacation rental properties, made a long-winded point about how the world had changed into a consumer culture, and that Seashell Bay needed to adapt to meet consumers' needs, especially the tourists who brought in so much revenue. By the time Calhoun wound up, Florence was so agitated that Holly was ready to get her out of there.

Then, to her shock, Micah raised his hand.

Chester blinked, clearly as surprised as Holly was. "Go ahead, Micah," he said, ignoring the other hands.

The room went silent as Micah rose. Though he was often in uniform at public events, tonight he wore old jeans and a brown, lightweight leather jacket over a black T-shirt. And boy, did he look hot. To Holly's growing cha-grin, Fitz apparently thought so too, since she was gaz-ing up at him with open admiration. As were all the other single women at the meeting—some married ones too.

Micah gave a friendly nod to the selectmen, then turned in a slow circle as he scanned the room, making eye contact with just about everyone in attendance. It was a powerful tactic that riveted their attention. If he didn't do it on purpose, he had mighty good instincts when it came to commanding a room. Then he turned sideways so he could speak to the front and still be mostly facing the locals.

"Thanks for the chance to say my piece. Folks, you know I usually don't say anything at meetings like this. I don't like taking sides unless I'm putting money down on college football." He flashed a rueful smile that surely melted the panties off half the women in the room.

Including Holly's.

"And you're not very damn good at that," Boone Cleary piped up.

Micah laughed along with the rest of the crowd. "You got that right. But I am going to take sides tonight."

Holly blew out a shaky breath, trying to relax, but she couldn't take her eyes off Micah. He was mesmerizing.

"Boyd, you and a couple of the others use the word *progress* a lot. Well, I guess it's pretty hard to be against progress." Micah lifted his broad shoulders in a dismissive shrug. "But what is progress? Is it building more subdivisions, destroying prime forests and farmland, and messing up our rivers and lakes? Is it building more and more roads so gigantic semis can haul more cheap goods to us even faster?" He gave his head a shake. "Lots of people would call all those things progress because they create business and make people money. I'm not denying that's a good thing, but there's a point where the downside outweighs the upside."

When he paused, the only sound in the room was the ticking of the second hand on the big clock behind the head table. People were hanging on his words.

"You talk about consumer culture—getting what we want, when we want it," Micah went on. "But to me, that means a race to get everything as cheap and as fast as possible, no matter the fallout. And that fallout comes down hard on small-business owners, people like Florence and Beatrice."

"You tell 'em, Micah," Brett Clayton said loudly.

Micah gave his friend a nod before continuing. "We all shop in the big-box stores in Portland, right? Sure, because they've got good prices and great selection. But what happened to all those small hardware stores, lumberyards, butchers, grocery stores, pharmacies, and other shops we used to see? Places run by owners who knew and cared about their customers. They're gone, and I bet a lot of you miss them. Call me old-fashioned, but I sure do."

"You know it, boy," Roy Mayo said in loud voice. "Last time I went to one of those big-box stores, I couldn't even find the damn bathroom. That's holy hell on an old dog like me."

Miss Annie smacked him on the arm. "Watch your language," she barked to a smattering of laughter.

When the chuckles died down, Micah looked straight at Kevin Archer, the rep from Night Owl. "Don't get me wrong, Mr. Archer. There's nothing the matter with Night Owl or any of those big stores. You're all just doing your thing. But the question is—do we need any of you in Seashell Bay?" He shook his head. "Not in my book."

Micah turned around and looked straight at Holly, Florence, and Beatrice. "But I'll tell you one thing we do need. We need the Jenkins General Store and Sam's Island Market. Those stores are part of the fabric of Seashell Bay, of our way of life. They're *us*. And they can adapt, *are* adapting. But if you grant this permit, soon Night Owl will be all we have left in Seashell Bay. Whether it takes a few months or a few years, it'll happen as sure as there'll be morning fog on the bay. Ask yourself, folks, is that really progress? To abandon those who've always been here for us?"

He directed his gaze at the selectmen. "It's not my definition of progress, that's for damn sure."

Before his butt even hit the chair, Holly jumped to her

feet and applauded harder than she'd ever applauded anything in her life. Micah, the most taciturn guy she knew, had hit it out of the park. Miss Annie raced up and hugged him, while Ryan and Aiden moved into the aisle to shake his hand. Roy Mayo stuck two fingers in his mouth and let out an earsplitting whistle.

But when her flush of euphoria died down, Holly realized that despite the raucous response to Micah's speech, little more than half the people in the hall had risen. Some had applauded but without a lot of enthusiasm. Only Chester Buckle among the selectmen was smiling.

Dammit.

"Thank you, Micah. You're next, Claude," Chester said.

"Claude will support us," Florence whispered to Holly. "He and I go back a long way."

Claude Dufresne was a burly man of around seventy who was well regarded by everyone. He'd lived in Seashell Bay all his life but ran a successful tour boat business out of Portland. While Dufresne sat near Holly and her aunts, as he spoke, he deliberately avoided their gazes.

"I'm afraid I have to support the permit application," he said regretfully. "And it just about kills me to go against Florence and Beatrice. But if there's one thing I've learned running a business, it's that you either adapt to change or you don't survive. My company almost went under ten years ago before I learned that hard lesson."

"Oh, Claude," Florence groaned under her breath. Holly felt like throwing up.

"We need new services on the island," Dufresne continued, "and if the other stores can't adapt like they should and go under, it'll be because they let it happen. Not because Night Owl pushed them out." He finally looked at Florence and Beatrice. "You know I love you ladies, but you need to face the truth."

Though hardly anyone applauded Dufresne's somber speech, it had caused quite a few heads to nod. Unfortunately, Selectman Hogan's grizzled head was one of them.

"Holly, I need to leave," Florence said in a reedy voice. "I'm not feeling well at all."

Chapter 18

$\mathcal{I}$ think I've died and gone to heaven." Morgan sighed as she put down her latte. "This is so unbelievably good."

When Holly punched a couple of buttons, her new Franke coffee machine started to brew a cup of decaf for her too. "I had a window banner made up in Portland claiming that we've now got the best coffee in the islands. Too much?"

Morgan laughed. "No way. Besides, the only other place to get coffee in Seashell Bay is the Lobster Pot, and that's basically swill."

Once Brendan had finished his top-notch renovations and the coffee machine and the new deli case had been professionally installed, Holly had set up displays by five Maine artisans in the new gift section by the door. She figured that she'd better give those goods pride of place in front if she wanted to attract sales from tourists and day-trippers.

Morgan went over to inspect the display of gorgeous stoneware from a well-known potter from the Rockland area. The small collection featured multicolored mugs in two sizes and a matching pitcher. If those pieces sold well,

Holly intended to expand the collection to include plates, cups, and saucers in varying patterns.

"Ouch, these are a tad pricey," Morgan said, checking the sticker on a mug. "But, hey, they're definitely awesome."

"You have to pay for quality," Holly said. "I'm counting on tourists wanting unique stuff. Hopefully, islanders will want that too. And speaking of quality, I've got a meeting in the city later this afternoon with a glass artist from Augusta who just got a big feature in *World of Glass* magazine."

"Cool," Morgan moved down to the display of bronze and sterling silver jewelry from an artist from Stonington. Most pieces were small, tasteful pendants on delicate chains. "Okay, this one is screaming that it wants to come home with me," Morgan said, practically caressing one gorgeous little piece. "Allow me the honor of being the first customer for your artisan goods."

Holly would have happily offered the piece to Morgan as a gift but knew her pal would be offended if she tried. "Thanks, but don't even look at the tag. For you, the price is our cost."

Morgan snorted. "As if. You're supposed to be making money, remember?" She peered at the attached price tag, then took her handbag off her shoulder and rummaged around for a moment before heaving a sigh. "Oops, it seems I'm a little challenged when it comes to cash. And I'm afraid I don't have my checkbook either."

Though the store accepted credit cards, Morgan always paid in cash or by check in order to save Florence and Beatrice the card transaction fees. "Oh, I think you're probably good for it," Holly said with a grin. She took the pendant from Morgan and went behind the counter to retrieve one of the small boxes the artist had left.

"I'll wear it to the meeting tonight," Morgan said, following Holly to the counter. "Maybe it'll bring us good luck."

Holly had been trying hard not to think about tonight's vote on the Night Owl permit. She'd wanted to skip the meeting, but Florence had insisted she was going with or without Beatrice and Holly. Holly was truly worried about the effect a bad outcome could have on Florence's health, but there was no way she could talk her stubborn aunt out of going.

"Any more gossip about the vote since the town hall meeting?" she asked.

Morgan shook her head. "As far as I know, even Chester has kept his mouth shut since. Miss Annie hasn't been able to worm a word out of him, which I find a bit weird."

Weird and worrying.

"I've been working hard to convince my aunts that the store will be able to survive no matter what. But Florence isn't really buying it." Holly grimaced. "And she's not very impressed with my changes."

She hated to admit it, but Claude Dufresne had been right about the need to change in order to survive. And Florence was fighting change almost every step of the way.

"I'm sorry, sweetie," Morgan said. "But they've devoted almost their whole lives to the general store, so even all the good things you're doing must be pretty hard to absorb. Change can be tough at their age. Heaven knows my dad tended to get stuck on the same old track at the B&B."

True, but with Ryan's help, Morgan had done an amazing job of revitalizing the B&B. It was doing great, and Holly saw it as a positive model of how to blend the old and the new in a community like Seashell Bay.

"All I can do is my best," she said with a sigh. "And if I

don't get down to New York soon, my new partners are going to throw me off the Brooklyn Bridge." She'd had another fraught conference call with them last night. To say the guys weren't happy with her was a massive understatement.

"Don't worry. You'll charm them out of the grumps," Morgan said loyally. "Now, to change the subject completely, are you and Micah still avoiding each other?"

Holly rolled her eyes. The only surprise in that question was how long Morgan had waited to ask it.

She and Micah had barely said hello at the town hall a few nights ago and hadn't laid eyes on each other since. While she was relieved not to have to deal with the crazy sexual tension between them, she missed him—a lot. And so did her body, which practically vibrated as she remembered every wonderful second of the evening when Micah transformed her anger and frustration into pure magic.

But that didn't mean she wanted to talk about it, even to her best friends.

"Why do you say *avoiding*?" she hedged as she fussed with tying a pretty pink ribbon around the gift box.

Morgan crossed her arms over her chest. "Really, we're going to play it like that? We've seen each other every day, but you haven't once mentioned his name. And he's been doing exactly the same thing, at least according to Ryan. Something happened during or after Lily's party, so don't even try to deny it."

While Holly had told her pals that Micah had driven her home that night, she'd withheld the rest. And that wasn't like her. Was she ashamed of the way she'd succumbed to the moment—and to him—and done something she'd vowed never to do? She'd asked herself that question many times, and maybe she was indeed ashamed. Micah deserved so much better than what she could give him. She'd hurt him, and that made her feel awful.

And not very eager to come clean with her friends.

"Nothing's going on," she said. "I'm sure we'll see him tonight at the meeting."

Morgan shot her another skeptical look. "Okay, you're obviously not ready to talk, so we'll leave it at that. For now." She took the box from Holly and leaned across the counter to kiss her cheek. "Your appointment with the glass artist this afternoon—it won't make you late for the meeting, will it? The selectmen like to start at seven sharp."

"No. I have to keep it short because I need to pick up a new prescription at Watson's for Florence before I catch the boat," Holly said. "Anyway, let's just pray hard that the selectmen will do the right thing. Florence is so nervous she can barely sit down, and I'm getting more and more worried about what might happen if the vote goes against us."

"Me too, but whatever goes down, remember that you're doing all you can," Morgan said firmly. "You're a wonderful niece and a wonderful person, and don't you forget it."

Micah had to resist the urge to pace along the back of the hall as he watched the rows of chairs slowly filling up with tense-looking islanders. At least a dozen people had already stopped to chat with him, but he'd been pretty terse in his responses. His nerves were buzzing like a hive full of bees on steroids.

He was keeping his eye on the door for Holly and her aunts. Unlike the last meeting, where Fitz had practically dragged him into the chair next to her, he had no intention of sitting with anybody but Holly. Yes, he ached to simply be near her, but he also had a bad feeling about how things were going to turn out tonight.

Rex Fudge, Amos's best friend, had let something out of the bag last night when Micah stopped to help him change a tire down on Collins Lane. Amos and Rex had shared a few beers at the Lobster Pot, as they often did, and Amos had let slip that he and another selectman had reached an agreement on the permit issue. Since Amos and Chester never agreed on anything, that meant he and Thor were now together, and that had to mean they were both on the dark side.

Unless old Rex was confused again, which was always a possibility.

If things did go sour tonight, as he feared, Micah wanted to be as close as he could to Florence and Beatrice—and to Holly.

Most of the seats were filled by the time she and her aunts arrived. The aunts looked pale and nervous as hell, but Holly looked gorgeous. Dressed in a short, cornflower-blue sundress that instantly drew Micah's eyes to her mile-long legs, she had her arm around Florence's waist. When she spotted Micah, she gave him a tight smile. All three women looked like they were expecting the worst.

"Jessie's been saving those seats," Micah said, pointing to the third-to-last row after they'd exchanged greetings. He'd staked out the chair directly the across the aisle by draping his sheriff's office jacket over it. "Are you okay?"

She grimaced. "Ask me in half an hour."

"Micah, I suppose you're never going to come around again now that the porch is finished," Florence said. "Beatrice and I can't help feeling rather abandoned." Despite her obvious worries, she managed to give Micah a mischievous wink.

What was he supposed to say—that he'd been busy? "I

figured you'd be sick of me after all those evenings banging away out there in back."

Florence rolled her eyes. "You are the world's worst liar, Micah Lancaster. We've missed him, haven't we, Holly?" She elbowed her niece, who looked ready to sink right through the floor.

"I think we've been enough of a burden to Micah, Auntie," Holly said. Her cheeks flushed a bright pink.

"Now *that's* a lie," Micah said. "Helping you ladies out made me happier than anything I've done for a long time."

Florence squeezed Micah's hand. "Thank you, dear. Now, I think I'd better sit down before I fall down. I'm still not feeling quite up to snuff."

Before Florence could sit, Kevin Archer from Night Owl appeared out of nowhere. "I don't mean to interrupt but I'd like to introduce myself." He extended his hand to Florence. "I'm Kevin Archer, ma'am."

Florence peered at him for a long moment before finally shaking his hand.

After he got Beatrice to shake, Archer turned to Holly. "And you're their niece, of course. I've heard quite a lot about you."

"Yes, I'm Holly Tyler."

"I know." Archer took her hand and held on too long for Micah's liking.

Micah stepped in and introduced himself. Archer briefly shook his hand and immediately turned back to Holly. "I'd planned to say hello the other night, but you folks left the hall so fast that I didn't get the chance. So, I thought I'd better take advantage of this opportunity."

"And so you have," Holly said, obviously trying to cut short the conversation so her aunt could sit down.

"I understand you've been making changes at your store," Archer said. "Good for you." He was so obviously interested in Holly that it made Micah want to toss the guy into a jail cell.

"You seem to be well informed, Mr. Archer," Holly said in a frosty voice.

The dude apparently took her remark as a compliment, giving her a broad smile. "At Night Owl, we always do our homework before getting involved in a new location. We study current and potential markets, the demographics, and our competitors. Pretty much everything that could impact our business."

"I do that for a living," Holly said, raising an eyebrow.

"And you have a fine reputation, Holly. We think it's wonderful that you're bringing your marketing expertise to your aunts' store."

"Are you serious?" Holly's skepticism echoed what they were all obviously feeling.

"Absolutely," he enthused. "Look, folks, I know what some people say, but Night Owl isn't in the business of trying to destroy its competitors. We believe there's going to be growth in Seashell Bay, enough to support more than one store. Maybe not three, but two shouldn't be a problem."

"Care to wager which one of our stores will go down the crapper first?" Florence asked in an acid tone.

Archer scowled. "I hardly think that's—"

"Is that anything more than a guess?" Micah interrupted.

"We don't guess a lot, Deputy," Archer said. "We know the new ecoresort is going to bring a lot of tourists to Seashell Bay, and that kind of stimulus is going to have an economic ripple effect across the island." He glanced behind him at the head table, where the selectmen were taking their seats. "And then there are the other projects."

Micah frowned. "What other projects?"

"There's nothing firm yet, but we're connected, and we hear some investors are starting to look at Seashell Bay more favorably."

More development battles on the horizon? Micah sincerely hoped not.

At the front, Chester cleared his throat. "Could everybody please take their seats?"

"Nice to meet all of you," Archer said. "Holly, I hope to see you again very soon." He flashed her a smile and then hurried to the front.

Micah took Beatrice's hand and helped her into the seat next to Jessie. After Florence sat, he murmured in Holly's ear, "I wouldn't believe a word that smooth bastard says, so don't let it get to you."

"What a tool," she said in a disgusted voice.

He couldn't hold back a smile.

She let out a weary sigh. "I just want all this to be over. At least then we'll know where we stand."

"I know, babe. Whatever happens, you know I'm there for you, right?"

Holly stared up at him, her beautiful eyes wide and full of emotion. "That's one thing I've never doubted, Micah. Not for a moment."

Chapter 19

We're going straight to the decision on Night Owl's application," Chester said. "I doubt you folks will want to hang around to talk about awarding the brush-clearing contract, will you?"

A handful of people chuckled, but it was clear to Holly that everyone in the hall was on edge.

Florence, who was gripping Holly's hand for dear life, was a wreck. Even the tranquilizers didn't seem to be making much of a dent in her anxiety. Then again, she didn't know for sure that her aunt was still taking them. Florence ferreted away all her pills in her bedroom. Holly had been tempted to check how many were left by rummaging around while Florence was downstairs, but she hadn't been able to bring herself to invade her aunt's privacy. Snooping in the store's financial files was one thing, but checking on the medications of a mentally sound seventy-year-old was quite another. Instead, Holly had restricted herself to asking Florence daily if she'd remembered to take all her pills.

Yes, dear, thank you for making sure I don't forget.

And damned if the woman wasn't a good enough actress that Holly was never quite sure if she was lying or not.

"The question before us is whether to grant the building permit requested by Night Owl for Lot 87 on Island Road," Chester said. "The application had already been judged to be in accordance with the requirements for Zone 1-B. However, the town's bylaws grant the selectmen full discretion when it comes to approval regardless of zoning."

Holly narrowed her gaze on Chester. He looked as nervous as everyone else, which wasn't a good sign.

"It's time to make a decision, so I'll lead off the voting," Chester said in a solemn voice. "Since I strongly believe that the majority of islanders are opposed to the construction of another store in Seashell Bay, I have to vote no." He thumped back down into his chair and wiped his brow with a handkerchief.

Florence exhaled a sigh. "Thank God."

Thor Sigurdsson stood up next. "I've heard a lot of loud voices and a lot of arguing, but I still can't see any decent grounds for denying a permit for a project that meets our zoning requirements. So I vote yes."

Just great. The vote was starting to feel like some TV show where the producers kept the audience on the edge of their chairs until the very end. She studied Amos, trying to gauge his reaction to Thor's announcement. But the old lobsterman remained stone-faced, his meaty, chapped hands clasped in front of him on the table.

"Amos?" Chester prompted.

Sighing, Amos hauled his rather squat bulk to his feet. Holly felt like she could hardly breathe. Beside her, Florence was perched on the edge of her chair, her eyes riveted on the man who would decide the issue. And maybe their fate.

"Please, Amos. Please, God," her aunt whispered.

Amos turned his unhappy gaze on Miss Annie, sitting only a few feet away in the front row. "I'm sorry, Annie, but Thor is right. I have to vote yes too."

"Oh, no," Florence cried, her body crumpling back against her seat.

Holly wrapped her arm around her aunt's shoulders and hugged her tight, trying to murmur some comforting words. Nobody in the hall cheered or applauded, but there were a good many groans.

On the other side of Florence, Beatrice dropped her head and started to weep softly.

"Bunch of damn idiots," Jessie Jameson snapped as she hugged Beatrice.

Miss Annie shot to her feet. "This is so wrong. You old fools can't just ignore what the people want. If you can't manage to do the right thing yourselves, you need to call a referendum on the issue right now. Let the people decide!"

"Damn straight," yelled Morgan, jumping up. "Let the people decide!"

Micah leaned across the aisle, looking worried. "I think we should get your aunts out of here. Florence is pale as a sheet."

"Yes," Holly said. She felt numb and more than ready to let him take charge. "Good idea."

When she tried to stand, Florence pulled her back down. "No, not yet, Holly. Referendum! Referendum!" she shouted. "Let the people decide!"

At least a dozen others took up the cry. Calls for a referendum echoed around the meeting room.

Chester stood again, holding up his hands for quiet. "Folks, folks. Please be reasonable. There can't be a referendum every time we make a decision you don't agree with. If you don't like what we're doing, then you can vote us out in the next election." He tried to smile. "If any of us is so foolish as to run again."

"But it'll be too late then, Chester," Gracie Poole said in a disgusted voice.

Holly heard a few muttered curse words around her. Although the decision sickened her, she hated the idea that another issue had again divided their usually tight-knit community.

"Thanks for sticking up for your own, Thor Sigurdsson and Amos Hogan," Florence called out bitterly. She turned to Holly. "Darned old fools. I've had enough of them. Let's go."

As Holly grasped Florence's arm, Micah stepped across the aisle. "Are you okay, Beatrice?" he asked.

"I'm fine, Micah," Beatrice sniffed, getting up. "Just see to Florence, please."

Micah nodded and took Florence's other arm. "I'll see you out to your car. You're going to be just fine. Everything's going to be fine."

Despite tonight's wrenching setback, Holly still had some degree of confidence that the general store could survive if everyone stayed on track with her plan. But in the end, the final outcome would depend on Florence and Beatrice and their willingness to embrace change and a different kind of future. Because soon Holly wouldn't be there anymore, and tonight more than ever, that reality left her sick with guilt.

"How is Florence?" Micah asked, hovering at the foot of the stairs as Holly came down from her aunt's room.

"We got a tranquilizer into her, but she's so . . . gray and worn looking," she said. "And her breathing is still a bit labored too."

On the short drive home from the town hall, her aunt had been sweating and sucking air like she couldn't get enough into her lungs. Micah had led them in his cruiser, and as soon as he saw Florence stumble out of the car, he'd wanted to call the paramedics. Florence had choked out a refusal, claiming she'd be perfectly fine after a little rest.

He followed Holly into the kitchen. "I still think we should get the paramedics to check her over. They won't mind coming out, even if it's not a true emergency, and they can be here in ten minutes, tops. It's just nuts to take chances."

"I agree, but when I said that, she yelled at me again." Holly leaned back against the kitchen counter, her stomach in a knot. "She looks terrible, Micah. I'm really worried."

Micah made an exasperated sound and pulled out his cell phone. "Screw it. She can yell at me if she wants, but I'm not waiting around for her to have a heart attack."

Holly nodded. "Do it."

Micah punched a number into his phone. "Jessie, I'm at Florence's place, and it's not good. You guys need to come stat, okay?"

He hung up and said, "Jessie's already on her way to the fire hall to pick up the rig, and she's calling the chief and one of the other EMTs. They'll be here real soon." He glanced at his watch.

"Why is she calling the chief?" Holly asked.

"So he'll make sure the fire rescue boat is ready if they need to take her into Portland."

"Oh, of course." She hated the idea of her aunt heading

back to the hospital, but it might be for the best. "Jessie is awesome, isn't she?"

"That's why I called her directly. It's not protocol, but no one's ever given me shit about it. And Jessie was just at the meeting with us, so I knew she wasn't tied up. Florence trusts her too."

Micah always thought of everything. "I'm so glad you came back with us," Holly said. "Thank you so much."

Micah smiled. "Not a problem. You know how I feel about your aunts." Then his smile faded. "And about you."

Micah stood in the fire rescue boat's stern, the wind whipping through his hair as the little craft cut through the water at a fast clip. Chief Frank Laughlin was at the helm of the boat, while Jessie Jameson and Brett Clayton were monitoring Florence inside the cabin. Both Holly and Beatrice were inside with her too. Despite the crowd, the chief hadn't offered any resistance when Micah insisted on coming along. He'd done that plenty of times when an islander or tourist had suffered a serious injury or illness.

As the boat angled toward Portland Harbor, Holly emerged from the cabin looking slightly less worried. She sat down beside him on the bench by the starboard rail. "She seems to be resting comfortably enough now. Her vitals are stable."

"Is she still giving you hell for calling the paramedics?" Micah asked, relieved.

"She's too out of it for that right now. But by tomorrow, I'll be deep in the shit again for sure. You too, buddy."

Micah had to laugh. "We'll be okay as long as we stick together."

"Deal." She gave him a fist bump.

God, he wanted to pull her into his arms and hug her close, giving her whatever comfort he could. "Are you cold?" he asked, as if that might give him an excuse. The evening had turned cool since the town hall meeting, and on the bay, it was blustery too.

"Not really. This is pretty warm." She tugged at the sleeve of her fleece-lined hoodie. Then she slumped a bit on the bench, staring wearily out over the water.

"I'm sure Jessie's got everything under control," he said, "and Maine Med is the best there is."

Holly sighed. "I can't stop thinking about what's going to happen next time."

He'd wondered the same thing but held his peace. He didn't want to add any weight to her already heavy load of guilt.

"I'm sure she's going to have more attacks," she went on gloomily. "Now that Night Owl's going ahead, it's just a matter of time."

"You can't be sure of that. You're putting the store on a better footing—even Archer said so. If Florence sees that it won't go under after Night Owl opens, the panic attacks should stop. Especially if she's responsible about taking her meds."

"Micah, those are some mighty big *ifs*. If she takes her meds, if the store doesn't go under. Yeah, I know I keep telling my aunts that it'll turn out fine, but I only half believe it myself. Honestly, I'm getting more and more scared about what's going to happen after I leave."

Then don't leave.

But as badly as he wanted to voice that plea, Micah knew better than to make that kind of mistake. She'd probably see it as him trying to pressure her for his own sake, something that he had to admit was at least partly true. "I get it," he said. "But Florence and Beatrice are adults. Don't forget that they were taking care of you way before you were taking care of them."

When she shot him a frown, he wanted to kick himself.

"I'm sorry," he said. "I just meant that they're going to be up to the challenge. They've managed to keep the store going for decades, so why won't they be able to pick up where you leave off?"

"I know, but—"

"Hey, you need to stop feeling guilty about having a career. Your aunts are really proud of you. They want you to do what makes you happy."

"But I owe them so much." Holly leaned forward and rested her forehead on her palms, obviously feeling pretty beat up. "Where would I have been without them? Fifteen years old and with no parents? I'm sure one of the reasons they're in such bad financial shape was all the help they gave me in college."

Now that was a surprise. Micah had always assumed she'd gotten a decent life insurance payout after her parents died in the crash.

"I didn't know they'd supported you," he said.

She sat up straight again, absently brushing hair from her face. He itched to stroke the silky fall that tumbled to her shoulders.

"They wouldn't take no for an answer," she said. "I told them I could manage on my own, but they insisted that they were doing fine and could afford it. If I'd refused, they'd have been mortally offended. You know how they are."

"Mainer pride."

"With a capital *P*. I wasn't willing to risk hurting them,

especially not after they insisted that they owed it to Mom and Dad to take care of me. They said there was no way on Earth that they were going to fail them."

"Okay, that would make me feel guilty as hell too. They haven't let you pay them back either, have they?"

"I gave up asking. They got so upset every time I brought the subject up. Like I was insulting them."

Micah got it. The Jenkins sisters had seen their duty and wouldn't let anything keep them from fulfilling it.

"So I'll take care of them no matter what," Holly went on. "Whatever they need, I'll find a way." Her voice rang with conviction and emotion.

Now he finally understood. "That's one of the reasons you're such a workaholic, isn't it? Why you're so focused on your career. You want to be able to support them if necessary."

"Sure, that's a big part of it. Don't get me wrong. I love my work, but I've always worried that something like this might happen. Not just a medical issue but a financial..." The words trailed off.

"Calamity?" he guessed.

She gave a solemn nod. "I couldn't do anything about my parents. The aunties, though...I need to be able to keep them safe and comfortable. I'm all they've got, Micah."

He put his arm around her shoulders, finally giving in to the impulse he'd been resisting for hours. Amazingly, she didn't pull back. Instead, she huddled under his arm, as if seeking warmth.

"You're wrong about that, honey," he said. "We've got a whole community here, people who dearly love your aunts. We'd do whatever had to be done to help them

out—to help *you* out. We'd make sure Florence and Beatrice were okay."

She turned her face into his shoulder. "I know, Micah."
Her voice came out slightly muffled. When she stayed
quiet, resting against him, he began to have some hope
that he was finally getting through to her.

But then she let out another sigh and pulled away from
him. He mentally cursed but let her go.

"I don't know," she said. "I'm starting to think that I
should really be putting all my efforts into convincing
them to sell the place while it still has some value. They
think they can't live without it, but Florence might not live
with it either. I could take care of them financially, especially if my new partnership lives up to its promise."

The boat slowed as they came into the harbor, and
she caught sight of the floating pier. An ambulance was
waiting on the street above, its bright, flashing lights illu-
minating the scene. A couple of city paramedics waited,
gurney at the ready.

Holly stood up, bracing herself. "I want my aunts to
live out their senior years in comfort, not lacking for anything. They deserve everything I can give them."

Chapter 20

$\mathcal{W}$hat's the latest on Florence?" Morgan asked as Holly brought over their lattes.

Holly placed the cups down on one of the new café tables she'd just set up outside the store and took a seat across from her pal. There hadn't been another customer besides Morgan for an hour, but that was no big surprise— business had been slow all weekend. With the Blueberry Festival on, most islanders and day-trippers were spending their time there and at the lobster boat races, not shopping.

"They're still doing tests," Holly said. "You know, checking for blockages."

Three days had passed since the fire rescue boat had rushed her aunt to Maine Medical. Florence had seemed to be recovering nicely, but yesterday, out of nowhere, she'd suffered what appeared to be a small stroke. Beatrice had made an incoherent phone call, asking Holly to come right away. Feeling frantic, Holly had called Micah and asked if he could run her into the city in his superfast motorboat instead of waiting for the ferry. He'd immediately raced her to the hospital to be with Beatrice.

"She didn't have an actual stroke though, right?" Morgan said.

"No, it's something called a TIA, and the effects do fade. But a significant percentage of people who've had a TIA go on to have a full-blown stroke, so they need to do a lot of testing to see what might have caused it. And then they can figure out the best treatment. Probably more drugs, I guess. Hopefully not surgery anyway."

Morgan grimaced. "Ugh, I feel so bad for her, and for you too. God only knows when you'll be able to get to New York now."

Holly was trying her best not to think about New York because it made her feel physically ill. She wouldn't call her partners again until she had a handle on what was happening with Florence.

"You seriously need a break," Morgan said. "You should come down to the festival with me and try to have a little fun."

"I'd like to, but I've already been closing the store quite a bit so I can spend time at the hospital with my aunts." Beatrice had again refused to leave her sister's side and was sleeping in a reclining chair in Florence's room. "Anyway, I'm feeling too grumpy to have fun."

"So you're going to leave me to face my fate in the charity dunk tank alone, are you?" Morgan said.

Holly laughed. "Oh, stop it. First of all, you've done your duty in that tank a dozen times. Second, if anybody gets fresh, I'm sure Ryan will be right there ready to pound them into dust if need be. And if he doesn't, Lily will."

"So true," Morgan said with a grin. "Oh, all right then. But I'm not taking no for an answer when it comes to the social. Ryan and I are picking you up, and that's all there is to it."

A social and dance traditionally marked the end of the festival. Probably half the island would be there at the VFW hall tonight. "I don't think so. I'm going to the hospital again, and by the time I get back, I'll be too tired."

Morgan rolled her eyes. "Oh, so lame. You're going to have to do better than that to get me off your case."

"Okay, how about the fact that I'd be lousy company, just staring at the dancers morosely and wallowing in my beer?"

"Even lamer. You're not going to make things any better for Florence by sitting around the house all night by yourself," Morgan said.

Holly could feel herself wavering. "Has Micah said anything to you or Ryan? About going tonight?"

"No, but I doubt he'll be there. He always likes to patrol the roads to make sure nobody drives home drunk."

"But I remember he dropped in for a while last year," Holly said. "Late in the evening."

Morgan studied her. "What exactly are you afraid of if he does show up?"

How good his arms had felt around me when he held me on that rescue boat ride into Portland. How I'd wanted so much to stay there forever.

Holly opened her eyes wide, pointing to her chest. "Me, afraid? Surely you jest."

"I call bullshit on that one, sweetie," Morgan said drily. "I know you too well." She finished the last sip of her coffee and stood up. "You'll be coming back from the hospital on the last boat, right?"

"Right."

"Okay, you'll need a little time to get ready, so Ryan and I will pick you up here at nine forty-five. And don't argue, because you're coming." Morgan shot her a sly grin. "You're going to have some fun even if I have to make you."

The festival organizing committee had decked out the VFW hall in a blaze of colorful, twisted streamers that met in the middle of the ceiling above a sparkling mirror ball. Two cash bars in opposite corners were doing a brisk business, with lineups stretching onto the parquet dance floor. A long table at the front of the room held a dozen trophies that had been awarded earlier in the evening to the victorious skippers in this year's lobster boat races. Holly was glad she'd missed the usual boring speeches from the president of the festival and reps from sponsoring businesses, although most of the other locals didn't seem to mind them.

Lily had reserved seats for her and Morgan and Ryan at one of the big round tables that seated ten. Laura Vickers and Brett Clayton were also there, along with Josh Bryson, Enid Fitzsimmons, and Father Michael.

At first, Holly had guessed that Fitz had come with Josh, and that had made her feel glad. Okay, kind of ashamed of herself because it was none of her business, but still glad. After the couple danced a few times, she'd relaxed even more. But when Josh wandered across the room and planted himself at another table, obviously flirting with a young woman Holly didn't recognize, her warm feeling fizzled. Clearly, Fitz was still on the market, which meant there was a chance she might end up with Micah after all, if he showed up. Speaking of which…

"I guess you were right about Micah," she said quietly to Morgan. "It's already eleven and no sign of him."

"Told you. But maybe you should slow down a bit.

That's the third beer you've polished off, and you don't exactly have a hollow leg."

"Yes, Mother."

Despite her joking response, Holly was drinking more than usual. First, Aiden had bought a round and then Ryan. The last beer came courtesy of an older dude from the mainland named Graham, who had already asked her to dance twice. Fortunately, he seemed like a nice guy. She'd danced with at least six or seven other guys too, all of whom she'd known for years. Despite her reluctance to come to the party, she was doing her best to forget about her troubles and have a good time.

Too bad it wasn't working.

Morgan cast her gaze toward the tables closest to the door. "Speaking of late arrivals, just check out that hottie sitting at Crystal Murphy's table."

Holly craned to look in that direction. Though it was dim in the hall, she couldn't miss the guy Morgan had mentioned. Very good-looking, he towered over the others at his table, like Aiden and Ryan did at hers. His short, black hair was trendy-spiky, and he was rocking a few days of dark scruff. He wore jeans and a black T-shirt cut high atop muscular biceps, and he was doing a pretty good job sporting a Mr. Dark and Dangerous vibe.

Holly had never seen him before but damned if he wasn't staring straight at her with a sly grin curving up the corner of his mouth. "Who is he?"

Morgan shrugged. "No idea, but he's kind of yummy, huh?"

Ryan glowered at his fiancée. "What did you just say?"

"Nothing, darling," Morgan said, batting her eyelashes at him.

"Maybe he came in for the festival," Holly said.

"Doesn't much look like that type to me. And he seems to know Crystal Murphy." Morgan's eyes widened suddenly. "Look, I think he's headed our way."

By the time Holly turned to look, the man was already standing beside Father Michael, and his eyes were locked on *her*.

"Would you like to dance?" he asked in a deep voice that managed to make the request sound like a come-on.

Holly had to admit there was something alluring about the guy, despite the bad-boy thing. She gave him a tentative smile and got to her feet because nobody refused an invitation to dance in Seashell Bay unless you were exhausted. One dance with him wouldn't kill her.

He led her onto the floor, where they started to dance to a mangled version of a Bon Jovi oldie, played by the local Portland band that usually got the festival gig. "I'm Logan," the guy said, leaning in close.

"Holly." She twirled around in a circle and put some space back between them.

"You run the general store, right?" He closed the gap again.

The question surprised her. "Temporarily. Have I seen you there?"

He shook his head. "A friend of mine told me that a tall, superhot babe was running the store these days. Described you perfectly, to tell the truth," he said with another rogue's grin. "But he can be pretty crude, so I'll spare you the X-rated details."

"Uh, thanks," Holly said. *Sheesh.*

They both shut up and danced until the music stopped. Holly said a quick thank-you and turned to start back toward her table, but Logan grasped her gently by the wrist.

"How about one more? And I mean just one, believe me. I'm damn sure every guy here must be waiting to dance with the most beautiful woman in the place." He followed the request with a rueful smile.

Oh, brother. If this guy wasn't trying to get in her pants, Holly was the queen of England. But he did have a way with a line. "Okay, just one. My girlfriend and I are leaving pretty soon anyway." *That should send a clear enough message.*

"Got it," he said. "Shame you have to bounce though."

Holly mentally groaned when the band chose that moment to play a down-tempo tune, though she supposed it shouldn't be surprising since it was getting late enough to start the usual slow stuff. That was what a lot of the older crowd preferred anyway. She glanced around as more couples suddenly headed onto the dance floor, including her best friends and their partners.

In one fluid motion, Logan swept her into his arms. His hand slid down her back, sinking possessively low. Again, Holly eased back a fraction.

"I heard the elderly lady who runs the store had some kind of attack," he said after a few moments. "Is she okay?"

"That would be my aunt, though she'd punch you in the face for calling her elderly."

He laughed as he guided her smoothly between couples, holding her tight but staying respectable. He was a pretty good dancer.

"Sorry. I hope she's going to be all right." He seemed sincere.

"She's still in hospital for more tests, but she's doing okay."

"Good. My friend said she's a nice lady. And the other one is too—her sister, I guess?"

Holly nodded. "Aunt Beatrice."

"So you're helping her run the store now?"

"I'm running it myself, actually, while Beatrice stays with Florence in Portland."

Logan was silent for a bit but then pulled her a little tighter. His right hand slid lower to rest not far above the top of her ass.

O-kay. If he moved his hand any lower, she was done with him.

"You're incredibly beautiful, Holly," he murmured in her ear. "You've gotta have a boyfriend, though it doesn't look like he's here with you tonight."

She was so not going there. Logan seemed okay, if a bit nervy, but she had absolutely no interest in dating him— or anybody else, for that matter.

Well, except possibly one persistent deputy sheriff.

"You're not from the island, are you?" Holly asked in the most pathetic segue ever.

"No, but I've been renting a place here for a few months," Logan said. "I'd like to move to the island permanently someday if I can."

When he pulled her closer still, Holly gritted her teeth and prepared to push back. It was time to draw the line.

But before she could, a deep male voice growled from behind her. "Let's just hope you can't."

Micah thought the top of his head would blow clean off when he walked into the hall and spotted Holly dancing with Logan fucking Cain, of all people. Fuming, he'd sat down beside Morgan for a few moments and barely said a handful of words as he glared at the dance floor. Then the music shifted tempo, and just about everybody else at the table got up for a slow dance. Fitz had looked at him with an expectant expression, but he'd been saved when Bram Flynn hustled over and asked her to dance. Micah had stood up then and moved nearer so he could watch Holly and the asshole with a close eye. Maybe a minute into the dance, Cain had more or less made a grab for Holly's ass, and it had been clear that Holly wasn't happy at the prospect of being groped.

"Micah?" Holly broke free from Cain and swung around. "What are you doing?"

"Yeah, what the hell *are* you doing, Deputy?" Cain said in close to a snarl.

Holly shot a startled glance at Cain.

"I'm cutting in," Micah said, taking a step forward. Which forced the guy to take a step back. "That's what I'm doing."

"You are?" Holly was peering at him like he was out of his mind.

"Nah, you can wait your turn," Cain said. "Though the lady did say that she wasn't sticking around for long, so you just might be out of luck."

"Then you should hurry up and leave us alone," Micah suggested.

"Get out of my face, dude," Cain shot back. "Like, now."

Holly sighed. Crossing her arms over her chest, she took a step back.

A few feet away, Ryan shot Micah a lift of the eyebrows that was clearly an offer—an offer to take care of Cain so Micah didn't have to risk his career by brawling at a public event. But Micah gave him a hand sign to signify he had things under control. He had no intention of touching Cain unless the guy did something truly stupid.

"See, Cain, all that crap does is show what a sad-sack outsider you are," Micah said in a pleasant voice. "You'd like to stick around Seashell Bay? Well, no guy on this island ever refuses a request to cut in on a dance. So learn that lesson and run along now." He paused for effect. "Or should I call your live-in girlfriend and bring her up to speed on what's been happening here?"

Holly stared, her mouth open. "Cain?" she blurted. Blanching, she turned to him. "Please leave now. I'm going to dance with my friend who, by the way, is a total gentleman, unlike you."

Cain stared at her for a long moment, and Micah saw something very dark behind his smug look. "Jesus, there's no accounting for taste, is there? Well, it's your loss, babe. You don't know what you're missing."

His fists still clenched, Micah didn't take his eyes off the man as Cain strode away, pushing through the dancers. Only after the asshole sat down beside Crystal Murphy did Micah turn back to Holly.

Crystal Murphy?

Micah made a mental note to follow up on that, but for now, he told himself to relax and focus on Holly. He smiled as he pulled her into his arms. She came willingly, slipping like silk into his embrace. Too bad she was still frowning.

"Cain's the guy you told me about," she said in a quiet voice as he settled her close against him. "The one you think had something to do with Fitz's robbery."

"Yeah, him and his buddy Horton. Too bad I don't have a damn bit of evidence to back it up. But when I saw him starting to grope you..."

"I'm really glad you cut in. I thought he was okay at first, but then he wasn't."

"It was my pleasure." Heat was spreading through Micah's chest, not to mention other parts of his body. "I thought I might lose it completely when I saw you dancing with him."

Or saw anybody but me touching you like that.

Holly gave his back a couple of comforting pats. "I'm sorry about that, but I can handle jerks like him."

Clearly, she thought he was upset because Cain was potentially a criminal, not to mention a dick. That was a big part of it, but there was way more to it than that. He didn't want *anyone* touching her with that kind of sexual intent.

She tipped her head back to look at him, finally smiling. "I didn't think you were coming tonight."

"Well, I always come late, if at all." He usually dropped in near closing time so he could tell anybody who was drunk not to drive home. In fact, he'd played chauffeur to plenty of locals over the years after the festival dance.

Tonight though, he'd been trying to stay away from Holly. For once, he was happy he had no self-control when it came to her.

"Oh, I thought you'd had some kind of premonition that a damsel might need rescuing," she joked.

He laughed. "Could be."

The music ended way too soon for his liking, and the dancers applauded the band.

Micah glanced over at Cain. The guy was back on his feet, looking like he might be getting set to leave. That was a good thing, since Micah was still tempted to throw him out on his sorry ass. "It looks like Cain's leaving," he said as the guy started toward the door. "Unless he's just heading out for a smoke."

"Maybe he should go home and spend time with his girlfriend," Holly said. "Can we sit down, Micah? I'm feeling a little . . . tired."

"Is that code for tipsy?"

"No getting anything past you, Deputy." Her tone was dry, but she still smiled at him. And it warmed him from the inside out.

He took her hand. "Why don't we grab a little air first? I bet you could use some."

"Okay."

Still holding her hand, Micah led her through the crowd and out the door. They stayed silent as they passed the parking lot on their way toward the VFW's dock. Micah made a quick scan of the lot to check for Cain but couldn't see either the man or his rusted-out Ford Explorer. Relieved, Micah led Holly down a flight of rickety wooden stairs to the VFW's small dock.

"Holly, you need to understand why I had to butt in like that back there on the dance floor."

She shot him a sharp glance before gazing out over Sunset Beach at the brightly lit ferry dock on the other side of the cove. "I think I get it."

"Sure, but there are a few details I'd like you to know, for your own sake."

With her profile to him, he took a few seconds to gaze at her. The breeze was ruffling her hair, and she looked so beautiful it damn near stopped his heart. The last time he'd been with her on a dock, she'd been wet and warm and as hungry for him as he was for her. He'd never forget that night if he lived to be a hundred.

"I'm not sure I want to know more," she said. She lowered herself onto the rough planks, the fabric of her soft skirt belling out around her legs. She dangled her feet over the water that gently lapped at the pilings several feet below. "I pity his girlfriend."

Micah sat down beside her. "Don't, because she's a real piece of work too. Brandy Keele's her name, and she's as rough and barnacled a keel as you'd ever want to run a scraper over."

Holly laughed. "God, that's a heck of a description. I take it you've met her."

"Met her? I came close to arresting her last night."

She twisted sideways to look at him. "Seriously?"

"At the Pot. The crazy woman had started screaming at Tessa Nevin in the restroom, accusing her of making eyes at Cain. Not that she used language that tame—the actual terminology was gross. Anyway, when I got there, Tessa told me she tried to get away from Keele, but the woman kept threatening to beat her up if she so much as looked at her boyfriend again. It was such an ugly scene that Laura called me, and fortunately I was close by."

Holly looked horrified. "Poor Tessa. That must have been awful for her. She's such a quiet, gentle person."

"Keele denied everything other than the fact that she and Tessa exchanged a few heated words in the restroom. And Cain pretended to be oblivious to it all, just drinking his beer."

The guy was such a douche that Micah had desperately wanted any excuse to haul his ass in. "Tessa said Cain had been coming on to her before Keele got there," he went on, "even though she hadn't given him the slightest encouragement. Sound familiar?"

She grimaced. "For sure, I'm sorry to say. But did Laura actually hear Keele make those threats?"

"She completely backed up Tessa's story."

"So you could charge her, right? Isn't threatening someone with bodily harm a crime?"

"It is. But prosecutors don't want police clogging up the system with that kind of charge unless things really were likely to end in physical violence. In most situations, especially arguments in bars, it's usually just a case of idiots blowing off steam. So I let her go with a warning but told her she wouldn't get a second chance."

"Okay, I'm glad you told me after all. I'll definitely give those two a wide berth," Holly said. "What a screwed-up pair."

"Maybe you've seen Keele in the store already. Short black hair, about five seven, big rose tattoo on her neck. Around twenty-six or -seven years old." She was pretty enough, but the woman had a mouth like a sewer and a personality to match.

Holly nodded. "Yes, I think she's been in once or twice. I guess I'm lucky she didn't show up tonight at an awkward moment."

His gut clenched at the idea of any harm coming to Holly. "I'll be watching her. If either she or Cain steps out of line, trust me, I'll be all over them."

Then he gave in to impulse and slid a hand under her jaw, nudging her to turn her face toward him. When she looked up at him, her eyes wide and vulnerable, it took a mighty effort of willpower not to cover her lush mouth in hot kisses.

"And you call me if you ever have any worries about them, hear me?" he said.

"I will," she said in a breathless voice.

They stared at each other, caught in the moment. For a

heart-stopping second, Micah thought Holly was going to stretch up and kiss him.

But then she sighed and edged away. "I think I'd better head on home soon. I'm pretty beat."

Or afraid, he suspected—afraid of giving in to her feelings and seizing the chance at what could happen between them if they took that next step.

Micah suppressed his disappointment as he got up to help her to her feet. Since she was clearly not ready to acknowledge what was still going on between them, he forced himself to back off.

"Are you planning to drive in that condition?" he asked in a mock hard-ass voice.

"Morgan and Ryan gave me a lift here. One of them will be happy to run me home now."

"Let me take you instead. No need to bother them."

Holly studied him for several seconds, then finally nodded. "Okay, but we need to go back inside for at least a few minutes. I have to get my bag and tell Morgan I'm going to be going home with you. And you can bet that everybody is going to want to hear about what happened on the dance floor with Cain."

"Yeah, you know it." Micah had no idea what would happen when they got to her aunts' empty house. Probably she'd just say good night and hurry inside, and he would end up feeling empty and frustrated again. Still, she hadn't said no to being alone with him, so that was something.

Chapter 21

$\mathcal{T}$aking a deep breath, Holly unbuckled her seat belt and glanced at Micah. "Cup of coffee?"

She had to be crazy for asking him to come in, but for whatever reason, she was going to do it anyway. Maybe it was the creepy little incident with Logan Cain that had spooked her. Or maybe she was still feeling too much on edge about her aunts and the store. But she wanted to be with somebody, and she wanted it to be Micah. Not Lily, Morgan, not anybody other than him.

Micah gave her a slow nod. "Sure, a quick one," he said, as if to reassure her that he wouldn't press her for anything more than a hit of caffeine. Trouble was, she was beginning to think that she wanted him to do a lot more than just drink coffee.

He followed her up onto the porch, big and silent behind her. Her hands slightly shaking, Holly retrieved her keys from her purse and unlocked the new dead bolt.

"I'm glad you finally convinced Florence to get better locks," he said.

"It was a titanic struggle, but Beatrice and I finally

prevailed." Holly pushed the door open. "I'm sure Florence gave in just to shut us up. She still thinks it's stupid to be afraid because of a couple of minor incidents, as she put it."

"The island isn't under some special cone of protection," he said. "It's probably as safe a place as there is, but it's still smart to be careful."

Holly led him to the kitchen. "No argument from me, Deputy."

Micah frowned as he headed over to the patio doors. "You didn't use the charley bar on the sliding doors tonight?"

"Uh, no." Actually, Holly hadn't used that security bar at all. She never thought about it, since neither she nor her aunts had bothered to lock any doors until after Fitz's break-in. And after the new hardware was installed on the exterior doors, she'd thought the house was secure—or at least more secure than just about every other dwelling in Seashell Bay.

When Micah slid the glass panel open, her stomach dropped. She knew she'd locked that door.

He walked across the screened porch and grasped the knob of the door that led outside. When that one opened too, Holly sucked in a harsh breath. "Micah, I'm sure I locked both those doors."

She spun and swept a frantic gaze around the kitchen. Nothing there seemed disturbed.

Micah came back inside. "Do your aunts keep their prescriptions in the kitchen?"

"No, in their bedrooms. And the over-the-counter stuff is in the bathroom."

"Let's go upstairs," he said, sweeping past her.

Holly hurried behind him, glancing into the living room as she passed. Nothing seemed out of place there either.

This can't be happening to me again. And not here—not in Seashell Bay.

Then she realized how stupid that was. Of course it could happen in Seashell Bay. There had already been two break-ins, and everyone was aware that her aunts were cooped up at Maine Medical. As for her, half the town knew she was at the social tonight, and the other half would likely have guessed as much. Breaking in through the porch would go unnoticed even in daylight. In the dark, a burglar could take his sweet time picking the locks.

"I know Beatrice grabbed most of their prescriptions before she got into the ambulance," Holly called out to Micah's quickly retreating back. He was running up the steps two at a time. "And she didn't ask me to bring anything else later."

"If he was after drugs, then I guess he picked the wrong house," Micah said over his shoulder.

"Not exactly. Beatrice had some she didn't take with her."

Grimacing, he headed into Beatrice's room while Holly hurried to Florence's. She flipped the light switch and slammed into a mental wall.

The room had been ransacked. The antique armoire had been emptied, as had the drawers from the matching walnut dresser and bedside table. The contents now littered the hardwood floor. The closet door had been yanked open, and her aunt's dresses, sweaters, and some coats were piled in a heap in front of it.

Holly glanced back at the dresser. Florence had kept her meds lined up there, but they were gone.

She felt like her heart was trying to punch its way out of her chest. "Oh my God, Micah."

"I know," he growled from down the hall, reading her reaction. "Beatrice's is trashed too."

She bent down and picked up Florence's mahogany jewelry box, desperately looking for the art deco diamond brooch from her aunt's grandmother. It was a beautiful piece, probably the only thing worth stealing in the room. That brooch was not only valuable—worth about ten thousand dollars, according to their insurance appraiser—it meant the moon and stars in sentimental value to Florence.

Holly rooted frantically around on the floor, but there was no sign of the brooch there either. Several other small pieces were gone too. Near the jewelry box rested a half-empty pill bottle she remembered seeing earlier, an antibiotic prescription filled almost a year ago. After putting the bottle back on the dresser, she went down onto her knees and retrieved a gold-framed photo that had been tossed halfway under the bed. The glass was shattered, so she held the frame carefully to avoid getting cut as she scrambled back up.

Her heart shredding, she stared at the faded color photograph of Florence, Beatrice, and Holly's mother, young and gorgeous and staring at the camera with a dazzling smile as they posed in front of Jenkins General Store. The picture had stood on her aunt's dresser for as long as she could remember.

Choking back tears, she carefully shook the broken glass into the wastebasket and set the frame back on the dresser. Somehow, it felt like a small act of defiance in the face of such wanton destruction.

"Holly, come to your room," Micah said in a calm voice. Too calm.

She wheeled and rushed down the hall.

Micah stood like a statue in her doorway, his dark gaze full of regret. He slowly moved aside to let her pass.

The pretty, cozy space was barely recognizable. Her clothes had been ripped out of the drawers and strewn across the floor and bed, and the closet emptied. The top of her dresser had also been swept clean, her books and cosmetics in a jumbled heap on the floor. A few bottles had cracked open, leaking concealer and moisturizer that made a mess on the polished floorboards.

Even worse, Drew's picture had landed in the corner opposite her bed, and the glass was cracked. She couldn't even bring herself to pick it up, knowing that looking at her husband's face right now would slice her heart in two. "The son of a bitch." Holly hardly recognized her own voice it was so choked with anger.

Micah came up behind her and put his arms around her, embracing her tightly. Holly gave in to furious tears then, turning into his chest as she tried to choke back the sobs.

"Just take some deep breaths," he said in a soothing voice as he gently stroked his hand up and down her spine. "Everything's going to be okay."

She wanted that to be true, but right now she felt shattered. How could this happen to her again? And what would it do to her aunts?

Holly pulled in a few shuddering breaths, then slipped out of Micah's grasp. He seemed reluctant to let her go.

The truth was, she didn't want him to let her go, but she needed to start dealing with the cleanup and aftermath.

She went down on her knees and began to sift through the mess. Of course, the two hundred or so dollars in cash she'd stashed in her top drawer was gone. The only other item of value she'd brought with her was a gold Tiffany pendant with pavé diamonds that Jackson had given her not long after they started dating. It was worth a considerable sum, and now she could kick herself for bringing it with her.

Fortunately, she'd left her computer and iPad locked in the store's office.

"See anything missing?" Micah asked, hunkering down beside her.

All her other jewelry was costume—cheap and cheery— and based on a quick look around, Holly suspected none of it had been taken. "A diamond pendant and about two hundred dollars cash so far."

Micah's eyes pinched shut for a split second. "I'm sorry, babe."

"The pendant was from Jackson, so at least there was no sentimental value," she said. "But Florence is going to be devastated to lose her grandmother's brooch."

"I'm sure. Anyway, you know you'll need to make a list of everything that's missing."

"Of course." She forced herself to say what they might both be thinking. "Cain could have come straight here from the dance."

He reached out and gently brushed her hair back over her shoulder. "Yeah, he could have."

"He was asking me a lot of questions about Florence and Beatrice."

If looks could kill, Micah's expression would be enough

to do it. "Cain or his buddy could have done this for sure, but thinking it is one thing and proving it is another." He helped her up from the floor. "I didn't see any drugs in Beatrice's room. How about in Florence's?"

"Just an expired antibiotics prescription." But she knew that Micah should have found one prescription bottle in Beatrice's room—the hydrocodone Holly had picked up only a few days earlier. Her aunt used it whenever her back acted up, and she hadn't taken it with her to the hospital. "But you're sure there's nothing in Beatrice's room?"

He frowned. "Are you saying she *had* drugs there?"

"There should be a full bottle of pain pills." She headed to Beatrice's room, where the mess was similar to the other two rooms.

Micah started sifting through the debris on the floor.

"We know he took them," Holly said morosely. "Why even bother looking?"

"You're completely sure Beatrice didn't take that bottle with her?"

"Of course I am." God, now she sounded like a bitch.

Micah got up. "Okay, I'm going to get my camera out of the car and take some pictures. After that, I'll take a good look around outside and talk to your neighbors up the street. Then I'll come back here."

She was glad Micah wouldn't be rushing off. "I doubt the neighbors will have seen anything. There's no line of sight to the porch."

"No, but they might have noticed a car parked nearby that they didn't recognize or someone hanging around the neighborhood who doesn't live here. Anyway, it's standard practice in a burglary case to talk to the neighbors as soon as possible."

"Okay, sorry to be so snappy."

Pulling her into a brief hug, he kissed the top of her head. "Don't be silly. You're doing great."

He let her go, taking all the warmth with him as he headed out to the hall. "I should take a quick look at Florence's room."

Still feeling shaky, Holly followed him.

Micah picked up the pill bottle and stared at the label. "Seriously? A half-used, year-old antibiotic prescription? Aren't you supposed to finish the whole thing?"

Holly let out a sigh. "Florence following doctors' orders? Please. But I'm sure she was going to take that bottle back to Watson's for disposal at some point. She and Beatrice always do that with their unused meds." She sank down onto the messy bed, trying to figure out where to start with the cleanup.

Micah eyed her. "Why don't you call Morgan or Lily to help you clean up the mess and keep you company? I really don't want you staying here alone tonight."

She tried to pull herself together. "I doubt the burglar will make an encore appearance. I'll be fine, Micah."

He propped his hands on his hips, scowling slightly and looking every inch a lawman. He also looked like everything she could want in a *man*—strong, dependable, protective, and loving. Concern for her came off him in waves.

"That's not what I'm worried about. I can barely imagine what it feels like to have your home invaded twice in one year. I'd like to not just arrest the guy—honest to God, I'd like to tear him apart."

Micah thrust out his jaw and clenched his huge fists, looking like he totally meant what he said.

"Me too," Holly said grimly. "But just catch him, okay?"

"You're damn right I will." Micah turned and headed for the stairs.

Holly listened to him jog downstairs, and then heard the front door slamming behind him. She dragged herself back to her room and, crouching down carefully, picked up Drew's picture. Only a few shards of glass were still attached to the damaged frame. In the dead quiet of the empty house, she gazed down into her husband's smiling eyes.

Shit, Drew. What do I do now?

Chapter 22

$\mathcal{F}$or the last half hour, Micah had cautioned himself to think like a cop, not like a man who wanted to beat the crap out of the guy who'd just hurt the woman he loved. Just because Logan Cain was a grade A jerk didn't mean he was a burglar. But his gut was pointing him more and more in the direction of Cain and his pal Horton as the guilty parties. Too many coincidences, especially for one little island.

And dammit, he *did* love Holly. He'd known that for a long time, but hearing her choked sobs as he held her in his arms tonight—as she was trying so hard to hold it together—had toppled all his emotional walls and cracked his heart wide open.

He'd do anything to protect her and help her get over what had happened to her both tonight and in the past. Anything.

But don't be stupid, dude. And sure as hell don't do something that might jeopardize a felony conviction later.

His tactical flashlight in hand, he'd spent about ten minutes carefully moving around the exterior of the house, looking for footprints or anything else that might even approximate a clue. He'd scrambled down the shallow rocky ledge to the shoreline below on the slight chance that the thief might have beached a boat down there and made his way up to the rear of the house. But he'd found no footprints there or anywhere else. And it might not have mattered much if he had anyway, since God only knew how long it would have taken to get a crime scene technician over to collect and analyze the evidence.

While he knew it would always be hard to get the kind of resources he needed to do his job in little Seashell Bay, he'd never had to confront the frustration until this series of break-ins.

After finishing his circuit, he'd walked up Island Road to the Garvey house, the closest to Florence and Beatrice's place. A pajama-clad Ken and Janet had welcomed him inside and offered coffee, which he'd declined. Neither had seen anything going on at the Jenkins house tonight. Janet did, however, mention that she'd noticed a man walking down the hill when she looked out an upstairs window as she was getting ready for bed. Because it was unusual for people to be walking about at midnight in Seashell Bay, Micah's ears perked up. Unfortunately, her description was almost uselessly vague. Fairly tall. Not fat, not thin, neither young nor old. Just a fairly tall guy wearing a baseball cap and a dark jacket.

Which described about half the men on the island.

Tomorrow, Micah would canvass more homes up the hill, hoping to find others who might have seen that lone man walking—or maybe parking a car. But he didn't need to wake those folks up tonight. Especially not when he wanted to get back to Holly as soon as he could.

Heading back down the slope, he tapped on her front door with his flashlight. When Holly threw the door open, she was barefoot and now wore black exercise pants and a yellow tank top—her bee outfit, as he'd heard her aunts call it.

Micah called it sexy as hell, especially with her hair down in a gorgeous mess around her shoulders.

Holly didn't hide the relief in her gaze and welcoming smile. "Find anything?" she asked as she stepped aside to let him in. She shut and locked the door behind them.

"Not much. Janet Garvey said she saw a man walking down the hill sometime before midnight, but her description isn't going to be much help."

"Could it have been Cain?"

He snorted. "It could have been just about anybody."

"Kind of an odd time to be going for a walk around here," she said, leading him into the kitchen. "Want some tea?"

Micah would have preferred a shot of whisky but nodded. "I'd have been a lot more excited if she'd seen a parked car and given me a decent description of it."

"For sure." She poured tea into a white mug.

"Did you call Morgan yet?"

"Micah, I know you think I should, but I'm going to be okay. Really I am."

"You don't sound okay to me." In fact, her voice sounded totally strained and she looked exhausted.

"I'm a little shaken up, but I'll be fine."

When she handed over the mug, he caught the slight tremble of her hand. "Okay, but then I'm not going anywhere tonight."

Her eyes popped wide. "What are you talking about?"

"I'll sit in the cruiser until you get up in the morning.

Because I'm sure you're not going to get a single minute of sleep if you're all alone here."

When she started to object, he held up a hand. "Come on, you know I'm right."

She sighed. "Micah, that would be crazy. It's incredibly sweet of you to offer, but—"

"It's not an offer, Holly. It's just a fact. It's what I'm going to do."

"Micah—"

"Look, I'd do the same for any islander. You know that."

She crossed her arms over her chest and studied him. Then her mouth parted in a smile so sweet it almost took him out at the knees. "Yes, I do. And I also know you're the most stubborn deputy sheriff on the whole darn planet, so there's no point in arguing with you. But you don't have to sit out there in the cruiser, you crazy man. You're welcome to sleep on the sofa."

Micah had figured she might say that. But there was no way he was going to spend the night in the house with Holly. He could barely keep his hands off her as it was. "I can't do that."

"Why not?"

"Because you've got to be feeling..."

Well, she was vulnerable now, and vulnerable people often did things they regretted later. They'd already played that song after that night at Jerry's dock. "Holly, it's just not a good idea."

A blush colored her pale cheeks as she shook her head. "That's very—"

"It's non-negotiable," he interrupted. He didn't want to hear her tell him how *decent* or *kind* he was, or some other shit like that. That wasn't what he wanted from her.

She nodded, looking a bit deflated. "Well, you at least have to let me give you a blanket. I can hear the wind off the bay, so it might get cold out there."

"Sounds good."

Keeping distance between them now was anything but good, but it was what he had to do.

Holly closed the door to her closet. Her room was looking fairly respectable now, as was Beatrice's bedroom. She'd been working steadily for over two hours and had cleaned up some of the worst damage. But it was late, and she should really try to get some sleep. She had to open the store in just a few hours.

Every time Holly thought about Florence's brooch, her stomach pulled into a sickening twist. Her aunt had proudly told her so many times that she'd be leaving it to Holly for her to pass along to her own daughter. How was she supposed to tell her poor aunt that her most cherished possession was gone?

She glanced out the bedroom window at Micah's cruiser, reassuring herself once again that he was still there. It had been hours since he'd holed up in the Tahoe, and she was increasingly resigned to a wakeful night despite his comforting presence outside. While every muscle in her body screamed out its exhaustion, her brain was on the hamster track—wired and more than a little paranoid.

How stupid was it to be worrying even one bit with Micah standing guard? Whenever she looked out the window, he was either reading something by the dim interior light or drumming his hands on the steering wheel. At one point he got out of the car and paced to the end of the driveway, glancing up and down the road, his broad shoulders hunched up against the stiff breeze off the bay.

And didn't that make her feel guilty as hell? It didn't matter that she'd told him to leave. Micah was a protector. He'd always been that way, even as a kid. He'd looked out for all his friends and for the younger kids on the island too. Even the bullies in school had known to give him a wide berth or face his righteous wrath whenever they picked on someone little or weak.

How some woman hadn't snatched him up years ago was an unfathomable mystery.

When she went back downstairs to put on the kettle for yet another pot of tea, she heard a car door slam. She lit the burner on the range and hurried to the front window, peering out to see if Micah was coming to the door or just making another circuit of the driveway.

She wanted it to be the former.

Micah apparently wasn't going anywhere though. He just leaned backward over the Tahoe's hood, like he was stretching out his back. He had something in his right hand—it looked like one of those exercise grips, the old-fashioned kind used to strengthen hands and wrists.

He stretched again and then twisted sideways, switching the grip to his left hand in the process. Then he tossed the thing into the cruiser, shook his arms out, and pulled off a few yoga moves—including the tree pose. Holly choked out a surprised laugh. Who'd have thought tough-guy Deputy Sheriff Micah Lancaster would be doing some yoga? It was incredibly endearing.

And pretty hot, actually. The guy was in phenomenal shape, and boy did he have some moves.

Then she realized that his unconventional exercise routine must be to help him fight sleep. And more guilt washed over her.

This is ridiculous.

Not bothering to slip on shoes, she opened the door and strode out onto the porch. "Micah Lancaster, get in here right this minute!"

He froze midstretch, staring at her.

"Don't make me come out there and drag you in," she threatened in a firm voice. She wanted him to come in, but she did *not* want him to think it was because she was needy or afraid.

Okay, maybe she was feeling needy, but she wasn't afraid. Especially not now, not when she was so close to him.

Needy, in fact, described what she was feeling quite nicely. Needy for him.

"Uh, Holly, like I told you—"

"No. In here. Now." She pivoted and marched back inside, leaving the door wide open. As she waited at the base of the stairs, her heart pounded with a spiraling mix of anxiety and anticipation.

A few seconds later, he appeared in the doorway but didn't come right in, instead bracing his hands on the doorframe. The unconscious pose did all sorts of enticing things to his brawny shoulders and chest, and Holly was overcome with an irresistible desire to rip off his shirt and run her hands over all him.

But then she suddenly realized that she hadn't thought through what she would say to him. She hadn't even been sure he'd come in.

His brow furrowed as he stepped inside. "Holly?"

"Micah, I...I...I wanted to tell you..." She threw her hands up in the air. "Oh, screw it."

She went at him in a rush, practically leaping on him. He huffed out a startled *oof* as she wound herself around him.

"Honey, what's the matter?" he asked urgently, folding her into his embrace. "Talk to me."

"No talk," she said. "Talk's not what I need. I need *you*."

She needed his arms around her, warm and safe and loving. He'd loved her for a long time, and he'd shown it tonight by protecting her even when she claimed she didn't need it. He knew better. He knew *her*.

Micah had worried that she'd be feeling vulnerable, and he hadn't wanted to take advantage of it. But she wasn't feeling vulnerable at all—it was the opposite, in fact. What she felt now swept over her with a power that ripped away all the reasons she'd shut him out for so long.

Micah sucked in a huge breath. "Holly, you're scared and upset. It's not the time—"

She reached up and grabbed his head, making him look at her.

"Please shut up now, Micah." Then she leaned in and kissed him with everything she had. When she slid her tongue along the edge of his lips, he opened to her pressure and let out a deep groan that made her knees shake. His hands slid down to her ass and nudged her against him. He was already hard.

As she wriggled closer, trying to get to the sweet spot, Micah pulled back. Holly swallowed a frustrated groan and curled her hands into his shoulders, holding tight. There was no way she was letting go, not this time. There was no reason to deny what they both wanted. And what they both clearly needed.

Okay, there were reasons. But she'd be damned if she paid attention to them.

You can worry about that tomorrow.

He stared down at her with a gaze alive with heat and wanting. His cheeks were flushed under his tan, and his mouth was damp from their kiss. Just looking at him made her heart pound, and made her go soft and wet between her thighs.

"Holly, are you sure?" His voice was rough and urgent. "Because I really need you to be sure."

She went up on her tiptoes and flicked her tongue over his lips, deliberately teasing him. When he sucked in a huge breath, she snuggled closer, rubbing her breasts against him.

"Well," he said with a shaky laugh, "I'd say that's a yes."

"You can take it to the bank," she whispered against his mouth.

"I'd rather take you to bed," he murmured, nipping her lip. "But I don't think I can make it that far."

Holly let out a squeak when he clamped his hands on her bottom and hoisted her up. Instinctively, she wrapped her legs around his hips. That brought him right up against her sweet spot, and she couldn't hold back a happy moan.

Micah carried her the few short steps into the living room and lowered her to the sofa. Then he came down between her thighs, pushing them wide as he knelt between them.

Holly braced herself on the cushions and stared into his heated gaze. He hadn't been kidding when he said they weren't going to make it upstairs. In fact, he looked like he was going to do her right here, right now—and that was more than fine with her.

"Man, I love how you look in these," he said, brushing his fingers down the center seam of her yoga pants. "I can imagine what every sweet inch of you looks like when you wear them."

"Okay, that's kind of embarrassing. You're not really supposed to see anything," she said, almost breathlessly.

No wonder she was losing her breath, since he was gently rubbing her most sensitive spot through the thin fabric.

He pushed her thighs a bit wider. "I have a very good imagination."

Holly fell back against the cushions and let the luxurious sensations wash through her. But even as she felt her tense muscles relax under his heated caress, another kind of tension started to pull her tight from the inside out—the kind that had her wanting to crawl all over his awesome body and have her way with him.

She dragged her eyes open, surprised to find she'd let them fall shut. His gaze was avid and intent as he stroked up the inside of her thighs, then gently rubbed her inner folds through the fabric. She jerked, the first hint of an orgasm sending out little ripples of gorgeous sensation.

"Hmm, that was nice," he murmured. She heard the satisfaction in his deep voice.

"Yeah, but I need more." And she needed it now. She pushed herself up and reached for him, grabbing his shirt to haul it up over his head with shaking hands.

Micah huffed out a gravelly laugh. "In a hurry, babe? What's the rush?"

She shook her head impatiently, nudging his arms up so she could slip the polo shirt from his body. It wasn't just lust that was driving her and making her hands shake. It was a craving for him that went so deep it almost scared her. It was like she could never get enough of him once they started.

Or like she could never walk away from him and be happy. Not after tonight.

He finished pulling the shirt over his head and tossed it to the floor. Holly let her hands drift over his shoulders and down his biceps. God, he was so brawny and beautiful that it almost made her feel faint, like some swooning heroine in an old fashioned novel. The sight of him looming over her set her heart to fluttering, that was for damn sure.

And it ain't just your heart that's fluttering, girl. Her insides clenched deliciously just looking at him.

Micah reached for her yoga top. "Let's get you naked too."

"But you're not naked yet," she protested.

"Details, details."

He eased the top over her head, taking her bra with it. Holly shivered at the flare of lust in his eyes as he took her in.

"You're so damn gorgeous, babe," he rasped out.

His hands shaped her breasts, tugging on her already-stiff nipples. Her body instinctively arched into his hands.

"I want to see all of you," he said.

A few seconds later, he had her out of her yoga pants and skimpy panties. Holly sat on the sofa, naked and spread wide, with him between her thighs. Micah looked almost . . . stunned.

A happy stunned, thank goodness—like he'd just woken up to the best Christmas morning ever. Holly had never felt so exposed, but she'd also never felt so sexy.

Giving in to impulse, she leaned back and draped her arms along the back of the sofa, curving her back into a gentle arch.

"Jesus," Micah groaned. "You're gonna kill me, Holly."

She flashed him a wicked grin. "Not before you take care of me, I hope."

"I'm not leaving this house until you're a hundred percent satisfied and then some," he said with a sexy growl.

Then he was on her, his mouth taking hers in a fierce kiss. She clutched at his shoulders, steadying herself, but she almost lost it a second later when he thrust two fingers into her body. Holly was already so wet and slick that he slid deep, making her almost come on the spot.

She cried out against his lips, but Micah showed her no mercy, driving her insane with ravenous, possessive kisses that left her breathless and aching for more. His fingers pumped into her, driving her toward a quick, desperate climax. Adrenaline surged through her body, and shivers raced across her skin. All the stresses of the last few weeks were blasted away under the heat of his big, talented hands on her body.

Micah pushed her right to the edge, and then suddenly, shockingly, he pulled back.

"What are you doing?" she cried out in frustration.

"I want to watch you," he said with a sensual growl.

He flashed a hot look at his hand between her thighs, then his gaze came back to her face. When his other hand settled on her breast, Holly let out whimper. *So. Damn. Good.*

Micah pressed his fingers deep, then pulled out to gently rub her. Holly gasped and curled forward, grabbing his forearms.

So close.

"Come on, babe. Let go," he whispered.

She let out a cry as sensation bolted through her body. Her muscles shook and she felt suspended in air, supported only by his strong hands. Then she slowly collapsed against the cushions, struggling to breathe.

"Oh my God," she gasped. "That was—"

"Just the beginning," Micah said in a gruff voice. He came to his feet and hauled her up into his arms. "We're going up to your bedroom and we're not leaving until I have my wicked way with you. Multiple times."

Holly managed a weak laugh as he swung her up into his arms. She didn't have the strength, or the will, to resist him.

Which was either the smartest or the dumbest move of her life.

Chapter 23

*M*icah pulled up to Crystal Murphy's trailer. It was early morning, but not as early as he'd planned to get to work on the case. Not wanting to be spied by any early risers, he'd intended to slip out of Holly's warm bed long before sunrise. Unfortunately, fate had had other plans about that.

Leaving her asleep—after a long, spectacular bout of lovemaking—he'd made a dash for his cruiser and pulled out to the end of the driveway at the exact moment Father Michael rolled past on his bicycle. Though the priest had lifted an ironic eyebrow, he thankfully didn't stop to chat, instead just giving him a cheery wave. Micah could only hope that the good father, on hearing about the burglary, would assume that Seashell Bay's deputy sheriff had simply been investigating the crime scene.

Yeah, right. At seven thirty in the morning.

Well, that was Micah's story, and he was going to stick to it. Though he didn't give a damn if the whole world knew that he'd had been with Holly, *she* would care. People would gossip, and there would undoubtedly be a few snide remarks about Micah's investigative technique.

Yeah, dude, you investigated all right. Investigated with your dick.

He could hear the ribbing now.

Last night, after he and Holly had gotten busy, they'd exchanged only a few words and then just let their bodies do the talking. And it had been amazing. Unlike that first time on the dock, they'd had so much more time to explore and experiment. Holly had been all over him, as focused on him as he'd been on her.

So why wasn't he feeling on top of the world this morning? Because his gut was telling him that Holly was already in retreat mode, just like she'd been after they had sex on the dock. He fully expected her to tell him that nothing had changed between them, at least in terms of the circumstances of their lives. He knew her damn well after all these years, and he knew that's where things were headed.

The hell of it was that he'd be more than willing to make changes—for his sake and for hers. But Holly wasn't there yet. He couldn't tell whether it was because she was afraid to risk her heart again after Drew or because she was too devoted to her career and new partnership to find time for a relationship. Or both. Micah honestly didn't know, and it was driving him nuts.

Since all he could do was give her some space to figure out what she wanted, he decided to focus on work. That now meant having a quick chat with Crystal Murphy. He'd obviously woken her up, since she pulled open the door of her trailer wearing nothing but a short nightgown that unfortunately revealed quite a lot.

Didn't need to see that.

Crystal wasn't pleased about seeing him either, since she glared at him through the screen as she lit a cigarette.

"Hey, Crystal, sorry about dropping over so early."

Crystal just shrugged and then took a long drag on her cigarette.

"I noticed you with Logan Cain last night at the social," he said, keeping his gaze fixed firmly on her face. "I've got a couple of questions."

Crystal still didn't say anything but slightly rolled her eyes.

"So how do you two know each other anyway?" Micah asked.

She blew smoke sideways out of her mouth. "I met him on the boat a while ago. He's easy to talk to."

"Has he sold you Oxy or anything like that?"

Crystal's eyes practically bugged out, and it took her a few long seconds to recover from his deliberately abrupt question. That reaction told Micah everything he needed to know.

"Hell no."

"Come on, Crystal, you're lying."

She looked around as if she expected somebody to be listening. "Well, okay, he gave it a shot," she admitted. "But I told him I have my own pills."

When Micah didn't answer right away, Crystal let out a weary sigh, looking like the weight of the world was bearing down on her. The woman did have a pretty tough life.

"That's the truth, Micah, I promise," she said.

He nodded. "Okay, I believe you. But I suggest you stay far away from Cain from now on."

She gave him a quick nod and shut the door.

Their brief interaction had at least given him a useful snippet of information. Cain obviously was trying to sell drugs to some of the locals.

Micah got back into the cruiser and pulled onto the road, heading for the construction site. As he rounded the curve near the B&B, he saw Morgan trimming the wild rosebushes at the front of the inn's yard, and she immediately spotted him too and waved.

Should he just wave and keep on going?

As much as he wanted to get to the site—and at Cain— he figured he'd better stop. Unless Holly had just called her in the last few minutes, Morgan was still in the dark about what happened last night. And she sure as hell wouldn't think he was much of a friend if he just breezed by her now.

He braked and turned into her driveway, parking in the small graveled lot.

"Good morning, Deputy," she said brightly as she strolled up to the cruiser. "I'm assuming you got my girl home safe and sound last night?"

The mischievous glint in her eye told Micah she was hoping he'd accomplished something more than simply playing chauffeur.

After a quick shower, Holly jumped into Florence's car and headed straight for the B&B. Last night had been wild for so many reasons, and she'd wanted only to be with Micah. Boy, had she wanted to be with him.

This morning, however, was another story. Now she really needed her best friend. Her life was so messed up, and that was not something she could discuss with the guy who'd taken her up into the stratosphere four times last night. The same guy she was going to have to drop down to Earth today.

Micah had ripped away all her defenses last night, or

so she wanted to tell herself. But she'd started it, brushing aside his concerns, and now she had to live with the emotion pouring out in a tidal wave that threatened to drown her. In some ways, last night had barely felt real. The ugly scene at the social, the break-in, and then the amazing night with Micah—she could almost convince herself that it had all happened to someone else.

But when she'd woken up this morning, alone and naked, everything had become real with a vengeance. The dominant question, of course, had been what she should do about Micah, whose touch was still branded on her very sated body. Other questions had then jostled their way into her brain, like how to deal with her aunts, the store, and her partners in New York. It all made her want to hide out in her bedroom for a week.

Absorbed by her thoughts, Holly almost missed the turn into the Merrifield Inn. Braking hard, she barely avoided swiping the mailbox before managing to straighten out and stop beside the old inn's front porch. Only after she started to get out of the car did she realize that she'd just blown by the sheriff's office cruiser. *Micah's* cruiser.

Damn, damn, damn.

She so didn't want to have to talk to him right now, not when she didn't have a clue what she wanted to say. Actually, she didn't even have a clue what she wanted when it came to him.

Okay, she did want to drag him back into the sack. That was a given.

Holly scrambled back into the car and shoved the keys into the ignition, thinking about the long odds on making a getaway without being noticed. Given the noise she'd just made with her botched turn into the driveway, those odds were probably close to zero. If she raced out now, she'd look like the lamest coward on the planet.

The issue became moot anyway when Micah strode out the front door and onto the porch. Though her mind froze, her body heated up in a nanosecond at the sight of him. Even though the guy had gotten virtually no sleep, he looked as sexy as ever. His heavy-lidded gaze and dark stubble made him look just a little rough and dangerous.

Dangerous to your heart, for sure.

He jogged down the steps to her car. Her legs felt like soggy spaghetti, so she didn't even try to get out.

"Hey, I thought you would sleep in a bit," he said with a warm smile. "You were really out."

"Yep, I was pretty tired."

He frowned slightly at her terse response. "Are you okay? I wanted to stay, but I also wanted to get out early. You know, keep the gossip down."

Holly nodded. He was being so sweet, which made her feel even worse. "I'm fine. Listen, thank you for... for everything, Micah. You certainly went above and beyond the call of duty." She mentally cringed at how awful that sounded, but nerves were twisting her tongue into knots.

He blew out an exasperated breath. "It was no duty, babe. The furthest thing from it."

They were treading into dangerous territory, so it was time to deflect. "Did you tell Morgan what happened last night?" When his eyebrows ticked up, she waved a hand. "About the break-in, I mean."

"Just the basics," he said drily. "About the break-in, I mean."

This time, she didn't manage to hide her wince.

"I'm afraid she's not real happy with you right now," he said.

"I should have called her," she said. "I'll talk to her now."

"I called the Cumberland County Sheriff's Office and spoke to one of the detectives about the break-in," he said. "Did you call your aunts yet?"

Good, back to business. "Yes, I spoke to Beatrice just before I left the house."

"How did she sound? It must have been a hell of a shock."

Totally freaked out. "She was very upset, as you can imagine. I told her there was no need for her to rush home, but she insisted on coming back for a while. She's going to catch an afternoon ferry."

He hesitated for a couple of moments. "Did you ask her about the hydrocodone?"

"Yes. That bottle was on her dresser, just like I said."

"Okay, I'll include that in my report." Then he sighed, suddenly looking very weary. "Man, what a mess."

Her chest pulled tight with a combination of worry and guilt. "Micah, I'm so sorry. I wish I could do something to help."

"You did a lot of helping a few hours ago," he said, his mouth quirking up. "That was amazing help."

Heat flushed through her body. She stared up at him, at a loss for words.

"You could probably use some space now," he said, taking a step back. "But if you want me to keep an eye on your place again tonight, just call, okay?"

He was letting her off the hook, and that, perversely, made her feel . . . deflated.

"Thanks, but Beatrice said she might stay the night.

She's been a total trouper through all this, but I think she's just about had it with trying to sleep at the hospital."

Micah briefly cupped her cheek. She wanted so badly to lean into his big hand.

"Okay, babe," he said. "But whatever you need, just ask."

She had to force the words past her tight vocal cords. "I will. Thanks, Micah."

He slid his sunglasses down and settled his gun belt on his hips.

The lawman has returned.

"Well, now it's time I said good morning to Mr. Cain and Mr. Horton," he said. "I'll keep you posted on what I find out."

A shiver rolled down Holly's back. The thief who had trashed her house struck her as a dangerous bastard. She hated the idea of Micah confronting either of those guys.

"Please be extra careful today," she said.

"Always." Micah turned and strode away to his cruiser, not looking back.

Chapter 24

I can't believe you didn't call me last night," Morgan affectionately scolded Holly at the door. "You should never have to go through something like that alone."

"I wasn't alone. Or didn't Micah mention that?"

"That's not the same. He's a *guy.*"

Yeah, I noticed. "Are you going to invite me in for coffee or interrogate me here at the door?"

Morgan gave her a sheepish smile. "Sorry, sweetie. Let's go sit in the kitchen and scarf down some blueberry scones."

"Thanks, but I'll stick to coffee. My stomach..."

"I'm sure. I probably wouldn't eat for a week if a break-in happened here." Morgan led the way to the kitchen and gently prodded Holly into a chair at the big table. "Micah told me about what the guy stole," she said as she poured coffee. "I'm so sorry, sweetie. And poor Florence...that gorgeous brooch. It had to be worth a bomb."

"I just wish I didn't have to tell her that now, not in her condition." Holly and Beatrice had talked about how to handle that problem and agreed that the news should come from both of them—but only after the doctors gave the go-ahead.

"So tell me exactly what happened," Morgan said.

Holly filled her in. Her pal shook her head and made sympathetic noises, occasionally patting her hand. Things started to get dicey, however, when Holly tried to dance around the issue of what happened later with Micah. Morgan was obviously trying not to be too pushy, but her expression of curiosity mixed with disbelief made it clear she was starting to figure things out.

Oh, what the hell.

"And then...I ended up sleeping with Micah," Holly blurted out.

Morgan blinked a few times. "Uh, okay."

"And don't ask me how it happened. It just did. It was insane, I know, but there it is. I have absolutely no reasonable explanation."

Except that Micah was incredibly sexy and wonderful, and the only man she'd ever met who could compare to Drew.

Morgan rolled her eyes. "No, it's completely understandable. To have something like that happen to you again is way beyond horrible. And Micah...well, he's Micah. Big and strong and super-protective, and dependable as the day is long. Not to mention the fact that he's been jonesing for you for years."

"Yes, and I took advantage of all that. I feel awful about it."

Not about the sex though, nor how good she'd felt wrapped in his embrace. No sane woman would feel bad about any of that.

Morgan scoffed. "Oh, stop it."

"And it wasn't the first time, I'm afraid."

Her friend jerked upright in her seat. "No!"

"Yes. We did it the night of Lily's party too."

No matter how much Morgan might press her, Holly would not reveal the details. What had happened with Micah that night felt too private and too special to talk about even with her best friend.

Morgan whistled. "Holy Mother Mary. You *have* been holding out on me big-time, haven't you?"

"I'm really sorry. It was only because it's not something I'm proud of. It's just I seem to get weak and stupid around Micah these days. When I'm with him, I want him so much." She sighed and rested her forehead on her palms. "But it's just not something that could work out in the long run."

"You're not stupid and you're not weak. And enough with the never-ending guilt trips, Holly. Seriously." Morgan poked her in the arm, making her look up. "All I want to know now is how it *felt* when Micah was making love to you. Not what you were thinking—what you were *feeling*. Because I bet you were feeling pretty damn good, and not just physically."

Holly couldn't deny that. She'd suffered a few pangs of guilt and anxiety during the night, until Micah started kissing her again. Then she'd been able to forget everything but the man beside her in bed.

Or on top of her. Or underneath her. They'd done it all, and Holly was still shamefully eager for more.

"*Pretty damn good* is something of an understatement when it comes to our deputy sheriff," she said, trying for a lighter tone.

Morgan lifted a hand. "I rest my case. And it happened

when you started to open up to him and listen to your heart, instead of coming up with reasons to push him away. It's okay to listen to your heart every once in a while. It's okay to be vulnerable."

Holly mentally grimaced. For years, she'd instinctively rebelled against that very thing. "Not to be too dramatic, but ever since Drew died, I feel like I've only got half a heart. And sometimes that even feels like too much." She scrunched up her nose. "I know that makes me a total wimp."

"Not even close. You've had way more loss at your age than anyone should have to bear. But to say you've only got half a heart is just crap. You've got a whole one, and it's a big, beautiful, generous heart that wants to love again."

Then her friend reached across and took her hand, looking her firmly in the eye. "You can't let Drew's death define you forever, because you deserve more than that. And I know Drew would agree with me."

Holly flinched.

"Yeah, I know, I'm an awful person and you should tell me to shut up," Morgan said quietly. "But I love you way too much to see you wasting your life on idiots like Jackson Leigh. All I want is for you to be happy again. And really happy, not just busy with your career. That's cool and all, but it doesn't get you where you live." She tapped her chest, right over her heart.

When Holly didn't answer, Morgan started to look impatient. "Look, Holly, I know you better than anybody. You need meaningful work but you need love too. And right now you've only got one of them."

Morgan was right, but the words of agreement seemed to stick in Holly's throat. She managed a tight nod.

"So you probably hate me now, right?" her friend asked, looking comically rueful. "Well, I have a pitcher of lemonade in the fridge. You can dump it over my head if it would make you feel better."

Holly choked out a laugh. "Stop being silly. I love you more than life itself, and I'm just glad and grateful that you're being honest with me. I mean it."

"Whew, that's a relief," Morgan said, fanning herself.

"You're probably right about everything," Holly said with a sigh. "Now I just have to find a way to actually believe it." She tapped her hand against her chest. "In my heart."

"Cain and Horton, round two," Micah said out the window of his cruiser.

Walter Okrent, the site superintendent at the ecoresort, rolled his eyes. "Jesus Murphy, man, you don't give up, do you? You're a pain in my ass, Lancaster. Don't you know we're trying to get a resort built here before the end of the century?"

Micah chuckled. "Just a few more questions, Walter. Ten minutes, tops."

The crusty old super took a step back from the Tahoe. "Okay, those two are doing some shoveling out front this morning." He waved at Micah to go ahead.

Micah parked as close as he could to the resort building and then headed toward the main entrance with its spectacular ocean view. A small crew was laying down crushed stone for the paved walkways, and a Caterpillar backhoe was digging a trench on the other side of the entrance. There was no foreman in sight.

He did, however, spot his two prime suspects.

Cain glanced up at Micah and poked his friend. Horton

looked startled for a few seconds, then shook his head disgustedly. Both men leaned on their long-handled shovels, trying hard to look both casual and badass.

And failing at both, as far as Micah was concerned.

"Wow, Deputy," Cain said with a smirk, "I guess you enjoyed my company so much last night that you couldn't stay away."

Horton looked sullen but kept his mouth shut.

"Over there." Micah pointed to a cleared area near the bluffs where they'd be out of hearing range of the other men in the crew. He turned on his heel and headed that way. Cain and Horton trailed behind him.

"There was another break-in last night," Micah said, after they'd come to a halt. "At the house beside the Jenkins General Store."

"So what?" Horton asked belligerently.

"Do you two have anybody who can vouch for your whereabouts between nine forty-five and twelve fifteen last night?" Micah flicked his gaze to Horton. "I guess I'll start with you, since you were so anxious to jump in."

Horton's fists clenched, his face reddening. "Fuck you. This is harassment. I don't have to answer a goddamn thing."

Cain gave his buddy a calming pat on the shoulder. "Jace was at a poker game with some of his friends, and it didn't break up until well after midnight. Isn't that what you told me this morning?"

"Five guys were at the table," Horton grumbled. "Call 'em if you want to waste even more of your time."

Micah drew out his notebook and handed it and a pen to Horton. "Write down their names and any phone numbers you know."

As Horton wrote, Micah focused on Cain. He was back to being the smooth operator, not the belligerent jerk he'd confronted at the VFW hall. "I know where you were between approximately ten forty-five and eleven twenty-five, but what about before and after?"

Cain heaved an aggravated sigh. "Oh, let's see. Well, first I was sitting on my ass in front of the TV watching the Red Sox game. When that was over, I was bored, so I decided to check out some dance I'd heard about. But some dumbass deputy fucked that up for me, so I went back home and sulked until my girlfriend got home. Then we…oh, well, you can guess," he said with a shit-eating grin. "What can I tell you? That hot babe I was dancing with got me a little worked up."

Micah wouldn't take that lame-ass bait. "No alibi then?"

"Nope. Stupid me," Cain mocked.

That was the damn truth. "So what time did your girlfriend get home? I'm assuming it was after you got back from the dance, or do you and Brandy have…what do they call it? An open relationship?"

Cain started to look pissed but had enough control to dial it back. "Must have been about twelve thirty. She's on the evening shift, and the last couple of nights she's had to stay late for inventory or something."

"There's no ferry at that hour, so how does she get home? Water taxi?"

"Yeah. Costs a bitch, but that's the price you pay for living out here in this little corner of paradise," Cain said.

Micah took his notebook back from Horton, noticing that he'd provided only one phone number. It was a start.

"By the way," he said to Cain, "where does Brandy work?"

The guy frowned. "What does that have to do with anything?"

"I'll need to confirm some of this with her employer. After the crap that went down at the Pot, I'm pretty interested in her whereabouts too. As a matter of fact, I intend to keep a very close eye on both you and Brandy Keele from now on."

"Just leave her out of this," Cain growled. "Your beef's with me, and it's obviously personal now. Maybe it's time I filed a harassment complaint with the sheriff's office."

"Sure, you do that. But right now, just answer my question."

"Here's your answer, Deputy—go screw yourself. You want to know anything else, you'd better arrest me."

Cain walked away. Horton flipped Micah the bird and followed his friend back to their crew.

Micah found it interesting that Cain got so riled at questions about his girlfriend. He'd even balked at telling him where the woman worked. It was weird, because Micah had probed about Brandy more out of thoroughness than any intention to spend a lot of time investigating her. But what Cain had just said, and even more what he refused to say, had sparked his interest.

Unless Brandy Keele was a liar—and knowing that would tell him something too—finding out where she worked should be a simple matter of one phone call.

Chapter 25

$\mathcal{D}$espite taking a shower and a short nap, Beatrice still looked haggard when she came downstairs to the kitchen. Worry for her sister and the stress of camping out at the hospital were leaving their mark. Holly hoped she could talk her aunt into staying home for a while. Florence would be quite all right without her, but convincing Beatrice of that would be an uphill battle.

"Can I get you something?" Holly asked as her aunt lowered herself onto one of the chairs at the kitchen table.

Beatrice gave her a wan smile. "A cup of tea would be lovely, dear."

"How about a blueberry scone? Morgan made them fresh this morning. It'll be a while until dinner is ready." She was making a mac and cheese casserole, one of her aunt's favorites.

"Maybe later."

Holly put the kettle on. "So it looks like Florence will be there at least a couple more days?"

"I'm afraid so," Beatrice said with a sigh. "You can imagine how she reacted to that news. But I think they finally convinced her that the extra tests really are necessary. And the doctor was quite blunt about her chances of a stroke if things don't change."

"Change meaning new medications and a lot less stress, right?"

Beatrice nodded. "But I'm not sure my sister is quite ready to hear that."

Holly had often wondered whether her tendency to stick doggedly to a chosen course had been passed down from Florence. Her aunt was the ultimate hardhead, but Beatrice almost always went with the flow. It wouldn't be a bad thing if Holly took after Beatrice a bit more.

"Oh, I almost forgot," her aunt said, perking up a bit. "Carrie Adams and Dottie Buckle were on the same boat as me. They'd spent the day shopping in the city."

"Uh-huh," Holly said, dropping a pair of tea bags in the pot.

"Well, they were certainly singing your praises, dear. They really like what you're doing with the store. They said they loved the pottery and the new coffee machine."

"Wow, that's really nice to hear."

"Yes, and they told me the store is practically the talk of the town. They meant that in a good way, of course. Dottie said she's sure tourists are going to flock here."

"Well, sales do seem to be picking up some." Holly had started to feel cautiously optimistic, although it was early days yet. "But I've still got a lot to do to round out a full selection of artisan works."

"I can't wait to tell Florence what they said. Maybe that will finally start to convince my stubborn sister."

They could only hope.

Holly decided to grab the bull by the horns. "I'm not

sure how much longer I'm going to be able to stay, Aunt Beatrice. I'm under terrible pressure from my new partners. If I don't get down to New York very soon, I..."

Holly wasn't quite sure what would happen. Would David and Cory cut her out of the partnership if she didn't start pulling her weight? When they'd approached her months ago, all they'd talked about was the trio's *awesome synergy*. Now though, they'd clearly started to question her commitment. She sensed they no longer fully trusted her.

From a strictly business standpoint she could see why, but their lack of understanding grated on her. The more she talked to them, the more she realized how little she actually knew about them as men, not just as dynamic marketing experts. What did they believe in on a personal level?

Holly couldn't pretend to have been a paragon of responsibility when it came to her own small family, but she'd always known she'd be there for her aunts whenever they needed her.

"I thought something like that must be going on," Beatrice said, frowning. "Since you've been home, you've looked worried the whole time. I hate that, Holly."

She couldn't deny that all the stress was taking its toll. And since she had a mirror, she knew she was beginning to look thin and worn down as well.

It's a wonder Micah even finds you attractive anymore.

Whoa. Where the heck had that thought come from? She forced the images of the sexy deputy to the back of her mind. "I'm trying to find ways of managing it all, Aunt Beatrice." The tea was finally ready, and she was tempted to add a splash of scotch to her cup.

"I'm sorry you've had to run the store all this time, Holly. We shouldn't have asked you to do that."

"Actually, I distinctly recall volunteering." Holly smiled as she sat opposite her aunt.

Beatrice ruefully acknowledged the point. "In any case, you really should be thinking more about your own business, not ours." She fixed Holly with a penetrating gaze. "That is, if you really do want to go to New York."

Holly stifled a sigh.

"I say that," Beatrice went on, "because the way you've been talking about it lately, I'm not sure you really do."

"But I have to, Aunt Beatrice."

"Why, dear? Is someone holding a gun to your head?"

Holly shifted in her chair. "You know I've always wanted my own firm."

"Yes, and your ambition does you credit."

"But?"

Her aunt gave the tiniest of shrugs. "I have to wonder what the point of success is if it doesn't make you happy."

Holly's fingers involuntarily tightened on her mug. "What makes you think I'm not happy?"

"Dearest, after all these years, I know when you're happy and when you're not."

Holly couldn't even convince herself, so how could she expect her aunts—who were effectively her mothers—to think she was happy? "Well, it's awfully hard after you lose your husband," she said, falling back into her old defensive pattern.

"Of course. But this isn't about Drew. Your work hasn't been making you happy for quite some time now, and that boyfriend of yours certainly hasn't either."

"Ex-boyfriend, you mean."

Beatrice's thin gray brows crawled up her forehead. Holly hadn't mentioned the debacle at Lily's party, nor of course had she said a word about soaking-wet sex on a private dock with the island's deputy sheriff.

Her aunt's worn face split into a grin. "Now that's progress. But I hope you'll think hard about that new job of yours too, because Florence and I wonder whether moving to New York will make you happy."

Holly had to smile back. "You've always been there for me. Always."

Beatrice started to look a little misty. "I wasn't lucky enough to get married and have children. But I'm so blessed to have my sister and my niece, and to be able to live in a place where people truly care for each other. Florence and I don't have much in the way of money, but we feel very rich anyway. And I'm happy. Florence and I both are, even though she doesn't like to let anybody think that. Your happiness is all we want now, Holly."

And what could Holly possibly say in reply to that, except that she wanted it too.

"At last," Micah said, answering his phone as he pushed his chair back from his desk. He'd been waiting for Griff Turner's call all day.

"Yeah, well, I was on the goddamn witness stand until five minutes ago," Turner said in a pissed-off voice. "And I have to go back again in the morning."

Micah sympathized. "That sucks. Anyway, I'm sorry to sound impatient, but I think I may finally have something on the break-ins here."

He filled Turner in on his conversation with Horton and Cain as well as a follow-up call to Cain's landlady, Sally

Christopher. "Sally's a real stickler for vetting her tenants, so I knew she'd have asked for background information on Cain and his girlfriend, Brandy Keele. She said she knew where Keele works without having to look up the paper-work. It's because Sally uses that pharmacy and has seen her there."

"Pharmacy?"

"Yeah, Keele's a pharmacy technician at Watson's. And that's the place where the victims in all three break-ins got their prescriptions filled."

"Okay, that's pretty damn interesting. But if the woman wanted to steal drugs, why wouldn't she just rip off Watson's?"

"Griff, when was the last time you had an in-house theft reported from a pharmacy?"

Turner hesitated. "Okay, it was quite a while ago."

"Yeah, because there isn't much employee theft going on anymore. Pharmacies have implemented tougher pro-tocols and really screen their prospective hires. I know for a fact that Watson's keeps tight control of their narcotics, and they have video surveillance too. They know exactly who's putting their hands on drugs like Vicodin."

"You're right, but if all you've got to go on is that the stolen drugs were prescriptions filled at the same drugstore..."

"No, that isn't all. Look, I know damn near everybody in Seashell Bay. These days, most folks go to Hannaford's or Walmart for their drugs because they're already shopping there for groceries and other stuff. I don't know too many that use Watson's anymore. I think it's mostly loyal customers who've been going there for years and years."

Turner's grunt seemed to signify acceptance of the point. "You think Keele steals from people who she knows have narcotics prescriptions?"

"I'm sure Cain does the break-ins—him or his buddy Horton. But we can check with Watson's to find out when Keele was working—I was planning to do that anyway."

"I'll handle that," Turner said. "My turf."

Micah was relieved to hear it. Griff obviously wasn't totally convinced, but he was getting into the case. "I'd like to be there when you do. And there's something else you should know too."

"Shoot."

"The last break-in was the real clincher for me. Cain knew Holly Tyler's aunts were at Maine Medical. He also knew that Holly was out at a local dance and that the house was empty. The fact that the Jenkins's prescriptions came from Watson's is just too big a coincidence in my book."

"Okay, I'm with you," Turner conceded.

"Griff, we really need a warrant for Cain's house now. That's the only way we're going to nail those guys."

"Yeah, but it's still going to be a long shot to convince a judge. Let's hold off until we talk to Watson's."

It wasn't ideal, but Micah would take it.

Chapter 26

$\mathcal{T}$he next day, Turner was waiting for Micah in his unmarked car on Commercial Street. He'd parked directly in front of the pharmacy, which was part of an old-fashioned but well-maintained cluster of stores only a few blocks from the pier where Micah had docked his boat. Turner had called him from the courthouse earlier and said he'd already arranged for them to meet the owner of Watson's at noon. Micah had headed immediately down to his marina and had docked in Portland twenty minutes later.

"Brandy Keele's not working the day shift," Micah said by way of greeting. "I was parked in front of her house most of the morning, and she didn't go anywhere."

"Good. Let's see what the owner has to say."

Turner opened the door, and they headed straight down the middle aisle to the pharmacy counter at the rear. The owner, Alf Watson, was typing into a computer behind the pickup area.

"Why don't we head back to my office?" Watson said after they exchanged greetings.

He led them past a series of high white metal cabinets, where a young woman appeared to be stocking and arranging meds, to a cramped office in a rear corner of the dispensary. Micah and Turner took seats in two steno chairs, while Watson sat behind his desk.

"You said this is about a theft of prescription narcotics?" the owner asked.

"Two thefts of opioids in Seashell Bay," Turner said. "Both prescriptions were filled here."

Watson's eyebrows lifted slightly. "Well, we do have a good many customers on the island."

"We want to talk to you about Brandy Keele. Is she scheduled to work today?"

Stiffening, Watson looked taken aback. "I believe she's on the late shift today, but I'll check. Carrie, could you come in here please?" Watson's words were loud enough to be heard across the dispensary.

In a softer voice, he said, "Carrie always knows the schedules, and she and Brandy are good friends."

"We need to see Keele's employment file too," Turner said.

Watson nodded and swiveled his chair around to pull out the top drawer of a low filing cabinet. He searched for a moment before extracting a file folder and handing it across to Turner.

At the same time, the petite blonde who'd been arranging the meds stuck her head in the door. "Yes, Mr. Watson?"

"Carrie, is Brandy working the late shift again?" her boss asked.

"Yes, sir. All week."

"Thank you," Watson said, dismissing her with a little wave.

After Turner asked a couple of questions about Kecle's background, Watson frowned. "Detective, I can't believe Brandy was involved in those thefts."

"Why not?" Turner asked.

"Well, it's just that I hired Brandy myself. She started out here as a clerk, and not too long after that, she went back to school at Northeast Technical, at my urging, by the way. When she got her certification, she had to go through a criminal background check, like everyone."

"How long ago was that?" Micah asked.

"About two years. And she's been a generally reliable employee since. She shows up for work every day and does her job competently."

"Our theory is that her boyfriend is the one doing the actual stealing," Micah said, "and that Brandy may be providing him with information. She would have access to all your customers' prescription records, right?"

"Of course." Watson frowned. "I'm not surprised about the boyfriend."

Micah and Turner exchanged glances. "What do you mean?" Micah asked.

"He appears to have had a considerable effect on Brandy."

"Such as?"

"Well, she's become obsessed with the man. According to some of the other staff, she talks about him constantly. Apparently, she's quite jealous and often very upset with him. We've all noticed quite a difference in Brandy since she started seeing him."

"Can you be more specific?" Micah asked.

Watson shrugged. "You should ask the staff who know her better than I do. But lately she's been too antagonistic for an employee who serves at the counter. I had to give her a written warning a few weeks ago after she was rude to one of our oldest customers. You'll see the letter in the file."

"We'll take the file," Turner said, rising. "We'll make copies of anything relevant and get it back to you."

"Could we talk to a couple of your people now?" Micah asked. "Carrie in particular."

"Of course," Watson said. "You can use this office. I'll send her right in."

"So Keele's apparently been a *generally reliable employee.* Hardly a ringing endorsement," Turner said after Watson went to get his employee.

"I've seen her temper myself, back on the island," Micah said.

Turner stood up. "It's still not going to be a slam dunk for a warrant, but it's good enough for me to give it a try. Can you follow up with the staff while I start tracking down a judge?"

Micah breathed a sigh of relief. "Sounds like a plan."

Progress, at last. For everyone's sake—but especially Holly's—Micah would like nothing better than to show up at Logan Cain's house with a search warrant. And then he'd wipe the smug grin right off the asshole's face.

Holly rang up the last of the purchases and handed the nicely packaged mugs to her customer, a thirtysomething woman who was part of a Portland cycling group. The club had spent the day riding on the island and had stopped at the store to pick up bottles of water and snacks for the ferry back to the city. To Holly's delight, they'd gone crazy over her new stock. The women oohed and aahed and snapped up a dozen ceramic mugs along with three suncatchers and six pairs of earrings.

It was the store's best day in a long time.

As the group reassembled outside, Micah's cruiser pulled up right next to them. He got out and said something to the closest rider, making her laugh. The rest of the women zeroed in on him like a pack of hungry wolves, and the animated little chat that followed went on for several minutes. He was still smiling when he opened the screen door and strolled in. "Hey, those women sure seemed pleased with their purchases. Said they really liked the new look of the store."

Seems like they liked the look of you too, Deputy Hottie. She certainly couldn't blame the women for falling all over the rugged, sexy lawman.

"I know," she said. "A couple of them even told me they were going to make sure the rest of their club knew about the store. That's good progress, I'd say."

He nodded. "Too bad Florence wasn't around to hear that. Is Beatrice still home?"

"No, she headed back to the hospital. I'm going to close up in a few minutes and go over too. I'll spend the evening with them and take the last boat back."

"I just got back from the city myself. Detective Turner and I had some questions for the owner and staff at Watson's Pharmacy. That's why I stopped by, to fill you in."

"Oh, okay," she said, feeling a bit deflated. Given how she'd been the one pushing him away, it was irrational to hope that he'd stopped by simply to see her.

"It turns out that Brandy Keele is a pharmacy technician at Watson's. We think she's been feeding Cain information on customers with narcotic prescriptions from Watson's—like Beatrice and Fitz."

Holly blinked. "Wow, that really sucks."

"Keele was apparently reliable until she took up with Cain, but she's been erratic since. Another technician told me she's over-the-top jealous about the guy because she doesn't trust him. Keele even said she'd kill herself if Cain ever left her."

"Yuck. He is such a creep," she said, remembering the jerk's behavior at the dance. "I can totally see him manipulating her."

"Turner is trying to get a warrant to search their house. When he faxes it to me, I'll be at Cain's place three minutes later."

She perked up. "Do you think you'll find Florence's jewelry?"

If Cain was guilty, he should be brought to swift and sure justice of course, but Holly couldn't help focusing on recovering her aunt's precious keepsake. It would mean the world to Florence.

"Hard to tell," Micah said. "Since it's been such a short time since the theft, the odds are obviously higher than if it had been longer."

"It's just that it would be so much easier on Florence if she knew the brooch was safe." She waved a vague hand. "I mean, obviously I really want you to catch the guy. But mostly now I'm worried about my aunt."

Micah nodded. "I get it."

They both fell silent. Micah stared at her with an intent look, as if he had something important to say. Sadly, Holly just felt tongue-tied and awkward. She and Micah would have to talk soon—really talk—but now wasn't the time.

At least that's what she wanted to believe. The truth was, she didn't know what she wanted from Micah. A big part of her wanted him in her life, but could she really give him what he needed?

More important, was she ready to open up her heart again?

A moment later, he breathed out what seemed to be a frustrated sigh. He took his sunglasses out of his shirt pocket and put them on, transforming back into the grim-faced lawman. "Well, I'd better get to the office and wait for that warrant."

At a loss for words, Holly just nodded.

He headed to the door, then turned back to her. "We will talk, Holly. Whenever you're ready."

She could only hope she'd be ready sooner rather than later.

Chapter 27

$\mathcal{O}$ne thing Holly had loved about her aunts' store was that she could glance out the windows and see the ferry docking. She'd gotten adept at waiting until the very last minute to head over there to catch the boat, often making the dash just before the crew hauled in the gangway.

She fast-walked from the parking lot, hurrying on board at the last minute. It was a beautiful sunny afternoon, and dozens of passengers had already lined the rails on the top two decks. Since both decks were crowded, she headed downstairs to the small open area at the stern, where she could enjoy fresh air and unobstructed views while avoiding the crowds. While there were a few people inside the lower cabin, she had the small, open deck all to herself, at least for now.

And boy did she need the peace and quiet, if for no other reason than to think through the situation with Micah—not to mention the rest of her increasingly complicated life. She took a few minutes to breathe in the sweet sea air, trying to calm the low-level anxiety that seemed to dog her almost constantly these days. Except, of course, when she was in Micah's arms, because then she felt wonderfully safe and...happy.

About ten minutes later, as the ferry slowed to line up with the small dock at Diamond Cove, Holly pulled out her phone to call Beatrice. Because the boat would discharge passengers from her side of the vessel, she headed for the opposite side, glancing into the cabin as she passed by.

And stopped dead in her tracks, as if she'd hit a wall.

Logan Cain.

A moment later her brain unstuck, and she took in the way he hovered over Brandy Keele, who was sitting on one of the benches, a small suitcase and a sports bag on the floor beside her. She looked nervous as hell.

Shit.

While Micah was waiting for a warrant so he could comb through their house for evidence, Cain and his girl-friend were on the ferry, obviously leaving the island. Maybe it was a completely innocent coincidence and they were just going on a planned trip. But Holly's head and gut told her they were skipping town.

No doubt with her aunt's jewelry and whatever else they'd stolen.

Whatever they were up to, Micah needed to know immediately that they were on the ferry. Holly slipped farther away from the cabin door and punched in his cell number.

He picked up after the first ring. "Holly?"

"I'm on the ferry," she whispered, as if Cain could hear her. It was silly, but she suddenly felt supernervous. "We're just about to dock at Diamond Cove. Logan Cain and his girlfriend are on this boat, Micah. And they've got luggage with them."

"Damn," he said, his voice a low growl. "Have they seen you?"

"I don't know. Maybe. They're inside the lower cabin, and I've been standing outside since we left Seashell Bay."

"Are there a lot of other people around?"

"Not out here," she said. "Some in the cabin."

"Then get up to a deck where you're surrounded by people. I'll call Turner and have him stop those two as soon as the boat docks in Portland. He'll hold them in custody until I've searched the house."

She nodded, as if he could see her. "I'll go upstairs right away. I have to say I'm a little creeped out."

"Honey, you'll be fine. Just don't go near them, and stay close to other people."

His warm, steady voice helped slow her racing pulse. "I will. But what if they get off before the city? I know it's unlikely, but this ferry stops again at Great Diamond."

"Okay, keep an eye on the gangway if you can and call me back if you see them getting off. But only if you can do it safely, all right?"

"I'll be careful. I promise." She risked a glance back into the cabin. Cain was staring right at her, his gaze narrowed and intent.

Uh-oh.

"Holly, I'm going to head right to—"

"He's spotted me, Micah. I have to go right now."

Holly disconnected but kept the phone in her hand. She fully intended to follow Micah's advice and get up to the crowded second deck as fast as she could. Unfortunately, to get back upstairs, she had to pass through the lower cabin.

Well, it's not like they're going to attack you or anything, right?

Screwing her courage to the sticking point, Holly strode to the cabin door and pushed it open.

Micah's gut was doing a high-wire act as he blasted north on Island Road and then cut straight across the island to the marina. Fortunately, he'd reached Turner right after Holly disconnected, and the detective had said he would personally intercept Cain and Keele at the Casco Bay Lines terminal in Portland.

Micah had every intention of joining that welcoming party—after he made sure Holly was safe.

Two minutes later, he wheeled the cruiser into Sea Glass Marina, parked in the closest open spot, and then raced down to the float where his boat was moored. With its massive 250-horsepower engine, he figured his Catalina stood about a fifty-fifty chance of catching up by the time Holly's ferry reached its Great Diamond stop. His plan was to board the ferry, stick close to Holly, and not let Cain and Keele out of his sight until Turner put cuffs on them. He didn't want to arrest them on the boat unless he had to, not when a confrontation could put the safety of the passengers in jeopardy.

And knowing that asshole Cain, he could be carrying a gun or other weapon.

If he didn't make it to Great Diamond in time, he'd just power past the ferry and wait with Turner at the terminal. But that was definitely not his preferred option. What he needed to do was get between Holly and Cain fast.

Holly hurried through the lower cabin and up to the second deck, not even glancing at Cain and his girlfriend. But when she reached the top of the staircase, she risked a look back.

Logan Cain was starting up the stairs behind her.

She rushed through the passageway and out onto the open deck. Dozens of people stood at the rail, taking in the sun-dappled blue waters of the bay and the islands in the distance. Holly headed for a group clustered around a baby stroller. A Border Collie was sitting like a guard dog beside it. Right now, she was wishing she had a dog too— a great big Doberman with enormous teeth.

When she reached the red metal railing, she turned around, trying to look natural.

Cain was heading straight toward her through the crowd. Despite the warm day, he wore a blue wind-breaker, partly zipped, and a black baseball cap. His right hand was stuffed into his jacket pocket. She couldn't see his eyes because he'd put on sunglasses, but he had a big, phony smile on his face.

"I didn't expect to see you here, Holly," he said in a friendly voice when he approached, as if they were old friends. "But I'm glad we ran into each other."

He gave the wagging dog a quick pat on the head and then leaned in close to Holly. "There's a big fucking knife in my pocket," he whispered, "and my hand's on it right now. So don't move or do anything stupid. I swear I'll cut you right here if you do."

His menacing tone froze her feet to the deck. She darted a glance to the group beside her, but no one was paying any attention.

This cannot be happening.

A few seconds later, her mental wheels started turning again and she heard the echo of Micah's words.

Do not take any risks.

He was right. If she just kept her mouth shut, Cain

would probably leave her alone. Doing something dumb now could endanger not just her but possibly others too, like that sweet baby in the stroller. The man was obviously crazy to threaten her in the middle of a crowd, so who knew what he would do if she defied him?

"Fine," she said. The word sounded like a frog's croak.

"Good. We're just going to have a quiet chat. Smile, okay?" He turned around so he was standing side by side with her, his back against the rail like hers. She could feel the hand in his pocket as it pressed into her side.

"What do you want?" Fear roiled her gut.

"I want your phone."

Her heart skipped a few beats. If he checked the call log, he'd see she'd just called Micah. But what choice did she have? She reached into her bag and pulled out her phone, handing it to him.

He hit a couple of buttons. "I know you were calling your boyfriend the deputy. You're not very good at hiding shit, Holly. It was all over your face."

Now she was starting to get pissed off, but she kept her mouth shut.

"I know he and that Portland cop are getting a warrant," Cain said, his voice still very soft but now flat. "So Brandy and me are heading out. Time to say good-bye to your weird little island and all the morons who live there."

"Guess we're not all morons," she said tersely. "What with you having to flee and all."

He ignored her jab as he fiddled with her phone. "Ah, there it is. Okay then. Now we're going to go back downstairs and sit for a while. And just before we get to Great Diamond, you're going to call Lancaster again."

Holly stared at him, struggling to understand. "Seriously?"

The bastard laughed. "Sure. And I'll tell you exactly what you're going to say. Come on, let's go."

"You're on a boat," she said in disbelief. "Where the hell do you think we can go?"

He took her arm in an unforgiving grip. "That's my problem. Now, move."

Chapter 28

$\mathcal{C}$ain pushed Holly onto the bench beside Brandy Keele and sat down, sandwiching her between the couple from hell. The few people sitting in the lower cabin paid them no notice. Everyone was either reading or looking at their phones or talking to the person beside them.

Holly had no intention of causing a scene anyway. Cain still held his hand against her side, and she could feel what she thought was the butt end of his knife.

"Stupid bitch," Brandy softly hissed at her. Her slender body was practically vibrating. "I told Logan he should push you overboard. Make it look like an accident. You deserve it."

Actually, going overboard would have been Holly's preferred option. She was a strong swimmer and would have been thrilled to get away from these two.

Maybe Cain and Keele were high on some drug. Holly had always been a straight arrow, so she didn't really know what to expect in terms of how they would look or act if they were, but Brandy did seem wired to the point of nuttiness. The woman's wild-eyed gaze and jiggling legs certainly made it clear she was pretty close to the edge.

Don't take any risks. Micah's voice filtered through her fear, calming her. Holly took a deep breath and felt her heart rate start to slow.

She glanced out the cabin window and saw they were getting close to Great Diamond.

Cain handed her the phone. "Here's what you're going to tell the deputy," he said quietly. "You're going to tell him the ferry's just pulled away from Great Diamond, and you thought he'd want to know that we didn't get off."

Damn. That meant they were planning to get off the ferry and wanted her to misdirect Micah. But what did they plan to do about her? They must know that as soon as they left the boat, she'd call Micah right back and tell him the truth.

Unless they intended to take her with them.

Her heart fluttered for a moment until she managed to tell herself that trying to take her with them would be really stupid. Logan Cain might be a dirtbag and a criminal, but he didn't strike her as stupid. No one in his right mind would try to kidnap someone off a public ferry, with only a knife to keep her in line.

Would they?

She sucked in a few more calming breaths to try to settle her stomach and clear her brain. Maybe Cain had a boat stashed away on Great Diamond. If so, they could be long gone by the time Micah or the Portland police could do anything about it.

"Did you hear what I said?" Cain's voice, low and hard, interrupted her thoughts.

"I heard you."

"Then call him now. Say what I told you to and get right off the phone. Make something up if you have to, but don't get in a conversation."

When Holly dialed Micah's number, he answered immediately. "Holly, what's happening?"

She tersely told him what she'd been instructed to say.

A moment passed before he responded. "I know he made you say that."

Holly nodded her head as if she was continuing to listen. Cain shot her an impatient look.

"Just hang on, babe," Micah said, his voice calm and low. "I'm in my boat not far behind you. I can see the ferry ahead."

Thank God. Micah could always tell when something was wrong. Ever since they were kids, he'd always known, even when she'd tried to pretend everything was fine.

"Yes, I'm absolutely sure they didn't get off," she said in a stronger voice. She gave a nod as if she were acknowledging a response and then said, "Okay, I'll meet you at the Portland terminal." She hung up.

"Good. Give me back the phone," Cain said.

He took it from her and shoved it in his jacket pocket.

When the ferry bumped against the dock, nobody in the cabin moved. That wasn't surprising, since hardly anyone got off at Great Diamond going in this direction. The stop would be just long enough to board a few more passengers heading to Portland.

As soon as the gangway banged down onto the dock, Cain stood up, followed by Brandy. He slung the sports bag over his shoulder while his girlfriend grabbed the suitcase.

"Get up," Cain said in that low, menacing voice. "You're coming too."

Holly's stomach dived. "What? Why?"

Cain grabbed her arm and made her get up, then pulled her along with him. His free hand—the one with the knife—dug into her side again. As he hustled her up the stairs and then across the deck and the gangway, she frantically tried to figure out what to do. Part of her wanted to struggle, fighting back and taking her chances, but another part of her was paralyzed with shock.

Cain hustled her over to a nearby ramp that led onto a small floating pier where a single motorboat was tied up. There, Holly's brain finally kicked back into gear. They were obviously going to take that boat and race off somewhere—there were certainly thousands of places to hide in the islands and coves all along the coast. But what did they intend to do with her? Let her go or make her go with them? Surely they must be thinking that, if they let her go now, they'd be long gone by the time she was able to alert Micah or anyone else.

Little did they know that Micah was closing in.

A moment later, Cain handed her off to his girlfriend—along with the knife—and jumped down into the skiff. Brandy held on to her arm while Cain flipped up the cover of the ancient-looking Mercury outboard engine. He was clearly intending to hot-wire the old thing.

Cain looked back up at Brandy. "Get her down here in the boat now and then untie the mooring lines."

Brandy gave Holly a poke in the side. "You heard him, bitch."

She stared at the two idiots. "You're really going to kidnap me?"

God, she was *so* seriously tired of bullies pushing her around. Like these two, and even people like Jackson and her business partners. Yes, the knife made her nervous—very nervous—but she had no intention of just caving in to these insane threats. She'd figured out what she had to do.

Micah should be appearing any minute now. He had one of the fastest boats on the bay, and he knew they were at or very near the Great Diamond ferry dock. All she had to do was get away from Cain and let Micah take care of the rest.

"Of course, you're our insurance," Cain snapped. "Now get in the goddamn boat."

Insurance? Clearly, Logan Cain had been watching way too many bad cop shows or thrillers, probably while he was stoned.

Muttering to herself, Holly climbed down into the small craft and sat on the bench in the bow where Cain had pointed. Fortunately, Brandy and the knife had remained on the dock, taking care of the ropes, so that would make things a whole lot easier.

As Cain turned away to focus again on the motor, Holly kicked off her shoes, preparing to get wet.

Micah figured Cain would try to get away in a boat—either one he'd left at Great Diamond or one he'd steal. He and Keele damn sure wouldn't stay where they were, since there was no way they could hide for long on the small island.

He guided the Catalina around Echo Point and spotted Cain and Keele at a small pier not far from the ferry dock. He was less than a hundred yards away now, closing in fast. Cain was sitting in a skiff while his girlfriend was still on the pier, struggling with a mooring line. The outboard's engine cover was up, which told Micah that Cain was trying to hot-wire it. But right now Cain's back was turned to the motor, and he was yelling at Keele. She was yelling right back at him, her face beet red.

Holly was nowhere in sight. Micah huffed out a relieved sigh. They must have let her stay on the ferry, and Holly was probably trying to borrow a phone to call him right now.

Still, it had been a few minutes since the boat docked, and she hadn't called yet, so that didn't seem right. Could they have hurt her? That thought made him want to smash something into little pieces. *Like Cain's face.*

He couldn't let himself think like that. *Just focus on the problem in front of you.*

Without cutting power, he blasted his boat straight across the harbor directly at the skiff. Cain turned back to work on the skiff's engine, and a few seconds later, it sputtered to life, belching out puffs of black smoke. Keele started yelling at Cain again, waving her hand and pointing in Micah's direction. When Cain whipped around to look, Micah could clearly see both shock and panic spread over his face.

With Micah's boat closing in so fast, Cain might be afraid it was about to ram him. If it did, while the Catalina would be badly damaged, the skiff and Cain would be blown to smithereens.

Barely slowing, Micah swerved hard to his right at the very last second, throwing up a gigantic wash that nearly overturned the much smaller boat. Craning to look over his shoulder, Micah saw Cain tumble over, scrambling for a hold so he didn't get tossed into the water. Even over the sound of his outboard, Micah could hear Keele shrieking at the top of her lungs from the pier.

Micah spun the Catalina around in a tight circle, blocking the wildly rocking skiff. He throttled to a stop and braced himself as he pulled out his service weapon. Cain stared, stunned, at the gun pointing right at him. Keele stood frozen above on the pier, her mouth agape.

"Hands up, both of you," he yelled.

Two sets of hands shot up in the air. Micah made a motion to indicate that he wanted them to climb into his boat. Once there, he intended to cuff them and head straight to Portland where Turner would take them into custody.

"Micah!"

Micah froze for a second at the sound of the voice, coming at him from the shoreline somewhere to his left. He glanced over toward the rocks near the ferry dock and, astonished, saw Holly there, soaked to the skin, her hair and clothes a bedraggled mess.

To Micah, she'd never looked more beautiful.

Chapter 29

With a weary sigh, Holly settled into her chair at the candlelit table for two in a quiet corner of one of her favorite Portland restaurants. She'd showered and changed at home after the marine patrol dropped her back in Seashell Bay. Then she'd hopped a ferry into the city and spent a couple of hours with Florence and Beatrice before heading over to meet Micah. To say it had been a long and tiring day was a vast understatement.

"So what happened after you got that horror show of a couple to the police station?" she asked.

"Cain lawyered up right away," Micah said as he studied the wine list. "But Keele caved the second Griff dangled the possibility of a plea bargain in front of her. She'll testify against Cain in exchange for a deal."

"I guess true love only goes so far."

He let out a sardonic snort. "She claimed Cain forced her to give him the names. At first he tried to force her to steal painkillers from Watson's, but she refused. I guess giving him information on customers with narcotics was a compromise. She said she had nothing to do with the burglaries. Cain and Horton did Fitz's place, and Cain did yours on his own."

"I guess I should have kept him dancing after all," Holly said drily. "But it still seems so crazy. They were risking a lot to get a few pain pills and some jewelry."

"Cain convinced her it would be dead easy in a place like Seashell Bay. Said there'd be almost no chance of getting caught."

She smiled across the table at him. "I guess he hadn't reckoned on Deputy Micah Lancaster, had he?"

Micah shrugged, looking a bit embarrassed by her praise—and still smokin' hot in his deputy's uniform, despite everything that had happened during the long day. Holly would never forget how he'd looked when he roared his boat up to that pier, blocking Cain's escape. He'd been the ultimate protective alpha male. And yes, he'd had a big gun to hold them at bay, but she had little doubt he would have taken them down with his bare hands if necessary.

Because nobody messed with Micah Lancaster's people.

"Speaking of jewelry," Micah said, "when deputies searched the bags Cain and Keele had with them, they found not just drugs but your diamond pendant and Florence's brooch."

"Oh, thank God," Holly said, so happy for her aunt. "I mean about the brooch. I don't much care about the pendant." She hesitated a moment and then said, "When do you think Florence will be able to get hers back?"

"Hard to say. I'll talk to Turner about it. Sometimes they'll just photograph evidence and let it go back to the owner. Other times, they need to keep the stolen item locked up as evidence right through to the end of the trial.

"Ugh. Florence won't be pleased if that happens, although at least she will get it back eventually. Maybe Cain will try to cop a plea too, once he knows his girl-friend is going to rat on him."

"Maybe," he said, as if it didn't really matter. "Anyway, I just wanted to tell you that I thought you were unbeliev-able today. I figure we make a hell of a crime-fighting team."

She'd obviously surprised him today. When he'd real-ized how she'd escaped, his mouth had gaped open for a moment before he flashed her a huge and obviously relieved smile. Holly had then rushed over to the pier to help him. Micah had quickly and efficiently cuffed Cain and his girlfriend and then called the marine patrol to pick Holly up. He hadn't wanted to leave her alone at Great Diamond while he took his prisoners into Portland, but she'd assured him she was fine.

"I didn't do anything special," she said. "You were the one who put your life on the line."

He scoffed. "Holly, all the guy had was a knife, and I'm sure he knew it was hopeless once I got there. You managed to keep those morons from spinning out of control, and you showed huge courage in getting away from them like you did. Hell, you were the one who took all the risks."

He obviously didn't get it.

"Micah, I wasn't afraid for myself," she said. When his eyebrows went up in an incredulous lift, she waggled a hand. "Okay, I was a bit afraid, although I really didn't think he'd use the knife on me. Cain's probably not that stupid."

"Don't remind me about the knife. If I'd known about it earlier, I'd have probably had a coronary."

"That's kind of how I felt when I saw you aim your boat at them," she said pointedly.

He frowned. "Why?"

She shook her head. "You are so dense sometimes. What if he'd had a gun, not just a knife? He could have shot you. Did you not even think of that possibility before you came charging in to the rescue?"

"Holly, I'm not an idiot. I went in really fast for that very reason. It's hard enough to hit a stationary target with a handgun, let alone a guy blasting toward you in a bouncing boat. And I knew the wash would knock him clean off his feet as I closed in and swerved."

"And what if he hadn't been in the boat? What if he'd still been onshore, holding on to me?"

His dark gaze narrowed, like it was something he didn't want to even think about. "I would have gotten the situation under control, regardless of the circumstances. That's what I'm trained to do."

"I'm sure Drew thought he had the situation under control until the second that RPG slammed into his helicopter," she snapped.

When he stared at her with disbelieving eyes, she wanted to kick herself. Why in God's name had she dredged that up?

You know why. Because she was starting to think about Micah the same way she thought about Drew—as if he belonged to her. And it had badly scared her to see him blasting in without a second's thought for his own safety.

She flapped her hands at him. "I'm sorry. I don't know why I said that, other than that it's been a long day."

"You really shouldn't worry," Micah said gently. "I've got a job to do, but I don't take unnecessary risks."

He must have seen the unspoken answer on her face. "Holly, I know what you've lost—all your friends do. And you're right to say that none of us can really understand. You've gone through some impossible things, but you can't keep pushing us away every time the subject comes up."

"Impossible things? But they happened to me," she countered.

"I meant impossible for us to grasp," he said patiently.

Holly had known what he meant. But she'd automatically flipped into defensive mode, like she was hardwired to respond that way whenever anyone crossed her self-imposed boundaries. It was not her best quality by a long shot.

She was trying to think how to respond without sounding like a total bitch, when their waiter came by and took their drink order.

"Look, babe," Micah said as soon as the waiter left, "I was just trying to say that I don't want to see you spend the rest of your life stuck on some merry-go-round of *what ifs*. What if Cain had a gun? What if I didn't get there when I did? None of those things happened, so worrying about them is pointless. You just end up feeling helpless and paralyzed."

She nodded, because her rational mind knew he was right. How she actually felt though? Different story. "I know. I suppose my reaction is partly because I never thought anything like this could happen in Seashell Bay. I'd expect it in New York or Boston, but here? It's almost like a...betrayal."

"Seashell Bay isn't under a dome. It's not immune from assholes like Logan Cain. Nowhere is, except maybe some outpost near the Arctic Circle. That doesn't mean it's not still safe or a great place to live."

"That's my point," she argued. "Terrible things can happen anywhere. People can get killed anywhere. In an instant, they can be taken away from you—forever."

And there it was, the fear that refused to leave her. She was so afraid of losing the people she loved—to the point that she didn't want to open her heart any more than she had to. And she did worry that it was crippling her.

Micah's calm nod seemed to acknowledge and accept her fears. "Sure, but we still have to live our lives, not hide from them. Cherish what we have, not obsess about what we might lose if the worst were to happen. To paraphrase the Dalai Lama, we have to live in the moment and be happy with what we've got."

She had to smile at that. "Well, look at you, Mr. Zen Master. Who knew?"

He flashed her a sheepish grin as the waiter approached with their wine. "Sorry if I sound preachy. I don't mean to."

"You're allowed. I know you do it because you . . . you care about me." She'd barely stopped herself from saying *love*.

"That's one way of putting it," he said in a wry tone.

Once the waiter had poured them each a glass, Micah cleared his throat. "How long are you going to be able to put off going to New York?"

Holly blinked at the sudden shift in conversation. New York seemed very distant at the moment. And the last thing she wanted to do was to think about her partners and all the challenges that awaited her in New York. Challenges that were now beginning to feel like the wrong ones.

Uh-oh. That thought was a no-go. Her career had saved her after Drew died. It meant everything to her.

"I don't know for sure," she finally said. "My partners are already hopping mad at me. Their idea of meeting family obligations seems to end at a weekend visit."

"That's just stupid."

"If you think I'm driven, you should meet David and Cory."

"You're not driven. You're just determined."

"That's one way of putting it," she jokingly echoed.

Micah shook his head. "I'm really going to miss you when you leave, you know."

Her throat went tight. "I'm going to miss you too, Micah. An awful lot."

He leaned forward. "Holly, are you sure this New York thing is really what you want? Because it seems to me that you're trying pretty hard to convince yourself, and maybe losing that argument."

Wow. Nailed that one, dude. Home run.

Holly didn't want to admit the true extent of her uncertainty—not even to herself, much less to Micah. She was in too deep with her partners to turn back now, or so it seemed. "Obviously I have some qualms about it. It's a huge step. But I don't want to stay in Boston much longer, and I really want to be a founding partner of my own firm. So how can I pass up an opportunity to do both?"

"I don't know. But the fact that you're asking the question instead of giving a direct answer tells me something."

She gave him a mock scowl. "It was a rhetorical question, you big jerk."

He rolled his eyes. "What I asked was if you're sure that going to New York is what you really want. Because

I get the strong feeling that you're *not* sure. Maybe you really don't want to go at all."

"You know nothing, Micah Lancaster," Holly said, trying to lighten the tone by imitating one of her favorite characters from *Game of Thrones*. Then again, that character had ended up dead, so maybe it wasn't such a good strategy.

He shot her a puzzled look.

"It's from a popular TV show," she explained, feeling even more embarrassed.

"You're really not going to answer, are you?"

"Micah, I don't think this discussion will get us anywhere."

His eyes narrowed with irritation. "Holly, I would be so damn grateful if you stopped trying to shut me down. I know you want me to let it go, and I would let it go if I didn't care so much. And I'd shut up forever if I thought you were happy. But you're not happy. Your friends know you're not, and I think you know it too. You're just too stubborn to admit it."

"Stubborn? Ha! That's the pot calling the kettle black, Deputy Lancaster. Besides, my friends support me completely. They couldn't be happier for me, in fact." She mentally cringed at how silly that sounded.

"Yeah, right. That's a crock, and you know it. We've all been worried about you these last few years—Morgan, Lily, your aunts, all of us. You're hiding from the people who love you, burying yourself in your work. Then you go and hook up with a creep who isn't worthy to clean your shoes."

She shot up a hand. "That would be the creep I broke up with?"

"Well, it took you long enough," he said bluntly.

Holly stared at him, dumbstruck. The unflappable Micah Lancaster had finally worked up a good head of steam. "I can't believe you're saying these things to me."

"I know," he said grimly. "And I'm probably an asshole for doing it. But we've all been dancing around the situation because no one wanted to hurt you. And we wanted to honor your love and grief for Drew. But it's been over four years, Holly. You can't keep hiding much longer from your emotions and from the people who care for you. Not without causing damage to both yourself and to those relationships." He paused. "And from what I knew of Drew, that's sure as hell not what he would have wanted for his wife."

"Really? What do you think *my husband* would have wanted for me?" she asked in a tight voice.

"I think I know what he wouldn't want. He wouldn't want you to have a life where you hide behind your work, too scared to love again, even to take the risk of trying to love again. Wasting yourself on dickweeds like Jackson Leigh."

She flinched as his words shot straight to their mark. Because everything he said was true. She knew it in her heart even if she couldn't admit it in her head. Drew would be very unhappy with more than a few of the choices she'd made.

And you should be unhappy too, because that's not really who you are, is it?

All at once it was too much, and Holly found herself blinking back a sudden rush of tears. Not very successfully, since she had to grab a napkin and blot her eyes.

"Oh damn," Micah groaned. "Please don't cry. I'm an

idiot and a jerk for laying all this on you right now. Especially after the day you've had. I'm sorry, Holly."

She gave an inelegant sniff and wiped her nose. She must look like a wreck by now, but she didn't really care. "It's fine. I'm fine, really."

"It's not fine. I was out of line." He grimaced. "I guess my only excuse was that I was pretty shaken up today too. I kind of let things get away from me for a minute now. You should give me a big kick in the ass, preferably with your pointiest shoes."

She choked out a laugh. "Maybe I'll take a rain check on that offer. And you weren't out of line."

When he raised his eyebrows, she shrugged. "Okay, maybe a little out of line, but most of what you said is true. Like you also said, I just don't want to admit it." She held out her wineglass for a refill. It was definitely going to be more than a one-glass evening.

After he topped her up, he stayed silent, watching her with a steady gaze. It was a look that said he was ready to hear whatever she had to say.

"It started out as a survival strategy," she said. "I'm sure you understand why."

"Of course I do."

"You remember what I was like after Drew was killed. I was a freaking basket case. It felt like my life was over. After I got past the initial shock and had to get on with things, all I hoped for was to be able to cope with the present. With the moment. The future felt completely out of my control. It felt . . . well, dangerous."

He nodded. "Sometimes it is."

"So I decided that all I could truly count on was myself and my work."

"You had your friends and your family," he said quietly. "You had Seashell Bay."

She nodded. "I did, and they saw me through the worst of it. But when it came to relationships . . . I wasn't going to take a nun's vows, but I wasn't going to get emotionally involved with a guy either. I just couldn't take the drama and the potential for more heartache. But I guess I started to believe it was the kind of life I really wanted, and that it wasn't just a coping strategy anymore." She wrinkled her nose. "I feel like a coward for saying this, but it was way easier."

"Loving someone can get you hurt, that's for sure," Micah said.

Holly mentally winced. He loved her, and she'd hurt him.

"So you shut down," he continued. "At a certain level, I mean."

"Let's just say I focused my energy on other things."

He leaned forward, resting his forearms on the table, his shoulders stretching the fabric of his shirt tight. He looked so handsome—and so serious—that it made her heart hurt. "You were willing to risk everything when it came to your career," he said, "but there was no way you were going to put your heart at risk. Am I right?"

She shrugged. "In a nutshell."

"Babe, give me your hand," he said, extending his across the table.

She hesitated a moment before resting her fingers in his palm.

"I love you, Holly Tyler," he said, "more than anything in this world. And if you loved me back, your heart would never be at risk. I would never, ever hurt you. And I would never let anybody hurt you. You can count on it."

Okay, this was the moment she should have been prepared for, because she knew he loved her that much. She
knew he wanted her and would do everything in his power
to keep his promise.

But no one in the world had that kind of power. And
she was *so* not prepared to deal with this conversation.

She squeezed his hand once and then tugged it free.
His frown told her how little he liked that.

"Micah, I hate to state the obvious, especially after
today's events, but you're a cop. So you might never hurt
me, but someone could hurt *you*. Which would then hurt
me." That sounded pretty muddled, so she tried again. "I
was already married to a guy who carried a gun for a living. I don't think I could do it again." She gave him a weak
smile. "It's kind of the ultimate in risk taking."

Micah blew out an exasperated breath. "I'm not going
to pretend I could never be in any danger as a Seashell
Bay cop, but Holly, a bus driver in Portland is more likely
to get hurt on the job than a cop on the island."

"Okay, how about today? Remember? Crazy drug
dealer with a knife?"

"You know as well as I do that most days fishing lobster is more dangerous than being a cop."

"Still, you've told me you might want to be a detective.
Or even join a big-city police force. That's a whole different thing."

Even she knew how lame she was beginning to sound.
Micah was right. She'd become so emotionally risk averse
it was almost crazy.

He thought for a long moment—so long that she started
to fiddle with the stem of her wineglass. Then he nodded,
probably more to himself than to her. "Holly, all I know

for sure is that I love you and want to be with you. I'd do whatever it took to make that happen. Hell, I'd probably go to New York and flip burgers in a diner if I thought you needed to be there to be happy."

Holly sagged back in her chair, stunned. "Seriously? Would you really give up being a cop?" Then her heart lurched at the implications—the responsibility it laid on her. "No, don't answer. I've got no right to ask that."

"Actually, you've got every right, because I just said I'd do whatever it took. And I meant it." Micah's eyes felt like laser beams trained on her.

Laser beams of love, girlfriend, and you know you want it.

Oh, man. Did she ever.

"Now what about you, Holly?" he asked, his quiet voice at odds with the intensity of his gaze. "What would you be willing to do for love?"

It was the million-dollar question, and she didn't have an answer.

Chapter 30

$\mathcal{H}$olly peered out the window and watched Morgan hop out of her little red pickup truck, her silver flip-flops sparkling in the glow of the store's floodlights. No doubt her friend would bust Holly's chops about her staying at the store so late, but she'd been too restless to return to an empty house after that intense dinner with Micah. It had ended on a question she still couldn't answer, so there was no way she could just go home and climb into bed despite her exhaustion.

The time spent alone in the store had calmed her down as she fiddled with the new displays and dusted the shelves. In many ways, it was still the same old cozy place she remembered from her childhood, and yet a page had been turned. Holly had turned it, and she felt proud about that. And she certainly hadn't run out of ideas for making the store even more attractive to customers, including using wall space to display paintings by area artists. Not only would it brighten things up even more, her aunts should pull in some commissions from sales.

But would Florence and Beatrice be able to keep the

momentum going? Florence's health was iffy, and Beatrice had never run things on her own. It was far from clear that they'd be able to keep the store moving forward in a way that would ensure its survival. She hated the idea of all her work going to waste. But far more, she hated the idea that the Jenkins General Store might soon be just history.

She opened the door for Morgan. "You probably think I'm crazy to call you so late."

"No, crazy was putting yourself in the middle of a shoot-out at Great Diamond." Morgan planted her feet wide and propped her hands on her hips. "Hell, girl, what were you thinking?"

Holly rolled her eyes and ducked behind the counter. "If it was a shoot-out, it was the lamest ever. I told you it was over before anything even happened. Micah made sure of that. Now, how about some coffee? I can make decaf."

"Better make it full strength," her friend said, leaning against the counter. "I'm betting you have a lot to talk about."

Holly started up the big machine. It made the usual soft hissing noises that signaled a cup of superb coffee would soon be on the way. "Yeah, about that. I did want to talk to you about Micah. I met him for dinner in town after I saw my aunts at the hospital."

A slow grin spread across Morgan's face. "Aha. I figured this might just be about him."

Holly nervously fiddled with some of the knobs on the coffee machine. *Might as well spit it out.* "Okay, well, here's the thing. He all but proposed to me over dinner."

Morgan's mouth dropped open. "No way."

"Way."

"Wow. I guess he decided it was time to fish or cut bait since you're leaving soon. But what the heck does *all but proposed* mean?"

Holly crossed her arms over her chest, frowning as she thought back to the scene in the restaurant, something she'd been doing constantly for the last two hours. "He didn't get down on a knee or anything, but it was clear what he meant. He said he loved me and that he'd do whatever it took to be with me. Go to New York. Quit being a cop. Flip burgers if he had to."

Morgan's eyes practically bugged out. "That is... unbelievable."

It was. The idea of Micah giving up his job to be with her was... well, *unbelievable* covered it pretty well. He loved being a cop, but Holly guessed he loved her more.

Since the machine was ready, she took a few moments to organize her thoughts as she prepared a cup and handed it over. "There was a catch to the New York part. He said he'd move there with me if he truly thought I wanted the partnership with David and Cory. But he was pretty blunt in saying he didn't think moving to New York would make me happy." She grimaced. "He thinks I've been kidding myself about a lot of things. Like that I don't really want the kind of life I've been trying to lead since..."

Morgan nodded. "Since Drew died. I can't say I'm totally surprised that Micah would put it out there."

"I guess not, since apparently you and Lily think pretty much the same thing."

Morgan winced. "Oh, crap. I guess I'll have to talk to our lunkhead deputy about telling tales out of school."

"Was he wrong? Is that how you guys feel too?"

Her friend reached across the counter and squeezed her shoulder. "Oh, sweetie, all Lily and I have ever wanted is to support you in whatever choices you make. But that doesn't mean we always agree with you."

"Well, you did make your feelings about Jackson pretty clear," Holly said drily. "Not that I blame you. I was obviously way off base on that one."

Morgan put her cup down on the counter. When she looked up, her gaze was almost as intent as Micah's had been a few hours ago. "He's just part of it, Holly. But are you sure you want to talk about this now? You've had a hell of a day."

"Yes, and please don't pull any more punches. I should have realized how much you've all been pussyfooting around me for the past four years, but I guess I've been too self-absorbed and scared to let it sink in. I let that go on for too long, and I'm mad at myself for shutting you guys out." She grimaced. "I'm really sorry about that."

Morgan emphatically shook her head. "No apologies necessary. We understood the changes in you after Drew's death, or at least we thought we did." She gave her a sheepish grin. "Though since Ryan and Aiden came back to Seashell Bay, we obviously have a lot better understanding about what real love is all about. We didn't before, but you certainly did."

After Drew was killed, Lily and Morgan had been as sympathetic and supportive as two friends could ever be, but they'd never been in love—at least not in the way they were now. They'd never truly known what it was like to invest all your hopes and dreams in a man and the future you thought you had with him—the future that had gone down in flames when an army officer and a chaplain had shown up on Holly's doorstop that awful morning.

"Thing is," Morgan said, "you always loved your job, but you sure didn't live for it. But after Drew died, you became a total workaholic. It was almost all you did, except for those few weeks every summer on the island."

Holly shrugged. "It was the only way I could keep from going crazy."

"That made perfect sense until it became the sole focus of your life in the long term too. But you *did* want more when you and Drew got married. You wanted a fulfilling career, which you sure as hell deserve. But you wanted a life with your husband too, and you wanted a family. Kids. You always wanted that life." Morgan drew in a deep breath, as if for courage. "You told me more than once how important family was to you, especially since you'd lost your parents. Remember?"

Holly felt her throat start to tighten.

Morgan clearly wasn't finished. "But after you lost Drew, all you wanted to do was date men who didn't want to get involved. We kept telling each other that it was the way you needed to cope for a while. But then we started to wonder if that really *was* all you wanted out of life."

"Why the heck didn't you say something then?"

"Believe me, we came close lots of times, but we always pulled back. We wanted to support you, not give you a hard time about something we couldn't truly understand."

"I suppose I'd have done the same thing," Holly said. "Besides, I'm not sure I would have been ready to hear it before now." She shook her head with disgust. "What an idiot I've been."

Morgan smiled. "You get a pass on this one. But unlike the rest of us cowards, Micah had the stones to actually tell you. Because he totally loves you, Holly. And you know you'll never find a better man anywhere than our big ol' sexy Deputy Dawg."

That was true, on both counts. But unlike the rest of her friends, Micah did have the courage to lay it all out on the line, even though the odds were good that she would reject him. Once again, he'd put her first—over his love for her and even risking their friendship, one that had been part of the bedrock of her life. She was stunned that she'd been blind to that for so long.

"I know," she said quietly. "Micah is…amazing." It was the only word that seemed to cover it. Okay, *smart*, *kind*, *generous*, *brave*, and *smokin' hot sexy* also applied, but *amazing* pretty much said it all.

And suddenly Holly realized how much she wanted *amazing* in her life once more. She thought she'd lost that forever when Drew died, but here it was again, right in front of her. That felt like a miracle of epic proportions.

"So, now that we've got that figured out," Morgan said, "what are you going to do about it? It seems like you've got a few decisions to make, not just about Micah but about where you belong. Got any ideas?" She crossed her arms and lifted a challenging eyebrow.

As Holly stared at her friend, finally, blessedly, the answer came through loud and clear. The answer that had been percolating inside her for a very long time. There was only one place in the world where she truly felt at home. It was long past time to cut the cords that kept dragging her away from the life she wanted.

It was time to stop being afraid.

Micah blinked at her, looking a bit stunned. He also looked wickedly delicious, wearing nothing but a pair of black gym shorts. Holly had to repress the impulse to fan herself as she took in his awesome body, remembering how wonderful all those hard muscles had felt when the two of them were naked in bed.

She hoped to feel that way again very soon.

"Surprise," she said in a cheery voice. "I know it's late, but how about a nightcap?" Holly held up the bottle of merlot she'd grabbed from the store after kicking Morgan out, telling her she'd suddenly developed other plans. "I never properly thanked you for buying me that lovely dinner."

Micah's eyebrows crawled up his forehead, but he quickly stepped back and held open the door. "Come in. You know you're always welcome here any time, day or night." He took the wine and headed toward the small kitchen at the back.

Holly kicked off her sandals and stepped inside, her heart fluttering like Old Glory in a stiff wind. She had so many things she wanted to tell him that she hardly knew where to start.

Or maybe she'd just lost the ability to think rationally due to her surging hormones. After all, the back view of Micah was just as good as the front view. She could barely keep her hands off his brawny shoulders, fine ass, and long, muscled legs.

Mercy. To think she'd almost let this man get away.

Micah was as fine a man as she could ever meet, and he clearly adored her. How had she gotten so lucky twice in her life? To have had her time with Drew, however short, and now the possibility of a future with Micah...it was truly humbling.

She leaned against a counter and let her gaze wander as he uncorked the wine and half filled a pair of large-bowl wineglasses. The simple all-white kitchen was like the man—clean, organized, practical, and utterly comfortable.

"Here's to a hell of a day," he said, holding up his glass. His smile held more than a hint of a question.

Holly gently tapped her glass against his. "Yes, but it's still not quite over." She took a hefty swallow, hoping for some liquid courage.

Micah's gaze warmed as it roamed over her, despite the fact that she was barely presentable in jeans, plain white T-shirt, and mussed hair. Then he took a quick glance down at his own body. She couldn't miss that it had started to respond to her presence.

"Hmmm. I guess I should either put on some more clothes or you should take some off," he said in a thoughtful voice. "The latter would be my strong preference."

Oh boy, mine too.

But not just yet. First, she had to own up, and it was turning out to be harder than she thought—her damn pride was getting in the way again.

"Micah, I need to tell you something. And I need to do it right now."

His sexy smile evaporated. "You're leaving sooner than you thought."

She shook her head. "No, I came to say that I hated the way we left things at the restaurant. The way *I* left things. Because you were pretty much right about everything. I knew it too but just couldn't admit it. I didn't know *how* to admit it."

He studied her for a few long moments before nodding. "Okay, maybe we should head to the living room and get comfortable. This doesn't sound like a kitchen conversation."

"No, please, Micah. Let me just get it out. I've kept all these feelings bottled up inside for so long…"

And dammit, there she was choking up again when she least wanted to. She was *not* some fragile creature they all had to tiptoe around. She was no longer afraid of taking risks, and she was determined to show him that.

Still, when he took her in his arms, she didn't resist. He cradled her to his chest, his strong arms wrapped tightly around her back. It felt so comforting, so right, that Holly didn't want to move—ever. But after a few moments, she found the strength to wedge her hands in between them and gently push him back.

"Okay, no more coddling me," she said. "I'm not going to break."

"Hell, I know that, especially after today. I've always known that, but I like coddling you anyway." He reached for her again. "And cuddling too. Cuddling's okay, right?"

She held up a restraining hand. "I'm trying to be serious here, Deputy Lancaster."

He leaned against the kitchen counter and crossed his arms over his chest. When he smiled at her, he was pure temptation. "Okay, Ms. Tyler. I'm listening."

She took in a deep breath. "Good. Well, you were right that I haven't been happy. And no, I don't believe New York is going to change that very much, even though I've tried superhard to convince myself otherwise. But being with you this summer, and with my aunts… seeing everything they're going through and how much they need me, it's made me finally face the truth. I know now that going to New York would just be another way to avoid feeling what I need to feel, what I *should* feel if I had the guts to face it." She shook her head. "I've been running away from myself for too long. I'm done with all that."

Micah gently grasped her shoulders. "Babe, don't beat yourself up over it. You did what you had to do to survive. We all knew that."

While what she'd done might have been right at the time, a necessary step on her path to healing, now she knew what she truly wanted. She wanted family and friends, people who counted for something and who loved her—people who would be there for her when she needed them. And, just as much, Holly wanted to be there for them when they needed her. It had taken four long years, but she finally realized that almost everything important to her was right here in Seashell Bay.

Starting with the man standing right in front of her.

"Micah, you told me you loved me tonight. You said you'd do whatever it took to be with me." She shook her head, awed by what he was willing to give up for her. "Well, I love *you* that much, and I'm prepared to do whatever it takes to be with you. Not for visits, but for always. Hell, I'll flip burgers in Portland if I have to," she joked, even though her throat was getting tight again.

"But what about your new partnership?"

Holly did hate the idea of disappointing David and Cory after she'd made commitments. But she had no choice. "The guys won't be happy, obviously, but they'll just have to accept my decision. Besides, I'm not exactly their only alternative for a third partner."

"Music to my ears," Micah said, giving her a smile so loving that it lit her up like a thousand firecrackers on the Fourth of July. "But I hope you don't think you have to give up the work you love."

"I've been thinking about that. I'm pretty darn good at what I do, if I do say so myself. So I figure I shouldn't have much trouble cobbling together work here in Maine. And it'll be fantastic to be able to stick around to help Florence and Beatrice and move forward with the changes to the store. I still have a lot I want to accomplish on that front."

Micah blew out a long sigh, as if he'd been holding his breath for a year. "Thank God. That is the best damn news I've ever heard." He rested his forehead against hers. "I really would have followed you anywhere though, Holly. Anywhere," he said softly.

She slipped her arms around his waist, imprinting the moment on her heart. It had been so long—a lifetime, it seemed—since she'd felt such happiness.

And a bone-deep certainty that the world was just as it should be.

But she knew if she tried to voice the depth of her emotions, she'd start crying. So instead she leaned back and smiled up at him. "Just shut up and kiss me, Deputy. And don't stop until I tell you to."

Micah laughed. "You know my motto—I live to serve."

Epilogue

October, Seashell Bay

Micah swung the cruiser onto the gravel road that led to the resort construction site.

"What are you doing?" Holly asked. They'd been heading to Lily and Aiden's house for a barbecue on a warm and perfect autumn day, but it looked like he was taking the scenic route.

He flashed her a smile—the one that never failed to make her go all gooey inside. Even though she'd been living with Micah for several weeks, the thrill of being with him had yet to wear off. She had a wonderful feeling it never would.

"I want to show you what the resort looks like now that it's almost finished. The view is pretty spectacular." He stopped the car in front of the chain-link fence. "I'll unlock the gate, and you drive through, okay?"

Holly came around to the driver's side while Micah opened a big brass padlock and then swung the gate open.

She inched through the gap and waited while he relocked the gate.

"I can't remember the last time I was up on these bluffs," she said after he got in the passenger seat. She wound the cruiser past several construction trailers, Dumpsters, and storage sites. "This was all Flynn land, and Aiden's dad didn't like kids poking around on his property."

Micah nodded. "Lily and Aiden really wanted that to change. So when the place opens in the spring, everybody will be able to enjoy it, not just resort guests. People can come for a meal or a drink or just to walk along the bluffs and enjoy the view."

After they parked in front of the hotel complex, they strolled down a graveled path that wound westward along the edge of a steep slope, lushly covered with bushes and sumac plants, already starting to blaze with autumn colors.

"Wow, what a view," Holly said, looking east toward the Atlantic horizon. Since it was Sunday, there were no fishing boats out on the placid blue waters. In fact, there were no boats at all. The quiet was almost eerie. There was no breeze, and she could barely hear the faint lapping of the sea against the huge rocks that dotted the driftwood-strewn beach below. For a moment, it felt like she and Micah had both the island and the ocean to themselves, as if they'd been marooned on a remote shore.

Micah gently turned her chin until she gazed at him. "Beautiful sea, beautiful island, beautiful woman," he said in a low voice. Then he took her in his arms and kissed her with a passion that made her knees go weak.

"For the strong and silent type, you are such a sweet-talker," she said after he let her up for air. "You brought me here to make out? I thought we did that all morning."

And most of the night.

They'd managed maybe three or four hours of sleep, then started up again when the sun finally woke them around seven. Holly had made pancakes while Micah cooked bacon, and then they'd headed straight back to the bedroom. Because she'd been so busy—first at the store and then at her new job with a Boston-based consulting firm that had just asked her to set up a Portland branch office—she and Micah hadn't seen much of each other this last couple of weeks. So when they did have a chunk of free time, they took advantage of every moment they had together.

"Are you complaining?" he said, nuzzling her neck.

"Not a chance, but I don't want to show up at Lily's looking like I've just gotten my ashes hauled. Again."

"You won't," Micah said with a laugh. "Let's walk."

His arm wrapped securely around her waist, he led her to a grassy area in the shadow of a pair of tall pines. Micah propped his back against one of the trees and settled Holly against his chest. She snuggled into his warmth with a happy sigh, content to quietly live in the moment as they took in the view.

Finally, Micah stirred. "I was thinking this morning about how cool it is that we've been getting more people moving back to Seashell Bay. A lot of locals worry about the island's future, but I think we might just get a little population boom in the next while."

"Well, I know Aiden and Ryan are certainly keen to do their part," Holly said drily. "Lily's already trying to get pregnant, and Morgan wants to have a big family too. I think it's just a matter of time before we have a new crop of Butler and Flynn kids populating the local school."

She felt him hesitate.

"And what about Lancaster kids?" he finally said. "Think they'll be showing up on the school playground at some point?"

Ah, there it is. She and Micah hadn't yet talked about children. She was sure he didn't know she'd been pregnant once, finding out shortly after Drew left for his final deployment. She'd suffered an early miscarriage a week after his helicopter was shot down, redoubling her misery. Holly had only told Lily and Morgan, and she'd sworn her friends to secrecy. At the time, the last thing she'd needed was more sympathy to remind her of everything she'd lost.

But she was done with secrets and with being afraid of living again.

"Micah, almost nobody knows this, but I was pregnant once. I miscarried right after Drew was killed."

His arms tightened around her, then he turned her in his arms. His eyes were dark with sympathy and worry. "Babe, I'm so sorry. I had no idea…"

"I only told Lily and Morgan because it was too painful to talk about. And too…"

"Private?" he guessed.

She managed a smile. "Yeah, you know me. Miss None of Your Business. But I was so miserable that I didn't even want to think about it, you know? And for a long time after that, I wasn't sure I would ever want to have children again."

He nodded, looking solemn. "And now?"

"I do want kids with you," she said. "Very much."

The tension bled away from his face. "That makes me very happy, but you need to know that it wouldn't make any difference if you didn't. Whatever is best for you— that's all I want."

Holly went up on her toes and kissed him. "You're a hell of a man, Deputy Micah Lancaster."

He smiled and nestled her under his arm so they could both look out over the ocean. "This area is where Aiden and Lily held the ground-breaking ceremony last fall. It was exactly one year ago today. I remember it so well."

Holly had missed it, too busy with work to make it up that weekend. "And?" She could tell he wanted to say more.

"Morgan and Lily were plotting about how they could lure you back to Seashell Bay. They said it would make things perfect if you came back."

Holly rolled her eyes. "Yeah, that's me. Perfection personified. And what did you say to that plan?"

"I was all for it but didn't say much. How could I?" He paused for a moment, his gaze drifting out to the horizon. "I wanted it so bad, but I never really thought it could happen."

Like he'd done to her a few minutes ago, she reached a hand up to nudge his jaw, making him look at her. "It all worked out in the end, didn't it?"

The shadows that lingered in his gaze vanished with his smile. "It sure as hell did. So...I've got something for you."

"A present?" she asked. He was always bringing home little things for her—flowers, her favorite bottle of wine, a pretty piece of sea glass to add to her collection.

"You might call it that."

"I hope it's good," she said in a joking voice. "My standards are high, you know."

When Micah pulled a small jeweler's box from the pocket of his leather jacket, Holly's heart practically stuttered to a halt. But when he went down on one knee in front of her, it kicked back into action at about a thousand beats a minute.

"Holly, I love you, and I'm going to love you until the end of time." He opened the blue box to reveal a truly stunning diamond ring set in white gold.

Wow. On top of everything else, the guy had amazing taste in jewelry. Holly instantly fell in love with it.

"I might sound like a total sap," he said in a serious voice, "but I want to raise our kids and grow old with you right here in Seashell Bay, surrounded by the people we love and who love us right back. So, how about you show off this ring at the party and make me the happiest guy in the world?"

He took the ring out of the box, ready to slip it on her finger. "Will you marry me, Holly Tyler? Will you spend your life with me here on this funny little rock in the Atlantic Ocean?"

Sucking in a huge breath, she tried to calm the tidal wave of emotion surging through her. She'd need to sort out some of what she felt later, especially her lingering sadness about Drew, but right now it was all good— perfect, as a matter of fact.

She extended a hand to pull him up. "I love you too, Micah Lancaster, and yes, of course I'll marry you. And thank you for never giving up on me. I promise to spend the rest of my life making sure you don't regret that for a single instant."

He slipped the ring on her finger and then swept her into a tight embrace. Holly hugged him back, torn between laughter and tears, reveling in the joy of the moment.

"I'll hold you to that promise, babe," Micah whispered in her ear. "And right back at you."

Aiden Flynn returns to Seashell Bay
to sell his family's coastal land
to a developer. But beautiful
Lily Doyle will do whatever it
takes to convince him to save
their island home—and
the love that still burns
between them...

Please see the next page
for an excerpt from

Meet Me at the Beach.

$\mathcal{A}$iden stared down into emerald eyes just as bewitching as he remembered—eyes that now also held a depth and maturity that sucked him right in. As much as he might have liked to deny it, he felt the pull toward Lily as strongly as he ever had, and he'd be willing to bet his parcel of land she felt the same.

But frigging darts...really? If Lily had no intention—sadly—of leaping his bones, he would have expected her to get down to business right away, pumping him for info about his position on the development project.

He glanced away from her challenging, amused stare to take in the avid gazes of the crowd, waiting with bated breath for his answer. And his destruction, he suspected, given the nasty smiles of anticipation that lit the faces of at least half the people in the bar. It was Thunderdome, Seashell Bay style, with Aiden tagged as the loser.

Just swell. Nothing like a little ritual humiliation to cap off his fabulous homecoming.

Lily Doyle had always had a touch with darts, just like Aiden had the God-given ability to hit baseballs. Most people thought it was simply a matter of natural coordination, but there was more to it than that. Lots of people had great coordination. Damn few, though, could hit a ninety-five-mile-per-hour fastball or throw a dart with perfect precision.

Lily had coordination in spades and a sweet, sweet form.

Aiden clapped a hand to his chest, trying to look like a wounded puppy. "Such a coldhearted way to welcome a native son back to the island. Since you're the top dog in these parts, I reckon you have some ulterior motive for wanting to whip my ass in front of the entire damn town."

Her gaze cut off to the side for a few seconds, surprising him. Lily was never one to dodge a question or a direct challenge. But then she looked back, dazzling him with a glorious smile that fried the logic part of his brain.

"Oh, I don't know," she replied with a throaty purr that made Aiden want to lift her over his shoulder and haul her out to his truck. "I guess I'm pretty good, but you're a *professional athlete*, after all. You're not afraid of a little old game of darts, are you, Aiden Flynn?"

"You tell him, Lil," Boone Cleary said, leaving his bar stool long enough to weave over and see what the fuss was all about. "Nobody walks away from a challenge on Darts Night. Not on this island, anyway." He belched as if to emphasize his weighty intervention, which prompted a whack to the back of his head from Miss Annie and a lecture on minding one's manners in public.

Bram whispered into Aiden's ear, "He's right, bro. Look, just keep saying stuff that'll get her rattled. You can start by reminding her of that time when you and me tailed her down to Bunny Tail Trail and saw—"

"Shut up," Aiden said through gritted teeth.

Lily had crossed to the dartboard but now came back to Aiden, still giving him that sexy smile that said, *What are you afraid of, big boy?* His brain might have been addled by waves of hot lust, but he couldn't shake the feeling she was somehow trying to manipulate him.

"Well?" She held her palm out, daring him to take the three darts that lay there.

Instinctively, he reached out, his hand swallowing hers and the red-tailed darts. Her skin felt hot and almost as smooth as he remembered from that long-ago night, when her hands had been all over him. That surprised him, given the work she did. Of course she wore gloves on the boat, but she set and hauled traps all day long. Both his dad and Bram had always suffered from unending cuts, scrapes, and chewed-up hands from snapping lobster claws.

He froze for a few seconds, her small hand trapped in his, and his mind became swamped with images of the battle-hardened warriors who fought the cold sea and the unforgiving elements to eke out their living. He could only imagine what Lily had gone through all these years he'd been away. While he'd been playing and partying in the glamor of big-city pro baseball, the slender, fine boned woman before him had toiled long and hard on her lobster boat, facing down the dangers—and the dangers were real and ever-present—of a brutally unforgiving family trade.

When Lily tilted her head, her half-smile curving with an unspoken question, he released her.

"You go first," he said, sliding his hand across the swell of her hip to gently turn her toward the throw line.

"You are such a gentleman, sir," Lily said over her shoulder, flashing him a mocking yet heated smile that went straight to his dick. "Okay, we play the usual rules here—501, straight start, double finish."

In that sultry voice, even the scoring rules sounded like an invitation to bed boogie. "Fine. Say, who's that girl keeping score?"

He nodded toward a tall, young woman at the side of the board who was staring intently at him as she gripped a black marker. She had cropped, dark hair and wore a black T-shirt and leggings so tight she couldn't possibly have been wearing a scrap of fabric underneath them. Though he didn't recognize her, she sure seemed to know him.

Lily swung around and shot him a look somewhere between puzzlement and annoyance. "That's Jessie Jameson."

Aiden couldn't hold back a disbelieving laugh. He remembered Jessie as a scrawny, preteen tomboy who hung around the boatyard. It was yet another lesson that not everything on Seashell Bay Island had stayed the same.

As Lily turned into the throw line, positioning her flip-flops at a slight angle, Aiden's eyes automatically locked onto the way her beautifully rounded ass filled out the little denim skirt. *Nice*, his libido muttered, imagining how easy it would be to slide his hands underneath that well-worn fabric and—

"Good one, Lily!" a blond woman said from a table near the board. "You give him holy hell!"

He jerked his attention away from Lily's very fine ass to the board. Her first dart had landed in the double twenty ring, no doubt exactly where she'd aimed it. She didn't turn around and gloat, though, instead giving her arm a little shake as she set up for her next throw.

Aiden glanced at the woman who'd shouted out the encouragement. "I know that blonde's a friend of Lily's, but I can't dredge up her name," he said to Bram at his side. It was starting to piss him off that he couldn't remember the names of people he'd known all his life.

"That's Morgan Merrifield," Bram said. "She's a teacher up the coast now, but she comes back every summer to help her dad at the B&B. Hell, she and Lily are so freaking close they might as well be married."

Aiden's mind went blank. "You don't mean that they're . . ."

Before he even finished his sentence, Bram looked at him like he was a freak. "What the fuck, bro? Did you get hit in the head with a baseball and not tell me? Lily isn't gay, and neither is Morgan."

"Nothing wrong about it if they were," Aiden said defensively. He didn't give a shit one way or another about anyone's sexuality, except for Lily's. That seemed to matter a lot to him at the moment, way more than it should.

Mumbling something that sounded like *fucking bone-head* under his breath, Bram turned to watch Lily while Aiden glanced discretely at Morgan. Now he remembered her. She, like Lily, had been a couple of years behind him in school. The girls had been close back then too. He probably hadn't recognized Morgan right off because she was thinner than she'd been in high school and because she'd worn wire-rimmed glasses back then.

Aiden returned his focus to Lily and watched as her dart just missed the double ring. A couple of seconds later, she sent her last one on a perfect arc into the double twenty ring again. Scoring one hundred on her first set was pretty sweet.

"Woo-hoo!" Morgan yelled. "Let's see you top that start, Mr. Big Shot."

Aiden ignored the taunt, just as he'd learned to ignore far worse from opposing teams' fans as he patrolled the outfield. Morgan was trying to rattle him, just as Bram had wanted him to do with Lily. But Lily's easy mastery of the game made it plain he was in over his head.

Story of his life, when it came to Lily Doyle.

"Let's go, Aiden! You can do it!"

He glanced to the bar where Laura was pumping her fist. He grinned at her, thankful that he had at least two supporters in the bar tonight.

Aiden held his first dart lightly in the pencil grip he favored. *Don't think, man. Visualize the tip of the dart hitting the target and just let it go.* He repeated that mantra twice and let the dart fly, a part of his mind jeering that he was taking a darts game so seriously. But it was Lily and it was Seashell Bay, so it mattered.

The dart headed straight for the top of the twenty but clanked against the double ring and dropped to the floor. *Bounce-out.*

Amid hoots from the crowd, Lily made a little shrug that held a lot more mockery than sympathy. Undaunted, Aiden launched his second dart. This time it angled perfectly between the wires for a double twenty.

Lily's eyes narrowed as she gave him a golf clap in response—all motion and almost no sound. Her cheering squad suddenly went quiet. Apparently the game mattered to them too.

Aiden took a deep breath and held it as he threw his last dart, this time aiming for the more difficult triple ring. How better to set sweet Lily Doyle back on her heels than to score a triple twenty the first time he was up?

And... *thunk*.

He did it. To the sounds of breath being sucked in from all sides, Aiden casually strolled over to the board, plucked out the two darts, and then bent to pick up the bounce-out. When he straightened, he gave Lily a deep, exaggerated bow. Damned if he didn't feel as good as if he'd just thrown out a runner at the plate.

"Jackass," Morgan Merrifield muttered from behind him.

Lily simply tilted her head, looking more intrigued than worried. "Decent," she finally said, then eased up to the throw line for her second turn.

Aiden moved in close, practically whispering in her ear. "Not to blow your concentration or anything, but why the hell was Miss Annie so freaked out just now? It's not like the stuff with the developer and the car ferry vote is a big secret."

Okay, maybe he *was* trying to blow her concentration, but as he inhaled her scent, the years melted away. He swore her hair smelled exactly the same as it had that last night in his car, when his lips were trailing kisses over her long, perfect neck and his hands were exploring the gentle swells of her breasts and ass. Her gleaming auburn hair was as sweetly fragrant as the roses that bloomed all over the island.

He couldn't hold back a smile. Yes, Lily had changed, had grown up. But she'd also remained essentially the same, and he found that incredibly appealing.

Clearly unfazed by his comment—or by the fact that he'd crowded her sweet bod—Lily launched her dart and then turned to face him. "I'm sorry about that. Granny's memory isn't what it used to be, and she sometimes thinks people are keeping her in the dark. You remember how much she hates not being in the know about absolutely everything that's happening on the island."

"Got it. But she sure still looks and sounds sharp to me." Annie Letellier might be in her eighties, but she looked like the same fireball he remembered from when he was a kid. He hated to think it might be otherwise.

Lily shook her head, her hair gently brushing over her bare shoulders. "She's definitely still our Miss Annie, but you'll notice some differences in her, for sure." For a nanosecond she looked sad, but then she lifted an eyebrow. "If you stick around long enough, that is."

She was probing for clues again, but he wasn't ready yet to give up that kind of info. "I don't know how long I'll be here. Depends on a lot of things," he said.

But after seeing you, babe, I may not be out of here quite as quick as I'd thought.

Lily let out a derisive little snort and turned to throw again, scoring a twenty.

"This match could be close," she said over a shoulder that Aiden wanted to caress.

"Don't count on it," he replied absently, letting his gaze drift down to her shapely ass.

She turned to him and blinked, as if startled that he stood so close. A faint blush washed over her cheekbones, but then she put her hands on her hips. "Then maybe we should make a little wager before we get too far in. What do you think, city boy? You up for the challenge?"

The gentle taunt in her voice tweaked his competitive instincts. "Name it," he said.

Lily tapped an index finger on her chin, as if pondering a weighty question. "Let's say if I win, my tab tonight is on you. If you win—like that's going to happen—I pick up yours."

"Even if I stay and close the place down?"

"Even if. In fact, be my guest. On Darts Night, I usually don't go home too early."

Which means you do every other night? He liked that idea. Lily tucked up in her bed safe and alone—preferably in a skimpy nightie that only he would ever see.

"You're on, then," he said.

Lily thought she'd done a fairly respectable job preventing Darts Night from deteriorating into full-blown war. Not that Bram would ever lay a hand on a woman, much less one almost three times his age, but Granny had lots of supporters in the Pot. Any one of them would have been more than willing to throw a punch on her behalf.

Aiden had done his bit to keep the situation under control too. He'd reacted calmly and decisively, keeping his stupid brother locked down and treating Granny with a sweet, old-fashioned respect.

And she had to admit that his understated confidence turned her on a little too.

Okay, he was pretty much melting her panties.

Once a high school hunk, Aiden had now matured into an incredibly sexy man with a laid-back assurance and masculinity that vacuumed up the attention of every woman in the bar but Granny. Every cell in Lily's overheated body was telling her that he felt the pull between them too, and that he was more than willing to act on it. Should she use that attraction to get closer to him and probe for info? She hated the idea of using such sleazy tactics, no matter how just the cause, and the idea of getting involved with Aiden was even more anxiety provoking. She felt pretty certain that would be a one-way boat ride to a whole lot of heartache.

But Gramps had made her mission crystal clear—find out where *the boy* stood on Seashell Bay's future. Would he honor his mother's inheritance, or would he side with his jerkwad of a father? From the few clues Aiden had dropped, she sensed that he had yet to make up his mind. Aiden wasn't the kind of guy to let his father—or anyone else—force him to make a decision before he was ready.

So there was time to push back, especially if he hung around for a while. And if he did, Aiden just might be a temporary fix for the other problem that was keeping her awake at nights.

If she could get him to agree to it, and that was a very big if.

She flashed him a bright smile when he hit the double ring to score another twenty-six points with the third dart of his turn. "Very nice."

Lily didn't need to fake her compliment—he was damn good. Now it would come down to the first person to hit the double needed in order to check out.

He casually rested his hand on the base of her spine as she took up her position. His hand, big enough to nearly span her lower back, sent heat through to her skin. The sensation forced her to lock her knees to hold her stance.

"Feeling the pressure yet?" His deep voice made her

want to press her thighs together. "You must really hate the thought of losing in front of the home crowd."

"Lose? In your dreams." She mentally winced at the squeaky note to her voice.

He was teasing, but his words contained an element of truth. Lily hated losing, and there were a few people watching who would find pleasure in rubbing it in. Folks in Seashell Bay took their darts seriously, and she'd been whipping their asses for years. Still, she'd developed a game plan, and she had to stick to it.

Think big picture and get over yourself, girl.

"Put him away, Lily," Morgan shouted, her face lit up with loyal enthusiasm.

"She's gonna bust," Bram retorted.

Lily shut everything out and threw three straight darts just outside the double nine, scoring zero for her turn. Perspiration prickled along her spine where Aiden's hand had rested only moments ago. It took skill to throw a game and not look suspicious.

"Ah, so close," Aiden said with a mock sigh as he moved up to the line.

"Let's see you do better, pal," Lily shot back, secretly hoping he'd put his first dart straight into the double seven to check out.

Deputy Micah moved in close, just off to her right beside Morgan's table. He scowled at the board like he wanted to pull out his gun and blast it. Given Micah's long-standing antipathy to the Flynns, she knew he was going to be pissed when Aiden won the match. Lily and Micah were old friends, and he wouldn't take kindly to Aiden beating her.

Despite the noise and catcalls, Aiden's hand was steady as he tossed his dart to score the double he needed. Just like that, the match was over, and Lily was on the hook for his beer tab.

Small price to pay.

"Yes!" Bram leaped out of his chair, knocking it to the floor. Once he finished pummeling his brother on the back, he swung around to sneer at Morgan and Micah. "How about that, huh? A Flynn wins!"

Aiden hauled him back. "It could have gone either way, bro. Lily just missed by an eyelash. She's a great player." Then he flashed her a seductive smile, turning her brain to fish bait. "Want to go again, Lily? Get your revenge on the city slicker?"

Morgan jumped up from her chair and whispered urgently in Micah's ear. Clearly, she'd figured out that Lily had tossed the game and wanted to keep Micah from acting like a bull-headed deputy.

"What? Now you want to stick me with Bram's beer too?" Lily said, struggling to find a light note.

Aiden shook his head. "No, and you don't need to buy mine either. I just like spending time with you. I always did." His voice was deep and sincere, a quiet undertone cutting through the raucous bar.

Lily was afraid she might melt on the spot, just when she most needed to focus.

"If you really want to give me a chance to get even, I just got another idea," she replied, trying not to sound breathless. She told herself the tight feeling in her chest was only about the crazy plan she was about to drop on him. "Are you up for a *real* challenge?"

He gave her a lazy grin that curled its way right down between her thighs.

Lord, the man could smile.

"Lily, have you ever known me to back down from any kind of challenge?" he asked.

She'd been counting on that, but not on the predatory heat in his gorgeous, dark eyes. He looked as if he was hoping she would suggest a wild night of strip poker as her next challenge. Now *that* would be a disaster. Getting a look at Aiden Flynn's naked body would be as dangerous as going out on the *Miss Annie* in a winter gale.

Bram was practically standing on his tiptoes behind his brother as he strained to eavesdrop. Micah started to move forward and Morgan scrambled after him, ready to run a little interference.

"You always loved watching the lobster boat races, right, Aiden?" Lily asked.

Every summer, up and down the Maine coast, various harbors hosted the races. Aiden's father had often raced his boat, though never once had the bastard allowed either of his boys to go with him. He'd been determined, she suspected, to keep any glory to himself.

"Sure," Aiden said, suddenly wary. "Who doesn't?"

Lily gave him an easy smile. "Well, the Seashell Bay races are this weekend, and I'll be racing my boat."

When Aiden's jaw tightened, she knew he'd caught her drift. "So?" he said.

"So, even though it hasn't raced in a while, I figure your dad's boat might still be one of the fastest out there. Right, Bram?"

Bram looked as stunned as a deer caught in headlights. "Uh, you know Dad can't race anymore, and neither can I."

"No, but this big, strong *professional athlete* surely can," Lily said, pouring on the sugar. "Do you think you could beat me, Aiden? Could you outrace a girl?"

Aiden let his thoughtful gaze roam over her. As always, he wouldn't rush to answer. "Let's just say for a moment that I agree to this little idea of yours," he finally said. "What kind of bet are we talking about? What would I win when I whip your butt?"

Oh, I think you'd like to spank my butt, wouldn't you?

Lily forced that too-enticing image from her mind. "Well, I was thinking the loser could grant the winner a wish. Say, something that involved a *personal service*." She tried for as much sexual innuendo as she could without going completely hot with embarrassment, hoping he would take the bait.

"Come on, Flynn. You're going to take that bet, right?" Micah needled, taking an aggressive, wide-legged stance. "Or has the Boy Wonder just come home to sign away his heritage and hustle back to the big city again?"

Crap. Lily had to repress the urge to smack Micah upside the head. If the well-intentioned loyalist of the Doyle clan managed to mess up her plans, she'd kill him. "Micah, come on. You know that's not the way we do things in Seashell Bay," she said in a firm voice. "Aiden will always be one of us."

Her friend grimaced but remained silent as he glared at Aiden.

Aiden's balled fists slowly opened, and he turned his gaze from Micah to Lily. He let the silence between them drag on for too long but then nodded. "I appreciate that, Lily. And if you want me to take a shot at the races, fine. As long as *Irish Lady* is up to it." He glanced back at his brother. "Can we get the old girl in shape by the weekend?"

If there was one thing the Flynns had in quantity it was

pride, so it was no surprise when Bram started to look enthusiastic. "It'll take some work, but damn right we can, bro. And it'll be great to kick some Doyle ass again, even one as sweet as Lil's."

Though Aiden was still looking wary and skeptical, Lily had been right in thinking he couldn't refuse the challenge. Especially from a girl, and worse yet, a Doyle.

But Mr. Aiden Flynn had no idea what he was getting himself into. After all, she'd won her class in the Seashell Bay boat races for the past two years.

And he'd be in for an even bigger surprise when she finally laid out the penalty for losing.

Fall in Love with Forever Romance

KISS ME IN CHRISTMAS
by Debbie Mason

Back in little Christmas, Colorado, Hollywood star Chloe O'Connor is still remembered as a shy, awkward schoolgirl. And there's no one she dreads (and secretly wants) to see more than her high school crush. While Easton McBride enjoys the flirtation with this new bold and beautiful Chloe, he can't help but wonder whether a kiss could have the power to bring back the small-town girl he first fell in love with.

Fall in Love with Forever Romance

PLAY TO WIN
by Tiffany Snow

In the third book of bestselling author Tiffany Snow's Risky Business series, it's finally time for Sage to decide between two brothers-in-arms: Parker, the clean-cut, filthy-rich business magnate...or Ryker, the tough-as-nails undercover detective.

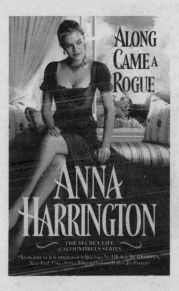

Fall in Love with Forever Romance

NECESSARY RISK
by Tara Wyatt

The first book in a hot new action-packed series from debut author Tara Wyatt, which will appeal to fans of Suzanne Brockmann, Pamela Clare, and Julie Ann Walker.

SEE YOU AT SUNSET
by V.K. Sykes

The newest novel from *USA Today* bestselling author V.K. Sykes! Deputy Sheriff Micah Lancaster has wanted Holly Tyler for as long as he can remember. Now she's back in Seashell Bay, and the attraction still flickers between them, a promise of something *more*. Their desire is stronger than any undertow... and once it pulls them under, it won't let go.

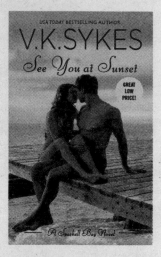